# THE BUSINESS

*A Novel*

## Iain Banks

Simon & Schuster

New York • London • Toronto • Sydney • Singapore

SIMON & SCHUSTER
Rockefeller Center
1230 Avenue of the Americas
New York, NY 10020

Originally published in Great Britain in 1999
by Little, Brown and Company

Simon & Schuster and colophon are registered
trademarks of Simon & Schuster, Inc.

Manufactured in the United States of America

1   3   5   7   9   10   8   6   4   2

Library of Congress Cataloging-in-Publication Data
Banks, Iain.
The business : a novel / Iain Banks.
p. cm.
1. Women executives—Fiction.
2. International business enterprises—Fiction.
3. Antarctica—Fiction.
I. Title.
PR6052.A485 B87 2000
823'.914—dc21
00-030785

ISBN 0-7432-0014-4

To Ray, Carole and Andrew
and again
with thanks to Ken

# PROLOGUE

'Hello?'

'Kate?'

'Yes.'

'Itsh Mike.'

'Mike?'

'Mike! Mike Danielsh! Chrisht, Kate, don't—'

'Mike, it's . . . it's four thirty-seven.'

'I know what time it ish!'

'Mike, I'd really like to get back to sleep.'

1

'I'm shorry, but it'sh fucking important!'

'You should get some sleep too, maybe whatever it is won't seem so important after you've slept. And sobered up.'

'I'm not drunk! Will you jusht lishten?'

'I am. I'm lishtening to a drunk man. Go to sleep, Mike. Hold on, aren't you due in Tokyo today?'

'Yesh!'

'Right. So get some sleep. I'm going to switch the phone off now, Mike. I didn't mean to leave it on in the first—'

'No! That'sh what I'm calling about! Tokyo!'

'What? What about Tokyo?'

'I can't go!'

'What do you mean? Why not? You have to go.'

'But I *can't*!'

'Calm down.'

'How can I be fucking *calm*? Shome fuckersh taken out half my teesh!'

'Say that again?'

'I shaid shome fuckersh taken out half my fucking teesh!'

'Is this some sort of joke? Who the hell is this?'

'It'sh me, for Chrisht'sh shake! It'sh Mike Danielsh!'

'It doesn't sound like the Mike Daniels I know.'

'Of courshe not! I've had half my teesh taken out! Fuck'sh shake, Kate, wake up!'

'I'm awake. Prove you're Mike Daniels. Tell me what you were going to Tokyo for.'

'Oh, Chrisht . . .'

'Ah, pull yourself together. Tell me.'

'Okay, okay! I wash going to Tokyo wish X. Parfitt-Sholomenideesh to shign the firsht part of the Pejantan Island deal with the Kirita Shinizhagi, Shee-Ee-Oh of Shimani Aero-shpace Corporation. Shatishfied?'

'Hold on.'

'What? What are you—? Hello? Hello? Kate?'

'. . .Okay. Go on. What's this about your teeth?'

'Your voish shounds echoey. You're in a bashroom, aren't you?'

'Very astute.'

'Where are you? You here in London?'

'No, I'm in Glasgow. Now tell me what the hell's going on.'

'Shome bastard'sh taken out half my teesh. I'm looking at it in zhe mirror now. My moush ish all pink and . . . the *fuckersh*!'

'Mike, come on. Get it together. Tell me what happened.'

'I wash out. I went to a club. I met zhish girl.'

'Uh-huh.'

'Well, we ended up back at her playsh.'

'Clubbing and picking up some floozy. Perfect preparation for the most important business trip of your career.'

'Don't fucking go shanctimonioush on me!'

'Don't go what?'

'Shanctimonioush! Shancti-fucking-monioush!'

'Right. So you went to a club and you scored. How did this lead to you losing half your teeth? Were they full of gold fillings?'

'No!'

'Well, was there a jealous boyfriend waiting for you back at her place?'

'No! Well, I don't know! All I remember ish having a shnog and a drink and then nexsht shing I know I'm waking up in my own flat and half my teesh are mishing! What the fuck am I going to do? I can't go to Tokyo like zhish!'

'Hold on, you woke up in your own flat?'

'Yesh! In my own bed! Well, on it. About ten minutesh ago!'

'Nobody else there?'

'No!'

'Have you checked your wallet?'

'Eh? No.'

'Check it now. And try to find your keys.'

The phone clunked down. I sat frowning at the tiles on the far side of the bathroom. Mike came back.

'All zhare.'

'Keys? Money? Credit cards?'

'Everyshing. All zhare.'

'Nothing missing in the flat?'

'Not zhat I can shee. Everyshing'sh here. Apart from my fucking teesh.'

'I take it you'd never met this girl before.'

'No, I hadn't.'

'Can you remember the address of her flat?'

'Notting Hill shomewhere. I shink.'

'Street?'

'I . . . No idea. I wash . . . I wash being dishtracted while we were in the takshi.'

'I bet. You go to that club a lot?'

'Fairly oshten . . . Kate? You shtill there?'

'Still here. Mike, are you in pain?'

'Mental fucking anguish. But my moush ish numb.'

'Bleeding much?'

'Nnn . . . no.'

'See any puncture marks on your gums?'

'What? Umm, hold on . . .'

I shivered. I pulled a towel from the chrome rack above the bath and wrapped it round myself, then sat on the toilet again. I could feel my frown deepening. I looked in the mirror. Not attractive. I pulled a hand through my hair with some difficulty.

On the phone, Mike Daniels said, 'Hnn. Could be. Few of zhem. Maybe four.'

'So your teeth weren't knocked out, they were extracted.'

'What short of fucking nutter takesh out half shomebody's teesh? Was zhish a *dentisht*?'

'Sounds like it. A central London dentist working serious overtime in the small hours of the morning. You better hope they don't send you the bill.'

'Thish ishn't funny!'

'No, actually your voice is quite funny, Mike. It's the implications that aren't.'

'Well, I'm sho fucking glad I'm shtill able to amushe you, Kasherine, but what the fuck am I going to do?'

'Have you reported this to the police?'

'The polishe? What, you mean shecurity?'

'No, the London Metropolitan Police.'

'Uh, no. I didn't think—'

'Have you told anybody else?'

'No, jusht you. Shtarting to regret it, now.'

'Well, it's up to you whether you call the civilian police or not. Personally . . . well, personally I don't know if I would. But do call company Security and let them know.'

'What can zhey do?'

'Nothing, I guess. But you'd better let them know. And call the company credit-card hot-line. It's twenty-four hours. You on platinum?'

'Gold twenty-four.'

'Well, if they give you any shit, tell them you're calling on my authority. They might be able to find you a dentist who can do something.'

'What, half a moushful of teesh before ten a.m?'

'Is that when the flight is?'

'That'sh check-in time.'

'You on scheduled?'

'Yesh.'

'Could we find you some more time by sending you on a company jet?'

'Been dishcushed before all zhis happened. Too many fuel shtopsh or shomeshing.'

'How long after you arrive are you supposed to meet Shinizagi?'

'About four hoursh.'

'Hmm. Mike?'

'What?'

'Exactly which teeth were removed?'

'Eh? Well, I don't know! I mean I don't know what zhare all called. One of my front teeth ... molarsh ... left wishdom ... jusht about half of zhem. Looksh random. Can't shee a pattern or anything. Disherent on top and bottom, disherent on each shide ... Well?'

'Well what?'

'Any ideash?'

'I've told you: call the hot-line. And call Adrian; Adrian George. You should have called him in the first place. I'm on sabbatical, remember?'

'I know you're on fucking shabbatical! I'm shorry I dishturbed your beauty shleep, too, but I shtupidly thought you might be able to help me.'

'I am helping you. I'm telling you to call Security, the company credit-card hot-line and Adrian. So do so. But, whatever happens, you have to make that flight.'

'But I can't go like zhish!'

'Stop wailing.'

'I'm not wailing!'

'Yes, you are. Stop it. You have to be in Tokyo tonight. Tomorrow night; whatever. It'll look very bad if you don't show up. Kirita Shinizagi is a stickler for these things.'

'A shtickler? A fucking shtickler? What about being a shtickler for executivsh having all their teesh? What if it'sh shome horrendous crosh-cultural inshult in Japan to turn up to shign a deal wish only shishty per shent of your shmile in playsh?'

'I thought as well as speaking the language you were well versed in Japanese culture, Mike. You must know whether that's the case or not.'

'Look, can't we shend shomebody elshe? It'sh Parfitt-Sholomenideesh who'sh doing the shining, not me; I'm jusht there ash a glorified bag-man.'

'I don't think so. You've been in on this from the start. Kirita Shinizagi trusts you. And Mr Parfitt-Solomenides doesn't speak Japanese. Frankly even if Mr Shinizagi wasn't expecting you, you'd have to go because Mr Parfitt-Solomenides's expecting you to be there and if you ever hope to leave Level Four, you don't go upsetting Level One executives because you have a dental problem. And Mr Shinizagi is expecting you. If you didn't show we might ... Never mind.'

'What?'

I didn't quite succeed in stifling a giggle.

'Are you— ? You're laughing! I can't fucking *believe* zhish!'

'I'm sorry, I was going to say we might lose face.'

'What? Oh, very fucking funny, Kate!'

'Thank you. Now, make those calls. And make that flight.'

'Oh, Jeshush.'

'This is no time for superstition, Michael. Orthodontics is your only hope.'

'You vishish bitch, you're enjoying zhish, aren't you?'

'Not in the least. And never call me a bitch again, Michael.'

'I'm shorry.'

'Make the calls, Mike, and be sure you have some pain-killers to hand for when the anaesthetic wears off.'

'Okay, okay. Shorry to have dishturbed you.'

'That's all right, given the circumstances. I hope it all works out, and give my regards to Kirita Shinizagi.'

'If I can shtill talk Japanezhe with no teesh.'

'Just do your best. I'm sure they have very good dentists in Japan.'

'Huh.'

'Good night, Mike. Safe journey.'

'Yeah. Good night. Umm . . . shanks.'

The phone went dead. I looked at it, wondering, then I switched it off. I draped the towel over the side of the bath, unlocked the door and returned to the bedroom, feeling my way across the unfamiliar space to the bed.

'What was that?' a deep, sleepy voice said.

'Nothing,' I said, slipping between the sheets. 'Wrong number.'

# CHAPTER ONE

My name is Kathryn Telman. I am a senior executive officer, third level (counting from the top) in a commercial organisation which has had many different names through the ages but which, these days, we usually just refer to as the Business. There's a lot to tell about this particular concern, but I'm going to have to ask you to be tolerant here because I'm intending to take things slowly and furnish further details of this ancient, honourable and – to you, no doubt – surprisingly ubiquitous concern in due course as they become relevant. For the record, I am one point seven metres tall, I weigh fifty-five kilos, I am thirty-eight years old, I have dual British/US nationality, I am blonde by birth not bottle, unwed, and have been an employee of the Business since I left school.

Early November 1998 in the city of Glasgow, Scotland. Mrs Todd the housekeeper cleared away my breakfast things and padded silently away across the pine floor. CNN babbled quietly from the television. I dabbed at my lips with a crisply starched napkin and gazed out through the tall windows and the light rain to the buildings on the far side of the grey river. The company apartments in Glasgow had been shifted a few years earlier from Blythswood Square to the newly fashionable Merchant City area on the north bank of the Clyde.

This building had been in company ownership since we built it, in the late seventeen hundreds. It was a warehouse for nearly two centuries, was leased out as a cheap clothing store for a decade, then it lay unused for a number of years. It was renovated in the eighties to create office and retail units on the ground and first floor and loft-style apartments on the three remaining floors. This, the top floor, was all Business.

Mrs Todd glided back to complete the tidying of the table. 'Will there be anything else, Ms Telman?'

'No, thank you, Mrs Todd.'

'The car is here.'

'I'll be ten minutes.'

'I'll let them know.'

My watch and mobile agreed that it was 0920. I rang Mike Daniels.

'Yesh?'

'Ah.'

'Yesh, "Ah" indeed.'

'They couldn't find you a dentist.'

'Zhey found me a dentisht but zhere washn't time to do anyshing. I shtill look like a fucking footballer.'

'Pity. Sounds like you're in a car. I take it you're on your way to Heathrow.'

'Yesh. Everyshing'sh on schedule.'

'Any pain?'

'A little.'

'Did you call Security?'

'Yesh, and Adrian G. Zhey were even lesh help than you. I don't shink Adrian George likesh me. He'sh calling Tokyo and Pee-Esh'sh offish to let zhem know, sho it won't come ash a shock.'

'Very considerate.'

'He shaid Shecurity would want to talk to me when I get back. Anyway, zhey're going to inveshtigate. Had to hand my flat keysh over to shome flunkey before I left thish morning. Oh, who'sh Walker?'

'Walker?'

'Shumshing to do wish Shecurity.'

'*Colin* Walker?'

'Thatsh him. Adrian G said he thought he'd sheen him in the Whitehall offish a couple of daysh ago. Sheemed to find it mosht amuzhing that he might be doing the inveshtigating.'

'I doubt that. Walker's one of Hazleton's people. He's his chief of Security. Well, more enforcement, in reality.'

'*Enforshement*? Oh, shit, ish thish shome department I haven't heard of? Shomeshing not for ush Level Foursh?'

'No. Officially Walker's Security. It's just he's usually regarded as Hazleton's . . . muscle.'

'Mushle? You mean like shum short of fucking *henchman*?'

'Henchman's a bit fifties B-movie-ish, don't you think? But I believe you could call him a person of hench. If we had hit-men, he'd be one. In fact, he'd probably be their boss.'

I know a little more about this sort of thing than most execs at my level because I started out in Security. That was before an interest in gadgets, technology and future trends got me angled across the company's career tracks and on to the plutocratic mainline. Maintaining contacts in Security may well prove to be one of the more astute investments I've made in my own future.

'Hazhleton. Shit. Ish he azh shcary azh everybody shesh?'

'Not normally, but Walker is. I wonder what he's doing in the country?'

'I heard a rumour zhere wash shome short of meeting nexsht week, at . . . umm, in Yorkshire.'

'Really?'

'Yesh. Shumshing to do wish the Pashific shing. Maybe he'sh here for zhat. Maybe Hazhleton's coming over from the Shtates. Advanshe guard. Checking out the grim old pile before Hazhleton showsh.'

'Mmm.'

'Sho, *izh* zhere a meeting, Kate?'

'Where did you hear this rumour?'

'Izh zhere a meeting?'

'Where did you hear this rumour?'

'I ashked firsht.'

'What?'

'Oh, come on! Ish zhere shome high-level meeting or not?'

'I'm sorry, I couldn't possibly comment.'

'. . . Shit, doesh zhat mean *you*'re attending?'

'Michael, you ought really to be concerning yourself with your own assignment.'

'Ha! I'm trying to take my mind off it!'

'Anyway, I have to go; there's a car waiting for me. Have a safe and productive trip.'

'Yeah yeah yeah. All zhat shtuff.'

I was on sabbatical. One of the privileges that comes with my rank is that I'm allowed one year in every seven, on full pay, to do just as I please. This has been a Business institution for those at my level and above for about two and a half centuries and seems to be working well. We'll probably keep it. Certainly I had no complaints, even though I had not taken what most people would regard as full advantage of such a serious perk.

Nominally and for tax purposes I was based in the States. I spent about a third of the year travelling, generally in the developed world. I was still enjoying this largely airborne lifestyle, but when I did want to feel the earth under my feet I could always retreat to the modest but comfortable cabin I owned in the Santa Cruz mountains just outside the town of Woodside, Ca, within easy reach of Stanford, Palo Alto and the rest of Silicon Valley (that's 'modest' and 'cabin' in the Californian Opulent sense, with a pool, hot tub, five bedrooms and a four-car garage). If home is the place that best displays your character, then this was my home. From the stuff on the shelves you could have told that I liked German composers, Realist art, French films and biographies of scientists. Also that I was addicted to technical journals.

My European base was Suzrin House, the company's monolithic warren of offices and apartments overlooking the Thames at Whitehall, which I preferred to our Swiss base at Château d'Oex. I suppose Suzrin House was my second home, though in terms of architectural cosiness that's a bit like regarding the Kremlin or the Pentagon as a *pied-à-terre*. Never mind. My job, wherever I might be, was to keep abreast of current and incipient technological developments, with the brief of recommending which of those technologies the Business ought to invest in.

I'd been doing this for a while. It was, I am pleased to say, on my advice that we bought into Microsoft on its initial flotation back in the eighties, and into the Internet Server companies at the start of the nineties. And – while many of the other computer and associated hi-tech companies we've put money into have gone quite spectacularly bust – a few of our investments in the computer and IT industries had produced returns sensational enough to make the whole investment programme one of our most worthwhile. In recent history, only the portfolios we developed in steel and petroleum during the late eighteen hundreds have yielded greater rewards.

My reputation in the company was, if I may toot my own tuba a tad, at least very secure and possibly – whisper it – even verging on legendary (and, believe me, we have a generous stock of living legends in the Business). I had achieved Level Three status ten or fifteen years earlier than I might have hoped for, even as a high-flyer, and, while it depended on the goodwill of my co-workers, I was fairly confident that some time in the next few years I would be promoted to Level Two.

A close inspection of my own personal Mammon graph would reveal even to the untrained eye that my remuneration package – including commission multipliers gained as a result of my successful forecasts regarding computers and the Internet – was already more generous than that of many of our Level Two executives. It had occurred to me a couple of years earlier that I was probably what the average person would consider independently wealthy; in other words that I could have existed comfortably without my job though, of course, as a good Business woman, that was all but unthinkable for me.

Anyway, you can't rest on your laurels. These successes with computer software and communications – lucky guesses if you wanted to be uncharitable – were all in the past, and I still had a job to do. And so it was that at that moment I had high hopes for our recently taken-up stakes in fuel cell technology and had been lobbying hard for more investment in private space concerns. We would see.

The Lexus hummed its way through the mirror-wet streets of Glasgow, heading east. People hunched against the buffeting wind-rush of rain; some carried umbrellas, others held folded tabloids or flapping carrier-bags over their heads as they waited at pedestrian crossings. I checked my lap-top for e-mail then read the newspapers. My chauffeur was called Raymond. Raymond was about half my age, tall and athletic, with short blond hair. He and I had developed what they used to call an understanding over the week or so I had been in Glasgow. Raymond was perfectly good behind the wheel, though I confess I preferred him between the sheets, which was where he had been the night before when Mike Daniels had called.

If Mrs Todd knew from the start that we were involved, she was able to pretend that she didn't because Raymond had so far always succeeded in waking up in time to slip away before she arrived in the morning.

An able if occasionally overly energetic lover at night, Raymond was the soul of driving professionalism and formal politeness during the day. When I was Raymond's age this sort of compartmentalisation of roles and relationships would have struck me as hypocritical, even deceitful. Now, however, it seemed quite the most convenient, even honest way to behave. Raymond and I could be prim and correct with each other while he performed his driverly duties, and as carnally abandoned as we desired when he took off his peaked cap and set his grey uniform aside. In fact I rather enjoyed the contrast: it lent a certain anticipatory frisson to the mundane condition of being taken from one place to another.

'Ah, Ms Telman?'

'Yes, Raymond.'

'Some bad traffic up ahead,' he said. He glanced at the car's navigation screen. 'Take a different route, aye?'

'Okay.'

Raymond whirled the steering-wheel to send us down a side road leading to the river. Raymond took this sort of thing seriously. Personally I have no interest in my route to a given destination, but some people like to be told why they're going one way rather than the other.

I scanned the newspapers. Mid-term elections in the States. Dow up. British chancellor makes an announcement today about extra government borrowing. Interest-rate cut expected later today. Footsie up, pound down.

Death and destruction in Central America, caused by the remains of Hurricane Mitch. Thousands buried under mudslides. Part of my mind scanned a mental list of company assets in the area, wondering how we might be affected, while my conscience shook its metaphorical head and tried to dredge up some human sympathy for the victims from the depths of my corporate soul. I could have logged on to the company Website and found out what exposure we had in Guatemala, Nicaragua and Honduras –

and, if our Web people were on the ball, what damage we'd taken down there – but I preferred to finish reading the papers first.

General Pinochet's appeal against his extradition to Spain was due to come up in the House of Lords that week. This was of more than academic interest for us as a company. Frankly the fate of one old fascist mass-murderer was irrelevant in business terms (though I don't doubt that as a company we kept on good terms with whoever was in power in Chile throughout the Allende years, Pinochet's regime and subsequently), but the whole issue of diplomatic immunity was one that exercised us at that point. Hence what Mike Daniels referred to as 'the Pashific shing'.

Personally I thought the Pacific thing was all a monumental irrelevance, but it was out of my hands – and I was probably not invited to the rumoured shindig in Yorkshire that weekend, no matter what Mike might think. That was Level One stuff, the preserve of the Hazletons and the Parfitt-Solomenides of the Business.

The chip factory lay a few miles outside Glasgow near the town of Motherwell. Standard low-level landscaping of clipped grass, ornamental water features and a scattering of thin trees, their leaves mostly gone to the autumn winds. They bent in the rain-heavy wind as the Lexus rolled up to the main entrance of the vast ochre shed that was Silex Systems' principal manufacturing facility. Raymond jumped out and was there with a golf umbrella, opening the door.

Mr Rix, the plant manager, and Henderson, his deputy, were waiting in the foyer.

'What happens to the chips that fail?'
'They're thrown away.'

17

'You can't recycle them?'

'In theory you could, but it would add a lot of cost. By the time they're at this stage they're already so materially complicated it would take a fortune to start reducing them to their individual constituents.'

I was standing with Mr Rix and Mr Henderson in one of the cleanest places on Earth. I was wearing something not far off a spacesuit. The closest I'd seen to it were the shiny things they wear in those rather forced Hey-we're-cool-really Intel ads for Pentium processors. The suit was loose and quite comfortable – as it would have to be if you were to spend an entire working day in it – with a full face mask incorporated into the helmet. Breathing seemed easy enough, though apparently I was doing it through a sub-micron filter. The suit's slipper-like shoes were built into the bottom of the legs, so that it felt a little like being a small child again, wearing pyjamas. When I changed into the one-piece, out of my white silk blouse and Moschino skirt and jacket, I felt a moment of regret at even temporarily giving up my clothes, until it occurred to me that the suit I was putting on was probably much more expensive than the one I was taking off.

We were deep in the giant factory, in a sterile room at the centre of three concentric levels of antiseptic cleanliness. I was looking through a glass screen at a complex and gleaming machine which was depositing CD-sized wafers on a platter, spinning them and then plopping liquid on to the centre so that it flowed, apparently instantly, to cover the whole shining surface; then a metallic arm quickly flipped the wafer over and into another part of the machine.

Around us, more spacesuited workers were gliding across the high polish of the tiles pushing tall carts of wafers, or sat hunched over microscopes on workbenches or staring at computer screens, the text and graphics reflecting off their face masks while their hands pushed mice around or gloved fingers fluttered over quietly rattling keyboards. The air transmitted a whole choir of subtle humming, whining noises to my shielded ears, and smelled a little like a hospital's, except cleaner. Everywhere, under the high, bright lights, surfaces glittered and sparkled.

Even without knowing the breathtaking scale of the investment a plant like this required, you could have smelled the money here.

'I hope you can stay for lunch, Ms Telman,' Mr Rix said. 'Just the usual canteen grub for us normally, of course, but we could go further afield if you liked. Can we tempt you?' Mr Rix was a big man, a head taller than me, and wide. His jowly face gleamed behind his mask, smiling from the eyes down. I felt quite cool in the air-conditioned, variously filtered atmosphere, but Mr Rix seemed to be sweating. Perhaps he was claustrophobic.

'Thank you, I'd be delighted. The canteen will be fine.'

'Do you often take these, ah, sabbaticals as a sort of busman's holiday, Ms Telman?' asked his deputy.

'This is my first sabbatical, Mr Henderson,' I told him. 'I haven't had time to establish a pattern.' Henderson was about my height, stockier. I started walking towards one of the parts of the clean environment we hadn't visited yet; the two men jockeyed for position between the workbenches and the humming machines; a robot delivery unit on a collision course sensed us approaching and glided to a stop until we passed by.

'I think if I had a year off I'd find somewhere better than Motherwell to spend it.' He laughed, and he and Rix exchanged glances.

'It is a sabbatical, Mr Henderson, not a holiday.'

'Oh, of course. Of course.'

'However, I did spend a month on a yacht in the Caribbean at the start of the year, without my phone or a lap-top; that got me nicely wound down,' I told them, smiling broadly behind the mask. 'Since then I've been taking the occasional little holiday to let me think, and I've travelled round a lot of the company sites I'd wanted to see but never got round to. Plus I have spent quite a while in the Library of Congress and the British Library.'

'Ah,' Mr Henderson said. 'It's just that I thought you must have seen the inside of a chip plant before, that's all.'

'One or two,' I agreed. Mr Henderson was right to be surprised. In fact he was right to be suspicious, if that was what he was: despite the impression I'd been careful to give, this was not at all a casual visit. I stopped outside a swipe-card protected door in a tall blank wall and nodded. 'Where does this go?' I asked.

'Ah, this is an area where we've got the workmen in at the moment,' Mr Rix said, waving at the door. 'Installing a new finishing line. Can't actually go through right at this moment in time. Too much dust and that sort of thing, you know.'

'Plus they're test loading some of the etching chemicals today, I think, aren't they, Bill?' Henderson said.

'Oof!' Rix said, taking a comic sort of step away from the door. 'I think we'll keep well away from that stuff, eh?' They both laughed.

In the safety briefing before we'd donned our spacesuits, as well as being told what to do in the event of a fire and where to run for a dousing if something acidic splashed on us, we'd been warned about various chemicals with very long names which were used in the chip-production process. They could, allegedly, sneak through the tiniest hole in a glove, soak instantly and unnoticed through the skin and get straight to work rotting your bones from the inside before going on to perform even more insidious horrors on your vital organs.

'Well,' said Mr Henderson. The two men started to pull away from the door. Mr Rix put an arm out as though to shepherd me away.

I crossed my arms. 'What's the likely life of the plant?'

'Hmm? Ah, well, with the new lines in place . . .' Mr Rix began, but I didn't pay very much attention after that. I had what you might call half an ear for his tone of voice and I was listening for certain keywords, but what I was really interested in was Mr Rix's and Mr Henderson's body language; their whole demeanour.

And all I could think of was, These guys are trying to hide something. They were frightened of me, which does – I confess – give me a buzz, but it went beyond the usual nervousness of local bosses used to total deference having to answer to somebody from higher up in the organisation who has come to pay a short-notice visit. There was something else.

Maybe they're both closet misogynists, I thought; perhaps their habituated reactions to women were derisory or even coercive (I'd looked at the files on this place: there was a slightly higher than average rate of staff turnover, especially amongst female workers, and there had been a few more complaints that had ended at industrial tribunals than one might have expected), but somehow that didn't feel like it would account for the edgy vibe I was getting here.

Of course, it could be me. I could be wrong. Always check the equipment for sensor error first.

I don't know whether I'd have dismissed the feeling in the end or not – I'd probably have decided they had some lucrative little scam going that could have got them cashiered, but not something it was worth my while bothering with, given that the plant's figures looked pretty good in general – but something happened that made me think about it all later.

A spacesuited woman came into view down an aisle. I could tell her gender from her gait as much as her shape. She seemed distracted, struggling to carry a lap-top, a plastic-wrapped metal briefcase, a thick, glossy-covered manual and heavy, straggling cables. I saw her first. Then Henderson looked round, casually back at me, and then quickly at her again. He started towards her, then glanced back at Rix, whose voice faltered momentarily before continuing.

The woman was fishing in a pocket of the spacesuit for something as she approached us while Henderson strode to meet her. Just before he got to her, she pulled out a swipe card on the end of a little metal chain.

Then Henderson intercepted her, one arm out as he nodded back in the direction she had come from. Her head came up as she noticed him for the first time. Mr Rix's arm extended again and, touching my right shoulder, gently but firmly pulled me round and away while his other hand waved through the air and he said, with just a little too much hearty bluster, 'While yet before they turn it into a battery-chicken shed, eh!' He clapped his gloved hands together. 'Well, now. Cup of tea?'

I smiled up at him. 'What a good idea.'

I had Raymond take us on a detour on the way back, to a nondescript field by what had once been a main road near Coatbridge.

'Come here, small girl.'
  'Whit?'
  'I said, come here.'

'Whit fir?'

'What? What did you say?'

'Eh?'

'Are you actually *talking* English, child?'

'Ahm no Inglish, ahm Scoatish.'

'Ah. Well, at least I understood that. I wasn't questioning your nationality, young lady. I was merely wondering aloud whether we shared the same language.'

'Whit?'

'Never mind. Look, would you kindly step closer to the car; I hate having to raise my voice ... I'm not going to bite you, child.'

'Who's he?'

'That is Gerald, my chauffeur. Say hello, Gerald.'

'Aye-aye. Y'all right, hen?'

'Aye ... Zat him fixin the tyre, aye, missis?'

'Yes. We had a puncture. He's changing the wheel.'

'Aw aye.'

'How are we doing there, Gerald?'

'Getting there, ma'am. Getting there.'

'Now, what is your name?'

'Ahm no supposed to talk tae strangers. Ma maw telt me.'

'Gerald, introduce us.'

'What's that, ma'am?'

'Introduce us, please, dear boy, as best you can.'

'Ah, Mrs Telman, this is, ah, the bairn you're talking to. Bairn, this is Mrs Telman.'

'Aw aye.'

'There. We've been introduced. I am not a stranger any more. Now, what is your name? ... Close your mouth, child. It's unbecoming. What is your name?'

'Ma maw sez . . .'

'Please, miss, her name's Katie McGurk.'

'Oh, hello.'

'Boaby Clark, you're just a wee clipe, so ye are.'

'Least ah've goat a da.'

'Ah widnae want a da like yours; he's just a waster.'

'Ah, still, but. At least ah've goat wan. More than you huv.'

'Just you fuck oaf, ye wee four-eyed cunt!'

'You're a wee cow! Ah'm tellin ma mum you said that!'

'. . . Katie?'

'Whit?'

'Here.'

'Whit's that?'

'It's a handkerchief. Go on. Take it.'

'No thanks.'

'I see. I take it that young man was Bobby Clark?'

'Aye. Wee shite.'

'Kate, I confess I am genuinely shocked. I didn't know children your age used the sort of language you did. Exactly how old are you, Kate?'

'Eight and a half.'

'Dear God.'

'How old are you, then?'

'My, you do recover quickly. You're very impertinent, too. Gerald, cover your ears.'

'Ma hands are a bit mucky, ma'am, but I shall endeavour to keep my lugs averted.'

'How gallant. I am forty-eight, Kate.'

'Goad, that's dead old, issit no? Ma gran's no that old.'

'Thank you for your thoughts on the matter, Kate. Actually it's not terribly old at all and I don't think I have ever felt better about my life. However. What exactly are you and your young friends doing over there?'

'Missis, we're havin Olympic Games.'

'Are you indeed? And I thought it was just a bunch of little kids playing on a bit of muddy wasteground in the drizzle. What sports are you playing?'

'Och, loads. Jumpin an runnin an that.'

'And what are you playing, Kate?'

'Ahm no. Ahm sellin the sweeties an stuff.'

'Is that what you have in your bag?'

'It's ma ma's. It's old, but. She said ah could have it. Ah didnae nick it or anyhin. Ah repaired the handle massel. See?'

'I see. So, you're running the refreshment concession, are you?'

'Whit?'

'Never mind. May I buy one of your sweets?'

'Aye. Ah've no many left, but. An there's nae fizz.'

'No fizz?'

'Aye. Nae Irn Bru, or American Cream Soda. Ah finished both bottles.'

'Just a sweet will do, then.'

'Whit dae ye want? Ah've Penny Dainties and Black Jacks. Or there's a few wee lucky-bag sweeties left.'

'I'll have a Penny Dainty, please.'

'That's a penny ha'penny.'

'How much?'

'A penny ha'penny.'

'A penny *and* a ha'penny?'

'Aye.'

'For a Penny Dainty?'

'That's the price.'

'But that's a fifty-per-cent mark-up on the normal retail charge.'

'Aye, still, but. That's the price.'

'So you said. Rather steep, though, isn't it?'

'Aye, but that's the price. D'ye want it or no?'

'Gerald, do you have any change?'

'Aye, ma'am. Hold on . . . Ah, I've got a thruppenny bit. That any use, ma'am?'

'Thank you, Gerald. Would you like a sweet?'

'Thanks, ma'am. Aye, wouldnae mind.'

'Tell you what, Kate. I'll give you tuppence ha'penny for two Penny Dainties. How's that?'

'Nut.'

'Why not?'

'Two's thruppence.'

'But I'm buying in bulk, relatively. I'm looking for a discount.'

'Whit? Whissat?'

'Didn't you get a discount for buying in bulk when you bought your stock?'

'Missis, ah goat these oot the machine at the bus station.'

'Ah, so you paid full retail. Still, that's your problem. My offer stands. Tuppence ha'penny for two.'

'Nut.'

'Kate, your little friends look like they're finishing their games. You might not sell much more. You could be left with unsold stock. It's a good offer. Here: take the thruppence. Then you give me two Penny Dainties, and a ha'penny change.'

'Nut. Two cost thruppence.'

'One can be too stubborn in the retail business, Kate. Flexibility is what carries a concern through changing circumstances.'

'Whit?'

'The rain's getting heavier, Kate. I'm sitting here in the dry. You're getting soaked and your pals are leaving. Two for tuppence ha'penny.'

'Nut.'

'You're being pigheaded, Kate. Maintaining or adjusting your margins should be a matter of practical calculation, not pride.'

'Ah know. Gie us the thruppence an I'll give ye the two Penny Dainties an ah'll gie a Black Jack as well. They're usually two fur a penny ha'penny or three fur tuppence.'

'Getting rid of more stock. Very sensible. Okay. It's a deal. There you are. Thank you. Gerald?'

'Ma'am?'

'Catch.'

'Thanks.'

'Here, Kate. You have the Black Jack back: I think it might stain my teeth . . . Now what?'

'Ma maw sez never take sweeties frae strangers.'

'Kate, don't be ridiculous: you just sold me this. However, your mother is quite right, I suppose. If you don't want it . . .'

'Na, okay, then. Ta.'

'My, you were hungry.'

'Aye. No much eatin in wan a those.'

'How's it going, Gerald?'

'Nearly there, ma'am. Just doin up the nuts. Be back on the road in five minutes.'

'Fine. Do you do this often, Kate?'

'Whit? Sellin stuff?'

'Yes.'

'Nut. Nivir done it before. Want tae know a secret?'

'What was that? A secret?'

'Aye. Promise ye'll no tell anybudy but?'

'I promise.'

'Cross yer hert an hope tae die?'

'Absolutely.'

'Ah goat the money frum ma uncle Jimmy. He let me play wi the pennies.'

'Oh. Really?'

'Aye, they're Irish pennies, cos he'd been tae Ireland on his boat.'

'Irish pennies?'

'Aye. They're the same shape as oors, an that, cept they've goat harps oan them. But the machine doon the bus station takes them fine.'

'And your uncle just gave you these? You didn't have to pay for them?'

'Nut. He just gied us them.'

'Ha! So you didn't pay full retail at all! Every penny you made was clear profit! You little rogue! Did you hear that, Gerald?'

'I'm shocked and appalled, ma'am. Enterprising wean, though.'

'Aye, but no fur everyhin. Ah had tae pay ma own money fur sum oh the sweeties, and the bottles oh fizz ah hud tae pretend ah wiz gettin fur ma maw. Ah've still tae take full yins back tae her.'

'And how much were you charging for the pop?'

'Penny a cup.'

'Those your mum's teacups?'

'Aye, missis. We'll no need thim till taenight.'

'I see. Oh, hello. Who's this, Kate?'

'This is Simon.'

'How do you do, Simon.'

'Hello, miss. Katie, it's affy wet. Ah want tae go hame. Zat okay? Ye cummin?'

'Aye. Here's the Penny Dainty. Dae ye want some lucky-bag sweeties an aw?'

'Aw aye.'

'Ah'll gie ye them when ah get hame, okay?'

'Aw aye, that's gret. Thanks, Katie. Can we go noo, though but? Ahm soakin. Ah fell in the water jump.'

'Ah-hah. Let me guess: Simon here is your security.'

'Nut. He's makin sure nun ah these wee shites nick ma money.'

'Same thing. Katie, I'm sure you won't accept a lift from a stranger, but could you tell me where you live? I'd like to talk to your mother.'

'Missis, you said ye widnae say anyhin! Goad'll git ye fur crossin yer hert an hopin tae die! Ye'll die, so ye will! Aye, an ah'm no fuckin kiddin!'

'Kate, Kate, calm down. I'm not going to say anything about the nature of your capital . . . about the pennies you used down the bus station. I swore I wouldn't, and I won't.'

'Aye, well, ye'd better no.'

'Kate, is your mother very young? I take it your father's not around, is that right? That's a nice wee dress, but it's a bit thin for this weather, and too small for you. You look hungry and too small for your age. Do you go to school every day? Are you doing well there?'

'Ahm goin hame.'

'Ready to roll, ma'am.'

'Thanks, Gerald. Just a minute. Kate, turn round. I'm serious. This is serious. Do you want to stay here for the rest of your life? Well, do you? Kate: what do you want to be when you grow up?'

'. . . Hairdresser.'

'Do you think you'll get to be one?'

'Mibby.'

'Kate, do you know of all the other things you could be?'

'. . . Ma pal Gale wants tae be a air hostess.'

'Mon, Katie. Ahm freezin.'

'There's nothing wrong with being a hairdresser or an air stewardess, Kate, but I think there might be a lot of other things you could be, if you wanted. If you knew. Let me talk to your mother. May I talk to her?'

'Katie, ahm fuckin freezin, so ah am.'

'Missis . . . you're no a bad wummin, are ye?'

'No, Kate. I'm not a saint, and I've used my share of Irish pennies in my past, but I'm not a bad woman. Am I a bad woman, Gerald, would you say?'

'Certainly not, ma'am. Always been very nice to me.'

'Katie, mon . . . 'sfuckin brass monkeys oot here, so it is.'

'Ye could gie us a lift, then. Zat okay, aye?'

'Really? Well, yes.'

'Aye. Come oan, Simon. We're gettin a ride home in this wummin's braw big car. Wipe yir feet.'

'Eh?'

And that is how I met Mrs Elizabeth Telman, a Level Two executive in the Business, one rainy Saturday afternoon in the autumn of 1968, outside Coatbridge, to the west of Glasgow.

Mrs Telman was one of those people who always seemed about six inches taller than she really was, to me. Even now when I think of her, she appears in my memory as a tall, elegant woman, as lithe and slim as my mother was wee and dumpy, yet the two were within a couple of inches of each other in height and not really that different in build. I suppose Mrs Telman just held herself straighter. She had long, raven hair which she only stopped dyeing, gradually, in her seventies (my mother was mousy brown, though I inherited hair somewhere between fair and blonde, apparently from my maternal grandmother). Mrs Telman had a wide mouth and long fingers and an accent that sometimes sounded American, sometimes English, and sometimes something else entirely, something tantalisingly foreign and exotic. There was a Mr Telman, but he lived in America; the two had been estranged since barely a year after their marriage.

Mrs Telman had Gerald drop Simon at his house and then took me to the local shop where I bought my two replacement bottles of fizz. We arrived at my house just as my mother was staggering up the path with her carry-out, fresh, if that's the word, from the pub.

I think Mrs Telman decided she wasn't going to get much sense out of Mother right then, and so arranged to return the following morning.

My mother threatened to slap me for talking to a stranger. That night, very drunk, she cuddled me to her, her breath sweet with the smell of fortified wine. I tried not to squirm, and to appreciate this unusually drawn-out burst of physical affection, but I couldn't help thinking of the rich, subtle, beguiling odours in Mrs Telman's car, some of which seemed to come from the car itself, and some from her.

She reappeared, to my surprise, the next morning, before my mother was up. Once my mother was dressed we went for a drive. I was given a Milky Way and got to sit up front with

Gerald, which was good, but I couldn't hear what was going on in the back because of the glass partition, which was annoying. Gerald kept me entertained by telling me what he thought the other drivers were saying and thinking, and letting me work the indicator switch on the dashboard. Meanwhile my mother and Mrs Telman sat in the back, swapping my mother's Woodbines and Mrs Telman's Sobranjes, and talking.

That night I got to sleep with my mother for the first time in years, all the way through to the morning. I was hugged even more fiercely, and I puzzled over her hot tears.

The next morning Gerald picked my mother and me up and took us through to Edinburgh, to Mrs Telman's huge, grand red sandstone hotel at the end of Princes Street. Mrs Telman wasn't there herself: she was off doing something important somewhere else in the city. We went to a big room, where – to my consternation and my mother's embarrassment – I was washed again by a large lady dressed like a nurse, given a medical inspection, and then measured and dressed in a scratchy shirt, skirt and jacket that were the first entirely new clothes I'd ever worn. Part of my horror at all this was because I thought we were in a public room where anybody might walk in and see me in my knickers; I didn't realise that these rooms were Mrs Telman's, that we were in her suite.

I was taken to another room where a man gave me lots of sums and other tasks to do; some were purely arithmetical, some were questions about lists, some consisted of looking at little diagrams and then looking at others and deciding which one fitted with the first lot, and some were more like little stories I had to complete. They were fun. I was left alone with a comic while the man went away.

Mrs Telman came and took us to lunch in the hotel. She

seemed very happy to see me, and she kissed my mother on both cheeks, which made me jealous, though I wasn't sure of whom. Over lunch, while my mother and I swapped conspiratorial looks as we tried to work out which cutlery to use, I was asked if I wanted to go to a special school. I recall being horrified. I thought special schools were where bad boys were sent for thieving and vandalising, but after this was cleared up and I was assured I would get to go home of an evening, I agreed, tentatively.

I started at Miss Stutely's School for Girls in Rutherglen the next day. I was a year behind the others, but physically no bigger than any of my classmates, and shorter than several of them. I was picked on for three-quarters of that first day, until I sent a girl home with a broken nose following a fight during afternoon play-time. I was almost thrown out and had to sit patiently through several stern talkings-to.

A tutor came to our house in the evenings to give me extra lessons.

Mrs Telman found my mother a job in an office-machine factory in Stepps; the same factory Mrs Telman had been on her way to inspect when her car had picked up a puncture. We ate better, we had proper furniture, a phone and, soon, a colour television. I found I had a lot fewer uncles than I'd thought I had, and Mother stopped walking into doors.

When I left Miss Stutely's and entered Kessington Academy in Bearsden, we moved from our terrace in Coatbridge to a semi in Jordanhill. My mother was now at another fac-tory, helping to make things called computers, not adding machines. She never married but we went on holidays with a nice man called Mr Bullwood. Mrs Telman came to visit us every few months, and always brought book tokens for me and record tokens, clothes and little things for my mother.

My mother died suddenly at Easter 1972, while I was on a school holiday in Italy. We had taken buses, ferries and trains to get to Rome, but I flew back alone. Mrs Telman and Mr Bullwood met me at Glasgow Airport and took me in Mrs Telman's car – still driven by Gerald – straight to the cemetery in Coatbridge. It was a warm, sunny day; I remember watching her coffin disappearing behind the curtains at the crematorium, feeling worried that I could not seem to cry.

A smallish man with shaking hands, wearing a shiny and badly fitting suit with a black armband up by one shoulder, came to me afterwards and breathed whisky over me, telling me with tears in his rheumy red eyes that he was my father. Mrs Telman put an arm round my shoulder and I let myself be guided away. The man shouted things at us.

Everything changed again. I was sent to board at an international school in Switzerland run by the firm Mrs Telman worked for; I was miserable there, but no more than I'd been in the months between my mother dying and completing the term at Kessington Academy. I studied for my baccalaureate and found a keen, solitary release in skiing and skating.

I was surrounded mostly by forbiddingly bright girls from families which seemed to possess infinitely deep reserves of money, taste and talent, and glamorous idiots with braying laughs who were destined to go straight to finishing schools and who had no ambitions beyond a rich marriage. I finished with a flourish and several academic prizes. Brasenose College, Oxford, awaited. Mrs Telman adopted me and I took her name.

I cried for both of them when she died last year.

*　　*　　*

The phone rang for a long time, well past the number of rings you'd normally allow before concluding that there was nobody present to answer it. Finally: 'Who is this?'

The voice – rich, sibilant and velvety – was that of an elderly man who was rather angry; the voice of a man answering a phone that rarely rang and which, when it did, was equipped to tell him the number that was ringing him, and from its memory also tell him to whom that number belonged. A phone which he expected to bring only important information.

'Hello. It's me.'

'Kate? Is that you, dear girl?'

'Yes, I'm using a call-box.'

'Ah, I see.' A pause. 'Does that mean that I was right and you've discovered something interesting?'

'Possibly.'

'Where are you?'

'Near where I've been all week.'

'I see. Would it be best to meet up?'

'I think it would.'

'Perfect, perfect. This weekend's definitely on. Can you still make it?'

'Of course.' My heart, I have to say, leapt. Uncle Freddy had told me a couple of weeks earlier that there might be a high-level meeting and general hoo-ha (to use his term) this coming weekend, and that I might be invited, but I hadn't liked to take this for granted. My contingency plans had consisted of surprising Raymond and spiriting him away for a couple of nights; I would do all the driving, we'd go somewhere discreet and expensive with a log fire and I'd feed us both lots of vintage champagne . . . but that would have to be put on hold. I would be going to Blysecrag.

'Good. Important get-together, Kate. The cherubim and seraphim of our tribe will be in attendance, not to mention more temporal powers.'

'Yes, there have been rumours.'

'Have there indeed?'

'Well, Mike Daniels had wind of something by last night.'

'Ah yes, the L-four whose teeth were stolen. What on earth was all that about?'

'No idea.'

'Well, the bush telegraph's obviously working. Still, be that as it may ... We'll need you here on Friday afternoon. Should all be finished by Sunday, but don't count on it. All right?'

'All right.'

'I should tell you your friend Suvinder will be there.'

'Will he now? Oh, joy.'

'Yes. Still coming?'

'Uncle Freddy, an invitation to Blysecrag is something I could never turn down. Oh dear, my money is running out. I'll be there on Friday. Until then.'

'Ha, right you are! Jolly good. 'Bye.'

What happened to your phone?
 This new one doesn't work out here. Can you believe that?
 Heads should roll. You need another phone. I believe they sell such things there in Tokyo. How did the signing go?
 Fine. KR loved his bottle of Scotch. Is it really 50 yrs old?
 Yep. PS get there OK?
 PS usual retiring self. Apparently the X stands

```
for Xerxes. Last seen escorting several geishas
back to his 737 to show them its circular bed. Boy
can that guy talk.
   Talking about talking . . .
   Oh, right. KR didn't seem to mind my slight
teeth-shortfall situation at all. Smiled and
bowed throughout. Probably thought it was a total
hoot; toothless gaijin. Recommended dentist.
Been there, done that, now got splendid set of
temporary Tokyo teeth. With Teflon. Now :-)
instead of : #
   Well, by gum.
   That took you 24 hours?
   I've been busy.
```

The origins of what we now call the Business predate the Christian church, but not the Roman Empire, to which it might fairly be said we owe our existence, and which, at one point – technically, at any rate – we owned.

Owning the Roman Empire, even if it was only for a total of sixty-six days, sounds wonderfully romantic; a real business coup. In fact we regard it as one of our greatest and most public mistakes, and it taught us a lesson we have never forgotten.

Most of the details are available in fairly digestible form in Gibbon's *Decline and Fall*, where it is recorded in Volume One, Chapter V (AD 180–248) that a 'wealthy and foolish' senator called Didius Julianus purchased the Empire at public auction from the Praetorian Guards, who had disposed of the previous ruler – one Pertinax – after he had proved too keen on tackling the empire's various corruptions (he'd lasted eighty-six days, beating our man by nearly three clear weeks). What only we

in the Business know is that the unfortunate Didius Julianus –
who became Emperor Julian when he ascended to the throne
– was merely a dupe; the front man for a loose consortium
of traders and money-lenders who had inherited a commercial
cabal already many generations old.

Possibly drunk on their success, certainly unable to decide
what to do with it, the squabbling merchants let the reins of
power slip from their fingers. Three generals – in Britain, on
the Danube and in the Eastern Empire – revolted, and limited
Emperor Julian's occupation of the Imperial throne to a little
more than two months. When he fell, so did many of those who
had supported him.

The Business had already existed for several centuries by then.
To Rome it had brought furs from Scythia, amber from the
Baltic, carpets from Babylon, and – in its most intense, risky
and lucrative enterprise – every year secured a host of spices,
aromatics, silks, gems, pearls and manifold other treasures from
Arabia, India and the Further East. Sensibly keeping away from
direct political power, all taking part had prospered; estates were
purchased, villas built, fleets constructed, herds increased, slaves
and works of art bought. With the Didius Julianus fiasco almost
all of that was lost. As I say, it was a lesson we have cleaved to
for the best part of two millennia (at least until now, arguably,
with the 'Pashific shing').

Documents – clay tablets, mostly – still stored in the closest
we have to a world headquarters, near Château d'Oex in
Switzerland, show that most of our original fortune was made
in trading, warehousing and lending money. There appear to have
been a few scams, too: shipwrecks that never happened, camel
trains that were robbed by our own people, warehouses that
burned down either with or without their contents, depending

whether you looked at one set of accounts or another; enough of that sort of thing generally to make us no better than most but sufficiently few for us not to have been the worst.

Allegedly we still store a few items which the Catholic Church and the Holy Roman Empire asked us to look after; sadly, nothing quite as dramatic as the body of Christ or the Holy Grail, but I've heard on good authority that we have in our possession at least one extra book the scholars don't know about which could well have made it into the Bible, a book of Leonardo cartoons, dozens of Michelangelo's pornographic paintings, various other art treasures and potentially valuable documents and several sets of crown jewels.

Rumours I've heard indicate that our Swiss Bank may be implicated, albeit marginally, in the recent Nazi gold scandal, which, aside from the morality of it all, is both careless and embarrassing, given the occasional co-operative venture we've taken on with the Rothschilds and the generally good relations we've enjoyed with Jewish enterprises over the centuries.

At any rate, one of the reasons that we are able to go quietly about our business as a company without too much intrusion or publicity – adverse or otherwise – is that we have at least a little dirt on almost everybody, whether they are other commercial concerns, sovereign states or major religions. There are other reasons, but we'll come to those later. All in good time (a resource which, given our longevity, we are obviously well used to working with in bulk).

# CHAPTER
# TWO

'Well, thanks for the ride.'

Raymond grinned. 'It was a pleasure having you in the back, Ms Telman.' He squeezed my hand rather harder than a normal handshake would have called for, then tipped his cap and swung his lithe form back into the Lexus. I permitted myself the briefest of lingering glances and a sigh, then followed the two footmen carrying my luggage into the vast symphony in grey stone that was Blysecrag House, while the car crunched over the pale stones of the driveway and set

off back through the deer-scattered parklands and forests for the main road.

'Kate! My girl! Good to see you!' Dressed in well-worn tweeds, waving a shepherd's crook with the thoughtless abandon of one brought up all his life under extravagantly high ceilings, attended by a brace of gangling wolfhounds leaving a double trail of whiskery grey hairs and saliva across the parquet, his own white hair seeming to float uncombed around his head as though in only casual contact with his scalp, Freddy Ferrindonald advanced down the length of the entrance hall, laughing, arms held wide.

He was lit from the side by the wintry sunlight pouring through a two-storey-high stained-glass window depicting a Victorian steel works; all gaudy reds, splashing oranges and sparking yellows with great roils of belching smoke issuing from huge machines, and small hunched human figures barely visible beneath the fumes and sparks.

A self-consciously eccentric dashing English toff of the old school, Uncle Freddy was genuinely an adopted uncle of mine, as he was a step-brother of Mrs Telman's, a familial relationship that he had never let stand in the way of sharing with me the odd toothily leering sexual innuendo, or giving my bum the occasional pat. Still, he was a laugh and – maybe because like me he didn't have much in the way of real family – we'd always got on surprisingly well.

'Welcome back!' Freddy hugged me as enthusiastically as his thin frame and eighty-plus years would allow, then held me at arm's length and looked me down and up. 'You're looking as lovely as ever.'

'As are you, Uncle Freddy.'

He seemed to find this hilarious, laughing loud enough to raise

an echo from the tiered upper galleries of the hall and exposing a wealth of variously angled and diversely coloured teeth. He put an arm round my shoulder and walked with me towards the distant foothills of the main staircase.

Miss Heggies appeared. Miss Heggies was the housekeeper of Blysecrag. She was small but formidable, with grey bunned hair, a steely stare, lips the colour and fullness of a small elastic band, artificial eyebrows and a voice to etch titanium. She also gave the impression of having a combined Transporter Room and Tardis buried somewhere in the house at her command, as she seemed to possess the gift of materialising at will wherever and whenever she wanted. The only difference was that in *Star Trek* or *Doctor Who* there was a cheesy sound effect and a vaguely human-shaped shimmer – or the sudden appearance of a Metropolitan Police box – to give you a few seconds' warning; Miss H had perfected the art of arriving instantly and without a sound.

'Ah, Miss H,' Uncle Freddy called out. 'Where's the lovely Kate billeted?'

Miss Heggies nodded to the expectant-looking footmen with my cases. 'Ms Telman's in the Richmond room,' she told them.

'Miss Heggies,' I said, with a nod and what I hoped looked like a respectful smile. Miss H is the sort of person it pays to keep in with.

'Ms Telman. Welcome back.' Miss Heggies allowed her head to incline downwards by about a degree, while the corners of her mouth twitched. This was her equivalent of a floor-deep curtsy and a broad but bashful grin. I felt truly honoured. We started up the stairs.

I threw open the tall windows and stepped out on to the

balcony, hugging myself as I drank in the cold air beneath a clear, cobalt sky. My breath smoked in front of me. Beyond the stone balustrade the view dropped sharply away in a series of sculpted terraces dotted with lawns, flower-beds, pools and waterfalls to the wooded floor of the valley where a few loops of river sparkled through the trees before decanting into the broad lake to my right, at the centre of which a single huge fountain towered. On all sides, the parkland spread away to the hills and crags beyond.

Looking along the cliff edge the house was perched upon, I could see a long structure like the top part of a crane laid along the lawn and jutting out over the drop. Steam drifted over it from behind, its rear obscured by a towered and crenellated wing of the house.

I rubbed my upper arms through my jacket and blouse, realising that I was smiling broadly at the view.

This was Blysecrag. It was begun in the early eighteen hundreds by the local duke, who was determined to create one of the great houses of England. He was responsible for the huge reservoir created in the hills five miles to the north of the house, which – via two valley-spanning aqueducts and a network of canals, cisterns and balancing reservoirs – supplied the water, and the pressure for the various water features in the house and grounds, of which the tall fountain in the lake was but the most immediately obvious.

The duke devoted all his time to the construction of the building but neglected to maintain the fortune that was supposed to pay for it. He duly went bankrupt. The estate was purchased by Hieronymus Cowle, an eccentric from a local mill-owning family who had made a second fortune in railways. He judged the already vast and rambling half-built structure to be a decent start, but insufficiently ambitious; many more architects, landscape gardeners, hydrologists, engineers, stone masons and artists would have to be thrown at the project.

By the time Hieronymus had finished, Blysecrag boasted three hundred rooms, eighteen towers, two miles of cellars, five lifts, thirty dumb-waiter shafts, a similar number of laundry-delivery elevators disguised as wardrobes, a water-powered funicular linking the house to its own railway branch line, a six-hundred seat underground theatre with a hydraulically driven revolving stage, numerous fountains and a mile-long reflecting lake. The place was equipped with a variety of systems for communicating with the staff, plus a pressurised petroleum-vapour lighting system powered by an early hydraulic turbine.

Hieronymus died before he could move in. His son, Bardolphe, spent most of the rest of the family fortune indulging a passion for gambling and aviation; he converted one of the ballrooms into a casino and adapted the reflecting lake – which was handily aligned with the prevailing westerlies – into a landing lake for his seaplane and, near one end of the lake, up a short incline, had installed the world's first land-based steam-powered catapult on the cliff edge, to launch the aircraft. It was this structure I could see from the balcony of my room, wreathed in steam. Uncle Freddy had just had it restored to working order.

Not content with being able to land his seaplane during the day, Bardolphe had devised a system of coal-gas pipes set just beneath the surface of the mile-long lake to release bubbles of methane which could be ignited during the hours of darkness to provide a flare-path for night landings. He died in the fall of 1913 trying to make his first such landing; apparently the wind blew out half the plumes of burning gas and ignited several piles of leaves at the side of the lake, causing him to fly towards the trees to one side and collide with the top of an ornamental pagoda. He was buried in a coffin that looked like a roulette table, housed within a seaplane-shaped mausoleum on the hillside looking over the lake and the house.

Blysecrag was used as a convalescent hospital during the Great War, then it and the estate fell into disrepair as the Cowle family struggled to cope with the ruinous costs of upkeep. It was an army training centre during the Second World War, then the Ministry of Defence sold it to us in 1949; we too used it as a training centre. Uncle Freddy bought it from the company in the late fifties and has lived here since the early sixties. The Business started the refurbishments but he completed them; the restoration of the steam catapult and the reflecting lake's underwater lighting system, recently converted to run on North Sea gas, was all his doing.

I returned inside and closed the windows. The servants had hung my suit carrier in one of the two huge wardrobes and left my other bags on the bed. I looked around but there was no TV in here: Uncle Freddy thought he was making a huge concession to modern technology by having a special room to watch television in. Blysecrag had speaking tubes, servant-signal wires, pneumatic delivery tubes, a domestic telegraph system and its own baroquely complicated field-telephone-based intercom network, but only a handful of TVs, and they were mostly in the servants' quarters. I'm a news junkie; normally the first thing I do in a hotel room is switch on the TV and find CNN or Bloomberg. Never mind. I shivered in my clothes, just briefly. Here I was in a huge house stuffed with antiques and swarming with servants, waiting for the vastly rich and powerful to arrive, and it was all entirely familiar to me. I had one of those moments when

I reminded myself how fortunate I'd been, and how privileged I had become.

As usual the first thing I unpacked, even before my toiletries bag, was a little netsuke monkey with a dolorous expression and eyes made from tiny chips of red glass. I placed it on the bedside table. I set the monkey – usually along with my watch and a torch – by my bed wherever I am in the world, so that I always have something familiar to look at when I first wake up. The sad-faced little figure was one of the first presents I ever bought myself after I left school. Embedded in its base is a thirty-five-year-old pre-decimal coin; the same twelve-sided thruppenny bit that Mrs Telman handed to me from her gleaming black limousine that wet Saturday afternoon in 1968.

Uncle Freddy wanted to fish. I dressed in some old jeans, a sensible shirt and a thick woolly jumper I found in a drawer; the house provided a life-jacket-equipped waistcoat with too many pockets, and a pair of thigh-length waders. An ancient jeep driven with geriatric abandon by Uncle Freddy himself bounced us down a grassy track to a boathouse by the broad lake with the fountain; the pair of wolfhounds bounded after us, scattering spittle to either side as they ran. In the boathouse we picked up two old cane rods and the rest of the paraphernalia associated with fly fishing.

'Are we likely to catch anything at this time of year?' I asked as we tramped along the shore, loosely accompanied by the dogs.

'Good god, no!' Uncle Freddy said, and laughed.

We waded into shady shallows not far from where the river met the lake down an ornamental weir decorated with chubby stone cherubs.

'Well, the bastards are up to something,' Freddy said, casting far out into the gentle current. I had told him about my visit to Silex Systems and the odd behaviour of Messrs Rix and Henderson concerning the locked door. He glanced at me. 'As long as you're sure you're not imagining all this.'

'I'm sure,' I told him. 'They were both perfectly polite, but I could tell they really didn't want me there. I felt about as welcome as a mole on a bowling green.'

'Ha.'

'I took another look at the plant's figures afterwards,' I said, making a reasonable cast myself. 'They show some odd fluctuations. They're like an oil painting: the further away you stand, the more convincing they look, but get up close and you can see all the brushstrokes, all the little blobby bits stuck on.'

'What the hell can they be up to?' Uncle Freddy said, sounding exasperated. 'Could they have another production line going in there? Could they be building their own chips and selling them independently?'

'I thought about that. Finished chips are worth more than their weight in gold, more than industrial diamonds, but I don't see how they could have hidden the capital plant. The raw-materials purchases would barely show in petty cash, but the machines, the whole line . . . they can't have hidden that.'

'Silex. They're not wholly owned, are they?'

I shook my head. 'Equal forty-eight per cent with Ligence US. The other four per cent is owned by the employees. Rix and Henderson are our guys, but via Mr Hazleton.'

'Shit,' Uncle Freddy said. Mr Hazleton is a Level One executive; a single level above Uncle Freddy and the highest of the high, one of the all-but-untouchable principal players of our company and a full member of the Board. He would be showing up later on today with some of the other power players. Uncle

Freddy – a frustrated Level One man if ever there was one – harboured certain resentments concerning Mr Hazleton. 'Do we have a legal route in there?' he asked.

'Only through Hazleton,' I told him. 'Or another Level One intervening.'

Uncle Freddy snorted derisively.

'Otherwise we'd have to wait until the elections next year,' I said. 'Though we'd have to start campaigning now. And I've no idea who might be plausible replacements.' (I'll have to explain about these elections later.)

'We should just get a chap in there,' Uncle Freddy said.

'I think so. Want me to talk to somebody?'

'Yes. Get a fellow from one of the European offices. Somebody who knows what they're doing. Scottish, I suppose, but not based there, or London.'

'I think there's someone in Brussels who might do. If you'll authorise it I'll see if I can persuade Security to put them on secondment.'

'Right you are. Yes. Think that's the least we should do.' Then Uncle Freddy's line, until that point lying in a lazily straightening S shape across the ruffled waters, jerked suddenly and disappeared under the surface. He looked surprised. 'Well, I'll be—!' he exclaimed, and braked the suddenly spinning reel.

'Let's hope that's a good omen,' I said.

The Business has understandings with several states and regimes, and over the centuries we'd carved out our own little territories in various places. We have, for example, a small factory in the US military base on Cuba at Guantanamo, which produces the only authentic Cuban cigars it is more-or-less legal to sell in the US (though they're so exclusive and expensive, and their production legality so ticklish, they're never advertised. Rumour has it that it was one of those which President Clinton . . . well, never mind).

Usefully close to Guantanamo is the small Bahamanian island of Great Inagua, which is not truly independent but has its own semi-autonomous parliament; we have interests there, too. On the US mainland, we own a couple of casinos and a few other business ventures in the Rez (as it's usually called; formally it's the Wolf Bend Native American Reservation) in a desolate corner of Idaho where – again conveniently – the full remit of US law does not apply.

We are the only non-governmental organisation to have a permanent base on Antarctica, in Kronprinsesse Euphemia Land, between Dronning Maud Land and Coates Land. Purchased from Argentina during the Junta, this is the closest we've come so far to having our own statelet and has the handy attribute of being both excruciatingly remote and effectively beyond the reach of international law. The more lurid company rumours have characterised Kronprinsesse Euphemia Land as our Siberia; our very own gulag. However, no one I know has ever heard of anybody being sent there against their will, so I reckon it's just a story to help keep people well behaved.

A few places have – for an arrangement, for services rendered or just outright bribes – allowed some of our most senior people to become accredited diplomats; hence our interest in the fate of General Pinochet, who was travelling on a supposedly diplomatic passport when he was arrested in London.

This seems to be the latest fad with our Level One execs; in the past we never used to bother. Perhaps it is simply that when you're so rich you can buy anything, all that's left is stuff that money normally can't buy. My own theory is that one of our

Level One people bumped into a high-ranking Catholic at a party once and discovered he was talking to a Knight of Malta, accredited through the Vatican to all the best diplomatic courts (Lee Iacocca, for example).

This would leave our Level One exec at a disadvantage, because only Catholics can become Knights of Malta, and there is a strict rule in the Business that all executives – anybody above Level Six – must renounce all religious affiliations, the better to devote themselves to pursuing a life dedicated to Mammon.

Anyway, some of our Level Ones possess diplomatic passports from some of the world's less savoury regimes, like Iraq and Myanmar, while some sport papers from places so little known that even experienced customs and immigration officers have been known to have to refer to their reference books to find them: places like Dasah, a trucial state on a small island in the Persian Gulf, or Thulahn, a mountainous principality between Sikkim and Bhutan, or the Zoroastrian People's Republic of Inner Magadan, between the Sea of Okhotsk and the Arctic Ocean, or San Borodin, the only independent Canary Isle.

These arrangements are useful, but they're expensive and fragile – regimes change, and if we can buy them now, who might buy them tomorrow? So there's another wheeze on the horizon; a fix for all this. We intend to buy our own state, outright.

Quite apart from giving us access to all the diplomatic passports we might reasonably require and allowing us unrestricted use of that perfect smuggling route called the diplomatic bag, we would also finally have what, according to some of the more enthusiastic Level Ones, we really need: a seat at the United Nations.

The candidate is the island of Fenua Ua, part of the Society

Islands group in the South Pacific. Fenua Ua has one inhabited island, two mined-out guano outcrops, and no natural resources apart from lots of sun, sand and salt and some only arguably edible spiny fish. They were once so desperate to generate income from any source at all they invited the French to come and blow up nuclear bombs beneath them, but the French refused. They used to have to import water. They now have a desalination plant but the water still tastes, apparently, on the salty side.

Their power plant works only intermittently, there is no natural harbour on the main island, barely space for a proper airport and the reefs make it impossible for cruise ships to call even if they want to (and as Fenua Ua is devoid of natural wonders and possesses no native culture whatsoever except that based around the removal of the spines from spiny fish, they don't want to).

The place's most pressing problem is that there is no ground on Fenua Ua higher than a metre and a half above sea level, and while its reefs protect the main island from waves and the Pacific swell, they will not be able to counter the effects of global warming. In fifty years' time, if present trends continue, the place will be mostly under water and the capital will look like Venice during an Adriatic storm surge.

The deal being suggested is that if we'll build them a sea wall which will girdle the whole island, the Fenua Uans will let us take control of the entire state. As there are only thirty-five hundred dispirited Fenua Uans, it has proved quite easy to bribe almost all of them. Three referenda in the last five years have backed our plans, by a huge majority.

This was, though, not proving an easy deal to complete. Various governments had got wind of the transaction and had been quietly trying to block it, offering various amounts of aid, trading credits and personal financial sweeteners to the Fenua Ua government. The US, the UK, Japan and France had proved particularly stubborn, and while we hadn't parted with any serious money yet – just a few skiing holidays in Gstaad, a motor cruiser or two, a couple of apartments in Miami and a few other expensive gifts – we'd invested a great deal of effort in all this, only to find that every time we thought we were on the brink of closing the deal, the Fenua Ua government came up with another objection, or pointed out that the French had promised to build them an international airport, or the Japanese would finance a better desalination plant or the US had offered them their own nuclear power station or the British had suggested they might be able to arrange a visit by Prince Charles.

However, according to the rumours I'd been hearing over the last few weeks, perhaps there had been some resolution of the problem at last, because the meeting at Blysecrag had seemingly been set up to bring the whole matter to a head. Pens might well be wielded, hearty handshakes shared and leather-bound document wallets exchanged, perhaps – I thought as I stood there in my waders watching Uncle Freddy reel in a lively little trout – that very evening.

'Ah,' said Uncle Freddy, throwing the car into a corner and twirling the steering-wheel until his arms were crossed. The Ferrari went briefly sideways and teetered on the edge of a spin. 'Come on, come on, old girl,' Uncle Freddy muttered; not to me, to the car. I clutched my purse to my chest and felt my legs pull up instinctively, squeezing the shiny shopping-bags behind my calves in the footwell. We continued to head for the hedge for what felt like a few seconds, then the Daytona seemed to gather itself just at the apex of the corner and its long red bonnet lifted as we roared on down the resulting straight. Cars were Uncle Freddy's weakness: the old stables at Blysecrag contained a collection of exotic automobiles – some of them very fast – that would have shamed most motor museums.

We were on our way back from Harrogate, which was about forty minutes' drive from Blysecrag, or half an hour if you drove like Uncle Freddy. He had offered to drive me into town to pick up a new dress for the formal dinner that evening. I had forgotten quite how enthusiastic a driver he could be. We had been talking – on my part largely to take my mind off the mortal peril Uncle Freddy appeared to be intent on putting us both in – about the Fenua Ua situation and I had expressed the cautious hope as detailed above that things might be settled tonight.

Then Uncle Freddy had said, 'Ah,' in that particular tone that made my heart seem to sink, while at the same time my curiosity suddenly awoke, sniffing something major.

I had been trying to distract myself from Uncle F's driving by counting the money I'd withdrawn from a couple of cash machines in Harrogate. The developed world divides people neatly into two camps: those who get nervous when they have too much money on them (in case they lose it or get mugged), and those who get nervous when they don't have enough (in case they miss a bargain). I am firmly of the second school, and my lower limit of nervousness seems to be way, way above most people's higher one. I tend to lose a lot in currency conversion charges but I'm never short of a bob or two. I blame my upbringing. I looked up from my purse at Uncle Freddy. '*Ah?*' I said.

'You bugger,' Uncle Freddy said, under his breath, as a tractor blocked the road ahead and a stream of cars coming in the opposite direction prevented him overtaking. He looked at me and smiled. 'Suppose you might as well be told now as later,' he said.

'What?'

'We're not really interested in Fenua Ua.'

I stared at him. I put the cash away, not fully counted. 'What?' I said flatly.

'It's all a blind, Kate. A distraction.'

'A distraction.'

'Yup.'

'For what?'

'For the real negotiations.'

'The real negotiations.' I felt like an idiot. All I seemed to be able to do was repeat what Uncle Freddy was saying.

'Yup,' he said again, throwing the Ferrari into a gap in the traffic and past the tractor. 'The place we're really buying is Thulahn.'

'*Thulahn?*' This was the tiny Himalayan principality with which we had – I had thought until now – a very limited understanding; just the usual money for diplomatic passports deal. Uncle Freddy had mentioned the day before on the telephone that Suvinder Dzung, the current Prince of Thulahn, would be in attendance at Blysecrag over the weekend, but I hadn't thought any more about this, beyond reconciling myself to an evening of unsubtle flirting and increasingly outrageous offers of jewels and royal yaks if I'd leave my door unlocked that night.

'Thulahn,' Uncle Freddy said. 'We're buying Thulahn. That's how we get our seat at the UN.'

'And Fenua Ua?'

'Oh, that's only ever been to throw the other seats off the scent.'

At this point I had better make clear that during the last decade or so, when the idea of buying our own country and securing our own place at the UN had been gaining popularity amongst the high-ups, we seemed to have started referring to sovereign states as 'seats'.

'What, right from the start?'

''Oh, yes,' Uncle Freddy said airily. 'While we got quietly on with the negotiations with the Thulahnese, we've been paying a chap in the American State Department a handsome sum every month to make sure they keep coming up with new ways of preventing us buying Fenua Ua. But I mean, pwah!' At this point Uncle Freddy puffed his cheeks out and lifted both hands from the wheel in a dangerously Italianate gesture. 'Who'd really want Fenua Ua?'

'I thought the actual place was irrelevant. I thought it was the seat at the UN that mattered.'

'Yes, but if you're going to buy somewhere you might as well buy somewhere decent, don't you think?'

'Decent? Thulahn's a dump!' (I'd been there.) 'They've so little flat land their single landing strip has to double up as their football park; the time I went we nearly crashed on our first attempt because they'd forgotten to remove one of the goalposts. The royal palace is heated by smouldering *yak* dung, Uncle Freddy.' (Well, bits had been.) 'Their national sport is emigration.'

'Ah, but it's very high, you see. No danger from global warming there, oh, no. Also very survivable in the event of a meteorite strike or that sort of thing, apparently. And we'll be levelling off one of their mountains to make a proper airport. Plan is to carve out lots of caverns and tunnels and shift a lot of archive stuff there from Switzerland. There's quite a lot of hydroelectric power, they tell me, but we've got a nuclear plant we bought last year from Pakistan just waiting to be installed. Oh, come on, get out the bloody way!'

This last was addressed to the rear of a caravan blocking our progress.

I sat and thought while Uncle Freddy fretted and fumed. Thulahn. Well, why not?

I said, 'The Fenua Uans will be upset.'

'They've done very well out of us. And we shan't be making a big fuss about buying Thulahn. We can keep the charade going with Fenua Ua until they have their airport or water plant or whatever from one of the other seats.'

'But in one generation they'll be under water.'

'They'll all be able to afford yachts, thanks to us.'

'I'm sure that will come as a great comfort to them.'

'Ah, bugger you,' Uncle Freddy muttered, and sent us sling-shotting past the caravan; a car approaching flashed its lights at us. 'And you,' Uncle Freddy said, before throwing the Ferrari into the fluted entrance to Blysecrag's estate. 'Excuse my French,' he said to me. Gravel made a noise like hail in the wheel arches as the car fishtailed back and forth before straightening, finding the tarmac that started at the gatehouse and roaring on down the drive.

I checked the time difference and then called one of my girl-friends in California.

'Luce?'

'Kate. How ya doin', hon?'

'Oh, fine and dandy. You?'

'Well as can be expected, given my boss-bitch from hell just beat me at squash.'

57

'How politic of you to let her triumph. I thought your boss was a guy.'

'No. It's Deana Markins.'

'Who?'

'Deana Markins. You know her. You met her at Ming's. Last New Year. Remember?'

'No.'

'The girls' night out?'

'Hmm.'

'You remember. We were splitting the check but they gave it to Penelope Ives because she was sitting at the head of the table and you said, Oh my God, they billed Penny!'

'Ah, that night.'

'Well, her, anyway. Oh, and my cat's in cat hospital.'

'Oh dear. What's wrong with Squeamish?'

'Serial fur balls. That's already more than you want to know, believe me. You still in Braveheart territory? They cun take ourr lives but they'll neverr take us serriously.'

'Luce, I swear you must have your own dialogue coach as well as personal fitness trainer. But no, I'm in Yorkshire, England.'

'What? This at the mega-house that belongs to your uncle?'

'The same.'

'Any chance your beloved will be there?'

'There, maybe; available, I doubt it.'

'What's his name again?'

'Gosh, I don't think I ever told you it.'

'Na, you didn't, did you? You're so cagey, Kate. So defensive. You should open up more.'

'That's what I keep offering to do for this guy.'

'Slut.'

'Chance would be a fine thing. But never mind.'

'One day your prince will come, kid.'

'Yeah. Funnily enough, tomorrow a real prince does arrive. Guy called Suvinder Dzung. I may have mentioned him.'

'Oh, yeah, the guy who made a pass at you in the scullery.'

'Well, it was the orangery, but, yes, that's my boy. I don't *think* that's why I've been invited, but I'm still just a little suspicious I've only been invited to keep him entertained.'

'This the Himalayan guy?'

'Well, as in hailing from, not in physical appearance. Yes.'

'So he's a prince of this place?'

'Yes.'

'But I thought he was the ruler.'

'He is.'

'So how come this guy's called a prince if he's the ruler? How come he's not the king?'

'No idea. I guess it's a principality, not a kingdom. No, hold on, Uncle F said it was something about his mother. She's still alive, but he was married briefly, so she's not the queen, but at the same time he's not the king. Or something. But, frankly, who gives a fuck? Not I.'

'Amen.'

# CHAPTER
# THREE

O ver the next few hours Blysecrag changed in character and became suddenly very busy. Cars, trucks and
coaches arrived separately and in convoy, thunder-
ing up the mile-long slope that was the finishing straight of
the driveway. Helicopters touched down briefly to disgorge
people on to the pad between the tennis courts and the polo
ground, from where the guests, security people, technicians,
entertainers and others were ferried to the house itself by a
pair of people-carriers.

Uncle Freddy was in nominal charge of all this, though as usual the people really masterminding everything were those of the Business's quaintly entitled Conjurations and Interludans division, or the Charm Monsters as they were commonly known within the company.

So up from London was flown one of the most famous chefs in the country, along with his entourage (an extremely annoyed and insistent fly-on-the-wall TV crew from the BBC were only prevented from accompanying him by being physically barred from the helicopter).

Arranged through long-predated paperwork in a manner that would make it look like a coincidence, a photo shoot with a similarly world-renowned photographer was set up for the weekend, too, by a fashion magazine belonging to one of our wholly owned subsidiaries. This was supposed to make look less sordid the fact that we had a house full of rich and powerful men, none of them accompanied by wives or partners, and a rather larger number of stunningly beautiful and allegedly unattached young women all desperate to make a name for themselves in the world of fashion, modelling, glamour photography, acting or, well, almost anything.

Additional cooks, servants, entertainers and so on decamped from a series of coaches and minibuses. I spotted Miss Heggies at one point, surveying everything that was going on from a third-floor gallery window. She looked like a proud, solitary old lioness whose territory had just been invaded by about three hundred loping hyenas.

Our own security people swarmed over the place, chunkily crew-cut and sober-suited to a man and a woman, most of them in dark glasses, all of them with a little wire connecting one ear and their collar and muttering into concealed lapel mikes. You could tell the ones new enough never to have encountered Blysecrag before by the sheen of sweat on their foreheads and their look of barely controlled professional horror. With all its lifts, cellars, walkways, passages, stairways, galleries, dumb-waiters, laundry-handling wardrobe hoists and complexly interconnecting rooms, securing the house in any meaningful sense was simply impossible. The best they could do was sweep the grounds, be grateful there was never less than a two-kilometre distance between the high wall that bordered the entire estate and the house itself, and try hard not to get lost.

Prince Suvinder Dzung of Thulahn arrived from Leeds–Bradford airport by car. Twenty years earlier, the Prince had lost his wife of a few months in a helicopter crash in the Himalayas, which was why he didn't arrive in one of the machines now. His transport was from Uncle Freddy's collection: a Bucciali Tav 12, which must count as one of the world's more outrageous-looking cars, having a hood – or bonnet, as we'd say here – about the same length as a Mini. Shortly after sending the e-mail to Brussels that would dispatch somebody Freddy and I trusted to Silex in Motherwell, I joined Uncle Freddy on the front steps to greet our guest of honour.

'Frederick! Ah, and the lovely Kate! Ah, I am so glad to see you both! Kate: as ever, you take my breath away!'

'Always gratifying to be compared with a blow to the solar plexus, Prince.'

'Hello hello hello!' Uncle Freddy shouted, apparently of the opinion that the Prince had become suddenly deaf and deserved greeting in triplicate. The Prince accepted a hearty handshake from a beaming Uncle Freddy and imposed a prolonged hug upon me before planting a moist kiss on my right middle finger. He fluttered his eyelids at me and smiled. 'You are still right-handed, my lovely Miss Telman?'

I pulled my hand away and put it behind my back to wipe it. 'In a fight I'm a southpaw, Prince. How nice to see you again. Welcome back to Blysecrag.'

'Thank you. It is like coming home.' Suvinder Dzung was a marginally tubby but light-footed fellow of a little more than average height with glisteningly smooth dark olive skin and a rakish, perfectly black moustache, which matched his glossily waved and exquisitely sculpted hair. Educated at Eton, he spoke without a trace of a sub-continental accent unless he was profoundly drunk, and when in England dressed in Savile Row's conservative best. His major affectation, apart from being a bit of a show-off on the dance floor, was his collection of gold rings, which glittered with emeralds, rubies and diamonds.

'Come in, come in, come in, old chap!' Uncle Freddy said, still apparently addressing a triumvirate of princes and waving his shepherd's crook so enthusiastically that it nearly felled the Prince's private secretary, a small, pale, beady-eyed fellow called B. K. Bousande, who was standing at the Prince's side holding a briefcase. 'Oops! Sorry, BK!' Uncle Freddy laughed. 'This way, Prince, we have your usual suite.'

'My dearest Kate,' Suvinder Dzung said, bowing to me and winking as he turned to go. 'See you later, alligator.'

I laughed. 'In a while, Cayman Isler.'

He looked confused.


'Well, thank God we didn't put much money into Russia!' Uncle Freddy exclaimed. He passed the port to me and picked up his cigar from the ashtray, pulling on it and rolling the smoke round his mouth. 'What a fucking débâcle!'

'I was under the impression we put quite a lot of money into Russia,' Mr Hazleton said, from the other side of the table, opposite me. He watched as I poured myself a small measure. I had permitted myself a relatively unphallic Guantanamo cigar along with my coffee.

The evening's fun was barely begun: we had been promised the run of the casino later, where we would each be given a stack of chips, plus there would be dancing. So far there had been no mention of anything as vulgar as our buying Suvinder Dzung's country off him. I handed the port to the Prince.

There were eight of us around a small dining-table in a modest room set off Blysecrag's cavernous main dining room. We had been many more for dinner, our fellow diners having included our titled photographer, a television presenter, a couple of Italian opera singers – one soprano, one tenor – a French cardinal, a USAF general, a pair of boyish pop stars I'd heard of but didn't recognise plus an older rock singer I did, an American conductor, a cabinet minister, a fashionable young black poet, a couple of lords, one duke and two dons; one from Oxford and one from Chicago.

After pudding, we had excused ourselves to talk business, taking the Prince with us, though as I say not much business had actually been talked so far. All this to impress Suvinder. I wondered if we weren't appearing a little desperate. Maybe we were anticipating problems during the negotiating sessions, which would start tomorrow.

There were a few of our own junior people present, too, lurking quietly in the background, plus a couple of the Prince's servants, and – standing with his feet spread and his hands clasped in the shadows behind his boss – the taut and bulky presence of Mr Walker, Hazleton's chief of security.

'Well, we did,' Uncle Freddy told Hazleton, 'depending on what you call a lot of money, but the point is we put in a lot less than most people and a hell of a lot less than a few. Proportionately, we're ahead when the pain's shared out.'

'How comforting.' Mr Hazleton was a very tall, very imposing man with a broad, tanned, slightly pock-marked face under a lot of white hair, which was as millimetrically controlled as Uncle Freddy's was wildly abandoned. He had a deep voice and an accent that seemed to originate somewhere between Kensington and Alabama. When I'd first met him he'd sounded like an archetypal smooth English toff (as opposed to Uncle F's batty variety), but, like me, he'd lived in the States for the last ten years or so and had picked up some of the local intonation. This gave him an accent that was either quite charming or made him sound like an English actor trying to sound like somebody from the Deep South, depending on your prejudices.

Hazleton was cradling a crystal bowl of Bunnahabhain in one large, walnut hand and pulling on a cigar the size of a stick of dynamite.

I've always found it hard to look at Level Ones like Hazleton without automatically multiplying the image they presented to me by their wealth, as though all their money, possessions and stock options acted like giant mirrors, proliferating them across any given social space like opposing mirrors in a lift. These days, we were getting close to being able to assume that anyone at Level One was a billionaire; not quite in the same financially stratospheric league represented by Bill Gates or the Sultan of Brunei, but not far off it; maybe a factor of ten away.

The only other Level One exec present was Madame Tchassot, a small, brittle-looking lady of about sixty who sported tiny glasses and wore her unfeasibly black hair in a tight bun. She had a thin, pinched face and was chain-smoking Dunhills.

Besides Uncle Freddy there were five other second level people, including the recently promoted Adrian Poudenhaut, Hazleton's protégé and main man in Europe. He was a tall but podgy Englishman with a mid-Atlantic accent who until I'd come along had been the youngest person to make it to Level Three. We'd never got on, though Uncle Freddy had a soft spot for him because he was another petrol head and so always got a tour of the car collection when he came to Blysecrag. He was rumoured to have some sort of thing going with Madame Tchassot, though nobody was sure, and as she rarely left Switzerland and he was often at Hazleton's side in the States, it could only have been pretty sporadic. Personally I found the very idea of the two of them bumping uglies profoundly unsettling.

The other Level Twos were M. M. Abillah, a small, mostly silent seventy-year-old Moroccan, Christophe Tieschler, a merry-looking German geezer of extravagant and seemingly self-satisfied plumpness, and Jesus Becerrea, an aristocratic-looking Portuguese with darkly hooded eyes.

There was only one other Level Three there: Stephen Buzetski, a sandy-haired, rangy-limbed guy with freckles, crinkly eyes, a few years older than me, whom I loved, and whom I'd loved from the first moment I'd set eyes on him, and who knew this, and who was obviously and genuinely flattered and embarrassed by this in equal measure, and who was so intolerably perfect and nice and lovable that he wouldn't cheat on his wife, to whom he wasn't even all that happily married, just faithful, the bastard.

'They do say the Russians need a strong man; their tsars, their Stalin,' Suvinder Dzung put in, letting one of his servants pour his port while he undid his bow-tie and unbuttoned his dinner jacket. The Prince wore a dark purple cummerbund secured by golden clasps. He was given to sticking both thumbs into the broad belt and stretching it against his belly. I wondered if he was trying to twang it; maybe he didn't know a good cummerbund doesn't twang. 'Perhaps,' the Prince said, 'they need another one.'

'What they might get, Prince, is the Communists back,' Hazleton drawled. 'If I didn't think Yeltsin was just an alcoholic clown I could believe he was secretly a Communist himself, supposed to appear to attempt capitalism but then make such a God-awful mess of it that the Brezhnev days look like a golden age in comparison and the Marxist-Leninists like saviours.'

'Ms Telman,' Madame Tchassot said suddenly in her sharp little voice, 'I understand you visited Russia recently. Have you any thoughts on the matter?'

I blew out some smoke. I'd intended to keep my head down for the rest of the after-dinner discussion, having earlier revealed myself to all as a dangerous radical. I'd contrasted, unfavourably, the West's reaction to a bunch of the already very rich getting caught out in their hedge-fund speculations with that of the response to the unfolding catastrophe caused by Hurricane Mitch. In one case a rescue fund of several billion US dollars was put together within a few days; in the other a couple of million had eventually been pledged as long as there was no dangerous talk about a debt moratorium or even – perish the thought – a total write-off.

'Yes, I was,' I said. 'But I was there to look at a few interesting technologies rather than at their society as a whole.'

'What's happened,' Adrian Poudenhaut said, 'is that the Russians have created their own form of capitalism in the image of what was portrayed to them as the reality of the West by the old Soviet Union's propaganda machine. They were informed that there was nothing but gangsterism, gross and endemic corruption, naked profiteering, a vast, starving, utterly exploited underclass and a tiny number of rapacious, vicious capitalist crooks who were entirely above the law. Of course, even at its most *laissez-faire* the West was never remotely like that, but that's what the Russians have now created for themselves.'

'You mean Radio Free Europe didn't convince them how sweet life here in the West really was?' Hazleton said, with a smile.

'Maybe it did,' Poudenhaut conceded. 'Maybe most thought it was diametrically equivalent propaganda and took an average.'

'The Soviets never slandered the West like that,' I said.

'No?' Poudenhaut said. 'I've seen the old films. Looked like it to me.'

'Very old, and not representative, then. The point is that the Russians don't really have capitalism at all right now. People don't pay their taxes, so the state can't pay its employees; the majority of people exist through self-sufficiency and bartering. And there's negligible accumulation of capital, reinvestment and development because all the money's siphoned off to Swiss banks, including ours. So what they actually have is barbarism.'

'I'm not saying many Russians believed life in the West was as awful as it was sometimes portrayed,' Poudenhaut said. 'There's just a nice symmetry to the fact that it's the caricature they're in the process of copying, not the reality. I don't think they understand it themselves.'

'Whereas you obviously do,' I suggested.

'Anything we could do?' Hazleton asked me.

'To profit us or to help them?' I asked.

'Well, preferably both.'

I thought. 'We'd probably be doing civilisation in general a favour if we had – ' (here I mentioned a fairly well-known Russian politician) ' – killed.'

Poudenhaut snorted with laughter. Hazleton's blue eyes partially disappeared; a fine network of lines appeared at the corners of his eyes. 'I have a feeling we may have had some sort of dealings with the gentleman already,' he said. 'He has his moments of slapstick, too, I'll grant, but he might not be quite as black as he's painted.'

I raised my eyebrows and smiled. One of the other gentlemen cleared his throat, somewhere down the table.

By my side, the Prince sneezed. A servant appeared flourishing a handkerchief.

'You think he is as black as he's painted, Ms Telman?' Hazleton said easily.

'I have this very odd feeling,' I said, 'that somebody like me – though probably male,' I added, with a general smile, just catching the concerned-looking gaze of Stephen Buzetski, 'was sitting here nearly seventy years ago saying the same sort of thing about Germany and a faintly comical small-time politician called Adolf Hitler.' It was really only at about this point that it struck me quite how outspoken I was being. I had to remind myself – a little late, perhaps – quite how powerful the people in this room were. Adrian Poudenhaut laughed again, then saw that Hazleton was looking very levelly and seriously at me, and stopped.

'That's quite a comparison to make, Ms Telman,' Hazleton said.

'*Hitler?*' Uncle Freddy said suddenly, as though waking up. 'Did you say *Hitler*, dear girl?' I was suddenly aware that just about everybody in the room was looking at me. Herr Tieschler was politely studying his cigar.

'Perhaps the trouble is you never can tell,' Stephen Buzetski said reasonably. 'Maybe if somebody had shot Hitler seventy years ago somebody else would have taken his place and things would have worked out much the same. It depends whether you believe in the primacy of individuals or social forces, I guess.' He shrugged.

'I sincerely hope I'm completely wrong,' I admitted. 'I imagine I probably am. But right now Russia is the sort of place that makes thinking along such lines seem quite natural.'

'Hitler was a strong man,' M. M. Abillah pointed out.

'He made the cattle trucks run on time,' I agreed.

'The man was an evil genius and no mistake,' the Prince informed us, 'but Germany was in a sorry mess when he took over, was it not?' Suvinder Dzung looked at Herr Tieschler as though for support, but was ignored.

'Oh, yes,' I said. 'It was left in a far better state after a hundred divisions of the Red Army had paid a visit and a succession of thousand-bomber raids had stopped by.'

'Well, now—' began Stephen Buzetski.

'Do you really think it is our business to go around having politicians shot, Ms Telman?' asked Jesus Becerrea, raising his voice to shout down Stephen.

'No,' I said. I looked at Hazleton, whom I knew had made a lot of money for himself and us in both Central and South America over the years. 'I'm sure that would never even cross our minds.'

'Or if it did we would swiftly dismiss it, Ms Telman,' Hazleton said with a steely smile, 'because acting upon such a thought would make us bad people, would it not?'

Was I being ganged up on? I was certainly being invited to keep deepening the hole I seemed already to be digging for myself.

'It might make us no better than everybody else,' I said, then looked at Uncle Freddy, blinking furiously beneath his cloud of white hair to my left. 'However, proportionately – to quote Mr Ferrindonald – we might hope to be ahead when the pain's shared out.'

'Pain can be a good thing,' Poudenhaut said.

'Relatively,' I said. 'In evolutionary terms, it's better to feel pain and rest up than to carry on walking and hunting on an injured leg, say. But—'

'But it's about discipline, isn't it?' Poudenhaut said.

'Is it?'

'Pain teaches you a lesson.'

'It's one way. There are others.'

'Sometimes there is no alternative.'

'Really?' I widened my eyes. 'Gosh.'

'It's like a child,' he explained patiently. 'You can argue with it and get nowhere, or you can just administer a short, sharp smack, and it's all cleared up. That applies to parents with children, schools ... any relationship where one half knows what's best for the other half.'

'I see, Mr Poudenhaut,' I said. 'And do you beat your other half? I mean, do you beat your own children?'

'I don't *beat* them,' Poudenhaut said, with a laugh. 'I give them the occasional slap.' He looked round the others. 'Every family has a naughty stick, doesn't it?'

'Were you beaten as a child, Adrian?' I asked.

He smiled. 'Quite a lot, at school, actually.' He lowered his head a little as he looked round the others, as though quietly proud of this proof he'd obviously been a bit of a lad. 'It never did me any harm.'

'My God,' I said, sitting back. 'You mean you'd have been like this *anyway*?'

'You don't have any children, do you, Kate?' he said, oblivious.

'Indeed not,' I agreed.

'So you—'

'So I don't really know what I'm talking about, I suppose,' I said breezily. 'Though I do seem to recall being a child.'

'I guess we all need to be taught a lesson,' Stephen Buzetski said casually, reaching for a large onyx ashtray and grinding out his cigar. 'I think I need to be taught that gamblin' don't pay.' He looked towards a rather slumped Uncle Freddy and grinned. 'That casino of yours open yet, sir?'

'Casino!' Uncle Freddy said, sitting upright again. 'What a splendid idea!'

'Just fuck me, Stephen.'

'It wouldn't be right, Kate.'

'Then just let me fuck you. You won't have to do a thing. I'll do it all. It'll be fabulous, dreamlike. You can pretend it never happened.'

'That wouldn't be right either.'

'It would be right. It would be very right. Trust me, it would be the rightest, sweetest, nicest thing that's ever happened to either of us. I know this. I do. I feel it in my water. You can trust me. Just let me.'

'Kate, I made a promise. I took these vows.'

'So? So does everybody. They cheat.'

'I know people cheat.'

'Everybody cheats.'

'No, they don't.'

'Every man does.'

'They do not.'

'Every one I've met does. Or would, if I let them.'

'That's you. You're just so enticing.'

'Except to you.'

'No, to me too.'

'But you can resist.'

'I'm afraid so.'

We were standing in the darkness by the stone wall at one end of the mile-long reflecting lake; the house lay behind us. Uncle Freddy had had the newly renovated gas flare-path lit for the first time that night; Suvinder Dzung had been allowed to ignite it, and a small plaque to this effect had been unveiled, to the Prince's obvious delight. Gas burbled with a comical farting noise from a hundred different patches of water. Flames burned above, detached torches on a wide obsidian floor fifteen hundred metres long. The converging florettes of yellow flame receded into the distance, becoming tiny, stitching the night.

If you looked closely you could see the little blue cones of pilot lights hissing away at the end of thin copper pipes, sticking out above the water in the middle of each darkly bubbling source of fire.

I had gambled in the casino (I was gambling now, though with no real hope of winning). I had talked to various people – I had even made some sort of peace with Adrian Poudenhaut – I had put off Suvinder Dzung as politely but firmly as possible when he'd tried to get me to come to his room, I had stood on the terrace with everybody else to watch fireworks crack and splash across the night skies above the valley, casually shooing off the straying right ring-encrusted hand of the Prince as he came to stand by me and tried to fondle my bum. Elsewhere in the main house there were rooms you could go to for drugs, and apparently there was one where there was some sort of live sex show going on, which might turn into an orgy later, depending on demand.

I had talked to the poet and the soprano, found myself being embarrassingly girly with the ageing rock singer, on whom I'd had a crush in my teens, and been chatted up by both the American conductor and the Oxford don. I had said hello to the monument in muscle and bronze Armani that was Colin Walker as he stood behind Hazleton, who was playing at the blackjack table, and asked him how he'd been enjoying his visit to Britain. He'd told me, in his soft, measured voice, that he had only flown in yesterday, but that so far it had been just fine, ma'am.

I had danced energetically to what I suppose was rave music in one of the small ballrooms with some of the younger execs and fellow guests, and more sedately to the music of the forties and fifties played by a big band in the largest ballroom, where most of the higher-level people were. Suvinder Dzung, twinkle-toed and undeniably impressive, had swept and dipped me round the room a couple of times, though by then, thankfully, he was starting to become distracted by a couple of lissom beauties, one blonde, one auburn, whom I assumed were the cavalry, dispatched to my rescue by Uncle Freddy.

It was there in the ballroom that I'd encountered Stephen Buzetski again at last and persuaded him to get up on to the floor and danced with him and eventually danced him out into the night air and then along a terrace from which we'd seen again the lights of the reflecting lake. I'd taken my shoes off and he'd carried them for me as we'd crossed the lawn.

75

It was cold, and my little blue-black Versace number didn't provide much in the way of warmth, so this had given me the perfect excuse to hug him and be hugged by him and have him put his jacket around me, which smelled of him. My shoes stuck out of his jacket pockets.

'Stephen, you're a rich and handsome man, you're a nice guy, but life's too short, dammit. What's *wrong* with you?' I balled a fist and thumped him gently on the chest. 'Is it me? Am I so unattractive? Am I too old? That is it, isn't it? I'm just too old.'

He grinned, face lit by the dully roaring yellow flames. 'Kate, we've been through this before. You are one of the most beautiful and attractive women I have ever had the good fortune to meet.'

I cuddled into him, hugging him tighter, pathetically, adolescently delighted by what had to be an outright lie. 'Nothing about my age, then,' I muttered into his shirt.

He laughed. 'Look, you're younger than me and you certainly don't look your age anyway. Satisfied?'

'Yes. No.' I pulled back and looked into his eyes. 'So, what? Can't you stand women who take the initiative?'

We had, as he'd said, been through all this before, but this too was a dance, something that had to be gone through. The first time we'd been over this ground, four years earlier, I'd suggested he might be gay. He'd rolled his eyes.

That was when I knew just how perfect he was, from the way he did that. Because rolling his eyes in that way – even if it hadn't seemed like an impossibly cute expression in its own right – just made it so obvious that this had happened to him before, that women had accused him of being gay in the past, in their confused and wounded pride at being rejected, and he was getting fed up hearing it.

That was when I knew it really wasn't just me; it was other women too, very possibly all of them. He really was faithful to his wife, and really not being either especially choosy or mildly sadistic. Which, of course, made him perfect. Because that's what we try to forget, isn't it? If he'll cheat on her with you, he'll cheat on you with somebody else, by and by.

So finding a man like this was like hitting the jackpot, discovering the mother lode, closing the deal of your life . . . only to find the pot had already been cleaned out, the claim had been staked by somebody else and the papers had already been signed without you.

My girlfriends and I had been over this territory often enough, too. By the time you got to our age all the good ones were gone. But until you got to our age you couldn't tell which ones *were* the good ones. What you were supposed to do? Marry young and hope, I suppose. Or wait for the divorcees and trust you got one who'd been a cheatee rather than a cheater. Or lower your standards, or settle for a different type of life altogether, which revolved around you as an individual and not you as one half of a couple, and which was anyway what I'd always thought I'd wanted, until I'd met Stephen.

'No, I find it flattering when women take the initiative.'

'You just never give in.'

'What can I tell you? I'm just a boring one-woman guy.' (Which meant, of course, as he was a very honest but also pretty smart guy, and he had chosen not to give me a straight answer, that he probably had strayed, once, and so knew what he was talking about, which only made me even more sad, because it hadn't been with me that he'd been unfaithful, and so I'd lost out not once but twice.)

'Everybody else is doing it, Stephen.'

'Hey, come on, Kate, what sort of argument is that? Besides, I'm not them.'

'But you're missing out. It's an opportunity. You're ... missing out,' I repeated, lamely.

'It's not some business thing, Kate.'

'Yes, it is! Everything is. Everything is trade, transactions, options, futures. Marriage is. Always has been. I'm offering you a deal that would be great for both of us, where neither of us loses: pure gain, total satisfaction on both sides; a deal you're crazy to turn down.'

'I've got my peace of mind to lose, Kate. I've got a whole guilt trip waiting for me if I did. I'd have to tell Em.'

'Are you mad? Don't tell her.'

'She might find out anyway. She'd divorce me, take the kids—'

'She'd never know. I'm not asking you to leave her or the children, I just want whatever I can get from you; anything. An affair, a single night, one fuck; anything.'

'I can't, Kate.'

'You don't even love her.'

'I do.'

'No, you don't; you're just comfortable with her.'

'Well, you know. Maybe that's what passion becomes, what it grows into.'

'It doesn't have to be. How can you be so ... determined, so ambitious in your business life and so meek in private? You shouldn't settle for so little, or if you need that bland comfort bit, you should have the passion too. With somebody else. With me. You deserve it.'

He let go of me gently, holding my hands in his and looking into my eyes. 'Kate, even with you I don't want to talk about

Em and the children.' He looked embarrassed. 'Don't you see? To me *this* is like having an affair; I get guilty just talking about this sort of thing with you.'

'So you've nothing to lose!'

'So I've everything to lose. Believe me, this guilt is barely registering on my in-built guilt-o-meter, but it still troubles me. If I climbed into bed with you it'd go off the scale.'

I sank back towards him, closing my eyes at the very thought. 'Believe me, Stephen, a lot would go off the scale.'

He laughed quietly and pushed me away again. I didn't think you could push somebody away tenderly, but he did. 'I just can't, Kate,' he said solemnly, and the way he said it just had that stamp of closure over it. We'd reached some sort of interim result, if not a conclusion. I could still choose to pursue the matter, if I insisted, but only at the risk of seriously pissing him off.

I shook my head. 'Guilt-o-meter. Really.'

'You know what I mean.'

'Yeah.' I sighed. 'I guess I do.'

He shivered in his white dress shirt. 'Hey, it's getting kind of cold out here, don't you think?'

'It is. Let's go back.'

'Think I'll go for a swim before I turn in.'

'I'll come and watch. May I?'

'Sure.'

Blysecrag's pool was only a little short of Olympic in size, buried underground at the end of a tangle of corridors and locatable principally by smell. I went arm in arm with Stephen down the carpeted corridors. The place was dark when we arrived and we had to search for the light switches, feeling round the walls until we found them and the lights flickered on, above and below the still water. The walls were covered with *trompe l'oeil* paintings showing pastoral scenes set in a landscape more gently rolling than that surrounding Blysecrag, and partially obscured by white Doric columns spaced every few metres. There were numerous tables, chairs, loungers and potted plants positioned near the walls on two room-long strips of Astro-turf, and a bar at the far end of the huge space. The arched roof was painted blue with lots of little white fluffy clouds.

I stood looking out over the calm blue surface while Stephen disappeared into the changing rooms. People had been here earlier – the tiled floor was puddled, there were towels and bits of swimming costumes scattered around, and a welter of pool-side-safe plastic flutes stood or lay by champagne buckets on the tables or had fallen to the pretend-grass floor – but the place was quiet and empty now and the waters lay level, undisturbed by even the slightest ripple now that the recirculating pumps had been switched off.

I looked at my watch. It was five fifteen. Much later than I'd intended to stay up. Ah, well.

Stephen appeared in a pair of baggy blue trunks, grinned at me and dived into the water. It was a beautiful dive, creating what seemed like far too small a splash, just a few tiny waves and a larger swell that moved languidly out from his point of entry. I watched his long tan body glide across the pale blue tiles on the pool's floor. Then he surfaced, shook his head once and settled into a powerful, easy-looking crawl.

I sat down by the edge of the pool, one knee drawn up under my chin, and just watched. He completed a dozen lengths then cut across the waves to me, sticking his elbows into the gutter that ran along the underside of the pool's edge.

'Having fun?' I asked.

'Yeah. Slow pool, though.'

'Slow? What? Is it full of heavy water or something?'

'No, but it's got this side wall,' he told me, patting the tiles above the gutter. 'The waves reflect back out into the pool so you're always slapping into them. Modern pools don't have walls; the water goes right to the top and spills into a flush trench under a grating.'

I thought about this. He was right, of course.

'Carries a lot of the wave energy away,' he said. 'Gives you calmer water. Makes the pool faster.'

'I see.'

He looked puzzled. 'Think you could swim in heavy water?'

'H two O two? Very buoyantly, I imagine.'

'Oh, well. Think I'll get out now.'

'I'll wait.'

He struck out for the chrome steps in one corner, lifted himself out in one exquisite, flowing movement and dripped away to the changing rooms.

I sat listening to the air-conditioning hum and watched the reflections the waters cast on the ceiling and walls; their long twisting veins of gold shimmered across the artificial sky and flickered amongst the grooved surfaces of the white plaster columns. I looked down at the chopping waters of the pool, recalling how perfectly still and calm they had been when we'd arrived.

Every wave, every ripple on that surface, as well as every dancing flick of light curving across the vault of sky and clouds above had been caused by him, by his body. His muscles, powering the shape and weight and surface of his frame through those waters, had spread that grace and effort throughout the pool and sent the light unwinding across the painted clouds and sky. I rocked forward, reaching one hand down to the water's surface, and let the liquid come up to meet my flattened palm, the little waves hitting my skin like a succession of soft caresses, their gentle, patting beat like that of an inconstant heart.

The waters calmed gradually again, the waves fell back and smoothed slowly out. The veins of light dancing on the ceiling became lazier and broader, like a river flowing towards the sea. The air-conditioner hummed.

'Okay?' Stephen said. I looked up at him.

One part of me wanted to let him go back by himself, so that I could stay here alone with the humming silence of the air and the slow averaging of the lulling waters, but his freckled face, tired though still smiling and open and friendly, would not let me. I accepted a hand up, we switched off the lights and returned to the main house.

He saw me to my room door, kissed me lightly on the cheek and told me to sleep well, which, eventually, I did.

'Mmm. Yes? Hello?'

'Kathryn, is that you?'

'Uh, speaking. Speaking. Yes. Who is that?'

'Me. Me . . . me, it is me.'

'Prince? Suvinder?'

'Yes. Kathryn.'

'Suvinder, it's the middle of the night.'

'Ah, no.'

'What?'

'I must . . . must correct you there. Kathryn. It is not the middle of the night, no no.'

'Prince, it . . . hold on. It's half six in the morning.'

'There. You see?'

'Suvinder, it's still dark, I've had one hour's sleep and I was hoping for a good five or six more, minimum. As far as I'm concerned it is the middle of the night. Now unless you have something very important to say to me . . .'

'Kathryn.'

'Yes, Suvinder.'

'Kathryn.'

'. . . *Yes?*'

'Kathryn.'

'Prince, you sound terribly drunk.'

'I am, Kathryn. I am very terribly drunk and very sad.'

'Why are you sad, Suvinder?'

'I have been unfaithful to you.'

'*What?*'

'Those two lovely ladies. I fell for their fanim . . . manifold charms.'

'You?'

'Kathryn, I am a man of easy virtue.'

'You and all the rest, Prince. Look, I'm very glad for you. I hope those two young ladies made you extremely happy and you were able to do the same for them. And you mustn't worry. You can't be unfaithful to me because I am not your wife or your girlfriend. We haven't made any promises to each other and therefore you can't be unfaithful. Do you see?'

'But I have.'

'You have what?'

'I *have* made promises, Kathryn!'

'Not that I was aware of, Suvinder, not to me.'

'No. They were made in my heart, Kathryn.'

'Were they now? Well, I'm very flattered, Suvinder, but you mustn't feel bad about it. I forgive you, all right? I forgive you for any previous and all future transgressions; how's that? You

83

just go on and have a whale of a time to yourself and I won't be bothered in the least. I'll be happy for you.'

'Kathryn.'

'Yes.'

'Kathryn.'

'Suvinder. What?'

'. . . Can I hope?'

'Hope?'

'That one day you will . . . you will look upon me kindly.'

'I already do, Suvinder. I look upon you very kindly. I like you. I hope I am your friend.'

'That is not what I meant, Kathryn.'

'No, I didn't think it was.'

'May I hope, Kathryn?'

'Prince . . .'

'May I, Kathryn?'

'Suvinder . . .'

'Just say that it is not a lost cause which I am pursuing, Kathryn.'

'Suvinder, I do like you, and I am honestly very flattered indeed that—'

'Always women say this! They say flattered, they say friend, they say like, and always later comes "but". *But* this, *but* that. But I am married, but you are too old, but your mother will put a curse on me, but I am too young, but I am not really a girl—'

'What?'

'—I thought you would be different, Kathryn. I hoped that maybe you would not "but". But you do. It is not fair, Kathryn. It is not *fair*. It is pride, or racism, or, or . . . or classism.'

'Prince, please. I've had a lot of disturbed sleep recently. I really need to get some quality rest in at some point.'

'Now I have upset you.'

'Suvinder, please.'

'I have made you upset with me. I can tell from your voice. Your patience is exhausted, is it not?'

'Suvinder, just let me go back to sleep, please? Maybe we should just, you know, stop now. We can talk about this in the morning. Things will look different then. I think we both need our sleep.'

'Let me come to see you.'

'No, Suvinder.'

'Tell me which room you are in, please, Kathryn.'

'Absolutely not, Suvinder.'

'Please.'

'No.'

'I am a man, Kathryn.'

'What? Yes, I know, Suvinder.'

'A man has needs . . . What was that? Did you just sigh, Kathryn?'

'Prince, I don't want to be rude, but I really need to get back to sleep now, and I'm asking you to say good night and let me get some rest. So, please, just say good night.'

'Very well. I shall go now . . . But, Kathryn.'

'Yes?'

'I shall not cease to hope.'

'Good for you.'

'I mean it, Kathryn.'

'I'm sure you do.'

'I do, I mean it.'

'Well, hurrah.'

'Yes. Well. Good night, Kathryn.'

'Good night, Suvinder.'

# CHAPTER
# FOUR

L et me explain some things about the way our company
works. The first thing to understand is that we are, up to
a point, democratic. Put simply, we vote for our bosses.
Never mind about that for now; we'll come back to it.

Secondly, we're quite serious about insisting that if people
want to rise above a certain level in the corporate hierarchy,
they must renounce any religious faith they have previously
espoused. In practice all this means is that an executive promoted
to the rank we once called *magistratus*, then Deacon, and now

call Level Six, has to swear they've given up their faith.

We don't insist that people stop going to their churches or their temples, or stop worshipping either in public or in private, or even stop funding religious works (though some sort of gesture in this direction is generally expected and appreciated); we certainly do not insist that people stop believing in their heads, or their souls if you will. All that's required is that people are prepared to swear they've stopped believing. This is quite sufficient to weed out the real zealots, the sort of people – admirable in their way if you esteem that sort of behaviour – who would prefer to be burned alive than switch to a different branch of the same church.

Thirdly, we practise total financial transparency: any company officer may inspect the accounts of any other. This has become much easier technically in recent years, of course, with the advent of computers and electronic mail, but the principle has been around since the first century AD. Its effect is to make corruption as a rule either unachievable or only possible at a trivial scale.

The main downside is complication. This was the case when people had to open up cabinets full of wax tablets for inspection, when they had to unroll papyrus scrolls, when they had to unchain books from counting-room desks, when they had to order old ledgers from storage, when they had to search through microfiches, and it is certainly the case now with computerised accounts; over two millennia, every technological advance that promised to make the task easier has been closely and seemingly inevitably accompanied by an increase in the complexity of the figures and systems involved.

Always looking for ways to cut costs, we've carried out trials which involve abandoning this practice for specific times and in certain places, intending to give it up entirely if the trials prove successful, but the results have always persuaded us that the benefits outweigh the costs.

Of course, corruption is always possible, and probably inevitable. A company worry has always been that one of our number might siphon off very small amounts of money over a long period and use that as seed capital for transactions which – though they exist outside the Business – are only possible thanks to the contacts, trust and information that person's membership of the company has brought and which grow exponentially until they distort the relationship between the apparent and real economic effect that person produces.

This sort of scam has been tried by various individuals in the past, but as a rule such perpetrators are discovered; unless they intend to bury their gains in the ground they have to do something with the profits, and an executive living significantly beyond their so easily checkable means has always been a sure sign some sort of chicanery has been going on. If somebody plays the long game of building up a big cash fund somewhere we can't see while continuing to live relatively modestly, and then retires early, suddenly seriously moneyed, to their own Caribbean island, we are not above indulging in our own style of chicanery to try and recover the funds we reckon belong to us. We aren't the Mafia and as far as I know we don't blow anybody's legs off, but it's surprising what you can do when you have your own Swiss bank and you're owed favours that go back in some cases for centuries. Actually, maybe it's not surprising at all.

Still, it is possible to beat the system, big time. In the late nineteenth century a certain Monsieur Couffable, one of our senior French executives, made a sizeable independent fortune on the Paris Bourse, which we didn't know about until he died. He'd spent every centime buying Dutch old masters, which he kept in a secret art gallery beneath his Loire château. So there you are; you do have to bury your money in the ground.

We never did get our hands on those paintings, despite having some very capable lawyers and the co-operation of the late Monsieur Couffable's widow (they were childless, he'd willed the secret collection to his mistress). Anyway, this practice has now become known as Couffabling. As a business, we try very hard not to get Couffabled.

Usually what's ours stays ours. A legitimately made fortune is never entirely personal in the Business, and specifically it is impossible to bequeath all you've made to your offspring or, indeed, anybody else who isn't one of us. The higher a person rises within our company, the greater becomes the proportion of their income paid in the form of stock options, pension rights, travel and other perks and so on.

So far so normal; lots of corporations limit the personal tax exposure of their senior people by giving them access to and often unlimited use of cars and drivers, apartments, mansions, aircraft and yachts. The Lear jet might belong to the company and be shown as a tax-liable item on the corporate books, but it's at the exclusive disposal of the CEO, who can use it to go shopping or golfing if he damn well pleases. In the same way, it's the company that pays for the box at the opera or the ball game, and the membership of the yacht or country club.

We do the same sort of thing, except perhaps more so.

The difference between us and others lies in the disposability of the assets that are nominally the property of the executive involved. Most of these can be sold back only to others in the Business, and even then there is a strict ranking of how much one can own according to one's hierarchical level.

What this means is that dynasties are difficult to establish and almost impossible to maintain; no matter how doting a father in the Business may be, he cannot pass on all his power and money to a favourite son just because he wants to. The father can make the son rich by most people's standards and he can attempt to further his boy's career in the company, but he cannot make Junior as rich as he has been or ensure that he too achieves the organisation's summit.

The vast majority of senior execs are quite happy with this arrangement, as they're usually the sort of people who believe that hard work and brains are the keys to success and have formed a dim view of any privilege which has been inherited rather than earned. This sort of attitude can actually be seen more clearly outside the Business, where quite a few very rich and successful fathers who've been in total charge of their own companies have left their children an only modest provision in their wills, not through general or specific vindictiveness but just to ensure that their offspring don't start out spoiled, and so that they too will know that if they do achieve anything it has at least partially been due to their own abilities rather than the sheer good luck of having a rich daddy.

Naturally, all this changes if the individual in the company invents something or has patents to their name. Take Uncle Freddy, for example. An Associate Level Two, he would probably only be a Level Five or Six but for the fact that he invented the chilp™. The chilp™ is the technical name (Uncle Freddy's own; I think he's a trifle sad it never caught on) for those little containers of whitish liquid that you get in tourist class in aircraft or in cafés, service stations and not very good hotels instead of a proper jug of milk.

The original things were those ghastly little pots with aluminium covers that it took both hands to open, if you were lucky, and which – even if you opened them carefully – usually splattered their contents over you. It was Uncle Freddy who came up with the much neater modern version, which opens cleanly and can be worked one-handed; one of those things most of us look at and think, Why didn't anybody think of that before? or, *I* could have thought of that ... Except that Uncle Freddy actually did.

Chilps™ are, literally, tiny things, but they're produced by the billion every year; the tiniest royalty on each one soon builds up to a very considerable fortune indeed, and as Uncle F invented the thing, he's got the patent and so he gets all the money; his promotion to Level Two in the Business was honorary. That kind of thing can throw out our system a bit, but somehow we manage to accommodate even the Uncle Freddies of the world. A better solution for us as a company, of course, would have been to have owned the patents corporately, and there are a few lucrative ones which we do own, and a few more we are cautiously optimistic about.

An example is the Incan™. This is a tube made from alu-minium, plastic or even waxed paper, designed to deliver two measured doses of finely ground powder into the nasal passages. It's registered with every major patent office in the world as a way to deliver either snuff or some sort of medicinal draught into the user's nose, but nobody who knows about it is under any illusions about its real rôle and we have no intentions of letting it be used for such mundane purpose.

It's a cocaine-delivery device for when, eventually, the stuff is legalised. You'll buy a pack of Incans™ no bigger than a pack of long cigarettes from wherever is licensed to sell them (by which time, of course, you may *not* be able to purchase legally a pack of tobacco cigarettes), pop the tab off one, snort, snort, and bingo!

No chopping, cutting and ploughing into stupid little lines on a mirror or the top of a toilet cistern, unless you're so into ritual you regard that as the best bit.

I've tried them at our labs in Miami; they work. (Best of all for us, they work only *once*; unless you're some sort of Unabomber-style micro-engineer you can't easily refill them.) The aluminium ones are very sleek and sexy and will be the original, premium product. They look a little like silver rifle-shell cases. We may do steel gold-plated versions for the luxury and exclusive gift end of the market. The plastic version is more mass-market, more blue collar. The wax paper ones are aimed at the more environmentally aware consumer and are biodegradable.

We have high hopes for the Incan™.

Back to the subject of corruption, racketeering, bribery, blackmail and other common business practices. Even though our organisation has always been tolerant of such victimless 'crimes' as prostitution, blasphemy, drug-taking, belonging to a trade union, sex and/or procreation outside marriage, homosexuality and so on, the societies in which we have to live and with which we have to trade have usually had other ideas, so secrecy and blackmail have never been entirely off the menu.

We are, above all, pragmatists. Corruption is frowned upon not because it is intrinsically evil but because it acts like a short-circuit in the machinery of business, or a parasite on the body corporate. The point is to reduce such behaviour to a tolerable level, not to attempt seriously to eradicate it utterly, which would call for a regime so strict and confining it would limit the abilities of the organisation to change and adapt, and stifle its natural enterprise even more severely than widespread corruption would. Even so, what we regard as a tolerable level of internal corruption is – thanks to our rules on financial transparency – positively microscopic compared to that in just about every other organisation we do business with, and it is a matter of considerable pride for us that in any given transaction or deal we will almost without exception be the most honest and principled party involved.

We're quite happy to deal with corrupt regimes and people, so long as the figures are all above board at our end. In many cultures a degree of what is termed corruption in the West has long been a respectable and accepted part of the way business is done, and we are ready, willing and able to accommodate this. (In the West, of course, it is just as common. It's just not respectable. Or publicised.)

In all this, of course, we're just the same as any other business or state. It's just that we've been doing it longer and are less hypocritical about it, so we're better at it. Practice makes perfect, even the practice of corruption. It ought to be one of our mottoes: Corruption – we deal with it.

Voting for your immediate superiors usually strikes outsiders as the most bizarre of our business practices. Manual and clerical workers tend to find the concept unlikely and bizarre, while those higher up have been known to react with outraged disbelief: how can it possibly work?

It works, I guess, because people generally are not stupid, and we do our best to recruit people who are smarter than most. It works, also, because we are used to taking, and are able to take, a long-term view, and perhaps because the practice does not extend into every other organisation we deal with and undertake joint operations with.

We have had several expensive but unpublished studies performed by highly respected universities and business colleges, which have tended to support our belief that letting people vote for their bosses means that a greater proportion of able and gifted people flourish and rise using this method than any other. The more usual system, where people are picked out from above, does have certain advantages – talented people can often rise more quickly, skipping several layers of management at once – but it is our firm belief that this leads to more problems than it solves, producing a culture where those on any given level within a company are constantly trying to find ways to flatter those above them, sabotage the careers of their colleagues on the same corporate rung, exploit, oppress and denigrate those on the levels beneath them and generally spend far too much time frivolously furthering their own selfish ends and their status within the company when they ought rightfully to be engaged in the far more serious and productive pursuit of making all concerned more money.

Our system doesn't put an end to all office politics, of course, nor does it reliably weed out every plausible rogue, gifted bully or lucky idiot, but it does make them easier to spot, control and ditch before they get too far. Gaining promotion by fooling your boss, especially one prone to flattery or sexual favours, can be relatively easy. Gaining the trust of those who work with you every day and will have to take orders from you if you are promoted is a lot more difficult.

The usual objection to all this is: Don't people tend to vote for people who'll give them an easy ride?

Sometimes they do, and a division of our company might suffer because there is a natural-born vacillator in charge, but people can be demoted by those immediately below them, too, or pensioned off, and – worst case – an entire department can be closed down from above, its structure dismantled, its duties redistributed and its personnel dispersed.

This almost never happens. People would rather elect to put

somebody in charge over them who knows what they're doing and whom they respect – even if they know that some of that person's later decisions will be disagreeable – than work under somebody who will damage all their interests by taking either no decisions or only easy ones.

We have works councils, too, in most of our wholly owned subsidiaries, though those tend to be at the sort of levels I'm not terribly familiar with.

None of this means that management is powerless: it's just that the spread of any given individual's power is different, tending to spread more upwards and less downwards compared to the standard model. It's still possible for senior people to encourage the careers of juniors and it's still possible for juniors to make themselves known to seniors and benefit thereby, it's just that neither can act without the tacit consent of those who will have to live with the effects of those actions.

We run, generally, a happy ship.

So why have you never heard of us, until now? We are not conspiratorial, or even particularly secretive. We don't believe in advertising ourselves, but we're sufficiently convinced of our own probity to be relaxed about any publicity that happens to come our way.

The most sinister reason given for our relative obscurity is that because we practise financial transparency and internal democracy while frowning upon conventional familial inheritance, the world's media – generally run by people for whom any one of these ideas is anathema – regard it as profoundly in their own interests to give us as little exposure as possible.

Another reason is that we undertake many more joint ventures than we do wholly owned ones, and in such situations we always let our partner company take the credit and deal with the exposure. We are a holding company, mostly, our interests lying in other companies rather than physically manufacturing products or providing services direct to the public. So we're partly invisible. Also, we have a variety of different company names and corporate identities for each individual branch of the business, all accrued naturally over the centuries, and so have no single name – apart from the Business, of course, which is so bland, general and vague it is almost a form of invisibility in itself. We do sometimes get confused with the CIA, though, which is silly; they're the Company. Besides, they're much more open than we are: there's no sign on the DC Beltway or anywhere else pointing to *our* HQ.

When somebody – sometimes a journalist, more usually a competitor – does start to investigate one of our concerns, they find that the ownership trail leads (sometimes straight, sometimes only after the sort of Byzantine flourishes and convolutions which are a good creative accountant's artistic signature) to one of those places that act as the commercial world's equivalent of black holes, into which public information might fall but from which none ever emerges: the Cayman Islands, Liechtenstein, or our very own Great Inagua.

We are not, however, totally invisible. There are articles about us occasionally in magazines and newspapers, sometimes there are television programmes that touch upon our interests, and every now and again a business book will mention us. The conspiracy theories are the most fun. There have been a couple of books and a number of articles, but the true home of those who would be our nemesis was the Net and now is the Web.

We have dozens of Websites dedicated to us, not one of which is our own. According to which one you choose to believe, we are either:

(a) the major force behind the New World Order (which appears to be what Americans too stupid to realise that the Cold War is over, they won, and the world is theirs, have adopted as the new bogey monster now that Ronnie's Evil Empire has a GNP a little less than Disney Corp.);

(b) an even more extreme, hideous and sinister branch of the International Zionist Conspiracy (in other words, the Jews);

(c) a long-term deep-entryist group of dedicated cadres charged by the Executive Council of the Fourth International to bring down the entire capitalist system from within by gaining control of lots of shares and then selling them all at once to produce a crash (which is the one I find most amusing);

(d) a well-funded cabal of the little known Worshippers of Nostradamus cult intent on bringing about the end of the financial world through a roughly similar strategy to that of the International Marxists (which may or may not imply a rethink for this plucky group of theorists if we do all make it past the millennium);

(e) the militant commercial wing of the Roman Catholic Church (as if, given the antics of the Banco Ambrosio and the Black Friars, they needed one);

(f) a similarly extremist Islamic syndicate sworn to out-perform, out-deal and out-haggle the Jews (probably the least plausible so far);

(g) a zombie-like remnant of the Holy Roman Empire, which has risen from the grave, unspeakably putrid but grotesquely powerful, to re-impose European dominance over the New World in general and the USA in particular through sneaky cosmopolitan business practices and the introduction of the Euro (top prize for invention, I feel);

(h) the front for a cartel of Jewish Negro financiers intent on enslaving the White Race (I confess I'm still waiting for my first introduction to a Jewish Negro financier, but maybe I just move in the wrong circles . . . except I don't);

(i) an alien conspiracy run from a spacecraft buried under the New Mexico desert, sent to bring about the collapse of (well, see any or all of the above) or

(j) just Bill Gates' retirement fund.

Heck, we've all been there; you've reinstated the underwater night-time flare-path and cleared the weeds out of your mile-long landing lake, some enterprising pilot's skimmed a dinky-looking dove-white Ilyushin seaplane successfully down over the hills and trees, kissed it on to the water and taxied noisily to the far end of the waterway to considerable applause from all those sports fans who've managed to prise themselves out of bed for the crack of noon, and then your steam catapult – guaranteed repaired by the best technicians money can buy just yesterday – suddenly goes on the blink. Hellish, isn't it? Actually I thought the pilot – a dashing Iranian – looked relieved.

'Bugger and blast!'

'Don't take it personally, Uncle Freddy.'

'Dammit, bugger and blast!'

Uncle Freddy's shepherd's crook decapitated two urns' worth of Michaelmas daisies and hydrangeas with one swinging swish.

Well, we missed the spectacle of an ex-Soviet navy seaplane being catapulted across the valley at the hills on the far side – if you looked carefully you could still see the craters where the engineers had fired old trucks loaded with steel plate into the woods to calibrate the catapult's throw – but we did get to play dodgems.

Being battered on all sides by over-enthusiastic revellers without either a decent hangover or the rudiments of driving ability while sitting in a small car resembling a garishly tin-plated slipper beneath an electrified metal grid is not necessarily my idea of the best way to ease myself back into sober normality, but it seemed only polite to Uncle Freddy to join in, after the disappointment with the catapult.

Re CW.
   Who what where?
   C Walker. Pay attention.
   What about him?
   Said Hi to him yesterday at Unc F's. Maintained he'd just flown in day before (ie Thursday). Does not compute.
   Oh right; more detail on Adrian George's spotting of CW. Original message was garbled (not at my end, obviously). AG saw CW while on *way* to office, not in it. Glimpsed presence in cab in street. Wednesday, this would be. So? Probably that aspect was garbled too.
   Never mind.
   OK. How's the party going?
   What party?
   You mean you're not @ B'crg @ the moment?
   OK, yes. Party usual low-key affair btw.
Where's your ass at?
   Singapore.
   Fun? I always thought it was a bit like the East would be if it was run by the Swiss. (This is not intended as a compliment.)

See your point. Did you know chewing-gum's
banned out here?

Yup. Lee Kwan U must have sat on a piece once and
got all upset.

Wonder if there's a flourishing smuggling
trade?

Careful, even talking about that sort
of thing's probably a crime, or at least a
misdemeanour.

Fuck em! I laugh in the face of their vicious
anti-chewing-gum laws!

Yeah, you're probably safe; they'd never make
it stick.

Ack. – (gags) – Goodbye.

'Kate.'

'Uncle Freddy.' I had been summoned to Uncle F's large and chaotic study in Blysecrag after lunch, while most people were still recovering from the excesses of one night and preparing themselves for those of the next.

'Jebbet E. Dessous.'

'*Gesundheit.*'

'Come now, dear girl. He's a Level One.'

'I know. Isn't he the one in Kansas? Collects tanks and stuff?'

'That's right. Made the news a while ago when he bought a couple of them what-d'ye-call-'ems. Rocket thingies.'

'Scud missiles?'

'That's right.'

'Was that him? I thought that was another guy, in Southern California.'

'Oh. Maybe the other chap got caught, then, and Jebbet didn't. That would be more like Jebbet. I can't remember.' Uncle F looked confused and stared at something long, grey and untidy on the floor, which turned out to be one of the wolfhounds. The beast stretched, yawned with a single echoing snap of its extensive jaws and then – such extreme activity having entirely exhausted it – rolled flopping back over with a long sigh, and fell asleep again.

Uncle Freddy opened his mouth as though to speak, then became distracted by something on his desk. Uncle F's desk was covered to a depth of several inches with a bewildering assortment of mostly paper-based rubbish. He picked up a long, elegant looking, Y-shaped piece of metal and turned it over in his hands, a look of intense concentration on his face, then he shook his head, shrugged and put it back again.

'Anyway,' I said.

'Anyway. Yes. Fancy paying old Jebbet a visit?'

'Do I have to?'

'What? Don't you like the fellow?'

'No, I've never met him, Uncle Freddy, though his reputation goes before. Why do I have to go and see him?'

'Well, he's sort of asked to see you.'

'Is that good or bad?'

'How d'you mean? For him or you?'

'For me, Uncle Freddy.'

'Ahm . . . pretty damn good, I'd say. Can't do any harm getting to know old Jebbet; very highly respected amongst the other top brass, he is, oh yes.' Uncle Freddy paused. 'Completely mad, of course. Thing is, you know his, umm, nephew or something, don't you?'

I said, 'Dwight?'

Now. There is a certain way of pronouncing Dwight's name that I find it hard to resist – sort of Dih-*Wight*? – when I'm trying to make it clear that the prospect of encountering the lad again has a coefficient of attraction roughly on a par with being invited to chew on a wad of silver paper. I made no attempt to resist that temptation here.

'Dwight.' Uncle Freddy looked puzzled, staring up at the study ceiling. 'Is that a real name, d'you think, Kate? That Eisenhower fellow was called that too, I remember, but then he was called Ike as well, and I could never work out which was a contraction of the other.'

'I think it is a real name, Uncle Freddy.'

'Really?'

'Yes. Don't worry. It's American.'

'Ah, I see. Jolly good. Anyway, Jebbet wants you to talk to the boy.' Uncle Freddy frowned and pulled on one pendulous ear-lobe. 'The nephew. Dwight. He's a playwright or something, isn't he?'

'Or something.'

'Thought that was the fellow. Is he any good, do you know?'

'As a playwright?'

'Hmm.'

'From what I've seen, no. But, of course, it's all very subjective. For all I know the boy's a genius.'

'Modern sort of stuff, is it? He writes?'

'Almost by definition.'

'Hmm.'

'Uncle Freddy, why does Mr Dessous want me to talk to Dwight?'

'Umm. Good question. No idea.'

'He couldn't phone, e-mail?'

Uncle Freddy looked pained and shifted uncomfortably in his seat. 'No, he definitely wants you to go there. But look, Kate.' Uncle F leaned forward and settled his elbows on the desk, causing a small landslide of papers, envelopes, old magazines, scraps of newspapers, bits of tissue and – by the sound of it – at least one until-then buried glass, which fell to the floor with a thud and a faint chinking noise. Uncle Freddy sighed and spared a glance at the stuff that had fallen. 'I think there is something Jebbet wants you to talk to the boy about; some mad idea he needs talking out of, but I've got a feeling he wants to talk to you himself as well. The nephew thing might be an excuse.'

'For what?'

'Well, Jebbet's word counts for a lot with the American people in the Business, from his own level, oh, well down past yours. Lot of these young Turk types, the keen brigade; they think the sun shines out of his behind, frankly. People like that, at the US end of things, they're making up the majority of your level these days, Kate. And the one below.'

'I know, Uncle.'

'Exactly. Exactly.' Uncle Freddy looked pleased.

'Uncle Freddy, you haven't actually answered my question.'

'What question was that, dear girl?'

'Why does he want to size me up?'

'Oh! For promotion, of course! Old Jebbet can put a lot of words in a lot of the right ears. As I say, the youngsters listen to him. He must have heard about you. You must have impressed him from afar. And good for you, I say.'

'I'm already at Level Three now, Uncle. I was expecting to wait a while yet before any more promotion. Right now I don't think even I would vote for me to step up another rung.'

'Think long, Kate,' Uncle Freddy said, and actually wagged

a finger at me. 'You can't get a good impression in too early, that's what I always say.'

'All right,' I said, half elated and half suspicious. 'Would the middle of the week be suitable?'

'Just about perfect, I should think. I'll check with his people.'


'You still in York State?'

'Yorkshire,' I said. It was late afternoon on the West Coast and I'd caught Luce on her way to her shrink. 'At Uncle Freddy's.'

'Yeah. Uncle Freddy. I was thinking: is this the old guy who used to molest you?'

'Don't be ridiculous, Luce. He pats my butt now and again. But that's all. He's always been really good to me, especially after Mrs Telman died last year. I cried on his shoulder, I hugged him. If he'd really wanted to try anything on that would have been the ideal opportunity, but he didn't.'

'I'm just concerned he might have abused you in the past and you're in denial about it, that's all.'

'*What?*'

'Well, you seem to just do anything he tells you to and you jump down my throat when I remind you this is the same guy who's sexually harassed you in the past—'

'What? Putting his hand on my backside?'

'Yeah! That's harassment! That'd get you fired from any office, most places. Interference with your fanny. Hell, yes.'

'Yeah, my American fanny.'

'Oh, Jeez, if it had been your British fanny he should have been locked up.'

'Well, call me less than a perfect sister if I let one old guy I happen to like a lot briefly touch my bum through a couple of layers of material, the point is I don't count that as abuse.'

'But you don't know!'

'I don't know what?'

'You don't know whether he abused you or not!'

'Yes, I do.'

'No, you don't. You *think* you know that he didn't but you don't really know that he didn't.'

'Luce, I think we're in the same boat here; neither of us knows what the hell you're talking about.'

'I mean, maybe he did much worse things to you in the past and you've repressed all the grisly details and even the fact that it happened in the first place; you're in denial about it all and it's fucking you up!'

'But I'm not fucked up.'

'Ha! That's what *you* think.'

'. . . You know, in principle this idiocy could go on for ever.'

'Exactly! Unless you take some action to discover the truth.'

'Let me guess. And the only way to find out is to go to a shrink, right?'

'Well, of course!'

'Look, are you on commission or something?'

'I'm on Prozac, so what?'

'I prefer prosaic. What I remember is what happened. Look, I'm sorry I bothered you, Luce. I'll—'

'Don't hang up! Don't hang up! Listen, this must have been meant to happen because I was just on my way . . . In fact I'm here, I'm at the place. Now look, Kate, I just think there's somebody here that you need to talk to, okay? Now, just a second. Just a second. Hi. Yeah, hi. Yeah. Yeah. That's right. L. T. Shrowe. Listen, I got somebody here on the phone I think really needs to talk to Dr Pegging, you know?'

'Luce? Luce! Don't you dare!'

'May I? He is? Oh, great.'

'Luce? Don't you fucking dare! I'm not – I won't – I'm putting the phone down!'

'Hi, Doctor. Yeah, it's good to see you, it really is. Look, I realise this is kinda weird, but I have this friend, right?'

'Luce! Luce! Listen to me, goddammit! This had better be a joke. You better be in the fucking supermarket or your manicurist's or something because I'm not going to—'

'Hello?'

'. . . ah.'

'Who am I speaking to?'

I looked through narrowed eyes at the far side of my room. *Okay*, I thought. I said, 'Oh, like, gee, are you another, like, *weirdo*?'

'I beg your pardon? My name is Dr Richard Pegging. I'm a psychoanalyst here in San José. And who might you be?'

'San José? Jeez, isn't that in, like, California or someplace?'

'Well, yes.'

'Okay, listen, Doc, like, if you really are, like, a doc, sorta like you said, then, like, I'm really sorry, okay? But, I mean, this woman, that woman who just, like, handed you the phone?'

'Yes?'

'Well, she's been calling me now for a coupla months. I mean, the first time she must justa dialled at random or something or got me out of the book, I dunno. Oh, sorry. My name's Linda? Linda Sinkowitz? I live here in Tuna County, Florida? And I'm just, like, here, you know? And then one day I get this phone call and it's this woman Lucy something and she thinks I'm her best fucking friend or something, excuse my language, and I tell her she must have, like, made a mistake only it goes on *way* too long for it really to be a mistake but so okay she calls off and that's fine

but then a few weeks later it all happens *again* and this is, like, the – Jeez, I dunno – the ninth or tenth time or something, you know? I mean, I guess she needs help or something, right, but if this happens again I'm gonna have to tell the phone company. I mean, you—'

'That's quite all right. That's fine, that's fine. I think I get the picture, Ms Sinkowitz. Well, it's been nice talking to you. Hopefully you won't be—'

'Kate!'

'Ms Shrowe, if you don't mind—'

'Doc, do *you* mind? It's my fucking phone! *Thank* you! Kate? Kate? What the fuck's this about Ms Sinkowitz?'

'Have a nice session, Luce.'

For the evening, we had a circus to entertain us.

The word was that during the afternoon – once Suvinder Dzung had been prised out of his bed and sobered up by his servants – Hazleton, Madame Tchassot and Poudenhaut had resumed negotiations with the Prince, his private secretary B. K. Bousande and Hisa Gidhaur, his exchequer and foreign secretary who had arrived that morning. This negotiating party was late for dinner, which was accordingly delayed for half an hour, and then went on without them. This was a little embarrassing as we had to entertain even more rich, famous and titled people that evening compared to the Friday; however, Uncle Freddy made some ridiculous excuse for our absentees, guffawed a lot and told a series of long-winded jokes, which kept everybody entertained in the drawing room until it was decided to go ahead with dinner anyway.

My beloved was gone: Stephen Buzetski had disappeared after breakfast that morning, called away to Washington DC.

The circus, in a tent on the lawn, was one of these extreme affairs where people dress as though auditioning for *Mad Max IV*; they juggled chainsaws, attached heavy industrial machinery to their sexual organs and rode very noisy motorbikes while doing unlikely things with knives and flaming torches. It was all terribly macho and camp at the same time and quite entertaining; however, I'd seen it all before several Edinburgh Festivals ago, so didn't stay long. I wandered back into the main house and took myself off to the snooker room.

I tend to play quite a lot of pool while trawling the in-play hang-outs in Silicon Valley. Most of the cutting-edge dudes are young and male, and find the idea of playing pool with a mature but well-preserved lady pretty cool. Often they'll drop their guard when they realise they're going to get beaten, or become a little too relaxed and open if I let them win against the odds.

Honing potting skills on a snooker or a billiard table is good practice for this sort of thing: if you can regularly make pots from across eleven and a half feet of green baize, switching to a pool table gives you the impression that the pockets have suddenly swollen to the diameter of basketball hoops.

Adrian Poudenhaut was there before me, also indulging in some solitary play. He looked tired. He was polite, almost deferential, and gave up the table for me, refusing the offer of a game. He exited the room with a wary but knowing smile.

I looked at my reflection in the room's tall windows. I was frowning. A tiny sparkle of light way in the distance caught my eye and I moved closer to the window. The snooker room was on the second floor of Blysecrag (third if you counted the American way), the last main floor before the servants' quarters in the attics. I remembered that from here, on a clear night, you could see the lights of Harrogate. Another distant blossom of light rose above the town. Somebody was letting off fireworks; it was two days after Guy Fawkes' Night, but a lot of people held their displays over to the Friday or Saturday after the more traditional 5th of November. I leant against the window-frame, arms crossed, watching.

'You look sad, Kate.'

I jumped, which is not like me at all, and turned round. The voice had been male, though I half expected to see Miss Heggies standing there, just re-materialised.

Suvinder Dzung, looking tired and a little sad himself, was standing by the snooker table, dressed in one of his Savile Row suits, tie undone, waistcoat unbuttoned, hair less than perfect. I was annoyed at myself for not having heard him or spotted his reflection. 'Did I look sad?' I asked, giving myself time to gather my wits.

'I thought so. What are you watching?' He came closer and stood beside me. I remembered watching our own fireworks the night before, on the terrace, and him putting his arm round my waist. I edged away from him a little, trying to make it look as though I was just making room for him, but getting the distinct impression that he was perfectly well aware of what I was really doing. He gave me a small, maybe apologetic smile, and did not try to touch me. I wondered if he even remembered our early morning telephone conversation.

'Fireworks,' I said. 'Look.'

'Ah. Yes, of course. Gunpowder, treason and plot, and all that sort of thing.'

'That sort of thing,' I agreed. There was an awkward silence. 'Pretty good view, for a billiards room,' I said. He looked at me. 'They're usually on the ground floor because of the weight,' I explained.

He nodded and looked thoughtful. 'Are you perhaps a Catholic, Kate?'

'What?'

'You looked so sad. The plot in which Guy Fawkes was taking part was an attempt to restore the Catholic succession to England, was it not? I thought perhaps you were lamenting to yourself his lack of success in blowing up the Houses of Parliament.'

I smiled. 'No, Prince. I was never a Catholic.'

'Ah.' He sighed and looked out of the window at the distant lights. He smelled a little of smoke and some old-fashioned scent. His eyes looked sunken and dark. He seemed lost in his own thoughts. 'Ah, well.'

I hesitated, then said, 'You look a little low yourself, Prince. Has it been a long day?'

'Most,' he said. 'Most long.' He stared out of the window. He cleared his throat. 'Ah, dear Kate.'

'Yes, Suvinder?'

'About our telephone conversation this morning.'

I held up my hands as though to catch a basketball at chest height. 'Suvinder,' I said. 'It's all right.' I hoped I might settle the issue with just that gesture and those words, plus a look of friendly sympathy and understanding, but the Prince had obviously already decided he was going to have his say. I hate it when people are so damn *programmed*.

'I hope you were not offended.'

'I was not, Prince. As I said at the time, I was annoyed at being woken up, but the sentiments were most flattering.'

'They were,' he swallowed, 'sincere, but ill put.'

'The sincerity was by far the more obvious quality, Suvinder,' I said, and even surprised myself at the way the words came out.

The Prince looked pleased. He gazed out the window again. We both watched the few rising sparks.

I was thinking about how high up we were, about the crags and cliffs and the undulating hills between us and the town when he said, 'It is all so flat here, isn't it?'

I looked at him. 'Are you homesick, Suvinder?'

'Perhaps, a little.' He glanced at me. 'You have only been to Thulahn once, haven't you, Kate?'

'Just the once, and very briefly.'

'It was the rainy season then. You did not see it at its best. You should return. It is very beautiful at this time of year.'

'I'm sure it is. Maybe one day.'

He gave a small smile and said, 'It would please me greatly.'

'That's very kind, Suvinder.'

He bit his lip. 'Well, then, will you tell me why you were looking so despondent, dear Kate?'

I don't know whether I'm just naturally reticent or it's some business-inspired wariness to do with giving people a handle on my possible weaknesses, but normally I'm loath to share any back-story (as Hollywood would call it) stuff. Anyway, I said, 'I suppose I always find fireworks kind of sad. I mean, fun, too, but sad all the same.'

Suvinder looked surprised. 'Why is that?'

'I think it goes back to when I was a little girl. We could never afford fireworks, and my mother didn't like them anyway; she was the kind of person who hid under the kitchen table when there was thunder. The only fireworks I ever had of my own were a few sparklers one year. And I managed to burn myself with one of those. Still have the scar, see?' I showed him my left wrist.

'Oh dear,' he said. 'Sorry, where?'

'There. I mean, I know, it's tiny, looks like a freckle or something, but, well.'

'To have no fireworks as a child, that is sad.'

I shook my head. 'It's not that, though. What we used to do was, on November the sixth each year my pals and I would go round the town where I lived, collecting spent fireworks. We'd dig the Roman candles up out of the ground and search for rockets in the woods and people's gardens. We tramped all over the bits of wasteground looking for these bright tubes of cardboard. They were always wet and soggy and the paper was just starting to unravel, and they smelled of dampness and ashes. We used to stick them in a big pile in our gardens, as though they were fresh and unused. The thing was to have more fireworks and bigger ones than your friends. I found it helped to go further afield, to where the better-off people had their displays.'

'Oh. So you were not just tidying them up?'

'I suppose we were doing that too, inadvertently, but really it was a kind of competition.'

'But why is that sad?'

I looked at his big, dark, melancholy face. 'Because there are few things more forlorn and useless than a damp, used firework, and when I look back it just seems so pathetic that we used to treasure the damn things.' I shrugged. 'That's all.'

The Prince was quiet for a while. A few more rockets lit up the skies above Harrogate. 'I used to be frightened of fireworks,' he said. 'When I was smaller.'

'The noise?'

'Yes. We have fireworks on many of our holy days and on the monarch's birthday. My father would always insist that I let off the biggest and loudest of them. It used to terrify me. I would never sleep the night before. My nurse would stop my ears with wax, but still when I set off the larger mortars the blast would all but knock me head over heels, and I would start to weep. This displeased my father.'

I didn't say anything for a while. We watched the tiny, silent sparks climbing, spreading, falling in the distance.

'Well, you're in charge now, Suvinder,' I told him. 'You can ban fireworks if you want.'

'Oh, no,' he said, and looked mildly shocked. 'I could never do such a thing. No, no, they are traditional and, besides, I came to tolerate them.' He smiled hesitantly. 'I would even say that now I love them.'

I put my hand out and touched his arm. 'Good for you, Prince.'

He looked down at my hand, and seemed to be about to say something. Then his secretary B. K. Bousande appeared at the door, clearing his throat.

Suvinder Dzung looked round, nodded, then smiled regretfully. 'I must go. Good night, Kate.'

'Good night, Suvinder.'

I watched him pad quickly, silently away, then turned back to look out of the dark window, waiting for more of the tiny lights climbing above the town, but there were none.

# C H A P T E R
# F I V E

'Y ou bitch.'
      'You asked for it.'
        'I was just trying to help.'
'So was I.'
'What do you mean?'
'Well, you spoke so highly of this Dr Pegging I thought I'd give him something more to work on. You can afford it. Think of the poor man's fees. And I think you've got a crush on him anyway. Gee, I imagine calling up a complete stranger thinking

115

they're your best friend is probably worth a whole year's extra treatment.'

'*Ex*-best friend.'

'Whatever.'

'Oh, Kate, don't be so *horrible*!'

'I'm sorry, Luce. Bygones?'

'I suppose.'

Word came through from Jebbet E. Dessous' people that the middle of the week was far too late to meet up; they wanted me there a.s.a.p.

So: Uncle F's Lancia Aurelia to Leeds-Bradford, where some sort of fuck-up by British Regional Aeroflot – a fairly regular occurrence judging by the bitter comments of some of my fellow non-passengers – meant I had to hire a helicopter from a company in the airport; I phoned our corporate lawyers to let them know we'd be charging BA for the relevant amount on my company credit card. I'm with the Prince on this one: I don't like helicopters either, or light aircraft for that matter, though in my case it's just because of the statistics.

Anyway, to Heathrow in a Bell Jetranger with a business-like pilot, who thankfully didn't indulge in any small-talk, then the tiny-windowed luxuriously upholstered cigar tube that is Concorde. No free seats and I was sat next to a smug advertising account director who was himself invasively well upholstered and determined to make the most of both the free champagne and two hours of enforced intimacy. I slipped my earphones on and turned up the Walkman. Sheryl Crow at volume shut him up.

I fell asleep after the album finished, and woke up as we were decelerating through bumpy clouds. I was in that drowsy, disconnected state where the bits of the brain that dream dreams and come up with crazy ideas haven't been brought back on message by the rational part, so that everything goes a bit haywire, and I remember watching the US coast, far, far below, and thinking, Well, here I am, and Stephen's in Washington DC; at least if there's some comprehensive world-wide catastrophe we'll be on the same continent. In the event of some deep-impact type disaster – if I survived – I could start walking and attempt to find him. Yes, and Mrs B might have died tragically and we could start a new life together . . .

I shook myself out of it and looked out my US passport, to speed the formalities when we landed.

JFK, an American 737 to Chicago (iffy lunch but the coffee had improved), a slim commuter Fokker to Omaha and a very noisy military-looking Huey to Jebbet E. Dessous' vast property on the Nebraska/South Dakota border; eighty thousand acres of plains, cattle, scrub, trees, roads like a map grid and all the dust you could eat. The co-pilot who helped strap me in insisted I wear a pair of heavy olive-green headphones for the journey. My hair, which had survived intact for four flights, one ocean and half a continent but which has always reacted badly to hats and serious headphones, was going to need fixing later on.

Half an hour in we hit some low-level turbulence over a series of pine-covered ridges. My lunch began to let me know it hadn't really settled down properly and was thinking of relocating. I considered the potentially onomatopoeic name of the helicopter I was travelling in, and tried to take my mind off my nausea by thinking of other modes of transport with dubious names, but only got as far as Sikorsky and the Cess in Cessna before we reached calm air again and my lunch decided that – on balance – it was happy where it was.

We landed in late afternoon in a dusty airport on the outskirts of what looked like a small deserted town, kicking up a great rolling ochre cloud.

'Welcome to Big Bend, ma'am,' the pilot said.

'Thanks.'

I took my time unclipping my harness and disconnecting the headphones while the dust settled. An ancient Willis Jeep in US army colours roared up and sat just outside the limit of the slowing rotor blades.

The breeze was cold and sharp and dry beneath a lapis sky stroked with feathers of high pink cloud. I could hear the steady crack-crack-crack of heavy machine-gun fire from some way off. The co-pilot dumped my bags in the back of the open Jeep and jogged back to the Huey, which was powering up again.

'Ms Telman.' The driver was a grizzled but healthy-looking guy a decade or so older than me, dressed in army fatigues. He stuck out one hand. 'Eastil. John Eastil. That all your luggage?'

'How do you do. Yes, it is.'

'I'll take you to your cabin. Hang on.' He spun the Jeep's wheel and gunned the engine; we roared away from the Huey. 'Sorry it's not a limo.'

'That's all right. Good to get some fresh air.' Actually I was pleasantly surprised by the way Mr Eastil drove: it was a lot more relaxing than Uncle Freddy's floor-the-pedal-and-damn-the-speed-bumps banzai style.

'Take you long to freshen up, Ms Telman?' Eastil asked. 'Mr Dessous would like to meet with you directly.'

'Five minutes.'

My cabin was a ten-minute drive away; a sprawling wooden thing set in amongst the pines overlooking a slow-flowing river winding through a shallow valley carpeted with long, pale grass. While Eastil waited in the Jeep outside I hung up my suit carrier, washed my face, squirted perfume behind my ears, dragged a brush through my hair, a toothbrush across my teeth and plonked the sad-faced monkey on a bedside table. The walk-in provided a skiing jacket, which I pulled on as I strode out to the Jeep.

We drove back into town, through its deserted streets and out the far side. We arrived at an old drive-in movie theatre; a huge field shaped like a baseball ground with the gantry for a vast screen at the wide end, though there was no screen, just the slim web of girders of its support structure. There were a lot of trucks and heavy rigs scattered around, and two big mobile cranes, one of them with its jib extended and its body raised up off the ground by its extended jacks.

Short rusty posts, which must once have carried the speakers for the parked cars, were arranged in serried rows across the weed-strewn lot. We parked alongside a handful of four-wheel drives and sport utilities by the projection building, which looked a lot like a concrete bunker, with no proper windows but a scattering of small rectangular apertures all facing in the direction of the absent screen. A long tube poked out of one hole.

'Miss Telman! Good to meet you. Jebbet E. Dessous. Call me Jeb, I don't answer to much else. I'll call you Miss Telman till I get to know you better, if that's all right with you. How was your flight? Cabin okay?'

Bustling out of a door in the projection building came a large, red-faced man dressed in the sort of speckled beige army fatigues the world has come to associate with the Desert Storm campaign. He wore a similarly camouflaged cap – incongruously, it was the

119

wrong way round, as though he was trying to look New York Hip of about five years ago – from under which stuck tufts of hair that might have been sandy or just yellowing white. He thrust out one massive hand.

His grip was delicate, even sensitive.

'How do you do, Jeb. Everything's been good.'

He let go and stepped back to look at me. 'You're a fine-looking woman, Miss Telman, hope you don't mind me telling you that. My opinion of my dumb-ass nephew has gone up, and that takes a lot of doing, I'll tell you.'

'How is Dwight?'

'Oh, still stupid.' He nodded at the Jeep. 'Come on, I'll take you to him.' He looked up at the sky with a frown, then pulled his cap the right way round.

Jebbet E. Dessous' driving style was more muscular than that of Mr Eastil, who sat in the back, holding on tight and chewing on a cold cigar.

'Sing us a song, John,' Dessous shouted, as we swung round the outskirts of the deserted town.

'What do you want to hear?' Eastil asked. I got the impression this was not an unusual request.

'Anything.' Dessous looked over at me and tapped the centre of the Jeep's bare metal dashboard. 'Can't get any sort of sound system in these things,' he said. I just nodded.

John Eastil launched into an enthusiastic – no, make that just loud – rendition of an old song I vaguely recognised but couldn't place until he got to the chorus, when I realised it was 'Dixie Chicken' by Little Feat. Dessous tried singing along too, but was patently tone deaf.

We headed along the bottom of a small dry creek towards the jumbled shape of a sprawling stone-and-log-built cabin, which looked like it owed something to Frank Lloyd Wright. Probably an apology.

'Boy comes here to write,' Dessous shouted at me.

'I see. How's he doing?'

'Oh, got some play opening in New York, so he says. Dumb-ass fool probably financed it himself. Still wants to make it in Hollywood, get his name above the titles. That's what – well, you'll hear.'

'Uncle Freddy seemed to think Dwight had some mad scheme you wanted me to talk him out of.'

'I don't want to prejudge anything here, Miss Telman. I don't know you, don't know which way you'll jump. I just want you to be honest with the boy. He talks about you a lot. Might listen to you. Sure as hell doesn't listen to me.'

'I'll do my best.'

'Yeah, well, just give it your best shot.'

We stopped outside. Eastil stayed with the Jeep again while Dessous jumped out, strode to the door, hammered on it once and marched in. 'Dwight!' he hollered, as I followed him. 'You decent, boy? I got a lady here to see you!' He pulled his cap off and ruffled his hair.

The cabin's shady interior was all long, low couches, split levels and rugs over naked concrete both underfoot and on the walls. From a distant room came a whoop, and Dessous turned in that direction.

'Hold on, hold on, just backing up!'

We found nephew Dwight in a bedroom with a view over the creek. The broad bed was covered in sheets of paper; on the desk by the window stood an elderly Apple Mac. Dwight was standing in front of the machine, clicking with the mouse. He glanced round. 'Yo, Uncle. Hi, Kate! How the hell are you?'

Dwight was a sharp-featured, awkwardly tall guy, only a little more than half my age; he was barefoot and wearing jeans and a dressing gown; his mid-length brown hair was half held in an unravelling pony-tail. He had a goatee beard and patchy stubble. He tapped the keyboard, turned the screen off and then came over to me, took both my hands in his and kissed me wetly on both cheeks. 'Mwah! Mwah! Great to see you! Welcome!'

'Hello, Dwight.'

'Your idea is *what*?'

We were sitting on a terrace overlooking the dry creek, Eastil, Dessous, Dwight and I, drinking beers. The stars were starting to come out. Thick jackets and a warm draught from the opened terrace doors kept us on the warm side of hypothermic.

'It's brilliant!' Dwight exclaimed, waving his arms about. 'Don't you think?'

I resisted the urge to suggest it was he who wasn't thinking, and just said, 'Run it past me again?'

'There's this, like, *thing* that looks like a ship's funnel or something, right? In Mecca, right in the centre. Where the Muslims go on pilgrimage to, okay? It's like the thing they're going there to see; this *rock*, inside this big sort of black shrouded building thing, in the centre of this humongous square in Mecca.'

'The Kaaba.'

'Cool!' Dwight looked delighted. 'You know the name! Yeah, the Kaaba, man. That's it!' He swigged from his bottle of Coors. 'Well, the idea for the movie is that . . . oh, yeah, like, hold on, this rock that's in the Kaaba, right? It's supposed to have fallen from the sky, be a gift from God, from Allah, right? I mean, obviously nowadays everybody knows it's a meteorite, but it's still holy, like, still venerated, okay? Or they *think* they know it's a meteorite,' Dwight said, leaning across the table and nearly putting one elbow in a bowl of dip. 'The idea for the movie is that it isn't a meteorite at all, it's a fuckin spaceship!'

'Dwight!' Dessous said sharply.

'Aw, Uncle,' Dwight said, with a sort of exasperated laugh. 'It's okay. Kate's cool about it. Sometimes even women cuss these days, you know?' He looked at me and rolled his eyes.

'You can swear in front of women if you want, nephew, but don't swear in front of women in front of *me*.'

'Yeah, right,' Dwight said, casting his gaze briefly towards the stars again. 'Anyway,' he said, and with gratuitous emphasis went on, 'the idea is that the *rock* inside the Kaaba *isn't* a rock: it's a *lifeboat*, it's an *escape pod* from an alien *spacecraft* that blew up above Earth fifteen hundred *years* ago. The lifeboat half burned up in the atmosphere so that's why it looks like a rock, or maybe it's *designed* to look like a rock, right, so nobody tries to look inside it – I mean, maybe all this happened in some sort of, like, *war*, okay? So it had to be *disguised*, right? Anyway, it crashed to the ground in *Arabia* and got taken for this incredibly holy, like, *thing*. And, like, maybe it *did* something, you know? Maybe that's why it was venerated and stuff, because it *did* something that rocks don't usually do, that even *meteorites* don't usually do, like float above the ground or dig itself out of the sand or something or zap somebody who was trying to cut into it. Whatever. But it gets taken to Mecca and everybody comes to worship it and stuff, but . . .' He chugged some more frothy beer. 'But, being a lifeboat, it's sent out a *distress* signal, right?" He laughed, obviously greatly taken with his own free-wheeling inventiveness. 'And it's, like, taken all this *time* until *now* for the distress signal to get back to aliens and them to get *here*. But as our story begins – I mean, we might have had some sort of

123

pre-titles stuff featuring the firefight between the spaceships and the lifeboat streaking down through the atmosphere, watched by shepherds tending their flocks by night, or whatever – anyway, as our story begins properly, the mothership's, like, *here*. And there's these alien guys *inside* the escape pod and they're just starting to *wake up*.' He sat back, eyes wide with enthusiasm. He spread his arms. 'What do you think? I mean, like, that's just the start, but what do you think of it so far?'

I stared at Dwight. Jebbet E. Dessous seemed to be gauging the width of his forehead with his hand. Eastil was blowing across the neck of his beer bottle, producing a low, breathy note.

I cleared my throat. 'Do you have any more of the story?'

'Na.' Dwight waved one hand. 'They have *scriptwriters* for that sort of stuff. It's the *concept* that matters. What do you think? Huh? Be honest.'

I looked at his eager, smiling face for a few moments and then said, 'You want to make a movie in which the holiest shrine of what is arguably the world's most militant and fundamentalist religion turns out to be—'

'An alien artifact,' Dwight said, nodding. 'I mean, Uncle Jeb's concerned that people might be upset by it, but I'm telling you, Kate, this is a *great* idea. I know people in Hollywood who'd *kill* to produce this movie.'

I watched Dwight carefully at this point for any sign of irony, or even humour. Not a sausage. I looked at Mr Dessous, who was shaking his head.

'Dwight,' I said. 'Does the word *"fatwa"* mean anything to you?'

Dwight started to grin.

'Or the name Salman Rushdie?'

Dwight hooted with laughter. 'Aw, Kate, come on, he was an Islamic! I'm not!'

'Actually I think he was sort of lapsed at the time,' I said.

'Well, he came from an Islamic family or whatever! I mean, he was from India or something, wasn't he? The point is I've got nothing to *do* with their religion. Hell, I'm not sure what I am – lapsed Baptist or something. Yeah, Uncle Jeb?'

'Your mother was a Baptist, I think.' Dessous nodded. 'I have no idea what your father thought he was.'

'See?' Dwight said to me, as though this explained everything.

'Uh-huh,' I said. 'Dwight, I think the point is that you might be seen as dissing their faith. That might not go down too well, regardless of your own belief or lack of it.'

'Kate,' Dwight said, suddenly looking serious, 'I'm not saying this movie isn't going to be controversial and cutting edge. I *want* this movie to be impactful. I *want* people to on-board this big-time, to sit up and think and overstand, you know? I want them to think, Hey, what if, like, our religions don't just come from *above*,' (at this point Dwight mugged staring nervously up at the near-black sky), 'what if they come from, like, the *stars*? You know?' He smiled widely and threw back the last of his beer.

I took a deep breath. 'Well, that's not exactly a new idea, Dwight. But if that's what you want to say, why not . . . well, do it through a different religion? Or even invent one?'

'*Invent* one?' Dwight said, frowning.

I shrugged. 'It doesn't appear to be that difficult.'

'But this idea *needs* the Kaaba thing, Kate, it *needs* this escape pod.'

'Dwight, if by some miracle you get to make this movie, you'll be the one who needs an escape pod.'

'Bull*shit*, Kate!'

'Dwight,' Dessous said tiredly.

Dwight looked genuinely sad. 'I thought you at least would understand! I'm an artist; artists have to take risks. It's my job, it's my calling. I have to be true to myself and my gift, true to my ideas, or what am I bothering for? I mean, why are any of us bothering? I have a responsibility here, Kate. I must be true to my muse.'

'Your *muse?*' Dessous said, almost choking.

'Yeah,' Dwight said, glancing from his uncle to me. 'Otherwise I'm just, like, a fake, and I won't be a fake, Kate.'

'Dwight, ah, there's a movie out at the moment called *The Siege—*'

'Yeah yeah yeah,' Dwight said, smiling tolerantly and patting the air as though pacifying an invisible dog. 'I know. Completely different sort of movie altogether. *This* movie's going to be big budget and ultra-spectacular, but it's going to be, like, *thoughtful?*'

'The people who made *The Siege* probably thought it was thoughtful, too. They probably didn't mean to upset the entire Arab-American community and have movie theatres picketed across America.'

'Well, across New York City, anyway,' Dwight said, shaking his head at my lack of understanding. 'You really on Uncle Jeb's side?' he asked me, disappointed. 'Frankly I was hoping you might help me talk him into putting some *money* into this project.'

This time Dessous did choke on his beer.

'I think you'd be mad to go ahead with this, Dwight,' I told him.

Dwight stared at me, aghast. Then he leant towards me, eyes narrowed. 'But you do think it's a great idea?'

'Brilliant. It's a breathtakingly good idea. But if you really want to put it to good use, find somebody in the movie industry you hate and would like to see ruined or dead and suggest the idea to them in a way that would let them claim it as their own.'

'And watch them pick up the Academy Award?' Dwight laughed at my naïveté. 'I think *not!*'

Dessous and I exchanged looks.

Dinner, an hour later, was in Jebbet E. Dessous' own home, an Italianate villa overlooking a broad lake on the outskirts of the deserted town, which was just what it appeared to be. Premier, Nebraska, had been a declining township on the fringe of Dessous' ranch for years before he'd taken over the spread on its other side; he'd bought the place up lot by lot and gradually moved people out until he'd created his own ghost town. The main reason he'd done this, he explained, while showing me round the villa before dinner, was so that he had the sort of room a man needs when he's using heavy ordnance.

Jebbet E. Dessous was into weaponry the way Uncle Freddy was into cars. Hand guns, rifles, automatics, mortars, heavy machine guns, tanks, rocket-launchers, he had everything, including a helicopter gunship stored out at the airfield where I'd landed and a motor torpedo boat which he kept in a large boathouse on the lakeside. Most of the heavier stuff – like the tanks, housed in a warehouse in the town – was old; Second World War vintage or not much later. He grumbled about the government's reluctance to sell tax-paying citizens main battle tanks and anti-aircraft missiles.

Dwight and I followed him round the stables attached to the main villa; this was where Dessous kept his collection of howitzers and field pieces, some dating back to the Civil War.

'See this?' He patted what looked like a load of long, open pipes mounted on a trailer. 'Stalin's organ pipes, they used to call these. The *Wehrmacht* were terrified of them. So were the Red Army; used to fall short too often. You can't get the rockets any more but I'm having a bunch of them made.' He slapped one of the dark green metal tubes with his giant hand again. 'Make a hell of a noise, apparently. Looking forward to letting these suckers off, let me tell you.'

'What's the biggest missile you've got, Jeb?' I asked, as innocently as I could, thinking of the Scuds he was supposed to have bought.

He grinned. He was dressed in a white tuxedo now – Dwight had thrown on a jacket, too – but Dessous still looked like a bucolic farmer dressed up and in town for a dance. 'Ah-hah,' was all he would say. He winked.

'Goddamnit, Telman, I thought you of all people would agree with that!'

So I was Telman, now. I had kind of thought that when Mr Dessous had said he'd call me Miss Telman until he knew me better he meant that in the fullness of time he might get round to calling me Kathryn, or Kate. Apparently not. Or maybe that would come later. The point at issue was how easy it was to bootstrap yourself out of poverty.

'Why, Jeb?'

'Because you came up out the slums, didn't you?'

'Well, if not slums, certainly a degree of deprivation.'

'But you did it! That's my point; you're here!'

Here was the dining room of the villa, which was fairly big

and untidily sumptuous. As well as myself, Dwight, Eastil and Dessous, there was Mrs Dessous, who was a stunning Los Angelino redhead about Dwight's age sheathed in silver and called Marriette. There were a dozen other people on Dessous' immediate staff, and a similar number of technicians and engineers, to whom I'd been introduced *en masse*.

The long table was stratified, with Dessous at the head dispensing Pétrus and the junior technicians somewhere at the far end swigging beer. The food had been Mexican, served by small and wondrously deft and inconspicuous Mexican men. I wondered if Dessous themed all his meals, so that if we'd eaten Chinese we'd have been surrounded by pigtailed Chinamen, while an Italian dinner would have been served by dark, slim-hipped young men called Luigi. The main course had been some very fine lean flag steak from one of Dessous' own herds, though I'd had to leave most of mine because there was just too much of it.

'I was extraordinarily lucky, Jeb,' I said. 'Mrs Telman's car blew a tyre near where I was playing with my pals. If it hadn't been for that piece of luck I'd probably still be in the west of Scotland. I'm thirty-eight. By now I'd have had three or four kids knocked out of me, I'd weigh another twenty or thirty pounds, I'd look ten years older, I'd smoke forty a day and eat too much chocolate and deep-fried food. If I was lucky I'd have a man who didn't hit me and kids who weren't doing drugs. Maybe I'd have a few high-school qualifications, maybe not. There's an outside chance I'd have gone to university, in which case it might all have been different. I might be a teacher or a social worker or a civil servant, all of which would be socially useful but wouldn't let me live the sort of life I've come to appreciate. But it's all based on luck.'

'No. You don't know. You're just making assumptions,'

Dessous insisted. 'That's the Brit in you coming out there, this self-deprecating stuff. I knew Liz Telman; she told me when she found you, you were selling candy at fifty per cent mark-up. You trying to tell me you wouldn't have learned something from that?'

'Perhaps I'd have learned how easy it was to rip people off, and decided never to do it again. Maybe I'd have ended up working in a Citizens' Advice Bureau or—'

'This is perversity, Telman. The obvious lesson to draw is how easy it is to make money, how easy it is to use initiative and enterprise to pull yourself out of the environment you find yourself in. You'd have done it anyway, with or without Liz Telman. And that's precisely my point, dammit. The people who deserve to will get out of their deprivation, they'll rise above any goddamn social disadvantagement, whether it's in Scotland, Honduras, Los Angeles or anywhere else.'

'But it's *not* the people who deserve to,' I said. 'How can you condemn the vast majority who don't get out of the slums or the schemes or the *barrios* or the projects? Aren't they going to be the ones who put family, friends and neighbours first, the ones who support each other? The ones who rise are more likely to be the ones who are the most selfish, the most ruthless. The ones who exploit those around them.'

'Exactly!' Dessous said. 'Entrepreneurs!'

'Or drug-dealers, as we call them these days.'

'That's evolution, too! The smart ones sell, the dumb ones use. It's vicious, but that's the state and its dumb laws.'

'What are we really saying here, Jeb? Societies are made up of a mix of people, obviously. There will always be people who basically accept their lot and those who'll do anything to improve it, so you've got a spectrum of behaviour, with total compliance at one end – people who just want a quiet life, who really only want to be left alone to raise their families, talk about the ball game, think about their next holiday and maybe dream about winning the lottery – and dissidence at the other. Within the dissidents, some people will still identify strongly with their friends and family, and struggle to improve the lives of all of them. Some will only be out for themselves and they'll do anything to achieve material success, including lying, stealing and killing. What I'm questioning is who amongst this lot could be termed "better" than the others.'

'Basically what you're saying is the scum rises and I'm saying the cream rises. Now, you tell me who's got the more optimistic vision here, and who's being defeatist.'

'Me, and you, Mr Dessous, in that order.'

Dessous sat back. 'You're going to have to explain that to me, Telman.'

'Well, scum and cream both rise, I guess, depending on the context. Actually I don't think either analogy is particularly helpful. The comparison you choose to make shows which way you've already decided. However, what I'm saying is more optimistic because it supposes a way forward for everybody in a society, not just its most viciously competitive percentile. You're being defeatist because you're just giving up on nine people out of ten in a poor society and saying there's no helping them, and that the only way they can help themselves is individually, by climbing out on top of those around them.'

'That's evolution, Telman. People get hurt. People strive, people succeed. Some strive and don't make it, and some succeed without striving, but they're the exceptions, and if you don't at least make the attempt then you don't deserve to succeed. You've got to have struggle. You've got to have competition. You've got

131

to have winners and losers. You can't just even everybody out; that's what the Communists thought you could do, and look what happened to them.'

'You can have fairness.'

Dessous roared with laughter. 'Telman! I can't believe I'm having to tell you this, but life isn't *fair!*'

'No, the *world* isn't fair, the universe isn't fair. Physics, chemistry and mathematics, they aren't fair. Or unfair, for that matter. Fairness is an idea, and only conscious creatures have ideas. That's us. We have ideas about right and wrong. We invent the idea of justice so that we can judge whether something is good or bad. We develop morality. We create rules to live by and call them laws, all to make life more fair. Of course, it depends exactly who draws up the laws who those laws are most fair to, but—'

'Selfishness is what drives people on, Telman. Not fairness.'

'And you accuse *me* of being pessimistic, Jeb?' I said it with a smile.

'I'm being realistic.'

'I think,' I said, 'that a lot of successful people are actually less hard-hearted than they like to think. They know in their hearts that people suffer terribly in poor societies through no fault of their own. The successful people don't want to admit that to themselves, they don't want to accept that really they're just the same as those poor people and they certainly don't want to face the horror of even suspecting that if they had been born into those societies they might have been stuck there and suffered and died, young and unknown after a miserable life, any more than they want to face the alternative of knowing that they could only have got out by being more competitively brutal than everybody else around them. So, to save their consciences, they decide that the people in the slums are there because they somehow deserve to be, and if they just tried hard enough they could get out. It's nonsense, but it makes psychological sense and it makes them feel better.'

'You accusing me of self-deception, Telman?' Dessous said, looking surprised but not angry. I hoped I was getting the correct impression here, that he was enjoying all this.

'I don't know, Jeb. I'm still not sure what you really think. Maybe you secretly agree with me but you just like an argument.'

Dessous laughed. He slapped the table and looked round the others. A few of the people nearest us had been following the argument. Down in their own relatively impoverished area, at the end of the table where the beer was, nobody was taking a blind bit of notice: too busy having a good time.

In the lounge after dinner, fuelled by fine wine and brandy, Dessous talked with some of the technicians who'd been at the other end of the table. He came back to where I was sitting with Dwight and Eastil, rubbing his hands and positively glowing.

'Mechanism's ready!' he announced. 'Screen's up. Ready for some target practice?'

'Betcha,' Eastil said, and knocked back his drink.

'I've got to see this,' Dwight agreed. 'Kate ... you ought to come.'

'Ought I?'

'Yee-ha!' said Dessous, turning and marching off.

'Yee-ha?' I said to Dwight, who just shrugged.

About a dozen of us drove to the drive-in movie theatre in three sport utes. The sky was clear, and Dessous, shucking off his DJ and pulling on a quilted jacket, ordered the other two drivers to leave their lights off. He drove in front, tearing along the road to town using only the moonlight and starlight, startling jack rabbits and discussing over the radio which way the wind was blowing.

We pulled up by the dark bulk of the projection building. While Dessous was cursing everybody for forgetting to bring a flashlight I pulled one from my pocket and clicked it on.

'Well done, Telman,' Dessous said. 'You always so well prepared?'

'Well, I usually carry a torch.'

Dessous smiled. 'I've got friends who'd tell you that ain't a torch, Telman. That's a flashlight; a torch is what you burn niggers with.'

'Would they? And are they really racist scumbags, or do they just enjoy trying to shock people?'

Dessous laughed and unlocked the door.

The lights flickered on in the projection building, bright after the blacked-out journey in the four-wheel drives. People flicked more switches, starting fans and heaters and powering up the two big 35mm projectors, which were aimed out through small windows at the distant screen, which was now in place.

I didn't notice anything odd at first: the place was all very techy in an old-fashioned sort of way, with exposed cables and ductwork and racks of film canisters against the walls and whole boards of clunky-looking industrial switches and fuses the size of your hand. At each of the two big projectors, two guys were loading film into the complicated pathways of rollers and guides. Then I saw what stood in between the projectors.

I stared. 'What the fff—?'

'Oerlikon twenty-millimetre cannon, Telman,' Dessous said proudly. 'Single mount. Isn't it a beauty?'

Dwight, standing on my other side and holding a half-full glass of wine, just chuckled.

Where a third projector might have stood there was, indeed, a very heavy machine-gun. It stood on a fluted mount bolted to the concrete floor, it had two padded brackets at the rear where it looked like you were supposed to rest your shoulders, and a big, almost circular drum of ammunition on the top. Its charcoal-coloured metal gleamed in the overhead lights. The long barrel disappeared out of a small window into the night, facing the huge screen in the distance.

The right-hand projector whined up to speed. Somebody handed out bottles of beer, somebody else dispensed ear-protectors.

The first reel was a Second World War dog-fight. It was black and white and looked like real camera-gun footage. Dessous took his place at the cannon and, after a deep breath, started firing.

Even with the ear-protectors on and the muzzle of the gun outside the building, the noise was pretty intense. I could see Dessous grinning like a loon and mouthing what I suspected were more yee-has, but his voice was entirely lost in the racket. A duct above the cannon's chattering mechanism sucked most of the smoke away, but the projection room soon stank of cordite and a thin grey mist filled the air. A big limp sack hanging on the other side of the gun from the magazine shook and pulsed as though there were a bunch of scared kittens inside it.

People were crowded round the remaining small windows facing out to the screen. I squeezed in beside Dwight, who put his arm round my waist. He bent his head to mine and shouted, 'Is this fucking crazy, or what?'

135

To my left, the surface of the projection booth was lit by the stuttering muzzle flash of the cannon. Across the gulf of darkness above the abandoned parking lot, the lines of tracer flicked, disappearing into the black and white skies of wartime Europe, where Mustangs and Messerschmitts dived and rolled and formations of Flying Fortresses laboured onwards through the clouds. Smoke drifting from the cannon in the near still air picked out the projector's beam. Then the gun fell silent.

There was a moment of quietness, then people cheered and clapped and whistled. Dessous, radiant, stepped down from the cannon, rubbing his shoulders, his face slick with sweat. He accepted congratulations and shook Eastil and a few of the technicians by the hand. His wife, silvery sheath of dress topped by a quilted jacket, went up on tippy-toes to kiss him.

Eastil was next at the cannon, once it had been reloaded, the sack full of spent cartridge cases had been emptied and another reel of film spun up to speed in the other projector.

We appeared to be progressing historically: this was Korean War footage of MiGs and Sabres. The cannon went crack-crack-crack, fast as a speeding heart. I watched the screen. There were a few small tattered holes starting to appear.

'You're our latest guest, Telman,' Dessous said, when Eastil had had his turn. 'Care for a shot?'

I looked at him. I wasn't sure whether I was expected to say yes or not. 'That's very kind,' I said. I watched another reel of film being loaded into the first projector. 'I imagine we're up to Vietnam by now.'

Dessous shook his big head. 'Not much dog-fighting there. We've gone straight to Yom Kippur.'

I had a very brief lesson in how to shoot the gun. This basically consisted of hold on, don't close your eyes, and press this trigger here hard. The cannon had a fairly crude sight which looked like the wire frame taken off a dartboard and shrunk to about the width of a hand. The gun smelled of oil and smoke; it gave off heat like a radiator. I settled into the padded shoulder rests and for some reason couldn't help thinking of the stirrups in a gynaecologist's. My mouth, I have to say, was quite dry.

The image across the drive-in lot flashed 5 + 4 + 3 + 2 + 1 +, with those reverse-sweeping clock roundels in between, counting down. Then we were in full colour above the sands of the Sinai peninsula and the skies were full of MiGs. I squinted through the sights and pulled on the trigger. The cannon shuddered and kicked back at me, nearly tearing my fingers away from the trigger. Tracer bullets lanced towards the screen and disappeared into the darkness beyond.

I tried aiming at the aircraft swirling in front of me, but it was hard. As long as I kept the bullets going through the screen and not into the framework holding it up I thought I'd be doing fine. The gun clattered to a stop. At first I thought it must have jammed, then I realised that I'd used up all the shells.

I staggered as I stepped down, my ears ringing, my arms tingling, my shoulders aching and my whole body seeming to buzz.

Dessous grabbed me briefly by one elbow. 'Whoa, you all right there, Telman?'

'I'm fine.' I laughed. 'Some kick.'

'Yup.'

The screen was starting to look a little frayed in the centre when we had our finale. Another three people had taken turns at the gun; both Dwight and Mrs Dessous had declined. Dessous took his place again, the projector powered up, and before the gun started firing I could hear a mixture of cheers and boos from the people clustered round the windows.

The unmistakable image of Saddam Hussein's face appeared on the screen, monolithically lugubrious, fixed and still. The gun launched 20mm cannon shells at it.

The rest of the short reel was Hussein in various settings, sitting talking to his military commanders, walking past crowds of cheering people, inspecting troops, and so on. Then it went back to the still of his face, looming a hundred feet high above the deserted lot. Dessous fired into the eyes until the silvery material of the screen there started to fall away and flap and tumble – dark, silver, dark, silver – towards the ground. Holes appeared in the vast nose, the deep brush of moustache and across the broad expanse of forehead. Finally, peppering the line between dress shirt and Adam's apple, Dessous must have hit some part of the framework around the screen's lower edge, because sparks burst out, and two of the tracer rounds suddenly ricocheted upwards into the night in a bright red V. The cannon fell silent again as flames started to lick up around the giant face still displayed on the screen, while flaps and scraps of screen folded and fell or were caught in updraughts and floated skywards.

More cheering and whooping and laughter. Dessous looked like a child locked in a candy store. He nodded and wiped his brow and took a lot of pats on the back and handshakes and just appeared utterly pleased with himself.

Across the lot, flames licked up around the huge, frayed, unsteady image.

Back in the villa, long past midnight, we sat in Dessous' den, just the man himself and I. The walls were covered in swords, hand-guns and rifles, all polished and gleaming and resting in little chrome cradles. The place smelled of gun oil and cigar smoke.

Dessous drew on his cigar, levered himself back in his giant leather seat with a creak and thumped his shoes on to his broad desk. 'You ever think of yourself as a socialist, Telman? You sure sound like one.'

'Briefly, at university. Do I really?' I tried the cup of coffee, which was all I'd felt like. Still too hot.

'Yup. You know how much you're worth?'

'Roughly.'

'Guess you can afford to be a socialist.'

'I guess I can.'

Dessous rolled the fat cigar round his mouth a couple of times, not taking his eyes off me. 'You believe in communities, don't you, Telman?'

'I suppose so. We're all part of communities. All part of society. Yes.'

'Are we your community?'

'The Business?' I asked. He nodded. 'Yes.'

'You're committed to us?'

'I think I've shown that over the years.'

'Just because of Mrs Telman?'

'Not just. That's the sentimental reason, if you like. I have others.'

'Such as?'

'I admire what the Business stands for, its—'

'What do you think it stands for?' he said quickly.

I took a deep breath. 'Reason,' I said. 'Rationality. Progress. Respect for science, belief in technology, belief in people, in their intelligence, in the end. Rather than faith in a god, or a messiah, or a monarch. Or a flag.'

'Hmm. Right. Okay. Sorry, Telman, I interrupted you there. You were saying.'

'I admire its success, its longevity. I'm proud to be part of that.'

'Even though we're vicious capitalist oppressors?'

I laughed. 'Well, we're capitalists, sure, but I wouldn't put it any stronger than that.'

'There's a lot of the youngsters – Level Six through Four – who'd think what you were saying earlier about initiative and drive and success and so on was something close to heresy; something close to treason.'

'But we aren't a religion, or a state. Yet. So it can't be either, can it?'

Dessous studied the end of his cigar. 'How proud are you to be part of the Business, Telman?'

'I'm proud. I don't know of any internationally accepted scientific unit of measurement of pride.'

'You put our collective good above your own interests?'

I tried my coffee again. Still too hot. 'Are you asking me to surrender some of my stock options, Jeb?'

He chuckled. 'Nope, I'm just trying to find out what the Business means to you.'

'It's a collection of people. Some I like, some I don't. As an institution, like I said, I'm proud to be a part of it.'

'Would you do anything for it?'

'Of course not. Would you?'

'No. So, I guess we're all in it for ourselves, aren't we?'

'Yes, but we rely on the support and co-operation of everybody else to help us achieve our individual goals. That's what communities are all about. Don't you think?'

'So what wouldn't you do for the Business?'

'Oh, you know, the usual stuff: murder, torture, maiming, that sort of thing.'

Dessous nodded. 'I guess that kind of goes without saying. What about this idea of self-sacrifice? What would you sacrifice something of your own for, if not for the Business?'

'I don't know. Other people, maybe. It all depends on the circumstances.'

Dessous grimaced and stared at the ceiling, looking suddenly bored with the whole conversation. 'Yeah, I guess it always does, doesn't it?'

I woke up. Very dark. Where the hell was I? The air outside the bed was chilly. The bed itself felt . . . unfamiliar. I heard a chinking noise like something hitting a window. I sniffed the air, suddenly afraid. Not in my house, not in London, not in . . . Glasgow or Blysecrag . . . Dessous' place. Big Bend. I was in Nebraska. The cabin on the ridge. The noise came again.

I felt for the light switch and touched the little netsuke monkey. The light was very bright. I stared at the curtains over the windows. I felt groggy and my head hurt; not badly, but enough to let me know I'd drunk too much. The noise at the window came again. I looked at the telephone on the other bedside table.

'Kate?' said a muffled voice.

I fastened the top button on my PJs top and went to the window and drew the drapes. Dwight's pale face stared back at me. I opened the window. Cold air spilled in.

'Dwight, what are you doing?'

He was wearing a thick jacket but he looked cold. 'Can I come in?'

'No.'

'But it's cold out here.'

'So you shouldn't have left your cabin.'

'I wanted to talk to you.'

'Haven't you got a phone?'

'No. That's why that cabin's so great. No phone. You can write.'

'What? You mean a letter?' I asked, confused.

Now he looked bewildered. 'No, I mean write treatments and shit, without distraction.'

'Oh. And what about your mobile?'

'I leave it switched off.'

'But . . . never mind.'

'Please let me in.'

'No. What did you want to talk about?'

'I can't talk out here! It's freezing!'

'I'm freezing too, so keep it brief.'

'Aw, Kate—'

'Dwight, I've had your uncle beating my ears all evening. If you have anything to say I'd really appreciate you saying it as concisely as possible so I can get back to sleep. I'm *very* tired.'

He looked pained. 'I was going to ask you . . . if you wanted to come to the première of my play on Broadway,' he said. He scratched his head.

'Your play?'

'Yeah,' he said, grinning. 'Finally got my name above the title on something. It's called *Best Shot*. It's brilliant! You'd love it.'

'When is it?'

'Next Monday.'

'I'll try.'

'You will? You promise?'

'No, I can't promise, but I'll try.'

'Right.' He hesitated.

I shivered. 'Dwight, is that it?'

'Uh, yeah. I guess.'

I shook my head. 'Right. Good night.'

'Umm. Okay,' he said. He started to turn away. I started to close the window. He turned back. 'Hey, ah, Kate?'

'*What?*'

'Do you, ah . . . Do you, like, want we should maybe, like, you know, spend the night together? Maybe?'

I stared at him. I thought of lots of things to say, but eventually I just said, 'No, Dwight.'

'But, Kate, Jeez, we'd be great together!'

'No, we wouldn't.'

'We would! I'm just so *admirative* of you.'

'Dwight, that's not a word, or if it is it shouldn't be.'

'But, Kate, I just find you so *attractive*, and I mean I *never* go for women your age!'

'Good night, Dwight.'

'Don't reject me, Kate! Let me in. I'm not going to be heavy, I'm not going to aggress on you or anything.'

'No. Now go home.'

'But— !'

'*No.*'

His shoulders slumped within the big jacket. His breath smoked down. He raised his head again. 'You'll still come to the play?'

'If I can.'

'Aw, come on, promise.'

'I can't. Now go home. My feet are turning blue.'

'I could warm them up for you.'

'Thanks, but no.'

'But you will try and come?'

'Yes.'

'You're not just saying that to get rid of me?'

'No.'

'As my guest, as my date?'

'Only if you can't find somebody your own age. Now, good night.'

'Excellent!' He turned to go, switching on a flashlight. I started to close the window. He turned back again. 'You really think my idea about the escape pod inside the Kaaba is that bad?'

'Not bad, just potentially fatal.'

He shook his head as he turned away into the night. 'Shit.'

My feet really were cold; so were my hands. I drew six inches of warm water in the bath and sat on the rim with my PJ cuffs rolled up, soaking my feet and hands to bring some blood back into them. I dried them and returned to bed and slept like a very tired log.

# CHAPTER
# SIX

It snowed later on during the night and when I opened the
curtains the next morning it was still snowing, turning
the countryside softer, brighter and silently beautiful. I
watched it snow for a while, then showered and dressed. The
cabin's phone rang while I was drying my hair.

'Telman?'

'Jeb. Good morning.'

'You want breakfast?'

'Yes, please.'

'Okay, dishing up in twenty minutes.'

'This is at your place, yes?'

'Yup, the villa.'

'Right. How will I get there?'

'Should be a truck in the garage.'

'Ah.'

There was: a big Chevy Blazer. I climbed in, it fired first time and rolled out into the snow. The garage door swung down automatically behind me. There was sat. nav., CB radio and a phone but I vaguely remembered the way and only took a couple of wrong turnings.

We were still in a Mexican groove, food-wise. I sat in the big, bustling kitchen of the villa with everybody else and tucked into my *huevos rancheros* while Dwight, sitting next to me, boasted loudly about all the famous people he'd met in Hollywood, enthused about his Broadway play and just generally acted like somebody shooting for most-favoured-nephew status.

'You ski, Telman?' Dessous shouted, from the head of the table.

'A little,' I said.

'Heading for the slopes in about an hour if the weather clears like it's meant to. Like you to come.'

'Happy to,' I said, feeling myself slipping into the way of Dessous' clipped syntax.

'Mind if I tag along?' Dwight asked, with a grin.

'Wouldn't want to cut into your muse time there, nephew.'

'That's all right, I could use a break.'

'Actually, son, I was being polite. There's only room for one more in the choppers, and Telman's just taken that seat.'

'Oh.' Dwight looked crestfallen.

'Still up for it, Telman?'

'Yup.'

The weather cleared from the west. Two dozen of us flew from the Big Bend air strip in a British Aerospace 146 into a vast blue space divided perfectly into blue sky and white earth. We landed at Sheridan, just east of the Big Horn mountains. Two Bell 412s were waiting on the tarmac; we loaded our skis into pods attached to the legs and were lifted to pristine snowfields lying beneath the high peaks. The Bells dropped us in the middle of their own little snow blizzard, their skis suspended just a foot above the surface while we jumped out and unloaded ours. Then they lifted away again and clattered down the valley.

Dessous got me to help him with a recalcitrant binding while everybody else swept off down the heft of icing-sugar white in a blur of multi-coloured shapes.

When we were alone, I said, 'There's nothing wrong with this binding, is there?'

'Nope,' Dessous said. He looked around. Our companions had disappeared into the broad valley beneath. The only moving things we could see were the fast-receding black dots of the helicopters, already too far away to hear. 'You want to sit down?'

We sat down in the snow, our skis planted, curved tips like plastic talons scratching at the blue. Dessous pulled out a leather cigar case. 'Smoke?'

I shook my head. 'Only after a drink. But don't let me stop you.'

'Well, I got a hip flask, too, but that's normally only for medical emergencies.'

'I quite agree.'

He prepared and lit a long cigar with some care, then said, 'How you think you're doing, Telman?'

'I don't know. What's the context?'

'Well, impressing me, I guess.'

'Then I've really no idea. Why don't you tell me?'

'Because I want to know how you think you're doing, dammit.'

'All right. I think you think I'm an opinionated socialist feminist, who's half American, half European, combines what you would regard as the worst aspects of both mentalities, has lucked out with some off-the-wall predictions and doesn't really respect the traditions of the Business the way I ought.'

Dessous laughed, and coughed. 'Too hard on yourself, Telman.'

'Good. I was hoping so.' This made him chuckle a little too. 'So, what is all this about, Jeb?'

'Not me who's going to tell you. Sorry.'

'Then who?'

'Maybe nobody, Telman. Maybe Tommy Cholongai. Know him?'

Another Level One: a Chinese-Malay shipping-line owner. I said, 'We've met.'

'Tommy and I have an agreement. Given there ain't much we ever agree on, this is something of an event in itself. Involves you, Telman. If we both agree, then . . .'

'What?'

He blew out a cloud of blue-grey smoke. 'Then we might ask you to do something.'

'Which would be . . . ?'

'Can't tell you yet.'

'Why not?'

'Can't tell you that, either.'

I sat and looked at him. He was staring up at the tall summit of the highest mountain. Cloud Peak, he'd said it was called, on the way up. Thirteen thousand feet; tallest of the Big Horn range. Custer's last stand had taken place a hundred klicks due north, in Montana. 'You know,' I said, 'all the secrecy surrounding this thing you can't tell me about might put me off whatever it is in the first place, if I ever do get to find out what the hell it is.'

'Yup. Know that. All the same.' He looked at me and grinned. I hadn't really inspected his teeth before: they were uneven, yellow-white, and so probably his own. 'Actually, Telman, I'd tell you now and get it over with but Tommy wouldn't appreciate that, and an agreement is an agreement.'

'So now I have to go see Mr Cholongai, would that be right?'

''Fraid so.'

I crossed my arms and looked around for a while. I was waiting for the cold to seep through my glossy red ski-suit and make my backside numb. 'Jeb,' I said, 'I'm junior to both you guys, but I am on sabbatical and, anyway, I thought I'd worked my way up in the company sufficiently not to get . . . passed around like this.'

'Better passed around than passed over.' Dessous chuckled.

'"Better looked over than overlooked,"' I quoted. 'Mae West, I believe,' I added, when he cocked an eye at me.

'Fine-looking woman.'

'Just so.'

We skied down to meet the others, were taken back up to more virgin powder and repeated the process, if not the conversation. Soon it was time for lunch, which we took in a Vietnamese restaurant in Sheridan. Dessous regaled us with his plans to develop the drive-in movie theatre/shooting gallery, which meant having a whole sequence of stacked screens ready to be dropped into place, or even a sort of roller system, like a giant scroll; once you'd shot the blue blazes out of one bit, you'd just haul it up or drop it down until you had a fresh area.

The conversation became even more ridiculous when Dessous talked about another project. He'd been taken with the sort of wheeze megalomaniac dictators were so fond of, involving a stadium full of compliant, well-drilled subjects and lots of big, coloured boards. The idea was to use the big, coloured boards to display what looked like a picture of something when seen from far enough away (the other side of the stadium, usually). I'd seen TV pictures of this sort of thing. As far as I could see the standard image was an image of whatever power-mad shit-for-brains was in control at the time.

Dessous thought this would be a fun thing to do, but he wanted to take it a step further and have *moving* images displayed.

The head technical guys who'd come skiing started to get excited, discussing how this could be done. The consensus seemed to be that you'd need a Third World country to get the requisite numbers of people, and that maybe it would be best just to hire an army division or so. Big cubes of expanded polystyrene with six different colours or hues on them just big enough to twirl round without interfering with a neighbour's would give you some degree of flexibility, though it'd be hard to get any control of saturation unless you could light them from inside, which would make them kinda heavy. The control system would be a bitch: you'd have to treat every goddamn person as a single pixel and they'd never be able to memorise more than a few changes. Some sort of individual signalling apparatus would be required. Serious programming of some sort.

I suggested they might call it a Lumpen Crowd Display, or possibly Large Ego Display; LCD or LED. This they thought a hoot, and only encouraged them. What would be their refreshment rate? Could you use all raster-farians? Hey, what if they all wanted a screen dump?

While the technical guys got on with this, Dessous was chairing another discussion group, which was trying to work out what images you could show on this widest of wide screens. Great sporting moments seemed to feature strongly.

I slipped away, stayed longer in the toilets than I really needed to, then stepped into the street outside where no one from the party could see me and checked my phone's signal strength.

'Hi, Kate. How are you?'

'Oh, sorry, Stephen, I . . . I didn't mean to call you,' I lied. 'Wrong button.'

'That's okay. You all right?'

'Yeah, yeah. You?'

'Fine.'

'Okay, then, sorry.'

'No problem. Where are you, anyway?'

'Place called Sheridan. Wyoming, I think.'

'You skiing with Dessous?'

'Yup. How'd you know?'

'Ah, just masculine intuition. I've been there myself.'

'Where are you now?'

'Ah, still in DC . . . And it looks like I've got where I'm supposed to be.' I heard the noise of traffic behind his voice as he said, 'Yeah, okay,' to somebody else, then, 'I've got to go,' to me. 'You take care now, okay?'

'Okay.'

'Don't break anything.'

'Yeah, you too,' I said.

Only my heart, I thought.

The following day I took the same Huey back to Omaha (those big olive green headphones again – for someone who tried to avoid helicopters I seemed to be spending a lot of time on the damn things), then a United 757 to LAX (stodgy muffin, steward with neat butt, brief snooze) and a Braniff 737 to San Francisco (mercifully quiet but overflowingly obese woman in seat alongside – smelled strongly of French fries). A hired car took me home to Woodside.

The place was warmer than Nebraska but the house felt cold. I watered my long-suffering cactuses and made a few calls. I met with some old friends in Quadrus, a Menlo Park restaurant popular with some of the PARC guys. I ate too much, drank too much and smoked too much, and babbled happily about nothing of consequence at all.

I invited Pete Wells back to my place. He's a research analyst and an old pal/lover, still a good-time guy and up for the occasional friendly fuck, though he is engaged to some lucky lass in Marin and so not for much longer. We made hazy, stoned, well-tempered love to Glen Gould playing J. S. Bach, listening to the man humming and singing along.

I slept well, apart from a weird dream about Mike Daniels searching my garden for his missing teeth.

The next morning, with Pete already gone and me both a little bleary and not particularly well rested, I repacked my bags – with DKNY, mostly – and took the Buick back to meet its buddies at San Francisco International's Alamo, then it was a JAL 747-400 to Tokyo via Hawaii (twenty minutes late leaving due to two tardy suits; I joined in the Mean Group Stare when they finally stumbled into First trying not to look sheepish and studiously avoiding everybody's eyes. Sushi very good. Played both Garbage albums, separated by Madonna's *Ray of Light*. Slept well). Cathay Pacific Airbus 400 from Tokyo to Karachi (shown how to play with game console in seat by Japanese kid; very good sleep later – worry that I may be turning into woman in a song I heard once who only slept on planes. Bumpy landing).

I had a feeling that whatever passport I chose for Karachi it would be the wrong one, but I decided on the British one and was pleasantly surprised: whisked through. The place was packed, the air was thick with a medley of smells, the humidity was stifling and the lighting in the arrivals hall was terrible. Over the crowds I spotted a board being held up with a rough approximation of my name on it. I hadn't been able to find a trolley so I held my suit carrier out in front of me and used it to work open a path in the right direction.

'Mrs Telman!' said the young Pakistani man holding the sign up. 'I am Mo Meridalawah. Very pleased to meet you!'

'It's Ms Telman, but thank you. How do you do.'

'Very well, thank you. Let me . . .' He took my bags off me. 'Follow me, please! This way. Out of the way there, coarse fellow!'

No, really, he did.

Hiltonised overnight, and restless, I got up, kicked the previous day's newspapers out of the way, booted the ThinkPad and spent some time on a few techy-oriented news groups before going back to more disturbed sleep. Mo Meridalawah reappeared mid-morning and drove me back to the airport through some of the most chaotic traffic I had ever seen. It had been just as bad the evening before but I had assumed then it was rush-hour.

There was no such excuse now, and it was even more terrifying in daylight; unbelievable numbers of bicycles, trucks belching black diesel fumes, garish buses, motorised trikes and cars driven seemingly at random in any direction as long as it was either directly across our path or on a collision course. Mo Meridalawah waved his hands about and chattered ceaselessly about his family, cricket and the incompetence of his fellow road users. Karachi airport was almost a relief.

Yet another helicopter: one of those ancient, tall Sikorskys with the engine in the bulbous nose and the flight deck up a ladder. The cabin was actually quite comfortably kitted out, but it all looked worryingly old-fashioned and well worn. Mo Meridalawah waved goodbye from the tarmac with a white handkerchief as though he for one never expected to see me again. We chopped out over the city, across dense green mangrove swamps, along the coast and then across the lines of surf and out over the Arabian Sea.

The *Lorenzo Uffizi* had been a cruise ship for nearly thirty years; before that it had been one of the last transatlantic liners. Now it was out of date, its powerful but old engines were hopelessly inefficient and the vessel as a whole was just too old to refit again economically. It was only worth scrapping, and it was to complete that process that it had come here from the yard in Genoa where its more valuable and salvageable fittings had been removed.

Sonmiani Bay is where a lot of the world's ships end up. The broad beach slopes smoothly into the sea, so that the vessels can be aimed at the sands, put to full speed ahead and then just run aground. On the vast beach there's plenty of room for whole fleets of obsolete ships, and in the countryside around there are hordes of impoverished people willing to work for a pittance, cutting the ships up with torches, attaching chains and hawsers to sections of hull and then – if they're quick enough – getting out the way in time when the giant winches further up the shore haul the pieces of ship off. More cutting, more dragging by winches, then the bits are craned on to rail flatcars and hauled to a quayside thirty miles away, where the scrap is loaded aboard ships bound for any one of a dozen steel mills throughout the world.

I had heard of Sonmiani Bay, I had read about it in a magazine twenty years earlier and just a couple of years ago I'd seen some TV footage, but I'd never been there. Now I was going to get to see it first hand, and I'd be arriving by ship. Tommy Cholongai was a Level One exec who could fairly be described as a shipping magnate. The first time I'd used this phrase in front of Luce she'd asked, did that made him anything like a fridge magnate. Normally I'd have said something, but as I recall I'd just asked her if she was still looking for Mr Cannon, and so my lips were tied. Today, I'd been told, Mr Cholongai was going to fulfil a lifelong ambition by being at the controls when the *Lorenzo Uffizi* hit the beach at full speed.

The *Lorenzo Uffizi* was still an impressive sight. It was about fifty klicks offshore, lying still in the water a few hundred metres from the comparatively toy-like shape of Mr Cholongai's own motor yacht. We circled the liner, level with its two tall funnels. The ship was creamy white, streaked here and there with rust; the funnels were blue and red and the stern funnel was the source of a thin streamer of grey smoke. Windows glittered with reflected sunlight. Empty lifeboat derricks stood like lamp-posts along the boat deck – there was just one lifeboat left on each side, up near the bridge – and its two drained swimming-pools gaped pale blue beneath the dazzling cloudless sky, Ballardesque.

The Sikorsky landed on the broad curve of a stern tier still marked out for deck games. One of Cholongai's assistants, a small Thai called Pran whom I vaguely knew from a company conference a few years earlier, slid the helicopter's door open for me and mouthed a welcome over the scream of the engine.

'I have wanted to do this for years,' Tommy Cholongai said. 'Captain, with your permission?'

'Certainly, Mr Cholongai.'

Cholongai took hold of the brass handle and, with a big grin on his face, moved the bridge telegraph indicator all the way down to the Full Ahead position. The telegraph made the appropriate ringing, chiming noises. He brought it back to All Stop to the sound of more bells, and then set it back to Full Ahead again and left it there. The rest of us – including the *Lorenzo Uffizi*'s captain and first officer and the local pilot as well as Cholongai's personal staff – looked on. A couple of Cholongai's PAs started clapping enthusiastically, but he smiled modestly and waved them to be silent.

Beneath our feet, the ship began to shudder as the engines spun up to speed. Mr Cholongai stepped to the ship's wheel, followed by the rest of us. The wheel was a good metre across, each handle tipped with brass. When the ship had some way on her, moving steadily across the gentle swell and still slowly gathering speed, Cholongai asked the pilot for the heading and then spun the wheel, watching the compass display in its overhead binnacle. The ship's course curved gradually, her bows turning to face the sands of Sonmiani bay, still out of sight over the horizon. At nearly thirty knots, our arrival ought to coincide with high tide.

Satisfied that we were pointing in the right direction, with approving nods from our captain and pilot, Mr Cholongai relinquished control of the wheel to a small, smiling Chinese seaman, who didn't look remotely big enough to handle it. 'You take good care now,' Mr Cholongai said to the seaman, patting him on the back and grinning broadly. The little Chinese guy nodded enthusiastically. 'I'll be back in a hour, yes?' More nodding and smiling.

He turned, scanning the faces gathered round him until he saw me. 'Ms Telman?' he said, and indicated the way off the bridge.

We sat on the sun deck just beneath the windows of the bridge, shielded from the ship's self-made wind by tall, sloped panes of glass, all streaked by dried salt and spattered here and there by birdshit. Above us a parasol provided shade, its edges rippling in the breeze. The two of us sat on cheap plastic seats around a white plastic table. A white-coated Malay steward delivered iced coffee.

The air felt thick and hot and the faint breeze curling over the glass barrier didn't seem cooling at all. I'd dressed in a light shot-silk suit, the coolest outfit I had with me, but I could feel sweat trickling down between my shoulder-blades.

'My friend Jeb tells me you are concerned, Ms Telman,' Cholongai said. He sipped his iced coffee. He was a dense-looking man, of average height and bulky but smooth-skinned with spiky grey hair. He'd put on sunglasses when we'd come outside. With so much sunlight and white paintwork around it was very bright even within the parasol's shade, and I was glad I'd remembered my own Ray-Bans.

'I seem to be,' I looked round at the paintwork's glare, 'getting kept in the dark, Mr Cholongai.' I smiled. I tried the iced coffee. Very cold, very strong. I shivered, the sensation of cold and the white blaze of light suddenly taking me back to the snowfields of Wyoming.

He nodded. 'This is true. One cannot tell everybody everything.'

Well, that was suitably gnomic. 'Of course,' I said.

Cholongai was quiet for a moment. He sipped at his coffee. I resisted the urge to fill the silence. 'Your family,' he said eventually. 'Do you still see them very often?'

I blinked behind the shades. 'I suppose I have two families,' I said.

'Truly you are blessed,' Cholongai said, without any obvious irony.

'I'm afraid I don't see either often. I was an only child, my mother was a single parent, she was also an only child, and she died some time ago. I met my father just once. Mrs Telman was like a mother to me . . . more like an aunt, perhaps. I only met her husband once, on the day of the court hearing when she – they – adopted me.' I was not, of course, telling Cholongai anything he couldn't find out from my personnel file; I didn't doubt that some underling had already briefed him on all this.

'That is very sad.'

'Yes, but I've been very lucky.'

'In your career, do you mean?'

'Well, that as well. But I meant that I was loved.'

'I see. By your mother, you mean?'

'Yes.'

'A mother should love her child.'

'Of course. But I was still lucky. She made me feel loved, and made me feel special, and she protected me. There were many men in her life and some of them were violent sometimes, but none of them ever touched me and she did her best to hide from me what they did to her. So, though we were poor, and things could certainly have been easier, I had a better start in life than some.'

'Then you met Mrs Telman.'

I nodded. 'Then Mrs Telman came along, and that was the single luckiest thing that ever happened to me.'

'I knew Mrs Telman. She was a good woman. It was sad she could have no children of her own.'

'Do you have a family yourself, Mr Cholongai?'

'One wife, five children, two grandchildren, third grandchild on way,' Mr Cholongai said, with a big smile.

'Then you are blessed.'

'Indeed.' He sipped his iced coffee. There was an expression on what I could see of his face that might have meant the coffee was giving him a toothache. 'Might I touch on a personal matter, Ms Telman?'

'I suppose so.'

He nodded for a while, then said, 'You have never thought of having children of your own?'

'Of course I've thought of it, Mr Cholongai.'

'And you decided not to.'

'So far. I'm thirty-eight, so I'm not in my prime for child-bearing, but I'm fit and healthy, and I reckon I could still change my mind.' In fact I knew I was fertile; I'd gone to a clinic when I was thirty-five, just out of curiosity, and been again a few months ago, and gotten a clean bill of reproductive health both times. Nothing wrong with my eggs or any part of the system, which made not having children my choice rather than an imposition.

Cholongai nodded. 'Ah-hah. This is awkward, I know, but, may I ask, was it simply that the right man did not come along?'

159

I tasted my iced coffee, glad to remain inscrutable behind my glasses. 'That depends what you mean.'

'You will have to explain. Please.'

'It depends on how you define the right man. The right man did come along, as far as I was concerned from a purely selfish point of view. But he turned out to be married. So, not the right man after all.'

'I see. I am sorry.'

I shrugged. 'One of those things, Mr Cholongai. I don't cry myself to sleep every night.'

He nodded. 'You are not, perhaps, a very selfish person: you give a lot of money to deserving causes, I think.'

This is the sort of thing you have to live with in the Business; that old financial transparency means there's no feeling quietly superior to somebody about things like this. If they have the slightest interest in your private affairs they'll already know exactly what causes you feel most strongly about, or what system of checks and balances you've put in place to square your conscience with your functional life.

'Actually,' I said, 'I'm very selfish. I only give to charities so that I can sleep easily at night. In my case the proportion of my disposable income I find I need to jettison is about ten per cent. A tithe.' More coffee. 'It's the closest I come to religious observance.'

Cholongai smiled. 'It is good to give to charity. As you say, all benefit.'

'Some think otherwise.' I was thinking of a few – mostly US-based – execs I'd met who had nothing but contempt for anybody who gave any money to any cause, with the possible exception of the National Rifle Association.

'Perhaps they have their own . . . indulgences.'

'Perhaps. Mr Cholongai?'

'Please, call me Tommy.'

'All right, Tommy.'

'If I may call you Kathryn.'

'I'd be honoured. But I'd like to know, Tommy, what all this has to do with anything.'

He shifted in his seat. He took his sunglasses off briefly, rubbing one knuckle into the corner of one eye. 'Can we talk in confidence, Kathryn?'

'I assumed we already were. But, yes. Of course.'

'It has to do with Thulahn.'

'Thulahn?' That threw me.

'Yes. We would like to ask you to change tracks.'

*What?* Maybe he'd meant change tack, but it worked either way. 'How do you mean?'

'In your career.'

I felt a coldness sweep over me, as though I'd drenched myself in iced coffee. I thought, What have I done? What can they do to me? I collected myself and said, 'I thought my career was going just fine.'

'It is. That is why it is difficult for us to ask this of you.'

My initial panic had subsided, but I was still not at all sure I liked the sound of this. My heart was racing. It suddenly struck me that a light silk blouse and unlined jacket were bad things to wear when your heart was thudding: people could probably *see* the fabric quivering. Maybe women and fat men suffered more this way; some sort of resonant frequency set-up magnifying the effect in your breasts. Breeze, I thought. There's a breeze. Should cover any signs. Calm down, girl. I cleared my throat. 'What exactly are you asking me to do, Tommy?'

'To become, in a sense, our ambassador to Thulahn.'

161

'Ambassador?'

'It is more than that.' (*More* than that? How could it be *more* than that?) 'At first we would ask you to go there to report. To look at the place and try to work out where it might be heading, to spot trends, in other words – social trends, if you like – in the same sort of way that you seem to be able to spot trends in technology at the moment. Do you see the connection?'

'I think so. But why?'

'Because we are entering a unique situation in Thulahn. By adopting it as our base we will be exposing ourselves in a way we have not done before. We will be making ourselves vulnerable in a manner we have not been since the fifteenth century.'

This was a Switzerland reference, of course: the late fourteen hundreds was when the place became effectively independent and the Business – always attracted to havens of stability, no matter how relative – had started to put down roots there. Cholongai's chronology ignored a dodgy moment in 1798 when the armies of revolutionary France invaded, but never mind.

'Don't we have people to do that sort of thing?' I asked. Surely either we did or we could employ the best. This was the sort of thing you could just throw money, university professors and battalions of post-grads at. Sociologists *loved* places like Thulahn.

'Not at the appropriate level, Kathryn. We need someone whom we can trust. That, of course, means someone in the Business whom we know to be profoundly committed to it. There are probably hundreds of people at the right level using that criterion alone. But we also need someone who can see things from a perspective outside the company, someone who will feel sympathetic towards the people of Thulahn. Someone who will be able to empathise with them, and advise us how best to incorporate their needs and wishes with those of the company itself.' Cholongai sat forward, clasping his hands on the surface of the white plastic table. Beneath our feet the deck buzzed and around us the plates and glass of the superstructure vibrated as the ship powered onwards, heading for the shore.

'Thulahn is not Fenua Ua,' Cholongai said. 'There are nearly a million Thulahnese. We cannot evacuate them all, or provide all of them with apartments in Miami. They seem a docile people, and devoted to their royal family, but if we are to make the sort of commitment to their country that we are anticipating making, then we need to be able to predict how they will feel in the future, and move to accommodate those feelings.'

'Such as, what if they decide they would like democracy?'

'That sort of thing.'

'So I'd be spying on them?'

'No, no.' Cholongai laughed lightly. 'No more than you already spy on those companies we consider investing in. What you would do would benefit the people of Thulahn as much as ourselves, perhaps more.'

'And only I can do this?' I tried to sound sceptical. It wasn't difficult.

'We think you would be the best person to do so.'

'What would it involve?'

'It would mean that you would have to relocate to Thulahn. It might be possible also to continue performing your present function for a while, but I would think that before too long it would become impossible to carry out both tasks satisfactorily.'

'You mean I'd have to live in Thulahn?'

Cholongai nodded. 'Indeed.'

Thulahn. Memories of my few days there came tumbling back. Thulahn (or at least Thuhn, the capital, because I hadn't really

163

been anywhere else): mountains. Lots of mountains. And rain. Mountains that – when you could see them through the clouds – made you crane your neck to see their snowy summits, even when you were already a mile or two high. Almost nothing level. That fucking football pitch that doubled as a landing strip. Lots of smoke – the smell of burning dung – tiny bright-eyed children plumped out by thick clothes, small men bent under huge bundles of firewood, old women squatting fanning stoves, shyly hiding their faces, goats and sheep and yaks, a surprisingly modest royal palace, the few dirt roads and the single stretch of tarmac they were so proud of, bizarre tales about the dowager queen I'd never met, huge monasteries barnacled across cliff faces, waking up in the middle of the night feeling breathless, the creak of prayer windmills, the bitter taste of warm milk beer. Not to mention my fan, the Prince.

I took a deep breath. 'I don't know about that.'

'It would seem to be the only way.'

'What if I say no?'

'Then we would hope that you would continue to do your present job, Kathryn. We would have to find somebody else – perhaps a group of people rather than an individual – to take on Thulahn in the way I have outlined.'

'I like my life, Tommy.' Now I was trying to sound regretful. 'I enjoy feeling part of the buzz in the valley. I like staying in London and travelling in Europe. I like travelling. I like the view over cities at night, and room service and long wine lists and twenty-four-hour supermarkets. You're asking me to settle down in a place where they're still struggling to come to terms with the flush toilet.'

'That is understood. If you took up this offer you would have complete freedom to work out the proportion of time you would spend in Thulahn and the proportion you spent elsewhere. We would trust you to resign if you found that the amount of time you felt able to spend in Thulahn was inadequate to fulfil the role you had taken up.' He paused. 'You would be made very comfortable. We could re-create your house in California, if that was what you wanted. You would have a company plane at your disposal. And a choice of staff, of course.'

'Those sound like the sort of privileges a Level Two could expect.'

'Level Two status would be assured.'

Good grief. 'Assured?'

'The importance of our association with Thulahn will surely be obvious to our colleagues at every level, once the deal has been struck and we are able to let everyone know. I cannot imagine that they would fail to promote you to a level your position in the country and importance to the company would befit.'

This was indeed as good as saying it was mine. 'But the deal with the Prince isn't done yet?'

'Not quite. Technically there are still a few details to be ironed out.'

'Would me agreeing to all that you're proposing happen to be one of those details?'

Cholongai sat back, looking surprised. 'No.' He looked up the not-quite-vertical slope of white superstructure towards the bridge of the ship. 'We are not sure if the Prince is simply holding out for better terms or whether he is genuinely beginning to have second thoughts. It is vexing. It may be that he is being struck by the enormity of what he is doing. He is ending several hundred years of tradition and taking something away from his own family, after all.'

'Just as well he's childless, then.' I was still a bit taken aback by all this. 'What exactly would be the set-up if we do take the place over? How do we make sure it's ours?'

Cholongai waved one hand. 'The details are complicated, but it would involve a sort of governing trust of all the Level Ones. The Prince would remain head of state.'

'And after him?'

'If he has no children, there is a ten-year-old nephew who is next in line. He is in one of our schools in Switzerland.' Cholongai smiled. 'He is making good progress.'

'Bully for him.' I tapped my fingers on the plastic table. I was thinking. 'Whose idea was this, Tommy?'

'What do you mean, Kathryn?'

'Whose idea was it to involve me in this way?'

He sat still for a moment. 'I do not know. That is, I cannot remember. The suggestion was probably made at a Board meeting, but when exactly, and by whom, I do not recall. Detailed minutes are not kept. That also is in confidence, by the way. Why does this matter?'

'Just curious. May I ask who knows about this?'

Cholongai nodded, as though he'd anticipated this question. 'Level One executives. I do not think anybody else does. J. E. Dessous and I have been delegated to take responsibility for the analysis and . . . decision.' He looked to one side as the steward approached with a large silver tray and what at first I thought was a lap-top sitting on it. It was a satellite phone. 'Excuse me,' Mr Cholongai said to me, and lifted the handpiece. 'Hello?' he said, then shifted into either rapid Chinese or Malay; I couldn't tell which.

He put the phone down and waved the waiter away. 'There is someone coming to see you,' he told me.

'There is? Here?'

'Yes. They have something for you. A present.'

I looked at him for a moment, glad that the Ray-Bans were hiding at least some of my confusion. 'I see.'

The noise of a helicopter thud-thudded unseen, somewhere behind us.

'Anyone I know?' I asked.

Mr Cholongai's head tipped to one side. 'Perhaps. His name is Adrian Poudenhaut.'

Pran and I watched Poudenhaut's helicopter land where mine had set down. His was a sleek Bell with retractable undercarriage (I felt jealous). Poudenhaut stepped out, dressed in a light blue suit. He held a slim Halliburton. Pran moved to take the aluminium briefcase off him, but Poudenhaut clutched it to his chest.

We walked away and the Bell lifted off, stowing its wheels and dipping its nose towards the land, which was just visible as a dark line on the horizon.

'Ms Telman,' Poudenhaut said.

'Hello again.'

'Thank you, that'll be all,' he said to Pran, who smiled and nodded and walked away across the deck. Poudenhaut reached into one pocket and extracted a sizeable mobile phone, then into another and took out an L-shaped attachment for it. Together they made an even dinkier satellite phone than Mr Cholongai's.

He pressed a couple of buttons then held the phone to his ear, looking at me all the time. I inspected my own sunglassed image in his shades.

The phone made a noise. 'I'm on the ship, sir,' he said. He handed me the phone. It was quite heavy.

167

'Hello?' I said.

It was, as I'd expected, Hazleton's voice on the other end. 'Ms Telman? Kathryn?'

'Yes. Mr Hazleton, is that you?'

'It is. I have something for you. Adrian will show you. The disc is yours afterwards.'

'Is it? Right.' I had no idea what the hell we were talking about.

'That's all. Nice to talk to you. Goodbye.' The line bleeped and went dead.

I shrugged and handed the instrument back to Poudenhaut. There was a bead of sweat in the hollow of his upper lip. 'I hope you know what's going on here,' I said, 'because I certainly don't.'

Poudenhaut nodded. He looked around, then pointed at a line of tall windows forward of where we stood. 'In here will do.'

The place must have been a lounge, perhaps a restaurant. The floor was bare metal plate with just a few strips of worn carpet and underlay strewn about. The suspended ceiling had been taken down and the light fittings removed. We sat in the gloom at the back by a small table attached to a metal column supporting the roof, surrounded by a forest of grey cables hanging from where the lights had been, all swaying slowly in the gentle swell.

Poudenhaut took off his shades and looked about. All around us were the grey fronds of the hanging wires. Forward of us there was a bulkhead with various hatches and doors set in it. In the other three directions, daylight glared through the windows like a vast, strident strip-light.

He flipped open the cover of the combination lock and clicked the three little wheels. He sprang the catches, opened the briefcase and lifted a little portable DVD player out.

'Oh, my,' I said. 'That's very neat, isn't it?'

'Hmm,' he said. I craned my head: there was nothing else in the briefcase. Poudenhaut frowned at me and clunked the case shut. He spun the little player so that it was facing me, hinged the screen up and – reaching over the top – stabbed at a button. The machine made discreet whirring noises and the screen lit up, though it stayed blank.

'I've been asked to show you what you're about to see,' Poudenhaut said. 'I need your word you won't say anything to anyone about this.'

'Okay, I guess.'

He looked like he wasn't sure whether this was really sufficient, but then said, 'Right.' He leant over and hit another button. The screen flickered.

Only I could see this: Poudenhaut was facing the rear of the screen. There was no sound. The picture was better than VHS, nearly broadcast quality. It showed a woman entering a building on a busy street. The woman was Caucasian, youngish and dark-haired. She wore sunglasses, a summer dress and a light jacket. Traffic was driving on the right-hand side of the street, and I guessed this was in the US somewhere from the automobiles. I got the impression the camera had been inside a vehicle. Small figures to the bottom right of the display indicated it was 10/4/98, 13:05; that would be April the way Brits show the date, but October if this was American; exactly a month ago.

The scene switched to a bedroom lit by sunlight on closed net curtains; the drapes moved slightly, as though the window was open behind them. It looked like the camera was sitting on top of a wardrobe or a cupboard, angled downwards. The image quality had deteriorated a little. No date/time display. The same woman – probably – led a tall man in a business suit to the bed and started kissing him. He was white, tanned, had black hair and a neatly trimmed beard. They slipped each other's jackets off, then they fell together to the bed. They started undressing each other, quickly. I looked up at Poudenhaut, raising my eyebrows. He stared back, impassive.

They both had good bodies. She sucked his dick (a little stubby for my taste, and with a distinct rightwards curve, but there you are), then they sixty-nined, then they fucked missionary position for a couple of minutes, without protection. Looked like they both enjoyed it. I cleared my throat. My, but it was hot in here. The screen flickered, and the couple were screwing again, him taking her from behind. They were both approximately facing the camera, but I got the impression neither of them knew it was there. I studied their faces. I had a vague feeling I knew the guy, but I wasn't sure. He took longer this time. It looked like real sex and not pornography because they just humped away with no cut-away shots of her face or his backside, and when he came he did so inside her, not over her face or her tits or anything crass like that.

Another few shots of them lying on the bed together, on top at first, then under a sheet, both talking and smiling and playing with each other's hair. Another flicker, then him leaving the apartment, hailing a cab. A yellow cab, so almost certainly the US. Possibly NYC. Flicker, then her leaving and walking away. The date/time display indicated they'd been together for just under two hours. Then, the end. Blank screen.

I sat back. Poudenhaut sat looking at me.

'Yes?' I said.

'It's finished?'

'Yes.'

'Would you eject the disc and take it out?'

I sat forward and inspected the machine, finding the eject button. The disc appeared and I slipped it out.

'Please keep it.'

I popped it into a side pocket in my jacket.

'Do you know what you've just shown me?' I asked.

Poudenhaut shook his head briskly as he turned the DVD player off, closed it and put it back in the briefcase. 'No,' he said.

'I just have this feeling it might not be what I was supposed to be looking at.' This was becoming more than slightly ridiculous: Poudenhaut with his fancy helicopter and his Hollywood-villain briefcase and minuscule sat. phone and spanking new DVD machine coming all the way out here just to show me a few minutes of amateur porn.

At least he had the decency to look confused. 'What—?' he began, then frowned. 'You . . . I believe you were supposed . . . expected to recognise a person.'

I thought back to the guy in the bedroom. *Did* I recognise him? I didn't think so. I shook my head.

'You sure?' Poudenhaut sounded worried now.

'I may forget a face, I never forget a . . . Never mind.'

Poudenhaut held up one hand. 'Would you wait a minute?' He moved about ten metres away through the pale grey fronds of the hanging wires. He stood with his back to me and tried to use the sat. phone. It didn't work. He shook it – which was, somehow, an encouraging thing to see – then tried again, once more fruitlessly.

'You'll probably find you have to go outside,' I called over to him. He looked at me. 'Satellite,' I said, pointing upwards. He nodded once and headed for the line of windows.

He stood in the sunlight, talked briefly and then started waving at me, motioning me to join him.

I left his briefcase where it was and strolled out. He handed me the phone. He was really quite sweaty about the face now.

'Kathryn?'

'Mr Hazleton?'

He laughed. 'Ah, the best-laid schemes, eh?'

'Gang aft agley,' I agreed.

'Hmm. One should not make too many assumptions. You aren't just teasing poor Adrian, are you? You really didn't recognise anyone in that little film?'

'Did I see what I was supposed to see?'

'A man and a woman having sex in a hotel? Yes.'

I smiled at poor Adrian, who was dabbing at his forehead with a handkerchief. 'I see. Well, no, I really didn't recognise either of them.'

'How embarrassing. After all that secrecy.' A pause. 'I suppose I could just tell you.'

'I suppose you could.'

'Perhaps it's better if I don't, for now. You may remember of your own accord, given time.'

'I'd rather you just told me.'

'Hmm. I'd appreciate it if you kept this to yourself for the moment, Kathryn. Don't show the disc to anybody else. You may well find it extremely useful, in due course.'

'Mr H, if you're not going to tell me, I might be tempted to post it on the Web and see if anybody else can tell me who these two young lovers are.'

'Now, Kathryn, that would be very irresponsible. Please don't be petulant.'

'I was supposed to know by now. Why not just tell me?'

172

Another pause. The ship's horn blared, above and forward of us. Poudenhaut and I both jumped.

'What was that?' Hazleton asked.

'Ship's hooter,' I said.

'Very loud.'

'Yes, wasn't it? So, who was I supposed to recognise, Mr Hazleton?'

'I suppose I am being overly secretive. It's just that there's no need for Adrian to know.'

I smiled at Poudenhaut. 'Fine by me.' I turned and walked a few steps away, then smiled back at Poudenhaut. His mouth set in a tight line. He retreated into the shade of the lounge and crossed his arms, watching me.

I heard Hazleton take a breath. 'You didn't even start to recognise her?'

So it was the woman. I thought hard. 'No . . .'

'When you met her she may have had blonde hair. Quite long.'

Blonde. I thought of the woman's face (annoyingly, the image that had chosen to etch itself on my memory was of her just as she was achieving orgasm, her head thrown back, her mouth open in a shout of pleasure). I tried to ignore this, and to edit out the shoulder-length black hair and substitute blonde.

Maybe, I was starting to think, I had seen her once, or met her. Maybe I had a bad association with that face. Something I didn't want to think about. Oh-oh.

'No further forward, Kathryn?' Hazleton asked. He sounded like he was enjoying this.

'I might be,' I said uncertainly. 'She might ring a vague bell.' Definitely a bad association here.

'Shall I tell you?'

173

'*Yes,*' I said (*you bastard,* was the bit I only thought).

'Her first name's Emma.'

Emma. Very definitely a bad association. Yes, I'd met her, just once maybe. But who the hell was she, and why the bad association?

Then I realised, just as he spoke her second name.

Half an hour later I stood on the bridge of the *Lorenzo Uffizi,* braced along with the others against one of the equipment consoles still ranged beneath the windows, while the coast swept forward to meet us at thirty knots. The *Lorenzo Uffizi* was headed straight for a broad gap between a half-demolished bulk carrier and a broad, unidentifiable hull that was all ribs and missing plates. Spread out on either side of us, for kilometres in each direction, were dozens of ships of every size and type and in every stage of dismantling: some freshly beached and barely touched, others reduced to little more than the spines of their keels and a few girders; tiny figures dotted the vast slope of oil-stained sand and infinitesimal sparks glowed sporadically amongst the hulks, while slanted pillars of smoke rose from a hundred different sites on the remains of the ships, the salvage-littered shore and deep inland.

The faintest of tremors shook the vessel. I watched the bows start to rise as the edge of the console pressed against my pelvis and belly. The telegraph rang for All Stop. A few people cheered. Tommy Cholongai, still holding on to the wheel, laughed and wheezed as the deceleration forced him forward into it. The ship groaned and creaked around us and from somewhere below there came a distant crashing noise, like hundreds of pieces of crockery falling. Shuddering mightily, the *Lorenzo Uffizi*'s bows rode further and further up the beach, gradually obscuring the view of the land dead ahead. Looking to port, I watched our wash go piling up against the rust-streaked hull of the bulk carrier in a great white sine of surf. Bangings and thuds sounded all around us, the deck seemed to flex beneath my feet and a window out on the far end of the bridge's starboard wing suddenly popped out of its frame and disappeared towards the glistening sands below.

The creaking and groaning and the steady pressure went on for a few more seconds, then with a final pulsing shake and a kind of softly transmitted thud that left me bruised for days and nearly hit my head on the window glass, the old cruise liner settled into her last resting place, the crashing noises ceased and the console stopped digging into me.

More cheering and applause. Tommy Cholongai thanked the ship's master and the pilot, and then with a flourish set the bridge telegraph to Finished With Engines.

I looked over at Adrian Poudenhaut, who had decided to stay aboard for the beaching but had looked distinctly green around the gills for the last ten minutes or so, calm seas or no. Still clutching his briefcase, he smiled wanly. I smiled back.

And as I smiled I thought, Emma Buzetski.

Because that was her name.

'Buzetski is her second name,' Hazleton had said on the satellite phone, half an hour earlier, just before he rang off. 'She's Emma Buzetski. You know, Stephen's wife.'

# C H A P T E R
# S E V E N

Just had a horrible thought.

You had a dream where you woke up and somebody had removed all your teeth last week. Michael, I have some bad news for you . . .

No, I'm serious. But it's about that. You recall the party I was going to see on the morning after that happened?

Yes. What about him?

He has a daughter. Very pretty, very Westernised,

very pleased to see me, once, when her dad wasn't
there. If you know what I mean.

Gosh, you're such a rake. Actually you're a
fucking cretin. You risked jeopardising a deal
that size by getting involved with a CEO's <u>KID</u>?
I can't believe you're telling me this. Is this
meant to endear me to you, Mike? Make me think
hey, here's one worth promoting, spread the word
around the Level Fours? Are you mad? Are you
drunk? DICKHEAD, Mikey boy.

Calm down, will you? Look, it just fucking
happened, all right? She came on to me. I mean
she's not a child or anything; 19 I think. But I
was practically raped.

Yeah, right.

Except she wouldn't actually let me — how shall
I put it, go the hole way?

Go on.

I used my mouth.

Ah. See your problem/worry. Except what was
done to you was done at this end, not that end. Of
the journey, I mean, not your bod.

Still. I mean, don't you think?

You said the party concerned wasn't too
bothered about your lack of dentition.

Quite unfazed.

Bad sign. Think back to your previous few
encounters with him, post your tryst with his
li'l girl. How was his attitude then?

Umm, well, frostier, maybe. I remember talking
about that. It felt like we'd slipped back a rung

or two in the negotiations. Thought it was just
a ploy. But he was always really polite to me, I
mean <u>really</u>.

You idiot. So he's frosty, then you lose half
your teeth and he's the one wreathed in smiles.
Didn't you ever suffer because of somebody, and
— even if you had to tolerate them because of
business — be really cold towards them, and then
have your secret revenge on them and suddenly
find it was easy, even <u>more satisfying</u> to be all
sympathetic towards them?

I am in the presence of the master, amn't I?
Or the mistress. Truly you are Yoda. Yodette,
anyway.

Displeased with you I am. I can't believe . . .
no, come to think of it, I can. You're a man. We're
probably lucky you didn't try to shag his wife
or have carnal knowledge of his favourite golf
course or something. I mean, eighteen holes; the
possibilities. Actually I don't know why I'm
making light of this. In all seriousness, I'm
very disappointed in you. That was a very stupid
thing to do. The deal <u>is</u> totally done, isn't it?
There isn't some last little tiny detail that
could explode — oh sorry, could that be ejaculate
— in our faces?

Yuk. Totally done, signed, sealed, delivered
and set in reinforced ferroconcrete. Look, I've
said I'm sorry, but at least I did tell you as soon
as I realised.

Ferroconcrete <u>is</u> reinforced. And I bet you did

179

not just think of this. And as I seem to recall telling you, Adrian G is your immediate superior while I'm on sabbatical, not me. Plus I just scrolled back through all this and you have <u>not</u> said you're sorry.

All right! I'm sorry! Really. Look, I don't have to tell AG, do I? He really doesn't like me. Say it ain't so. I'll make it up to you. This is all off the record, obviously.

Helps to say that at the start. You do have a lot to learn. How did you get to be an L4? Anyway, I won't tell AG, but in the event that anything does happen with the deal concerned, you're going to have to confess all to the relevant authorities. As the deal's done, and the CEO was apparently happy, we're probably OK, honour satisfied. But, like I say, in the event, you'll have to own up. And another thing: have you talked to the girl since? Has she said she confessed all to her pa? I mean it looks like he found out, but through her?

She won't return my calls. I'm starting to regret telling you this. Look, if something did go wrong later, this could end my career. You won't grass on me will you? Kathryn; please.

I'm not promising anything. If all you pay for this is losing a few teeth, we'll all have got off lightly.

Who's this We, white man? Might I point out that I've taken <u>all</u> the shit here; as far as the biz is concerned the phrase Scot free comes to mind, my little Caledonian chum. You, ie the company has lost fuck all.

Yes, and you'd better pray it stays that way.

I thought you were an atheist.

It's just a form of words; don't get hot under
your dog or any other collar. Where the hell is
your dumb ass — sorry, arse — anyway?

Home in a dark and rain-swept Chelsea. You?

I'm in Karachi, and a quandary.

Oh. Isn't that the new Toyota?

Never mind. You should be asleep. Do try not
to fuck up any important mega-deals or lose any
major body parts while in the land of nod.

Make it so, number one. Oh, forgot: Adrian G
changed story again. Apparently it definitely and
definitively was _not_ our large secure friend Mr
Walker he saw in that taxi the other day. My fault
for getting totally the wrong end of the stick,
allegedly. Just thought I'd tell you.

Right. So now we know. Night, and then again,
night.

We'd been lifted off the *Lorenzo Uffizi* by the helicopter from
Tommy Cholongai's yacht. For a while I'd wondered whether
we'd be taken straight to the yacht and never actually set foot
on the sands of Sonmiani Bay, but we did, plucked from the
deck and lowered to the beach in groups of four, and stood
in the shade of the enormous stem of the old liner while Mr
C glad-handed the boss-men of the ship-breaking concern that
would be scrapping the vessel.

Even while we stood there, the water still drying on the vessel's
patchy red hull-bottom paint and draining from the weeds and

encrusted growths that had accumulated under the waterline since her last scraping, a squad of little men and skinny boys pushing oxyacetylene cylinders on trolleys came jogging past us. They split into groups of two stationed every hundred feet or so down the length of the hull exposed above the now retreating tide, ignited their torches, flipped dark goggles down and started cutting into the ship's plates to form a series of beach-level doors.

The Pakistani bosses were all smiles and politeness and invited us to take tea in their offices further up the beach, but I got the impression they just wanted rid of us so they could get on with the job of taking the ship apart. Mr Cholongai declined their offer gracefully and we were all ferried out to the yacht in the little Hughes, apart from Adrian Poudenhaut, who was picked up by his fancy Bell-with-the-retractable-undercarriage, the swine.

There was a feast arranged on board the yacht, and something of a party. The *Lorenzo Uffizi*'s captain and first officer and the local pilot received presents from Mr C. They didn't unwrap them but they seemed very happy with them all the same. Gorgeously attractive Malay girls wandered the teak decks and main lounge, serving cocktails and seafood.

'Mr Poudenhaut did not stay long,' Tommy Cholongai observed, joining me at the port deck rail. Most people were either in the air-conditioned lounge or on this side, in the shade. Even in the shadows, with a gentle breeze produced by the yacht heading parallel with the coast towards Karachi, it felt fiercely hot and humid.

'A man with a mission,' I said, and sipped my margarita.

'A present, I understood.' He held a glass of iced coffee.

'Yes,' I said, aware of the weight of the disc in my jacket pocket.

'From Mr Hazleton, it would be obvious to infer,' Cholongai said, nodding thoughtfully. He smiled. 'Forgive me if I'm being too nosy, won't you?'

'That's all right. Mr Poudenhaut was delivering something Mr Hazleton thought I ought to see. I take it you weren't aware of what it was.'

'Indeed no. Mr Poudenhaut's visit was as much a surprise to me as it was to you.' He glanced at me. 'It was a surprise to you, wasn't it?'

'Yes.'

'I thought so.' He looked out towards the shore. We had left behind the last of the scrapped ships' ragged outlines a few minutes ago. A thin, dark line of mangrove trees had replaced the tawny sands. 'Of course,' he said, 'given what I have told you about today, and given that the Level One executives all know of this matter, there is bound to be, oh, how would one say it? Some jockeying for position.'

'I think I'm starting to appreciate that, Tommy.'

'We shall be staying in harbour in Karachi for a day or two. I have to entertain various worthy but not very sparkling industrialists this evening; you are certainly invited, though I think you might be bored. However I would be honoured if you would join me for lunch tomorrow.'

'If I have time to do a little shopping when we get ashore I'll happily join you for both. Boring industrialists hold no terror for me, Tommy.'

Cholongai looked pleased. He glanced at his watch. 'It would be quicker to send you ahead in the helicopter.'

'Oh,' I said. 'Good.'

Having been met by Mo Meridalawah at the airport and

transported across the ocean of poverty that was Karachi to the archipelago of shops where serious money could be spent, I had time to buy a new frock, a satellite phone and a DVD player.

'Hello?'

'Mr Hazleton?'

'Yes. Who is that?'

'Kathryn Telman.'

'Well, hello. Have you a new telephone, Kathryn?'

'Yes. A satellite phone. Thought I'd test it out. This is my first call.'

'Oh. I suppose I ought to feel honoured, oughtn't I?'

'You rang off rather abruptly yesterday.'

'Did I? I'm sorry.'

'Why did you want me to see that, Mr Hazleton?'

'What? The scene in the hotel? Oh, I thought it might come in useful for you.'

'It's blackmail material, Mr Hazleton.'

'It could be used as such, I suppose. I hadn't really thought of that. You weren't thinking of using it as such, were you?'

'Why should I use it at all, Mr Hazleton?'

'Oh, that's up to you, Kathryn. I simply thought to provide the material. How you use it is up to you.'

'But why, Mr Hazleton? Why did you provide it?'

'I'd have thought it was rather obvious, Kathryn. So that you would feel beholden to me, so that you would be well disposed towards me. It is a gift; I'm not asking for anything specific in return. But I know about the task that Tommy and Jebbet will have outlined to you by now, and it is a very important one for the company. That will make you a very important person. In a sense, it already has, even if you have not yet come to a decision. Have you, by the way?'

'Not yet. I'm still thinking.'

'That is sensible. It is a big step. A step that I, like the others, would like you to take, but you're right not to make the decision without serious thought. I'm sorry if I've given you even more to think about.'

'Did you set this up, Mr Hazleton? I mean, the filming.'

'Not I. You might say that the material fell into my hands.'

'And why do you think that I in particular might be interested in it?'

'Kathryn, it's not exactly common knowledge, but I think I know how you feel about Mr Buzetski.'

'Oh, you do, do you?'

'Yes. I like Stephen, too. I admire his integrity, his principles. It would be a pity if those principles were founded, as it were, on false premises though, wouldn't it? I thought that, as this piece of film existed, it might be of value to you. The truth can hurt, Kathryn, but it is usually preferable to falsehood, don't you think?'

'Mr Hazleton, do you hold any evidence of a similar nature concerning me?'

'Good heavens, no, Kathryn. This is not something I have any regular part in, or wish to encourage. As I said, the film fell into my hands.'

'And what exactly makes you think I feel anything in particular for Stephen Buzetski in the first place?'

'I'm not blind, Kathryn, and I am human. The same goes for the people who work for me. They understand emotions, they can empathise with people. Of course they make it their business to know how people in the company feel about their colleagues so that one doesn't accidentally place together people who hate each other. Just good business practice, really, and of genuine benefit to the individuals concerned, too. I'm sure you can appreciate that in the circumstances one doesn't have to try to discover who's attached to whom, to find out *en passant*, as it were. It just happens.'

'I'm sure it does.'

'Quite. So, you have the film, or video disc or whatever it's called. Frankly all this technology is beyond me. How you use it is up to you, though of course I entirely understand that you may wish not to use it directly, as it were. You may think it would be better if Stephen found out what has been going on without any reference to you, in which case I'm sure that a way could be found for him to discover the truth without you being involved in any way. All you would have to do would be to let me know.'

'You make it all sound very reasonable, Mr Hazleton.'

'Good. I'm glad.'

Stephen, help.

How?

I'm in a quandary. Where are you, anyway?

Home. Where are you?

Karachi, Pakistan. Everybody OK there?

Fine. Wow, you are trotting that old globe. What seems to be the problem, ma'am?

New job offer.

New job offer? What the hell can it be?

Well, for one thing it's in confidence.

You got it.

And also it's in Thulahn.

You have got to be kidding. No, you've got to be
being kidded. That's the place in the Himalayas,
right?

The same.

Explain. I can't wait. This isn't demotion is
it? You haven't done anything foolish have you?

Oh, it's not demotion. And I have done lots of
foolish things, but enough about my sex life. They
want me to, well, it's hard to explain. Scout the
place out. I can't give you all the details, but
they want me to settle there. Live there, get to
know the people, try and suss how they're going
to react to future changes, anticipate their
collective mood, I guess.

But there's nothing there, is there?

Mountains. Lots and lots of mountains. And nine
hundred thousand people.

How much can't you tell me? Rough idea. Promise
it'll go no further.

Shit. Well, it's important. And it would be
good for my career, I'm told. But it's a totally
radical change. It means giving up the way I live
my life, it means giving up what I'm good at,
job-wise, it probably means giving up seeing my
friends as much as I do at the moment and that's
already barely enough. With the job, I don't know
I'd ever be able to step back into it. I mean what
I do now is all so techy and it's all moving so
fast I probably can't leave it for more than about
— you guess — maybe a year? Eighteen months max
and everything I know will probably be obsolete.

187

What they're proposing is, well, big, so it'll easily go over that eighteen months. Cutting to chase, the point is this is one of those Warning — Not Undoable decisions.

Lordy mama. Don't know how to advise. Sounds like only you are in possession of the full facts.

Wish same could be said for my faculties.

It can. What's your gut feeling?

I must have become a ruminant because I seem to have at least two different gut feelings. One says Fuck it, take it, other just scrunches up into little ball in corner and squeals No no no no no! But which is the real me?

I know which one I'd go for.

Ah, Stephen, if only.

Emma's here at my side, so I'll just ask her . . . only kidding. When do you need to give them a reply?

Indefinite. They'd like some sort of provisional idea in the next couple of weeks, but I could probably stall into '99 if I wanted.

You're in Karachi. Close to Thulahn. Worth taking a few days there.

Well, about 2000 km, but yes, wasn't that convenient? Ah, well. You're right. I probably will. Only the Prince could be a problem.

Oh yes. He greatly admires and respects you, doesn't he?

Has the hots for me, yes.

Oh, Kate; you dismiss any and all professions of love as just lust. Maybe one of these guys is

genuinely head over heels for you. Maybe they
all are. It's a subtle form of self-denigration
you're indulging in here, Kate.

Oh, suddenly I'm on line to Dr Frasier Crane.
You're listening. I'd no idea.

So defensive, Kate.

Well, maybe in the words of the immortal
Whitney Houston, I'm saving all my love for
somebody else.

Anyway. I'm sure you can handle the Prince.
Ahem.

I'm sure too, but seriously, it's a
consideration.

Take that holiday, or whatever you want to call
it. You're still on sabbatical, aren't you?

Doesn't feel like it, but yes.

So go.

Good idea. Hey, I'd get to choose staff. You
wouldn't want to move to Thulahn, would you?
I mean not now but if all this happens? (Just
kidding, really.)

Kind of got commitments here. Schools, you
know. Plus Emma not too keen on any incline beyond
one in twenty. Probably a girl thing. High heels
and stuff.

Yeah, commitments. Like I said, just kidding.
You could always visit though, yeah, yeah,
huh, huh?

Surely.

Don't call me . . . actually you can call
me anything/time you want. Ah, dear. I think

tiredness is catching up on me. Bed beckons. I
shall to my sheets. Thinking of you. Have a nice
day, and from this end, good night.
   You are a rascal. Sweet dreams.

Sweet dreams indeed. I put a finger to my lips and kissed it, then touched the tip to the screen on the words 'Sweet dreams'. Then I laughed at myself and shook my head. I closed the lap-top's lid. The machine beeped at me and the glow of light from the screen cut out just before it came down to meet the keyboard. Only the TV's screen was left on now, tuned to Bloomberg, sound off. I looked out at the lights of the city, and then up at the cornice of the room, between wall and ceiling. Everything was built in. Nowhere to just plonk a camcorder. Come to think of it, it had probably been something more sophisticated that had spied on Mrs B and her lover: you could put a camcorder lens into a pair of glasses these days so maybe the camera had been concealed in a smoke alarm or something and the rest of the mechanism housed somewhere its bulk didn't matter.

I lifted the lap-top's lid up again; the screen flicked back on. I looked at the last few lines we'd exchanged. Commitments.

'Oh, Stephen,' I whispered, 'what am I to do?'

The DVD player was still in its box: I hadn't had the time or the inclination to try connecting it to my lap-top yet. The disc Poudenhaut had given me was still in my jacket pocket, hung up inside the wardrobe and smelling of smoke (all the industrialists on Mr C's yacht were heavy smokers). I didn't need the disc, or the DVD player. I could see Mrs Buzetski silently mouthing *Oh, oh, oh,* very clearly indeed, thank you.

I didn't save our exchange to the lap-top's hard drive; I

just powered down. First the machine, then, after a shower, me.

Well, now, here was an interesting little treat: that nice Mr Cholongai had loaned me his company Lear. It was a good one, too; actually had facilities. The first time I was offered a lift on a private jet I was appalled to be told it might be an idea to visit the airport loo before we left as the plane didn't have a toilet. Finding that your ultimate corporate status symbol has less in the way of amenities than a modern express coach can take the gloss off the experience.

I should be old enough not to want to do this sort of thing, but, well. I discovered my ordinary mobile phone would work and attempted to call my pal Luce back in California. Voicemail. I tried another of my girlfriends in the valley. She was on an exercise bike in the gym and was suitably impressed when I told her where I was, but too breathless to be able to talk much. Still in a telephonic mood, I drew various blanks, machines and more voicemails, then got through to Uncle Freddy.

'Guess where I am, Frederick.'

'No idea, dear girl.'

'In a Lear jet, all by myself, flying across India.'

'Good heavens. I'd no idea you knew how to fly.'

'You know what I mean, Uncle Freddy.'

'Oh, you're a passenger?'

'I am *the* passenger. I am outnumbered two to one by the crew.'

'Well, good for you. I suppose there are times when it's good to be in the minority.'

'Oh, really? Name one other.'

'Umm . . . Troilism?'

\*    \*    \*

Given that only a few months earlier both India and Pakistan had been trading underground nuclear tests, it was probably a sign of how good our relations were with both states that the Lear was cleared straight through across both air spaces to a small airport at Siliguri, situated in the little bit of connective tissue that winds round the northern frontier of Bangladesh and beneath the southern limits of Nepal, Thulahn and Bhutan to join the main body of India with the appendage of Assam. The Himalayas, visible in the distance to the north throughout most of the flight as a deep sweep of glaringly white peaks, gradually disappeared under a layer of haze. I started playing *Jagged Little Pill*, but it was entirely inappropriate. Besides, I'd grown fed up with Alanis Morissette's little end-of-phrase gasps and hadn't forgiven her for entirely confirming the Brit prejudice that Americans don't know the meaning of the word irony.

I looked through my discs and decided I didn't have any music suitable for this view. Instead I fired up the DVD at last and put it through the lap-top, glancing at the film of Mrs B and her lover (like Emma, it did come with sound – the volume just hadn't been turned up before), then clicking through the documentary and photo files on the rest of the disc. Depressing. Soon enough we dipped towards the ambiguous landscape that was neither plains nor foothills around Siliguri.

I had to change planes here. The Lear couldn't land at Thuhn: it needed about four times the length of runway there and it also wasn't really happy landing on anything other than smooth tarmac. As Thuhn's airstrip was composed of the sort of uneven gravelly earth that was pretty crap as a football park, let alone an airfield, this meant that the very nice young Norwegian co-pilot had to lug my bags across to the scruffy

Twin Otter I recognised from the last time I'd made this trip.

This two-engined Portacabin was the pride and joy of Air Thulahn, and indeed the only aircraft it actually possessed. There was a little socket just outside the pilot's sliding window; jamming a stick in there with the Thulahnese royal flag attached instantly converted the plane into the Royal Flight. The plane was wittily nicknamed Otto. It didn't really look all that primitive – well, apart from the props and the fixed undercarriage and the odd dent or two in the fuselage – until the ground staff opened up the nose (which I'd fondly assumed might contain radar, direction finders, instrument landing gear, that sort of thing) and dumped my luggage in the empty space revealed.

The last time I'd climbed aboard Otto, at Dacca airport, in Bangladesh, fresh off a PIA DC10 (terrible flight, perfect landing), I'd had to share the cabin with a gaggle of drunken Thulahnese bureaucrats (there were six of them; I later discovered this constituted about half of the entire Thulahnese civil service), two saffron-robed priests with funny hats and plastic bags full of duty-free cigarettes, a couple of peasant ladies who had to be dissuaded from lighting up their kerosene stove for a bowl of tea while in-flight, a small but pungent billy goat and a pair of vociferously distressed and explosively incontinent piglets. Oh, and there was a crate of hens, every one of which looked distinctly dubious about trusting their necks to such a patently un-airworthy craft.

What a fine old time we had.

On this occasion I was the only passenger, though there was a pile of crates secured by webbing behind the last row of flimsy seats and various sacks of mail occupying the front two rows. The pilot and co-pilot were the same two small, smiling Thulahnese guys I remembered from the last time, and they greeted me like an old friend. The preflight safety briefing consisted of telling me they suspected the last seat-pocket safety instruction card had been eaten by either a goat or a small child, but if I did happen to find another one on the floor or anywhere, could they have it back, please? They were due an inspection soon and these Civil Aviation Authority people were such blinking sticklers!

I promised that in the unlikely event I opened my eyes at any point during the flight, I'd keep them peeled for laminated cards or indeed photocopies floating past on the breeze or stuck to the ceiling during a section of an outside loop.

They thought this was most amusing. While my new flight-deck crew tapped gauges, scratched their heads and whistled worriedly through their teeth, I stuck my nose as close as I dared to the suspiciously smeared surface of the window and watched the sleekly gleaming Lear swivel its electronics-crammed nose round, briefly gun its twin jets and taxi towards the end of the runway. I suspect my expression at that moment would have displayed the same despairing regret of a woman who has in some moment of utter madness just swapped a case of vintage Krug for a litre of Asti Spumante.

'You want we leave the door open?' the co-pilot said, leaning round in his seat. He'd been eating garlic.

'Why would you do that?' I asked.

'You get better view,' he said.

I looked out between him and the captain at the tiny wind-screen, only a metre and a half away, imagining it entirely full of rapidly approaching snow and rocks. 'No, thanks.'

'Okay.' He pulled the door to the flight deck shut with an

uneven, flapping thump. The sun visor on your average family saloon gave a greater impression of solidity.

'Uncle Freddy?'

'Kathryn. Where are you now?'

'In a flying transit van heading straight for the highest mountains on Earth.'

'Thought it sounded a bit noisy. In Tarka, are you?'

'Tarka?'

'Oh, no, wait, that was the plane before this new one.'

'This is the *new* one?'

'Oh, yes. Tarka crashed years ago. Everybody killed.'

'Well, that's encouraging. I hope I'm not disturbing you, Uncle Freddy.'

'Not at all, dear girl. Sorry if I'm disturbing you.'

'Don't worry. I won't pretend this isn't partly to take my mind off the flight.'

'Quite understand.'

'But also I forgot to ask about the Scottish thing we discussed, remember, when we were fishing?'

'Fishing? Oh, yes! Who'd have thought you could nab a trout at this time of year, eh?'

'Who indeed. You do remember what we were – *ah!* – talking about?'

'Of course. What was that?'

'Air pocket or something. Hold on, a mail sack's just landed on my lap. I'm going to strap it into the seat beside me . . . Right. Did you get in touch with Brussels?'

'Oh, yes. Your man is on his way to, umm, where you were.'

'Good. Jesus *Christ*!'

'You all right, Kate?'

'Mountain . . . kind of close there.'

'Ah. Yes, it is a rather spectacular flight, isn't it?'

'That's one word for it.'

'Your pal Suvinder back there yet?'

'Apparently not, he's in Paris. Back in a few days. I may leave before he arrives.' ˙

'Don't forget to watch out for the prayer flags.'

'What?'

'The prayer flags. At the airport. All around it. Terribly colourful. They put flags wherever they think people need spiritual help.'

'Really.'

'Still, it's true what they say, isn't it? You're more likely to be killed in a car than a plane.'

'Not when you're *in* the plane, Uncle Freddy.'

'Oh, well, I suppose. If you're going to look at it that way.'

'Right, just thought I'd check. How are things in Yorkshire?'

'Bit rainy. GTO needs a new big end.'

'Does it? Right. Okay.'

'You sound a bit tense, old girl.'

'Ha! Really?'

'Try having a snooze.'

'A *snooze*?'

'Works wonders. Or get absolutely filthy drunk. Of course, you have to do that a good while before the flight.'

'Uh-huh?'

'Yes. Equip yourself with such a bloody awful hangover that a fiery death in the mangled wreckage of an aircraft seems like a merciful release.'

'I think I'm going to ring off now, Uncle Freddy.'

'Right you are! Get some shut-eye. Good idea.'

The final precipitous roller-coaster descent into Thuhn was even more terrifying than I remembered. For one thing, I could see it this time; on the previous occasion we'd been in cloud until the last thousand feet or so and I'd ascribed the wildly uneven flying of that part of the flight to yet more severe turbulence. Approaching in mid-afternoon on a clear day, it became all too obvious that going into a succession of stomach-churning nose-dives and standing the Twin Otter on its wingtips was simply the only way for the tiny craft simultaneously to lose enough height and avoid a succession of towering knife-sharp obsidian cliffs and seemingly near-vertical boulder fields full of vast rocky shards like ragged black shark's teeth.

It was probably just as well there was an air of unreality about the flight. I felt woozy. I had the beginnings of a headache; it was probably the altitude and the thin air. They said it was better to take your time getting to somewhere as high as Thuhn; drive up, or take a donkey, or even walk. That way your body adjusted gradually to the thinning air. Flying in from sea level was precisely the way not to do it. Still, at least we were descending now. I shivered. I'd dressed in jeans and a cotton blouse and kept a few clothes by my side which I'd gradually put on during the flight – a plaid shirt, a jumper, gloves – but I still felt freezing.

The plane levelled out in that last thousand feet of its approach, if you can call hurtling down at an angle of about forty-five degrees levelling out. I watched a stone shrine, a stupa, flashing past the window on a spur of rock level with the plane. I looked down. If we were at forty-five degrees, the slope was at about forty-four. I did not need to be a geometrician to know that the brown blur of broken ground was getting closer all the time.

The shadow of the plane – worryingly sharp and close to life-size – flickered over rocks, lines of prayer flags and straggling walls made from rough round boulders. Some of the tall bamboo masts anchoring the lines of prayer flags were about twice as far off the ground as the Twin Otter. I pondered Uncle Freddy's words about the siting of prayer flags, and the possibility of dying in a plane crash caused by well-meaning believers hoisting a fresh set of flags in the last obvious space around the airport, only to snag the plane and cause the disaster they were hoping to avert.

Suddenly there were buildings underneath, opposite and above us – I glimpsed an old man looking down at us from a window and could have told you the colour of his eyes if I'd been paying attention – and then I was terribly heavy, then light, and then there was a thump and a furious shaking and rumbling that meant we'd landed. I opened my eyes as the plane rattled and banged across the landing ground, raising dust.

There was a cliff edge about three metres away, and a drop into a deep, wide valley where a white-flecked river wound through sinuous fields of grey gravel, its banks terraced with narrow fields and dotted with sparse trees. Grey, black and then utterly white mountains rose beyond, their peaks like a vast white sheet hooked in a dozen different places and hauled sharply up to heaven.

The plane wheeled abruptly, engines roaring and then cutting out. That left only the roaring in my ears, then. The co-pilot appeared, looking pleased with himself. Through the plane's windscreen, not far in front, I could see a set of soccer goalposts. He kicked open the door, which whammed down and jerked on its chain like a hanged man. 'Here we are,' he said.

I unbuckled, rose unsteadily and stepped out on to the dusty brown ground. I was suddenly surrounded by a sea of knee- and thigh-high children kitted out to resemble small cushions, while a crowd of adults dressed in what looked like colourful quilts appeared and started congratulating the flight crew on another safe landing. The terminal building was still the fuselage of a USAAF DC3 that had crash-landed here during the Second World War. It was closed. A wind as cold and thin and sharp as a knife cut across the landing strip, raising dust and goose pimples. I patted a selection of worryingly sticky little heads and looked up past the jumbled buildings of the town to the steep slope of chaotically fractured rocks over which we had made our final approach. Prayer flags everywhere, like bunting round a used boulder lot. Beneath my feet were the markings for one of the football ground's penalty boxes. One of the male quilt-people came up to me, put his hands together as though in prayer and bowed and said, 'Ms Telman, welcome to Thuhn International Airport.'

I successfully resisted the urge to laugh hysterically in his face.

'I say, did you know that you can count up to over one thousand just using your fingers?'

'Really?'

'Yes. Can you guess how? I bet you can't.'

'You'd . . . use a different base, I suppose, not ten. Ah, of course; binary. Yes. It'd be . . . one thousand and twenty-four.'

'One thousand and twenty-three, actually. Zero to one thousand and twenty-three. Gosh, though, well done. That was

very quick. I must have bored you with this before. Have
I?'

'No, Mr Hazleton.'

'Then I'm impressed. And you know my name, and here I am
and I've very rudely forgotten yours, though I'm sure we were
introduced earlier. I do hope you'll forgive me.'

'Kathryn Telman, Mr Hazleton.'

'Kathryn, how do you do. I do believe I've heard of you.'

We shook hands. It was November 1989, in Berlin, the week
the wall came down. I'd squeezed myself into a Lufthansa flight
from London (jump seat, snooty stewardesses) just that day,
determined to be there for a bit of history that had seemed
unthinkable just a few years earlier. A whole bunch of the
more adventurous Business high-ups had had exactly the same
idea – Tempelhof and Tegel must have been double-parked with
executive jets for those few days – and as a result almost by
default there was a sort of impromptu meeting of various Level
Twos and Ones set up for that evening. I'd decided to try and
gatecrash that as well, and succeeded.

We were sitting down to dinner in a private room in the
Kempinski after a chaotic evening in a collection of limos and
taxis, touring the various places where people were swarming
over the wall, attacking it, demolishing it, wheeling bits of it
away and pocketing it. Everybody was a bit drunk, and, I
suppose, infected with the heady, almost revolutionary – make
that counter-revolutionary – atmosphere of that particular time
and place.

I had indeed been introduced to Hazleton at the reception
before dinner. He was a Level Two at the time, but marked out
for still greater things. He'd looked me over in an automatic,
unfocused way. I was twenty-nine, already a Four, thanks to my

inspired guesses about computers and IT. I looked pretty good; better than I had at nineteen. Hazleton might have forgotten my name but he hadn't forgotten what I looked like. He'd made straight for the seat at my side. Well, fairly straight: he bumped a couple of gold-painted chairs on the way.

He'd just nodded at me as he'd sat down and then ignored me throughout the first course, as though he'd really chosen this seat at random or had taken it reluctantly, then suddenly he'd come up with this unlikely chat-up line about digital digits. I had become used to this sort of thing from upper-class Englishmen. At least he had used the second person, rather than 'one'.

'And if one used one's toes,' he said, 'one could go up to over a million.' (Oh, so we *were* using 'one', were we?)

'Impractical, though,' I said.

'Yes, you'd have to take your socks or stockings off.' (Back to 'you', then.)

'I was thinking,' I said, 'of the difficulty of articulating your toes.'

'Oh. Yes. How do you mean?'

'Well, you can use your fingers to count because you can alter their state, bend each one to show whether it's a zero or a one, but very few people can do anything similar with their toes. They just sort of sit there, don't they?'

He thought about this. 'I can put my little toes over the ones next to them.'

'Really? On both sides?'

'Yes. Good, eh?'

'Then assuming you can put each of your big toes over the one next to *them*, you could count to, what, just over sixteen thousand.'

'I suppose so.' He contemplated his entrée for a moment. 'I can wiggle my ears, you know.'

'Never!'

'Yes. Watch.'

'Good heavens!'

We amused each other with a selection of childish antics like this for a while, then got on to puzzles.

'I've got one,' I said. 'What are the next two letters in this sequence? S, T, N, D, R, D?'

He sat back. I had to repeat the letters for him. He looked thoughtful. 'S, D,' he said.

'No.'

'Yes, it is. It's "standardised" with all the vowels taken out.'

'No, it isn't.'

'Why not?' he asked indignantly. 'That's a perfectly good answer.'

'The correct one's much better.'

He made a noise which sounded suspiciously close to a 'harrumph', and sat back with his arms crossed. 'Well, so you tell me, young lady.'

'Want a clue?'

'Oh, if you insist.'

'First clue. I'll write it down.' I took my napkin and lipstick and wrote: S T  N D  R D  _ _.

He bent over the napkin, then looked up at me sceptically. 'That's a clue?'

'The gaps, the spacing. That's the clue.'

He looked unconvinced. He carefully extracted a pair of half-moon glasses from his breast pocket and put them on. He peered at the napkin over the top of them.

'Want another clue?'

'Wait, wait,' he said, holding up one hand. 'All right,' he said eventually.

'Second clue: it's a very simple sequence.'

'Really? Hmm.'

'The simplest. That's your third clue. Actually it's your fourth clue, too, and I've already given you the answer.'

'Uh-huh.'

He gave in at last. 'Well, I think the answer *is* S, D, and you're just being a tease,' he told me, folding the glasses and putting them away.

'The answer is T, H.'

He looked at the napkin. I wrote the last two letters into the space. 'No,' he said. 'I still don't see.'

'Watch.' I wrote a large 1 in front of the letters ST. I didn't need to add the 2, the 3 or the 4.

'Ah,' he said, nodding. 'Very clever. Haven't heard of that one before.'

'You wouldn't have. I made it up myself.'

'Really?' He looked at me. 'You are a clever little thing, aren't you?'

I used my wintry smile.

I woke up in darkness, breathless. I was gasping for air, drowning in what felt like a semi-vacuum beneath a huge and terrible weight. Darkness. Not just ordinary darkness but total darkness; profound and utter and somehow intensifying the breathlessness. Where was I? Berlin? No, that had been a dream, or something remembered. Blysecrag? Chilly enough for one of the turret rooms. I looked for my watch. The bed felt small and cold and odd. Nebraska? The air outside the bed, as well as feeling absurdly cold, didn't smell right. The bedclothes were far too heavy. My breath hurt my throat. There was a very strange smell in the air. Where the hell was I?

I extended my left hand and found cold, stone-solid wall. I reached up and touched wood. I saw a small glowing circle nearby on my right and leaned across to it. It felt like I was wearing all my clothes. My fingers closed around the watch. It felt very cold. According to the Breitling it was four fifteen. I tried to remember whether I'd reset it for the right time zone. Clattering across an uneven wooden surface, my fingers encountered the familiar lumpy shape of the netsuke monkey figure, and then the ribbed casing of my little flashlight. I clicked it on.

My breath smoked in front of me. I was in some sort of bed alcove. The ceiling of the room was painted bilious yellow and livid green. A row of demonic faces glared down at me, painted red, purple, black and orange. Their brows were arched, their ears were pointed, their eyes were huge and glaring, their moustaches were curled like waxed black hooks and their fang-like teeth were bared behind snarling carmine lips under cheeks as round and green as avocados.

I stared at them. The little Aspherilux threw a tight, even spot of light. The spot was shaking. I must still be dreaming. I really needed to get back to sleep properly and wake up again.

Then I remembered. Thulahn. I was in Thulahn, in the capital city of Thuhn, in the Palace of a Thousand Rooms, which had exactly sixty-one rooms. The bizarre painted wooden heads were there to ward off demons while the honoured guest slept. There was no light because (a) it was night, (b) there was no moon, (c) the room's window was covered by both curtains and shutters, and (d) the palace electricity generator shut down at midnight when the Prince was in residence; at other times, like now, it was turned off at sunset. I was cold because I was in a place where central heating meant having a full stomach. I was breathless because I'd come from hot and humid sea level yesterday morning to nine thousand feet by teatime. By the side of the bed there was a small oxygen cylinder and mask, just in case. No TV, of course.

I remembered the airstrip, being welcomed by a polite little quilted Thulahnese guy of indeterminate age called Langton something or other, walking with him at the head of a procession of adults and chattering children and being shown around the ramshackle town, entering the palace complex through brightly painted wooden gates and having a tour of its impressive state rooms before sitting down to dinner at a long table with what looked like a bunch of monks dressed in primary colours, none of whom spoke English. I'd sampled various consistencies and hues of beige food, drunk water and fermented milk beer, then suddenly it was dark and apparently it was time for bed. I'd felt wide awake – bewildered, dizzy, not connected to the world, but wide awake – until I'd seen the little cot-bed, and then I'd suddenly conked out.

I clicked the torch off. My feet felt down to the bottom of the bed and touched the cork-stoppered china hot-water bottle. It was still warm. I hooked it with one foot and brought it up towards my bum as I curled up again and closed my eyes.

Why had I been dreaming of Berlin and Hazleton?

Because I'd been talking to Hazleton the day before, I supposed. Because that dinner was the first time we'd exchanged more than a few words. Obvious, really. Except that it wasn't. Some bit of my brain didn't like this explanation and kept insisting there was more to it. I put it down to lack of oxygen.

Hazleton had felt my knee beneath the table later, and insisted he would see me back to my room that evening. I'd run away.

Why couldn't I dream of Stephen?

Stephen, married to Emma. Emma who went Oh, oh, oh, in total silence. Emma who was having an affair with Frank Erickson, a corporate lawyer for Hergiere Corp, who lived in Alexandria, Va, with his wife Rochelle and three children, Blake, Tia and Robyn. He and Emma had met in various hotels within the DC Beltway, usually around lunchtime, and had managed two weekends together, one in New Orleans when he was attending a convention and she had claimed to be visiting an old schoolfriend, and one at the Fearington House, an elegant country inn tucked away in the woods near Pittsboro, North Carolina.

I had the zip code and the telephone number for the inn; I even knew what they'd had to eat for dinner on the Friday and Saturday night and which wines they'd chosen to accompany their meals; I could have called the place up and asked them to reserve the same suite and put a bottle of the same champagne on ice.

There were no videos of their tryst there, but I had a scanned copy of the bill. The DVD Poudenhaut had given me contained photographs of that bill, various restaurant cheques – all matched to still photos or other short pieces of video of the adulterous couple in those restaurants – receipts for flowers to be delivered to Mrs Buzetski's office in the graphic-design company she worked for, a receipt for a five-hundred dollar négligé in Mr Erickson's name, which I suspected his wife had never worn, and a whole variety of other bits and pieces of film and documentation that chronicled their affair in excruciating detail.

The film of them fornicating in the DC hotel room (the Hamptons Hotel, Bethesda, room 204, to be precise) was just the cherry on the cake. Somebody had gone to a huge amount of trouble over a considerable period of time to gather that evidence, and the more I thought about it, the less I believed Hazleton that the disc had just fallen into his hands.

How much of this sort of stuff went on? Was it just Hazleton, or were the rest at it as well? Did they have anything similar on me? Unlike Stephen, I'd never taken any vows, never made any promises, legal or otherwise, but what about the people I'd slept with? I tried to review the list of sexual partners I'd had over the years, looking for any that could be blackmailed or otherwise compromised.

As far as I could remember there shouldn't be a problem: I'd always tried to avoid married men just as a matter of course, and on the few occasions when I'd ended up in bed with one it had been because the bastard had lied (well, once or twice I might have *suspected*, but never mind). Come to think of it, Stephen ought to be grateful and flattered I was prepared to make an exception for him.

Maybe this had all been done for me, I thought. Maybe Hazleton really didn't make a habit of this sort of thing, but had set up this particular surveillance operation because he knew how I felt about Stephen, knew how Stephen felt about adultery and had seen a way, perhaps, to give my beloved to me and so leave me for ever in his debt.

I was too hot. The air outside the bed was still sharply chilly, but underneath the Himalayan pile of bedclothes it had suddenly become sweaty. I pulled off my jumper and thick socks. I kept them in the bed with me, in case I needed to put them on again later.

What the hell was I going to do?

Should I tell Stephen about his wife? Shit, it wasn't just the dishonesty or any advantage I might gain, it was safety: Emma and Frank hadn't used any protection that I could see.

I could phone Stephen right now. I could tell him the truth, that I had the evidence and Hazleton had given it to me. That was the most honest course, the sort of thing you could imagine justifying in court. But if I did? Maybe he would blame me, maybe he'd stick by her, maybe he'd think I was just trying to wreck his marriage. No win.

Or I could – even more easily, because it would take a single sentence with no angst, no trauma involved – ring Hazleton and say okay, do it. Let it happen. Let Stephen find out the truth and see what he did next, hoping that he'd turn to me, sooner or later. Maybe even arrange to be nearby when he heard the news, and so be the most obvious shoulder for him to cry on; up my chances at some little risk.

Or do nothing. Maybe he'd find out anyway. Maybe Mrs B would be discovered some other way, or Mrs Erickson would find out and tell Stephen, or Mrs B would grow tired of living a lie and announce she loved somebody else and wanted a divorce – hell, she knew a good lawyer. That was the best outcome: doing nothing and still coming out ahead; a low reading on the guilt-o-meter. But that still left me knowing and not doing anything.

I tossed and turned in the bed, still too warm despite the chilly air. I slipped off my loose cotton pants and rolled them up. I had my PJs on underneath.

The Palace of a Thousand Rooms. With sixty-one rooms. Ha: Blysecrag had more than that in one wing.

That would be the other reason I'd recalled my first proper meeting with Hazleton and the thing about counting to a thousand on your fingers. The Palace of a Thousand Rooms was called that because whoever had first built it had counted in base four, not base ten, so that – if you chose to translate it that way, and they had – their sixteen was our hundred and their sixty-four was our thousand. So the palace had been built with sixty-four rooms. Except that three rooms had dropped off during an earthquake in the nineteen fifties and they hadn't got round to replacing them yet. Different bases. That must be the explanation. That was why I'd had that dream-memory of dinner in Berlin, the week the wall came down.

Only it still wasn't. In all my billions of neurons and synaptic connections, it seemed like it only took a few determined troublemakers to distract me from the sort of things I ought to be thinking about, like whether to tell my beloved he was being cuckolded, or whether I should abandon my brilliant career and move to Thulahn (What? Was I mad?).

Think around the problem. Don't call Stephen. Call his missus. Call Mrs B. Tell *her* you know.

No, call her – or have somebody else call her – anonymously and let her know only that somebody knows. Bring things to a head that way. Maybe she'd confess all (yes, and then Stephen – just, gee, a big soft galloot – forgives her and, heck, if their relationship doesn't, like, gather strength from the experience).

I could see that.

Or maybe she'd leave him. I could see that, too. Maybe she'd leave him and take the children. Maybe she'd leave him and take the children and leave the poor, gorgeous sap with nobody to turn to . . . (but wait! Who's that in the background? Yes, her, the attractive thirty-eight-year-old blonde – oh, but looks younger – with the Scottish/Bay Area accent?).

Well, heck, a girl could dream.

Shit, none of this was getting me anywhere, and I wasn't even sleepy any more. Tired, yes, but not sleepy.

I felt for the flashlight again. I switched it on, let the beam travel round the room while I took in where everything was, then switched it off again. I pulled on my socks, trousers and jumper, stuck my head under the covers. The warm air smelled muskily, pleasantly of perfume and me. I took a few deep breaths, then jumped out of bed, putting the covers back.

I felt my way to the window. I pulled back the thick, quilted drapes, folded the creaking wooden shutters to each side and opened the wooden-framed windows with their bottle-bottom panes.

No moon. But no clouds either. The town's roofs, the river valley, crumpled foothills and crowding mountains were lit by starlight, with eight and a half thousand feet less atmosphere in the way to filter it than I was used to. I couldn't see any other lights at all. A dog barked faintly somewhere in the distance.

The breeze flowed into the room like cold water. I stuck my hands into my armpits (and suddenly remembered that when I was a little girl we used to call our armpits our oxters) and leaned forward, sticking my head out into the view. What little of my breath the altitude hadn't already taken was removed by the sight of that darkly starlit gulf of rock and snow.

I stayed like that until I started to shiver, then shut everything up with numbed fingers and crawled back into bed, keeping my head under the covers to warm it up again.

I shivered in the darkness. The capital city, and not a single artificial light.

Tommy Cholongai had given me an encrypted CD Rom with details of what the Business was planning for Thulahn. There would be another all-year road to India, a university and a modern, well-equipped hospital in Thuhn and schools and clinics in the regional capitals. We'd build a dam in the mountains behind Thuhn that would provide hydro power and control the waters that washed over the broad, gravelly valley I'd seen from the airstrip, allowing the waters there to be channelled to one side so that a bigger airport could be built, one that would take jets. Big jets.

During the summer months the hydro plant would produce much more electricity than Thuhn would need; the surplus would be used to power giant pumps, which would force specially salinated water into a huge cavern hollowed out in a mountain high above the dam. The idea was that this water wouldn't freeze, and in the winter, when the main hydro plant was useless, this saline solution would flow down through another set of turbines and into another dam so that Thuhn would have power all year round. All power lines would be underground wherever possible; a minimum of disfiguring poles and wires.

Also on offer was a network of tarmac roads connecting the capital with the main towns, plus street-lights, a water treatment plant, drains and a sewage works for Thuhn initially, with similar improvements scheduled for the regions later.

The plan was to skip conventional wire or terrestrial microwave telephony entirely and go straight to satellite phones for every village and every important person. The footprints of various satellites we controlled would be adjusted to take in Thulahn and so provide additional digital Web and TV-based information and entertainment channels for those who wanted them.

Then there was the stuff the Business intended just for itself: a whole network of tunnels and caverns in Mount Juppala (7,334 metres), a few kilometres north-east of Thuhn in the next valley.

211

That was where, if possible, the PWR would go. Ah, yes, the PWR. At no point in the CD-Rom was that particular acronym explained; even in a CD-Rom that had serious encryption, ran to maybe a dozen copies in the world and was restricted rigidly to those who needed to know, it seemed we didn't want to spell out the words Pressurised Water Reactor. This was the Westinghouse unit we'd bought from the Pakistanis and had mothballed.

There was some serious engineering involved in all this: basically we'd be turning quite a lot of Mount Juppala into something resembling a Swiss cheese. A hand-picked team of our own engineers and surveyors armed with everything from rock hammers to magnetic and gravitometric arrays had already probed, drilled, sampled, analysed, shaken, mapped and measured the mountain to within a millimetre of its life (only we knew it was three and a half metres higher than the guidebooks and atlases said).

The CD held several impressive sets of plans drawn up by some of the world's foremost engineering firms, each of whom had carried out feasibility studies on turning this vast lump of rock into a small self-contained city – none of whom, however, had been told where this mountain actually was. It was a big job. We'd be buying a couple of specially modified Antonovs to move all the heavy plant and machinery in. We reckoned we'd built up a fair knowledge-base concerning heavy engineering in extreme cold, thanks to our Antarctic base, but even so the whole Mount Juppala project might take a couple of decades. Just as well we thought long-term.

Was any of this something I wanted to be part of? Were we doing the right thing in the first place? Was the whole Thulahn venture just a huge act of hubris by billionaires with a bee in their bonnet about having a seat at the UN? Did we have any right to come in here and take over their country?

In theory we could build our new HQ with almost no impact on Thulahn: there was a contingency plan for building the new airport in the same valley as Mount Juppala; it would mean levelling off a smaller mountain, but it was less than had been done for the new Hong Kong airport, and we could afford it.

Doing all we could do, undertaking every improvement we were prepared to offer, would change the entire country, and especially Thuhn, probably for ever, which sounded terrible given how beautiful and unspoiled it was and how happy the people seemed to be. But then you looked at the infant-mortality rate, the life-expectancy figures and the numbers who emigrated. If we only offered these changes/improvements, rather than imposed them, how could it be wrong?

I had no idea. At the very least, before I decided anything, I needed a while here, just to start getting the feel of the place. This process was due to start tomorrow, with a visit to the apparently fearsomely weird queen mother, in her own palace, further up the valley.

Legend had it she hadn't left her bed for the last twenty-six years. I curled up under the weight of bedclothes and cupped my still cold hands, rubbing them and blowing into them and wondering why staying in bed for as long as humanly possible was considered even remotely weird in Thulahn.

# C H A P T E R
# E I G H T

**Y**ou rise with the sun in Thulahn. The same as any
place where artificial light is still a novelty, I suppose.
I woke to find a little fat quilted lady bustling round
my room, slamming open the window shutters to let in some
eye-wateringly bright light, talking away either to herself or
possibly to me and pointing at the washstand, where a large,
gently steaming pitcher now stood beside the inset bowl. I was
still rubbing my eyes and trying to think of something rude
to say, like, When were your people thinking of inventing the

215

Door Lock, or even the Knock? when she just bustled straight out again and left me alone and grumpy.

I washed with the warm water in the bowl. There was a bathroom down the end of the hall with a large fireplace in one corner and a rather grand scroll-topped bath on a platform in the middle of the room, but it took a lot of water-pitchers to fill it and the palace servants clearly required advance notice to organise both the fire and the water.

Technically my room was *en suite*, if a cubicle the size of a telephone box with the end of a pipe sticking up between two shoe-shaped tiles counts as *en suite*. There was real toilet paper, but it was miniaturised and unhelpfully shiny. I flushed with the water out of the washing bowl.

Breakfast was served in the room by my little fat quilted lady, who arrived talking, talked as she plonked down the plates and jugs and kept talking as she nodded to me and left. I could hear her talking all the way down the hall. Maybe it was a religious thing, I thought; the opposite of a vow of silence.

Breakfast consisted of stiff fried pancakes and a bowl of watery porridge. I tried a little of each, recalled the variety of mono-taste beige food from the evening before and was reminded that managing my weight, and indeed even losing quite a few pounds in a matter of days, had proved remarkably easy the last time I'd visited Thulahn.

'Her Royal Highness is looking forward to meeting you.'

'Is she? That's nice.' I grabbed a strap and hung on.

Thulahn had cars before it had roads. Somehow, this came as no surprise. Well, it had a car, if not in the plural: a 1919 Rolls-Royce Silver Wraith purchased in India by the Prince's great-grandfather when he was King. It had been dismantled and carried across the mountain paths by teams of sherpas and eventually reassembled in Thulahn the following summer.

There was, however, nowhere to drive it, a point which had perhaps escaped the then King when he'd made the purchase. At the time a main road in Thulahn consisted of a boulder-strewn pathlet wandering along the side of a steep hill with broader bits every now and again where two heavily laden porters or yaks could pass without one knocking the other off the cliff, while a principal street in Thuhn was basically a shallow V between the randomly sized and sited buildings with a stream-cum-sewer in the bottom and lots of little paths strung out along the sides.

As a result, the Roller sat within the main courtyard of the palace for five years, where it was just about possible to run it in a figure of eight providing the wheel was kept at full lock the whole time and the transition from left to right or vice versa was accomplished without undue delay. Hours of fun for the royal children. Meanwhile a road, of sorts, was constructed, from the floor of the valley where most of the farms were, through Thuhn and on up to the glacier foot, where the old palace and the more important monasteries clung like particularly determined limpets to the cliffs.

I was in that car, on that road, now. My driver was Langtuhn Hemblu, the man who'd greeted me at the airstrip the day before and given me the rapid guided walking tour of the city and palace before abandoning me to the colourful monks.

'You mustn't worry,' Langtuhn shouted.

'About what?'

'Why, about meeting Her Royal Highness.'

'Oh, all right, then.' Well, I hadn't been. Langtuhn caught my eye in the rear-view mirror and smiled in what was probably meant to be an encouraging manner.

As far as I could tell his title was Important Steward. I strongly suspected he'd never taken a driving test. It wasn't even as though there was no other motorised traffic around any more: registered in Thuhn alone there were now at least seventeen other cars, buses, vans and trucks to have collisions with, most brought in during the heady days of Thulahn's motoring Golden Age, between the summer of 1989, when a supposedly permanent road had been completed direct from Thuhn to the outside world, and the spring of 1991, when a series of landslides and floods had swept it away again.

There were a few more roads within the kingdom nowadays, and except in the depths of winter (when it was blocked by snow), or during the monsoon (when it tended to get washed away) you could drive from Thuhn down the valley through various other, lower towns, then on down the course of the Kamalahn river and into Sikkim where, season permitting, you actually had a choice: turn left for Darjeeling and India, or right for Lhasa and Tibet. There was, still, a track direct from Thuhn back over the mountains that almost encircled the capital and which allowed a very determined driver to bring a four-wheel drive in over the passes from India, but even that meant sliding the vehicle across in a cradle slung under a wire hawser over the river Khunde.

The Roller bounced and lurched. I clung on. It felt very strange to sit in a car with no seat-belts. Grab-handles and straps didn't give even the illusion of safety.

I'd dressed in as many layers of the clothes I'd brought with me as I could. Even so, I was glad of the little wood-burning stove in one corner of the car's rear compartment. This looked like an after-market accessory and I doubted the boys at RR would have approved, but it helped stop my breath freezing on the windows. I made a mental note to buy some warmer clothes in the afternoon, assuming I survived that long.

The road which wound up through the capital consisted of big flat stones laid across one of the main V-shaped streets-cum-streams-cum-sewers. Langtuhn had explained that as there was just the one main road, it had been designed to take in as many important buildings as possible *en route*, hence the tortuous nature of the course it took, which often involved doubling back on itself and heading downhill again to take in buildings of particular consequence, such as the Foreign Ministry, the important consulates (this seemed to mean the Indian and Pakistani compounds), an especially popular temple or a much-loved tea house.

Most of the buildings in Thuhn were constructed, for the first one or two storeys at least, from large, dark blocks of rough stone. The walls were almost vertical but not quite, spreading out at the base as though they'd started to melt at some point in the past.

They generally looked worn but tended, and most had fresh-looking two-tone paint jobs, though a few sported patches and friezes of brightly painted plaster depicting scenes from the Thulahnese version of Hinduism's idea of the spirit world, which – from the gleeful illustrations of people being impaled on giant stakes, eaten by demons, torn to pieces by giant birds, sodomised by leering, prodigiously endowed yak-minotaurs and skinned alive by grinning dragons wielding giant adzes – looked like the sort of place the Marquis de Sade would have felt thoroughly at home in.

The top storeys were made of wood, pierced by small windows, painted in bright primary colours and strewn with long prayer flags twisting sinuously in the wind.

We skidded round a corner and the Wraith's engine laboured to propel us up the steep slope. People ambled or jumped out of the way – depending on how soon they heard us coming – as we rumbled and bounced across the uneven flagstones.

'Oh, I have your book!' Langtuhn said. 'Please. Here.'

'What book?' I reached out to the opening in the glass partition and accepted a small dog-eared paperback with a two-colour cover.

'The book you left on your last visit.'

'Oh, yes.' *A Guide To Thulahn*, the cover said. I'd picked it up in Dacca airport four years earlier and vaguely recalled leaving it in my room in the Grand Imperial Tea Room and Resting House – a sort of de-glorified youth hostel – which had been my base the last time I'd been here. I remembered thinking at the time that I had never encountered a book with so many misprints, mistakes and misspellings. As quickly as I could without taking my gloves off I flicked to the work's notoriously unreliable 'Top Tips and Handey Phrases' section and looked up the Thulahnese for *Thank you*. 'Khumtal,' I said.

'Gumpo,' Langtuhn said with a big smile. I had the worrying feeling that this was the sixth Marx Brother, but it turned out to mean 'You're welcome'.

We cleared the city; the road stopped twisting wildly at random and started twisting wildly at regular intervals, zigzagging steeply up the boulder-littered side of the mountain. Dotted along the roadside amongst the houses were more tall masts, prayer flags, squat stone bell-shaped stupas and thin wooden prayer-windmills, their sails painted with dense passages of holy script. The houses themselves were sporadically spaced, turf-roofed and, from a distance, easily mistaken for piles of stones. People walking downhill under dripping, small but heavy-looking packs, or trudging uphill under huge and heavy-looking bundles of wood or dung, stopped and waved at us. I waved back cheerfully.

'Do you yet know how long you will be staying with us, Ms Telman?' Langtuhn shouted back.

'I'm still not sure. Probably just a few days.'

'Only a few days?'

'Yes.'

'Oh dear! But then you might not meet the Prince.'

'Really? Oh, what a shame. Why? When is he due back?'

'Not for a week or thereabouts, I am told.'

'Oh, well, not to worry, eh?'

'He will be most disappointed, I'm sure.'

'Really.'

'You cannot stay any longer?'

'I doubt it.'

'That is a shame. I suspect he cannot come home any earlier. He has been away on business, looking after all our interests.'

'Is he, now?'

'Yes. I understand he has said that soon we may all start to benefit from greater outside investment. That will be good, will it not?'

'I dare say.'

'Though of course, he is in Paris, or some such French place. We must hope he does not gamble it all away!'

'Is the Prince a gambler?' I asked. I'd watched him at the blackjack table in Blysecrag; if he was a gambler he wasn't a very good one.

'Oh, no,' Langtuhn said, and took both hands off the steering-wheel to wave them as he looked back at me. 'I was making a joke. Our Prince enjoys himself, but he is most responsible.'

'Yes. Good.'

I sat back in my seat. Well, not a despot, then.

The road grew tired with making wild zigzags up an increasingly steep slope and struck out ambitiously along a notch cut in a vertical cliff. A hundred metres below, the river lay frozen in the bottom of the gorge like a giant icicle fallen and shattered amongst the sharp black rocks.

Langtuhn didn't seem to have noticed the transition from a steep-but-ordinary road to a slot-in-a-cliff. He kept trying to catch my eye in the rear-view mirror. 'We have been hoping that one day the Prince would come back from Paris with a lady who might become his new wife,' he told me.

'No luck yet?' I looked away, hoping this might encourage him to return his attention to the business of keeping the car on the narrow road. The view down into the chasm was not an encouraging one.

'None whatsoever. There was a princess from Bhutan he seemed most sweet upon a few years ago, they say, but she married a tax-consulting gentleman from Los Angeles, USA.'

'Smart girl.'

'Oh, I do not think so. She could have been a queen.'

'Hmm.' I rubbed the red tip of my nose with one gloved hand and looked in my guide-book for the word for frostbite.

The old palace canted out over a deep, ice-choked gorge a mile down from the glacier foot, its haphazard jumble of off-white, black-windowed buildings supported from beneath by a half-dozen enormous charcoal-dark timbers, each the size of a giant redwood. Together they splayed out from a single jagged spur of rock far below, so that the whole ramshackle edifice looked like a pile of ivory dice clutched in a gigantic ebony hand.

This was where the dowager Queen lived, the Prince's mother. Even higher up the mountainside, at the head of tumultuously zigzag paths, monasteries lay straggled across the precipitous slopes in long, encrusted lines of brightly painted buildings. We passed a few groups of saffron-robed monks on the road; they stopped and looked at the car. Some bowed, and I bowed back.

Langtuhn parked the car in a dusty courtyard; a couple of small Thulahnese ladies-in-waiting in dramatic carmine robes met us at the doors and led us into the dark spaces of the palace, through clouds of incense, to the old throne room.

'You will remember to address the Queen as ma'am, or Your Royal Highness, won't you?' Langtuhn whispered to me, as we approached.

'Don't worry.'

Guarding the doors was a massively rotund Chinese man, who wore camouflaged black/grey/white army fatigues and a jacket made of what looked like yak fur. He was sitting in a chair reading a manga comic when we approached. He looked up and rose carefully, taking a pair of minuscule glasses off his nose and leaving the comic open on his seat.

'This is Mihu,' Langtuhn whispered to me, 'the Queen's manservant. Chinese. Very devoted.'

Mihu moved in front of the double doors, barring the way to the Queen's chamber. The two ladies-in-waiting bowed and spoke to him in slower-than-normal Thulahnese while gesturing at me. He nodded and opened the doors.

Langtuhn had to stay in the antechamber with the two ladies. Mihu came into the room with me and stood with his back to the door. I looked around.

I hadn't really believed that the dowager Queen had stayed

in bed for the last two and half decades, since the death of her husband but, then, I hadn't seen the bed.

The ceiling of the huge state room was painted like the night sky. Its two longer walls were lined by bizarrely proportioned sculptures of snarling warriors, two storeys tall. These were covered in gold leaf, which had started to peel so that the soot-black wood underneath showed through like dense sable skin under flimsy gold armour. Tissue-light, the strips and tatters of glittering leaf waved in the faint draughts that swirled through the vast room, setting up a strange, half-heard rustling, as though hidden legions of mice were all crumpling Lilliputian sweet-wrappers at once. Snow-white daylight spilled in from the wall of windows, which looked across a terrace to the valley; its glare glittered back from the rustling scraps of gold like ten thousand cold and tiny flames spread out across the walls.

The bed sat in the centre; a painted wooden construction for which the term four-poster was entirely inadequate. I had seen houses smaller than this. It took three tall steps just to get level with the base. From there more steps led up through lush velvet drapes and heavy brocade hangings to the surface of the bed, while from the cantilevered canopy a network of dyed ropes and loops of printed silk hung like a profusion of jungle creepers.

Big bed, big bedspread: a vast embroidered purple cover stretched from each corner and edge of the bed, rising like a perfect Mount Fuji of lilac to its central summit, where the Queen Mother's head – pale and surrounded by ringlets of white hair – stuck out of a hole in the middle like a snowy summit. From the angle of her head it was hard to tell whether she was lying, sitting or standing. I imagined it was perfectly possible to do all three in there.

According to Langtuhn the Queen Mother didn't even have

to stay inside if she didn't want to. The whole bed was mounted on trolley wheels running on rails leading to the tall, wide set of double doors set in the west-facing wall of windows, beyond which lay the wide balcony with the view over the valley below. Trundling the whole apparatus out to the sunlight would be a task for Mihu, I imagined. With the bed out there and the bed's canopy rolled back, the old lady could get a breath of fresh air and take the sun.

There was nowhere to sit, so I stood facing the foot of the bed.

The little snowball head, about a metre higher than me in the centre of the bed, spoke. 'Miss Telman?' Her voice was thin but still strong. The Queen Mother spoke excellent English, because she was. She had been the Honourable Lady Audrey Illsey until she'd married the late King in 1949.

'Ms, yes, ma'am.'

'What?'

'I prefer the title Ms rather than Miss, Your Highness.'

'Are you married?'

'No, ma—'

'Then you are a Miss, I think.'

'Well,' I said, wishing now that for once I had shut the hell up about the Ms/Miss thing, 'there's been a change in the way people relate to each other, Your Highness. In my generation, some of us decided to take the title Ms, as a direct equivalent of Mr, to—'

'I don't need lessons in recent history, young woman! I'm not stupid, or senile. I have heard of feminism, you know.'

'Oh. Have you? I thought perhaps . . .'

There was a commotion in one side of the slope of the mauve hillside of bedcover, just down from where the dowager Queen's right shoulder must be, as though a volcanic side-vent was about to erupt. After some flapping and muttering, a small white hand appeared from an embroidered slit in the cover clutching a rolled-up magazine. A thin arm clad in lacy white waved hand and magazine. 'I can read, Miss Telman,' she told me. 'The post may take a while but subscriptions do arrive eventually. I am rarely more than a month behind the times.' Another thin white arm appeared from the bedclothes; she opened the magazine out. 'There you are; last month's *Country Life*. I don't suppose you take it, do you? You sound rather American.'

'I have met one or two US citizens who subscribe to the magazine, ma'am, however I am not one of them.'

'So you are American?'

'I'm British – Scottish – by birth. I have dual British-US nationality.'

'I see. Well, I don't see, really. I don't see how one can be of dual nationality, apart from purely legally.' Both arms and the magazine disappeared under the covers again. 'I mean to say, who are you loyal to?'

'Loyal to, Your Highness?"

'Yes. Are you loyal to the Queen, or to . . . the American flag? Or are you one of these absurd Scottish Nationalists?'

'I'm more of an internationalist, ma'am.'

'And what's that supposed to mean?'

'It means my loyalties are contingent, Your Highness.'

'Contingent?' She blinked rapidly, looking confused. 'Upon what?'

'Behaviour, ma'am. I have always thought that believing in one's country right or wrong was, at best, sadly misguided.'

'Oh, you have, have you? I must say you are a very opinionated young woman.'

'Thank you, ma'am.'

I watched her eyes narrow. One arm reappeared with a pair of glasses, through which she surveyed me. 'Come closer,' she said. Then added, 'If you please.'

I stepped up to the base of the giant bed. There was a strong smell of incense and mothballs. The fluttering scraps of gold leaf on the walls set up a distracting shimmer on either side.

The Queen brought out a white handkerchief and polished her glasses with it. 'You have met my son.'

'Yes, ma'am.'

'What do you think of him?'

'I think he is a credit to you, Your Highness. He is charming and . . . responsible.'

'Responsible? Ha! Either you know nothing or you're one of the useless ones. One of the lying ones. The ones that say what they think I want to hear.'

'Perhaps you're confusing lying with politeness, ma'am.'

'What?'

'Well, I don't really know your son all that well, Your Highness. As far as I can tell he seems a gentleman. Well-bred, polite . . . Oh, and a *very* good dancer, great poise and extremely light on his feet.' (The Queen's brows furrowed at this, so I didn't continue with the topic.) 'Ah, he seems sad, sometimes, and he is a little flirtatious, perhaps, but not rudely or aggressively so.' I thought back to what Langtuhn had said in the car. 'He doesn't seem to be too extravagant, which is always a good thing in a prince, I think, especially when they are away from home. Ah,' I said, struggling to end on a positive note, and failing, 'I suspect the responsibilities of his inheritance lie heavily on him.'

The old Queen shook her head as though to dismiss all

this. 'When is he going to get married? That's what I want to know.'

'I'm afraid I can't help you there, ma'am.'

'Not many can, young lady. Do you have any idea how few princesses there are in the world these days? Or even duchesses? Or ladies?'

'I have no idea, ma'am.'

'Of course you wouldn't. You're just a commoner. You are just a commoner, aren't you?'

'I have to confess that any position I've achieved has been attained through merit and hard work, ma'am, so, yes, I'm afraid so.'

'Don't flaunt your inverted snobbery at me, young woman!'

'I'm not usually given to flaunting, ma'am. Perhaps it's the altitude.'

'And don't be downright cheeky either!'

'I can't imagine what's come over me, ma'am.'

'You are a very disrespectful and impertinent girl.'

'I did not mean to be disrespectful, Your Highness.'

'Is it so terrible for a mother to worry about her son?'

'Not at all, ma'am.'

'It would be terrible not to, I think.'

'It would indeed.'

'Hmm. Do you think he's marriageable material?'

'Well, of course, Your Highness. I'm sure he will make some lucky princess, or lady, a wonderful husband.'

'Platitudes, Miss Telman. That is the sort of thing my courtiers tell me.'

I wondered if Mihu and the two little red-clad ladies counted as her courtiers. The palace had seemed quite empty apart from them. I cleared my throat and said, 'He is your son, ma'am.

Even if I thought he'd make an absolutely awful husband I'd be unlikely to say so right out without at least softening the blow a little.'

The Queen Mother sounded exasperated. 'Then just tell me what you *feel*!'

'He'll probably be fine, ma'am. If he marries the right person. Isn't that all one can say of anybody?'

'He is not just *anybody*!'

'Any mother would say the same, ma'am.'

'Yes, and it would be sentimentality! Motherly instinct or whatever you want to call it! Suvinder is heir to a *throne*.'

'Your Highness, I'm not sure how much help I can really be to you in this. I'm not married, I don't expect to marry, and so I don't tend to think in those terms, plus I don't know your son or the international royal-matrimony circuit well enough to comment.'

'Hmm.' The Queen put her glasses away again. 'Why are you here, Miss Telman?'

'I thought I had been summoned, Your Highness.'

'I meant here in Thulahn, you idiot!' Then she sighed and her eyelids fluttered closed for a moment. 'I beg your pardon, Miss Telman. I should not have called you an idiot. Do forgive me.'

'Of course, ma'am. I am here in Thulahn to decide whether I ought to accept a post which will mean coming here to live.'

'Yes, you are one of these mysterious business people my son talks about in such admiring tones. Who are you really? Are you the Mafia?'

I smiled. 'No, ma'am. We are a commercial concern, not a criminal one.'

'My son says that you want to invest what sound to me like

229

most unlikely amounts of money in our country. What's in it for you?'

'We'd like to use Thulahn as a sort of base, Your Highness,' I said, trying to choose my words with care. 'We'd hope that we might be welcomed by your people and that some of us might become citizens. There would be more trade and more dealings in general with other countries, thanks to the improvements and investments we'd like to offer, and so we hope, and we think, it would be appropriate that some us might be allowed certain diplomatic posts so that we could represent Thulahn abroad.'

'You're not backed by those bloody Chinese, are you?'

I wondered if Mihu, still standing by the door, understood English. 'No, ma'am. We're not backed by anybody, in the way I think you mean.' If anything, I thought, we were the ones who tended to do the backing.

'Hmm. Well, it all sounds jolly fishy to me.'

'We mean only to help Thulahn, Your Highness. The improvements to the infrastructure and so on would be offered, not—'

'Family, faith, farms and fealty,' the dowager Queen said, releasing one arm to wag a finger at me.

'I beg your pardon, ma'am?'

'You heard. That's what matters to these people. Those four things. Nothing else. Everything else is irrelevant.'

'Well, perhaps better water supplies, a few more primary schools, more primary health care, too, and—'

'They have water. No one dies of thirst. They have all the education they need. Do you need a degree to walk behind a plough? No. And health? It will always be hard to live here. It's no place for the weak. We all have to die, young woman. Better to work hard, accept the consolation of one's faith and then go quickly. All this hanging around's just vulgar. People are so greedy these days. Accept your lot and don't insist on extending the misery of those who'd be better off dead. There. That's what I believe. Oh, and you needn't try to hide your feelings. I know what you're thinking. Well, for your information, I have not seen a doctor since I took to my bed, and I will not in the future, no matter what. I've been waiting to die for a quarter of a century, Miss Telman. I believe the good Lord is keeping me alive for his own good reasons and so I shan't hasten the process of dying, but I shan't do anything to delay it, either, once it begins.'

I nodded. 'That's very stoic of you, ma'am. I hope anybody would respect your choice.'

'Yes?' she said slowly, suspiciously. 'But?'

'I . . . think it would only be right to offer the Thulahnese people a choice as well.'

'A choice of what? Will they want television? Burger bars? Jobs in factories and supermarkets? Salaries in offices? Motor cars? They will doubtless choose all that, if they're offered it. And before you know it we will be just the same as everywhere else and we'll have homosexuals, AIDS, socialists, drug-dealers, prostitutes and muggers. That will be progress, won't it, Miss Telman?'

By now even I was beginning to suspect that there was no point in continuing this argument. I said, 'I'm sorry you feel that way, Your Highness.'

'Are you? Are you really? Try telling the truth.'

'I am. Truly.'

The Queen looked down at me for a while. Then she nodded. She leaned fractionally towards me. 'It is a hateful thing to grow old, Miss Telman. It is not an enjoyable process, and it will come to you one day. I don't doubt you think me an appalling old reactionary, but there is this consolation for me that there may not be for you: I will be glad to leave this stupid, hurtful, degrading world.' She straightened again. 'Thank you for coming to see me. I am tired now. Goodbye. Mihu?'

I turned round to see the big Chinese man silently opening the doors for me. I looked back to say goodbye to the Queen, but she had closed her eyes and her head had drooped, as though she had been a marionette in a fairground booth all the time and now my money had run out. I took a last look round the strange room with its glittering, whispering walls of flaking leaf over black wooden flesh, then turned and left.

Langtuhn Hemblu almost had to run to keep up with me as I strode back to the car.

'My, you had quite a long time with the Queen Mother!'

'Did I?'

'Yes! You are very privileged. Isn't she a treasure?'

'Oh, yes, a treasure,' I said. Pity she's not buried, I thought.

When I got back to my room in the palace at Thuhn, all my stuff had gone.

I stood in the doorway and looked around. The little cot bed in the alcove had been made up. The cupboard where I'd hung my suit carrier and clothes was open and empty. The satellite phone, my computer, my toiletries; all gone. The little table by the bed had been cleared too; my netsuke monkey had disappeared with everything else.

A swimmy sort of feeling came over me. No phone, no contact. Just what I stood up in. In my pockets, a billfold and two shiny discs.

Had I been robbed? I'd assumed this was one of those places where you didn't need to lock anything, and that was why there was no way of securing the room door. But, then, how much were the satellite phone and the ThinkPad worth, compared to what the average person here made in a year? Maybe somebody had been just too tempted, and I too careless.

Or had I made *that* bad an impression on the Queen Mother? Was this some sort of instant revenge of hers for speaking back to her? I turned to try and find somebody to help, and heard a voice in the distance coming closer. The little quilted lady who didn't stop talking appeared at the end of the corridor. She came up, took my hand and, still talking, led me off to another part of the palace.

The door had a lock. The floor was carpeted. My suit carrier hung in a wardrobe that could have come out of a Holiday Inn. The window was a triple-glazed sealed unit. Under the window was a radiator, plumbed into pipes which disappeared discreetly through the carpet. The bed was a standard double with ordinary pillows. The netsuke monkey had been placed alongside my flashlight on the bedside table. The computer and satellite phone sat on a little writing table with a mirror over it. Through an open door I could see a tiled bathroom with a shower and – glory be – a bidet. Still no TV, mind you.

The little quilted lady bowed and left, talking.

There was a business card on the writing table beside the sat. phone. Joshua Levitsen, honorary US consul, would like to meet me tomorrow; he suggested breakfasting at the Heavenly Luck Tea House at eight.

I went to the window. Same view, a storey higher. The room was warm; a faint thermal was drifting up from the radiator. I turned it off and tilted the heavy window open.

\* \* \*

My e-mail included a plaintive note from Dwight Litton reminding me that I was missing the première of his Broadway play. I didn't bother to reply.

How you doin?
   That line work on all the girls?
   So they say. I wouldn't know.
   No, of course not, Stephen.
   So how is Shangri-La?
   Cool.
   Think you might want to stay?
   Too early to tell yet. Saw the Queen today;
a character. I'll tell you about it later; you
won't believe. I've been moved within the palace
from a rather spartan but characterful room
to something that looks like it's been filched
wholesale from the nearest Ramada. How's things
with you?
   Fine. Working on a big restructuring exercise
for two of the biochemical multis. Also taking
part in (mostly e-mail) discussions about MAI
fall-out. Domestically, looking after bambinos
while Emma visits old girlfriend in Boston . . .
Hello? Kate? You still there?
   Sorry. Sorry for the hiatus. Some sort of glitch
at this end. Had to reconnect.

I awoke, breathless again.
   Where was I? Where had I been?

I couldn't even remember what the original problem had been,

234

what slight or remark, what insult or minor injury had occasioned the incident. All I remembered was that I had gone to Mrs Telman for comfort, and received a strange sort of it.

She held me. I sobbed into her bosom. It was probably a very expensive blouse I was soaking with my tears, but at least I was too young to be allowed to wear mascara; the marks of my fury and despair would soon dry and leave no mark.

We were in the hotel in Vevey where Mrs Telman stayed whenever she came to visit me at the International School. Lac Léman was a dark presence in the night, its white-flecked surface visible by moonlight between the wintry showers that fell upon the waters from the mountains. I was fourteen or fifteen. Young enough still to need to be held sometimes, old enough to be troubled by, even ashamed of such a need. She smelled of the exotic perfumes I remembered from her car, six years earlier.

'But it's not fair!'

'Life is not, Kathryn.'

'You're always saying that.'

'When it stops being true, I'll stop saying it.'

'But it should be fair!'

'Of course it should.'

'Well, then, why *can't* it be?'

'Why can't we all live in palaces and never have to work? Why can't we all be happy and never have to cry?'

'I don't know,' I said defiantly (I'd begun to get used to this sort of rhetorical defence). 'Why can't we?'

Mrs Telman smiled and offered me her handkerchief. 'There are two schools of thought.'

I rolled my eyes dramatically. She ignored me and went on.

'Some people will tell you that we can never have true fairness, or justice, or happiness, or freedom from having to work. We are sinners and we deserve no better anyway. However, if we do as we're told, we may achieve perfect happiness for ever after our own death. That is one point of view. Another is that we may begin to attain all those goals in this world if we apply ourselves, even if the final fulfilment of those dreams will certainly take place after our own death.

'I prefer the second outlook, though I accept I could be wrong. But, Kathryn, in the meantime, you must understand that the world is not fair, that it does not owe you a living or even an apology, that you have no right to expect happiness, and that all too often the world can seem like a mad, bad place to be.

'When people behave rationally, kindly, generously and lovingly towards you or those you care about, be grateful; appreciate it and make the most of it at the time, because it is not necessarily the normal way of things at all. Reason, kindness, generosity and love can seem like very rare resources indeed, so make the most of them while they are around.'

'I just don't know why people have to be horrible to other people.'

'Kathryn, unless you are a saint, you must know.'

'But I don't!'

'You mean you've never been horrible to anyone? Never teased other girls, never been unkind, never been secretly delighted when something bad happened to somebody you don't like? Or are you going to tell me there's nobody you don't like?'

'But they were horrible to me first!'

'And they probably thought they had their reasons. You're very clever. Some people resent clever people; they think they're showing off.'

'What's wrong with being clever?' I asked indignantly.

'A lot, if you're not a very clever person yourself and you

236

feel that a clever person is showing off or trying to make you look stupid. It's like a strong person showing off how strong they are.'

'But I don't care if people are strong! They can show off how strong they are as much as they like; I won't care.'

'Ah, yes, but then you're clever.'

'But that's not— !' I did not say the word 'fair'. I balled the handkerchief she had given me in my hand and thudded my head against her chest again. 'That's not right,' I said lamely.

'It's right to them.' She held me and patted me on the back. 'And that's all that matters. To themselves, people are usually right.'

I felt for the bedside table. I was in Thulahn, in Thuhn, in the royal palace. I found the little monkey and rubbed it between my fingers.

In my dream the old Queen had been a cross between one of the demon-warriors that guarded her bedchamber, and the netsuke monkey that guarded my bedside. There was some sort of fading thing about monkey guards my subconscious had probably filched from *The Wizard of Oz*, but it was all already pretty vague and strange and just not of this world. In my dream I had been trapped inside a dark, cold palace carved within a mountain. It was full of smoke and I had been stumbling around trying to find the Queen but then I'd been chased through the fume-filled halls by . . . something. Or a lot of somethings. I could hear them whispering but I couldn't make out what they were saying, because somebody had pulled out half their teeth. They kept the removed teeth in little pouches on their belts, where the teeth clicked and rattled in a jittery accompaniment to their lisping voices.

Whatever they were, I knew that if they touched me there was something in their touch, in their sweat, that would burn and burrow down to my bones and poison me and make me one of them; dark wraiths of pain consigned to wander the hollowed-out palace for ever.

They could run faster than me, but there was some sort of rule – or some sort of effect or gift that I had – that meant they couldn't bear the gaze of my eyes, and so I had to run backwards, keeping them always one corner or room or corridor or door behind, and running backwards had been slow and difficult and scary, because I couldn't be sure that there weren't any of them behind me too, lying in wait for me to run backwards into them, and so I had to keep glancing over my shoulder to make certain, and that gave the ones I was running away from in the first place a chance to catch up. All the time I kept shouting, 'It's not fair! It's not fair! It's not fair!' while my feet clattered in the silence of the shadowy halls.

The dream ended unresolved, before they could catch me or I could finally make my escape to the world outside. I awoke remembering my meeting with the Queen and the words of Mrs Telman, and needing to touch the little monkey, which was my guardian, just to know that it was what it was; something inanimate and fixed and incapable of malice or love, but, if anything, something on my side as well as by it, something made reassuring just by its familiarity, and talismanic by the illusory fidelity gained through the long continuity of its presence.

# CHAPTER
# NINE

I'd shopped in the afternoon, picking up a trail of small
pillow-children who'd seemed determined to follow me
everywhere as soon as I'd stepped outside the palace gate.
The last time I'd been here, shopping in Thulahn meant forgetting about credit cards and using cash. Luckily – I thought
– I'd remembered this and brought vast amounts of US dollars
from Karachi. Only to discover that some of the more up-to-date
retailers in the capital did now take plastic. The main foreigners'
outfitters in Thulahn was the Wildness Emporium, a huge stone

barn of a place, which smelled of kerosene and was full of very expensive Western hiking and climbing gear. It was run by two turbaned Sikhs who'd looked like they were fed up explaining that, no, it wasn't meant to read the Wilderness Emporium.

I'd picked up a very thick and much-pocketed mountaineering jacket in yellow and black, a matching pair of insulated dungarees and another set of padded thermal trousers in vivid red. I'd also bought a pair of no-nonsense hiking boots that looked like old Timberlands but had less fiddly laces that went through hooks instead of eyes at the top, a complicated multi-coloured hat with ear flaps, velcro chin flaps and an adjustable peak, and a pair of stiff black ski-gloves with draw-strung gauntlet extensions that came up to my elbows. A fleece in aquamarine, a couple of pairs of thick socks and two sets of vests and long johns completed my new wardrobe. The two Sikhs – brothers as it turned out, once we'd got talking – had happily relieved me of a bothersomely bulky wad of bills and urged me to come again anytime.

I'd staggered into the street, wearing some of this gear and carrying the rest, and been mobbed by children once more. They'd insisted on helping me carry my stuff. Heading back up to the palace I'd taken a different route and discovered a shop that sold native Thulahnese gear, so we stopped off there and left with a gorgeous black fur hat I felt only a little guilty about buying, a matching hand muff, a pair of black hide boots with fur on the inside and fifty-millimetre-thick soles made from layers of auto tyres (which makes them sound horrible but actually they were beautifully stitched and finished), a little satin jacket with mandala designs, and a long red quilted jacket with matching trousers.

And all for not very much money at all, really. In fact, for so little that I'd tried to leave a tip, but the old Thulahnese couple who owned the place had just looked mystified. I'd felt so bad

I'd taken another turn round the stock and come back to the counter with the most expensive-looking thing I could find (and, trust me, I'm *good* at spotting this sort of thing): a long, slim, silk and satin jacket, jet black with gold and red dragons sewn into it, delicately quilted and sparkling with gold thread.

Seeing what I'd selected, the old couple had made a show of having synchronised heart-attacks, puffing out their cheeks and shaking their heads and bustling amongst the racks to bring me much cheaper jackets that were almost as nice, but I'd clutched the one I'd chosen to my breast and refused to let it go regardless of all cajolings and remonstrations until, eventually, with much puffing and shaking and hand-waving, I'd been allowed to buy this beautiful, beautiful thing for, well, still not very much money.

The only thing I forgot to buy was a big bag or rucksack to carry it all back in. Usually I remember to do this when I've made a lot of purchases abroad.

But for the children I'd have needed a wheelbarrow to take all my new clothes back to the palace. I didn't know whether to offer them money or not, and in the end they'd just left me at the gates with lots of bowing and smiles and nervous giggles.

I confess that I had briefly worried that one of my bags might not make it all the way back with me, or that something would disappear from one of them, and so felt quite utterly mortified when, in my room, after checking the bags were all there, I opened them up and discovered that not only did they contain everything I'd bought, several of them held more: little home-made sweets and savouries wrapped in carefully folded greaseproof paper and tied with ribbon, and tiny artificial flowers made from wire and cut silk.

*       *       *

The weather early the next morning was appalling: a furious snowstorm whirled outside my triple glazing. I could hear it through the glass, through the stone walls. I had mixed feelings about this sort of weather. It would make getting around difficult but on the other hand it might hold off the Prince for another day or two. At least it hadn't stopped the palace generator from working. Electric power: hot water and a working hair-dryer. I treated myself to my second shower in twelve hours, lost myself within the comforting hum of the hair-dryer, then hesitated when it came to dressing. Western or ethnic?

I chose Western, so pulled on the dungarees, seriously pocketed jacket and fake Timbies, and plonked the complicated hat upon my head. As an afterthought, just before I left the room, I stuck one of the little wire and silk flowers in the velcro fastening of one of the jacket's pockets.

By the time I was squeaking through the snow in the main courtyard the weather had abated somewhat; the wind had dropped and only a few flakes were falling, though the mass of cloud above the valley looked low and dark and heavy with more snow.

Children met me at the gates again, appearing from every direction. To my shame, I realised I had no idea if they were the same ones as yesterday or not. It was time to stop treating them as a mass, I guessed. I hunkered down and smiled and started trying to find out names.

'Me, Kathryn,' I said, pointing at myself. 'Kath-rin.'

They giggled and looked down and snorted and shuffled their feet. Eventually I worked out what I hoped were a few of their names and got them to understand I wanted to go to the Heavenly Luck Tea House. I tied a few pointy hats on properly and wiped a couple of snotty noses with a paper handkerchief.

I stood up, took two of the offered chubby little hands and we tramped downhill through the snow.

'Ms Telman. Hi. Josh Levitsen.'

'How do you do.' We shook hands. Mr Levitsen was not what I'd been expecting at all. He was young – though his tan skin was deeply lined – he was full-bearded, blond, and wore a slightly grubby fawn parka with a matted fur hood lining, and a pair of leather-sided circular mountaineering glasses with surfaces like oil on water.

'Fine. Just fine. You having breakfast? I've got tea here for both of us.'

The Heavenly Luck Tea House was within a skyed penalty shot of the football field/air strip, with a view over that and the snow-filled valley. It was warm and steamy and full of people, mostly Thulahnese. Polished wood was everywhere and the floorboards creaked like a swamp full of demented frogs.

'What do you recommend?'

'Rikur saraut, champe and thuuk.'

'What's that?'

'Corn pancakes – they keep syrup behind the counter just for me and my guests – porridge and thick noodle soup; kampa – spicy – if you like.'

'Perhaps a very little of each. I'm not terribly hungry.'

He nodded, waved one arm and shouted the order. He poured us both some strong tea into cups with no handles but little ceramic tops. We exchanged a few pleasantries and agreed to use first names before he sat forward and lowered his voice a little. 'Just to let you know, Kate, I used to be with the Company.'

'The CIA?' I asked quietly.

He grinned. 'Yeah, but now I'm with the Business.' He lowered his glasses to wink.

'I see.' This had, of course, been mentioned in the CD-Rom Tommy Cholongai had given me: Mr Levitsen wasn't actually an employee of ours, but we did pay him quite a lot of money and he had a vague idea that we were interested in the place for more than the odd diplomatic passport.

'You let me know if I can be of any help.' He spread his arms wide. 'I am at your disposal, Kate. I have a lot of contacts. Smoke?' He pulled a little painted tin from one pocket of the grubby parka and took out a slim hand-rolled cigarette.

'No, thank you.'

'Mind if I do?'

I glanced round at the counter. 'I take it you're not expecting the quickest of service.'

'Ten, fifteen minutes on a good day.' He lit the roll-up with a Zippo. Some smoke rolled across the table. Not a cigarette, then, a joint. He must have seen me sniff. 'You sure?' he asked, through a smoke-wreathed grin.

'A little early in the day for me,' I told him.

He nodded. 'Heard you saw the old lady yesterday.'

'The Queen Mother? Yes.'

'Is that a weird fucking set-up, or what?'

'Weird just about covers it.'

'She say anything about the Prince?'

'She wanted my opinion on his marriageability.'

'Yeah, she's been talking about that a lot recently.'

'Do you visit her often?'

'Na. Just been the once, when I first got posted here, three years ago. But, like I say, I got contacts everywhere.' Above the oil-on-water glasses, his sun-bleached eyebrows arched. 'So, what's happening with the Business here? I keep getting hints there's some sort of major shit coming down, or maybe not shit, maybe more like major manna coming down, you know?' He pulled the mountaineering glasses down again and gave me what could almost have been a leer. 'You part of that? Bet you can't tell me even if you are, right? But you're here, and you're, what, a Level Three, yeah? Best looking L-Three I've ever seen, by the way – uh, hope you don't mind me saying so.'

'No, I'm flattered.'

'So, what's happening?' He leaned closer again. 'What was all that stuff out on Juppala last year? And down on the valley floor here and upstream. All that laser range-finding and drilling and surveying shit. What's all that about?'

'Infrastructure improvements,' I said.

'On Mount *Juppala*? You kidding me?'

I sipped my tea. 'Yes.'

He laughed. 'You aren't going to tell me a damn thing, are you, Kate?'

'No.'

'So why did they send you?'

'Why do you think anybody sent me? I'm on sabbatical. I can go where I like.'

'Weird time of year for a holiday.'

'A sabbatical isn't a holiday.'

'So why did you come?'

'To see what the place is like at this time of year.'

'But why?'

'Why not?'

He sat back, shaking his head. He attached a roach clip to the remains of the joint and sucked hard, brows knotted with either concentration or the sharpness of the hot smoke. 'Whatever,' he said, on an in-drawn breath on top of what he'd already smoked. He pinched the roach out and left it folded in the teacup's saucer. 'So, where do you want to go?'

'When?'

'Whenever. I got a Jeep. Get places Langtuhn's limo won't. Anywhere you want to go, let me know.'

'That's very kind. I may take you up on that. Are you free this afternoon?'

'Sure. Where to?'

'You're the local knowledge. Suggest somewhere.'

'Well, there's – ah-hah! Hey, that was quick. Here's breakfast.'

'Uncle Freddy?'

'Kate, dear girl. You made it to Thulahn then, yes?'

'Yes. Managed to avoid the prayer flags. Been having a look round. Done the palace and bits of the city, seen the old Queen and had a guided tour of the lower valley and the nearest town just this afternoon. The weather's atrocious now. Nearly didn't make it back '

'Prince returned yet, is he?'

'No. He's not due back from Paris for another few days.'

'Oh, he wasn't going to Paris, dear girl. He was in Switzerland,' Uncle Freddy said. 'At CDO.' CDO is what we usually shorten Château d'Oex to.

'Oh. Well, no, he's still not due back until next week.'

'Jolly good. Did you give the Queen Mum my regards?'

'No. I didn't know you knew her.'

'Audrey? Oh, golly, yes. From way back. Meant to say. Thought I had. Senility, probably. Still. She didn't mention me, then?'

'I'm afraid not.'

'Not to worry. Heard she'd gone a bit batty actually, if not totally ga-ga. How did she seem to you?'

'Eccentric in that sort of feral way that old English ladies go sometimes.'

'Probably the altitude.'

'Probably.'

'Who was your guide if the Prince isn't back?'

'The honorary US consul. Youngish chap, second-generation hippie. Secured me a breakfast that was surprisingly edible and then took me down to Joitem in his Jeep. It's a bit like Thuhn except lower down and flatter and surrounded by rhododendron bushes. Visited an abandoned monastery, saw a few farms and prayer windmills, nearly skidded off the road into ravines a few times, that sort of thing.'

'Sounds terribly exciting.'

'And you? I've tried you a few times and you never seem to be in.'

'Oh, just fafing about as usual. Driving.'

'You should get a mobile.'

'What? One of those things you hang above cots?'

'No, Freddy, a phone.'

'Pah! And disturb a good drive by having a phone go off in my ear? I should cocoa.'

The skies were clear the next day, though confusingly (for me and probably no one else in Thuhn) snow swirled everywhere for a few hours beneath that cloudlessness; a stiff, freezing wind blasted down from the mountains and across the city and the palace and seemed to scour most of the snow away, brushing it off down the valley in tall, white, dragging shrouds and gathering it into huge drifts beneath the river's steeper banks.

Josh Levitsen had warned me about wind chill the day before and, anyway, this wasn't the first time I'd been in a cold place. I made sure I had a scarf over my mouth and nose when I went out, dressed in Western gear again, but even so the ferocity of the chill was stunning.

The children were nowhere to be seen. The city seemed deserted. My eyes watered in the icy blast and the tears froze almost instantly on my skin; I had to keep turning and bending and brushing drops of salty ice away and rubbing feeling back into my cheeks. I pulled the scarf up higher and eventually found my way down to the Wildness Emporium, where the Sikh brothers fussed over me and poured me warm paurke – tea with roasted barley flour and sugar in it; it tasted much better than it should have. There also I bought a polarised ski mask for my eyes and a blue neoprene thing that fitted over the rest of my lower face and made me look a little like Hannibal Lecter but which was much more effective than the scarf.

Suitably kitted up, with not a square centimetre of bare skin left exposed to the elements, I left the brothers happily counting even more of my dollars and set off into the wind again.

People were keeping indoors. It was the best time to see the city just as a set of buildings and the spaces in between them. I walked all over it until hunger and chance brought me within sniffing distance of the Heavenly Luck Tea House around lunch time, and then sat, extremities tingling, tucking into dhal bhut (sticky rice with lentil soup poured over it) and jakpak kampa (spicy stew with mystery meat). A watery yoghurt called dhai – pretty similar to a plain lassi – washed it all down.

The other diners – all seriously quilted, mostly male, some

still wearing pointy hats – laughed and grinned and talked at me in machine-gun Thulahnese and I just grinned like an idiot and laughed when they laughed and made dumb faces and fanned my mouth in what was apparently a quite hilarious manner when I bit on a chilli in the stew and nodded and shrugged and mugged and whistled and just generally behaved like a complete cretin for about forty minutes, and then finally left the place with a huge smile on my face under the blue neoprene Hannibal Lecter mask, feeling full, content and warm as well as perfectly, blissfully happy and with the sense that I'd just spent one of the most pleasantly communicative and life-affirming lunches I'd ever experienced.

'Kathryn?'

'Mr Hazleton.'

'You are well, I hope?'

'I'm fine.'

'And your stay in Thulahn, is that going well?'

'Very well.'

'I've never been. Would you recommend a visit?'

'That depends on your tastes, Mr Hazleton. It's fine if you like lots of mountains and snow.'

'You don't sound very enamoured of the place, Kathryn.'

'I like lots of mountains and snow.'

'I see. I was wondering. I was trying to decide whether you'd decided. Trying to make up my mind whether you had made up your mind, or not.'

'Uh-huh.'

'You're being very reticent, Kathryn.'

'Am I?'

'Is there somebody else there in the room with you?'

'No.'

'You're upset with me, aren't you?'

'Upset, Mr Hazleton?'

'Kathryn, I do hope you believe me when I say I had nothing to do with the contents of that disc. It came into my possession and I confess I thought to turn it to my advantage, but what else was I supposed to do? ... Kathryn, if I'm wasting my time with this call, tell me and I'll hang up. Perhaps we can talk again later.'

'What was the purpose of your call, Mr Hazleton?'

'I wanted to know if you'd come to a decision regarding the contents of the disc I had delivered to you. Have you decided to do nothing, or are you still mulling it over?'

'Oh, I'm mulling. Mulling away furiously here.'

'Are you, Kathryn?'

'Would I lie to you, Mr Hazleton?'

'I imagine you would if you thought it was the right thing to do, Kathryn.'

'Well, I'm still thinking.'

'The problem hasn't gone away, I'm afraid. Right now, even as we speak, Mrs Buzetski is—'

'Boston. She's in Boston, and she's not really visiting an old school chum at all.'

'Ah. You know. You must have spoken to Stephen. How is he? Do you think he suspects anything yet?'

'I'm sure I couldn't say, Mr Hazleton.'

'I'd better go, Kathryn. Give my regards to the Prince when he gets there, will you?'

In the late afternoon Langtuhn Hemblu appeared and announced he was to take me to the Foreign Ministry for the formalities to be completed. I was to bring my passport. I asked him to wait and changed into my ethnic clothes, then we took the Roller a short distance down into the crowded city to a squat building with plain-painted walls.

I was shown into a large room where a bulbously tiled cylindrical stove in one corner radiated heat and four young, yellow-robed clerks perched on high stools behind tall desks. All four stared at me and then put their heads down and scribbled furiously when a tall, bald, orange-robed man appeared from a door to one side of the big stove, announced he was called Shlahm Thivelu, Senior Immigration officer, and invited me into his office.

We sat on either side of an impressive desk topped by a curved gallery holding lots of compartments containing rolled-up documents. Mr Thivelu put on a dainty pair of glasses and inspected both my passports as though he'd only ever seen one or two such odd documents before.

The last time I'd been here I'd gone through immigration control and customs in the arrivals hall at the airfield. This had consisted of ducking through the cargo door of the crashed Dakota, giving my name to an adolescent sitting behind a tiny rickety desk and shaking his hand. Obviously things had become a lot more formal since then.

Mr Thivelu nodded, searched about the desk for a while, muttered something about a damned stamp, then shrugged and wrote something into my UK passport before handing both back and wishing me a pleasant stay.

As I stepped out of the ministry I looked at what he had written. He'd printed the date and *Welcome To Thulahn*.

Langtuhn held the Roller's door open for me. He was smiling widely. 'You look happy,' I said, as we set off back up the hill.

251

'Oh, yes, Ms Telman!' Langtuhn said, his face positively radiating happiness from the rear-view mirror. 'His Holiness the Prince will now be returning tomorrow!'

'Yes, unfortunately I'm not sure – *what*?' I jerked forward in my seat. '*Tomorrow*?' I'd thought I'd have at least three more days here before having to worry about Suvinder showing up.

'Yes! Isn't that wonderful news? Now you will get to see him after all! He too will be happy to see you, I'm sure.'

'Yes. Yes, I expect he will.' I watched the Wildness Emporium slide past. One of the Sikh brothers saw me; he smiled and waved enthusiastically. I waved back feebly.

I couldn't even get the plane out; it had been and gone again since I'd arrived and tomorrow's inbound flight bringing the Prince was the next one. The alternative to flying was finding some motorised transport and taking the long road north and west and eventually south and back to India. Days of hair-raising travel and nights in dubious rest-houses, from what I'd heard. Or I could hike straight out, if the passes were open, which was unlikely at this time of year. I'd done some trekking in Nepal in my early twenties so I wasn't totally inexperienced, but I wasn't hill fit either, or that young any more. Anyway, I supposed it would look terribly rude.

'What brings the Prince back so early?' I asked.

'We do not know,' Langtuhn admitted, hauling the ancient car straight as we passed a butcher's and skidded on a patch of what looked like chicken entrails. He laughed. 'Perhaps he has run out of money in the Paris casino.'

'Ha ha,' I said. I sat back. Suvinder. Oh, well.

Maybe having the Prince here wouldn't be so terrible. He wasn't that difficult a guy to deal with and he would, I assumed, make it even easier for me to travel round the country and gain access to, well, whatever I needed to gain access to. So, not such a bad thing after all.

Look on the bright side, I told myself.

The Prince arrived back the following morning. What seemed like most of Thuhn turned out to watch the plane land. It was another clear but bitingly cold day, though the wind was barely more than a breeze. Langtuhn Hemblu, wearing a slightly threadbare chauffeur's outfit, which was a size or two too big for him and which included tall boots, jodhpurs and a peaked grey cap, drove me down to the airfield in the Rolls Royce but explained apologetically that I would have to make my own way back to the palace, as the car would be required by the Prince and his entourage. I told him this was fine by me and joined the crowd on the banking above the football pitch/airfield like everybody else. They'd removed the far set of goalposts, I noticed.

Some of my little pillow friends appeared – Dulsung, Graumo and Pokuhm, if I'd got their names right – and we stood together, though they couldn't see very well over all the adults in front. Dulsung was the smallest, so I lifted her on to my shoulders. She giggled and slapped a pair of sticky hands on to my forehead, below my black fur hat. The two boys looked up enviously at her, put their pointy-hatted heads together and conferred for a moment, then each tugged at the nearest pair of quilted trousers, pointed meaningfully up at Dulsung, and after some teasing were duly hoisted on to neighbouring sets of shoulders.

Everybody else seemed to see the plane before me. People started pointing and a few cheers rang out. Then I saw the tiny scrap of metal against the grey-black rocks of the mountains high above and away to one side, its dark shadow flickering over ridges and gullies as it tipped and fell towards us. It looked about the size of a small bird of prey. The sound of its engines was still lost in the spaces between the mountains.

I looked up towards Dulsung, pointed at the aircraft and said, 'Aeroplane.'

''Roplane.'

The plane raced down, wheeling and stooping through the winds, no longer making straight for us but heading diagonally across the sky above the ice-choked gorge. It curved out to one side of the city, turned sharply over the gravel beds in the valley downstream and came flying back straight towards us. The wind, I realised, must be in the opposite direction from when I'd landed. The square-sectioned, hunched-looking craft seemed almost static in the air, the drone of its engines audible now.

The plane jiggled, riding waves of wind and shaking its wings as though it was shrugging. It seemed to be about to overshoot and go round again, then it dipped suddenly and flared, wheels smacking the far end of the field in a cloud of dust and gravel with a thud, just about where the goalposts would have been. Everybody seemed to take this as a cue to start clapping; even Dulsung removed her hands from my forehead to slap them together a few times. Over this racket, the plane's engine note had changed and swelled and the machine seemed to bow, compressing the nose wheel's landing gear as it rushed towards us with a swirling grey-brown cloud rising behind it.

I could see the two pilots in their seats. I got ready to run. The engines screamed, the whole plane shuddered and slowed, and then it turned, tipping slightly and skidding to a halt, still not quite into the nearer penalty box and a good fifty metres away from where I stood.

I joined enthusiastically in the applause while the cockpit

window slid open and a Thulahnese flag on a stick was jammed into its hole. A small line of welcoming officials formed up on the gravel and Langtuhn Hemblu manoeuvred the Roller on to the touchline near a couple of four-wheel-drives and then got out and stood, cap under arm, by the rear door.

The Prince was first out of the plane, waving from the doorway, dressed in what looked like a niftily tailored dark blue version of the traditional quilted trousers and jacket. People waved back. Some were drifting away already; presumably those who came only to watch the plane, or hard-line republicans disappointed to have witnessed another safe royal landing. More people spilled out of the aircraft behind the Prince.

I glanced up at Dulsung. Her muddy boots were leaving marks on my quilted red jacket. I pointed. 'The Prince,' I said.

'Thirp Rinse.'

Suvinder looked around, seemingly distracted, as he progressed down the line of bowing officials. He motioned Langtuhn Hemblu over while everybody else was getting themselves and their luggage organised. Langtuhn and the Prince talked briefly then Langtuhn pointed at our bit of the crowd and they both shielded their eyes and stared in our direction. They weren't looking for me, were they?

Then Langtuhn looked right at me, waved and called out. He touched the Prince's sleeve and gestured in my direction. In front of me, heads were starting to turn. The Prince caught my gaze, smiled broadly and waved, shouting something.

'Shit,' I breathed.

'Shit,' said a little voice quite clearly above me.

'It is so good to see you again!' the Prince enthused, clapping his hands and smiling like a schoolboy. He wasn't wearing any

255

rings, I noticed. There were seven of us squeezed into the back of the Roller, bouncing uphill to the palace. I was thigh-to-thigh with Suvinder, who was relatively comfortable in the middle of the rear seat with B. K. Bousande, his private secretary, on the other side. Hisa Gidhaur, the exchequer and foreign secretary whom I'd last seen at Blysecrag, sat directly across from me. Hokla Niniphe, the home secretary, was sitting sweating next to the cabin's stove, while Jungeatai Rhumde, the prime minister, and Srikkuhm Pih, commander of the militia, had been the last two to get in and so had to squat each with their backs to a door. I'd have assumed they'd be better off in one of the two four-wheel-drives following us up the hill, but apparently there was some big protocol thing about travelling with the Prince.

I'd been introduced to the officials and dignitaries I hadn't met before and they'd all been very polite and cordial before we clambered into the back of the car, but I sincerely hoped I wasn't inadvertently treading on as many metaphorical toes as I had physical ones.

At least they all seemed happy enough, sitting or squatting hunched in their thick clothes with big smiles on their round, hairless faces, nodding at me and making appreciative noises. I put it down to the understandable euphoria of at last having their chunky Thulahnese asses only half a metre above the ground in a vehicle travelling at little more than a fast walk which, if it broke down, would just sit at the roadside decorously wisping steam rather than plummeting abruptly towards the nearest patch of icy rock.

'You have seen my mother,' Suvinder went on. 'She is well?'
'Yes, I think so.'
'How did you get on?'
I thought carefully. 'We had a full and frank discussion.'

'Oh, very good!' Suvinder looked delighted. I glanced round the others. The cream of the Thulahnese hierarchy looked appreciatively on, nodding their approval.

The Prince's suite was in the same recently modernised section of the palace as my room, though a floor higher. The whole royal complex was suddenly full of people dashing about, slamming doors, waving bits of paper, carrying boxes and clattering open shutters. I stood with B. K. Bousande in the lounge of the Prince's private suite, watching servants I'd never seen before rushing round the room distributing bits of luggage and straightening pictures.

The lounge was relatively modest, even restrained. Plain walls held a few gauzy watercolours; a polished wood floor was scattered with intricately patterned carpets, a couple of big cream-coloured settees and a few pieces of what looked very old and elaborately carved wooden furniture including a low central table.

A servant carrying a bunch of fresh flowers appeared through the door and set them in a vase on a sideboard. I straightened the little wire and silk flower I'd worn the day before and had transferred to my red quilted jacket, then noticed again the muddy grey marks Dulsung's boots had left by my lapels. I brushed them off as best I could and dusted my hands.

'You must tell me all you have done since you arrived!' the Prince called out from somewhere beyond the bedroom door. Judging from the echo, from the bathroom.

'Oh, just sightseeing.'

'You will not be rushing away, I hope? I would like to show you more of Thulahn.'

257

'I can stay a few more days, I guess. But I wouldn't want to interfere with your duties, sir.'

There was a pause, then the Prince stuck his head round the door from the bedroom, frowning. 'You do not call me "sir", Kathryn. To you I am Suvinder.' He shook his head and disappeared again. 'BK, deliver my invitation, would you?'

B. K. Bousande bowed to me and said, 'We are holding a reception to celebrate His Highness's return this evening. Would you be his guest?'

'Certainly. I'd be honoured.'

'Oh, good!' the Prince called out.

*The high valleys were torn ribbons of scrappy green rammed between the force of mountains pitched tumultuously against the sky. In them was a whole raised world of tenaciously adapted bushes, trees, birds and animals somehow able to grow and multiply in this winded sweep of gust-eroded ice, naked rock and barren gravel.*

The reception was held in the palace's main hall, a relatively modest space not much larger than the throne room in the old palace, but much less bizarre in its decoration, with a stalactitically carved wooden ceiling and walls covered by what looked like crosses between Afghan rugs and tapestries.

After consulting with Langtuhn Hemblu on the propriety of the little blue-black Versace – regretfully deemed too short – I'd chosen a long green silk sleeveless number with a high Chinese collar. This is the sort of dress that makes me look long and hard at myself; however, I passed the inspection of my own in-built body-fascist program and, happily, people did later compliment me on the dress in that way that means they think you look good in it, and not in the way that means they're astonished how tolerable a job it's doing of making mutton look like lamb.

There were perhaps two hundred people present at the reception. The majority were Thulahnese but there were a couple of dozen Indians and Pakistanis and a smattering of Chinese, Malays, other Oriental people whose nationalities I wasn't so sure of and some Japanese. A lot of Westerners seemed to have crawled out of the woodwork, too; I hadn't known there were so many in Thulahn, let alone Thuhn.

I was introduced to the Indian High Commissioner, the Pakistani and Chinese ambassadors, and various consuls, honorary and otherwise, including Josh Levitsen, who looked awkward in a three-piece suit that had probably last been fashionable about the time of his senior prom. Perhaps to take his mind off this he was already quite drunk when we shook hands.

The Prince guided me round his ministers, advisers and family members. This last category included his rather subdued brother and sister-in-law whose son was the heir to the throne if Suvinder didn't have any children and who was at a Business-run school in Switzerland. I also met representatives of the other noble families, of which there were about a dozen all told, a swathe of subtly varied saffron-clad lamas, a couple of Hindu priests clad in borderline-garish, and I was introduced to the remainder of the Thulahnese Civil Service that I hadn't met in either the Twin Otter four years earlier or the Foreign Ministry the day before.

I made a point of bowing and smiling a lot. A gift I've always been very grateful for is never forgetting a name, so I was able to greet people like Senior Immigration Officer Shlahm Thivelu, Home Secretary Hokla Niniphe and Prime Minister Jungeatai Rhumde without having to be prompted. They all seemed pleased. I spotted a female face I knew I'd seen before but couldn't place until I realised it was one of the old Queen's ladies-in-waiting.

The remaining foreigners included a clutch of VSO Brits and Peace Corps Americans – all appropriately young, enthusiastic, naïve and full of energy – a few teachers, mostly English and French, a couple of Ozzie doctors and one Indian surgeon, some Canadian rough-diamond type engineers and contractors engaged on relatively small-scale infrastructure work, a handful of sweaty mixed-European businessmen hoping to land contracts with the various Thulahnese ministries, and a physically attractive but corrosively smug Milanese geology professor with his own little entourage of students, all female.

*Only when you started to look, only once you'd had your fill of gazing at the dazzling white peaks above and refocused your sight to what was really around you did you see the variety of forms displayed.*

'They are very bad workers.'

'Are they?'

'Impossible. Quite useless. They cannot keep time. I think sometimes they cannot tell time.' The speaker was a tall, bulky Austrian businessman with a tight grip on his cocktail glass.

'Oh dear,' I said.

'Yes. We have a factory – just a very small concern you understand, something quite tiny, really – in Sangamanu making eyeglasses and ethnic jewellery. We received funding from the World Bank and various NGOs and the project was seen as a way of providing much-needed employment. It could be acceptably profitable, but the employees are quite hopeless. They forget to turn up, many days. They wander off before the clocking-off time comes. They seem unable to understand that they must be there five or six days out of seven; they go ploughing fields or gathering wood. It is quite unacceptable, but what is one to do? This factory means nothing to my company. I say nothing, of course it means something, but really it is so small in scale that it means next to nothing. But, you see, in Sangamanu it is the biggest employer. These people should be grateful that it is there and do their best to make it a success, as we have done, but they do nothing. They are just pathetic. They are a very childish sort of people, I think. They are immature, yes, like children are.'

'Really,' I said, shaking my head and looking as though I found this fascinating. I created an excuse to get away from the guy shortly afterwards, leaving him agreeing sternly with a German surveyor that, yes, the people here were just impossible. I went in search of anybody not conforming to their own national or cultural stereotypes.

I spotted Srikkuhm Pih, the militia commander, standing stiffly in his rather grand ceremonial uniform, which looked as if it might have been fashionable in the British Army about a hundred years earlier.

'Mr Pih,' I said, bowing.

'Ah, Miss Telman.' Srikkuhm Pih was old, slightly stooped, shorter than me and had the greyest hair of any Thulahnese I'd seen so far.

'I very much like your outfit. You look terribly grand. That sword's quite wonderful.'

Mr Pih responded very well to flattery. Apparently as well as being commander of the militia he was Minister of War, Secretary of Defence and Chief of Staff of the Armed Forces. After he'd shown me the dazzlingly bright and beautifully inscribed sword – a present to one of his predecessors from an Indian maharaja at the turn of the century – we were soon talking about the ticklish nature of his job and the generally unwarlike nature of the average Thulahnese male.

'We very bad soldiers,' he said, with a happy shrug.

'Well, if you don't need to fight . . .'

'Very bad soldiers. Monks best.'

'Monks?'

He nodded. 'Monks have competition. Of this.' He mimed drawing a bow.

'Archery competitions?' I asked.

'That right. Four time year. Each . . .'

'Season?'

'That right. Four time year they competition, all sampal, all monk-house against all other. Arch. But always get drunk first.'

'They get drunk first?'

'Drink khotse.' This was the local brew, a fermented milk beer that I'd tried exactly once when I'd come to Thulahn the first time. I think it's safe to say that even its greatest fan would agree it was an acquired taste. 'Get drunk,' Srikkuhm Pih continued, 'then they fire arrow. Some very good. Hit middle of the target, bang spot on. But. Start good, then drunk, end not good. Laugh too much. Fall over.' He shook his head. 'Sorry state of affairs.'

'You can't use the monks as soldiers, then?'

He mugged horror and dread. 'Rinpoche, Tsunke, head lama, chief priest man, they not let me. None of would. They are most . . .' He blew out his cheeks and shook his head.

'Didn't you have sort of samurai or something? I thought I read about a warrior caste. What were they called? The Treih?'

'They no good either. Worst. All gone soft. Very soft peoples now. Too much of living in houses, they say. Just not officer material, don't you know.' He shook his head again and regarded his empty glass. 'Sorry state of affairs.'

'What about the rest of the people? Where do you get your soldiers?'

'Not got soldiers,' he said, shrugging. 'Got none. Not a bean.'

'None at all?'

'We have militia; I am commander. Men have guns in house, we have more gun to give, here in palace, also in Government House in each towns. But not barracks, not standing army, not professionals or territorials.' He tapped his chest. 'This only army uniform in country.'

'Wow.'

He gestured to where Suvinder was talking to a couple of his ministers. The Prince waved. I waved back. 'I ask Prince for money for uniform for men,' the militia commander went on, 'but he say, "No, I am afraid not yet, Srikkuhm old fellow, must wait. Maybe next year." Well, I am very patient. Guns more important than uniforms. Not wrong there.'

'But if, say, the Chinese invaded, how many men could you put up? What would be the maximum?'

'Government military secret,' he said, slowly shaking his head. 'Very top secret.' He looked thoughtful. 'About twenty-three thousand.'

'Oh. Well, that is a fairly respectable army. Or militia.'

He looked dubious. 'That how many guns. Men not supposed to sell them or use them for other thing, like for plumb in house, but some have.' He looked glum.

'Sorry state of affairs,' I said.

'Sorry state of affairs,' he agreed, then brightened. 'But Prince always is saying he happy to have me most unemploymented man in Thulahn.' He looked around, then leaned closer and dropped his voice. I bent to hear. 'I get performance-relate bonus every year there no war.'

'Do you?' I laughed. 'How splendid! Well done.'

The militia commander offered to refresh my glass, which didn't need refreshing, then wandered off in the general direction of the drinks table, looking pleased both with himself and the financially agreeable absence of war.

I did some more circulating and found myself talking to one of the teachers, a young Welsh woman called Cerys Williams.

'Oh, Cerys, like the girl in Catatonia?'

'That's it. Same spelling.'

'I'm sure you get asked all the time, but what's it like, teaching here?'

Cerys thought the Thulahnese children were great. The schools had very little equipment and the parents were inclined to keep children away from lessons if there was anything that had to be done on the farm, but generally they seemed very bright and willing to learn.

'How long do they get in school? How many years?'

'Just primary, really. There is secondary education, but you have to pay for that. It isn't a lot, but it's more than most of the families can afford. Usually they educate the oldest boy up to third or fourth year, but the rest tend to leave when they're eleven or twelve.'

'Always the boy, even if there's an older girl?'

She gave a rueful grin. 'Oh, well, almost always. I'm trying – well, we're all trying, really, but I think I'm trying hardest – to change that, but you're up against an awful lot of generations of tradition, see?'

'I'll bet.'

'But they're not stupid. They're coming round to the idea that girls might benefit from higher education; we've had a few successes. It still usually means only one child per household goes to secondary, mind you.'

'I imagine there might be a few eldest boys who feel resentful because of that.'

She smiled. 'Oh, I don't know. They're happy enough to leave school when the time comes. I think most of them would much rather it was their sisters who had to stay on.'

More circulating. The Prime Minister himself filled me in on the workings of the Thulahnese governmental system. There was a form of democracy at the most local level, where people in each village and town elected a head man or mayor, who then chose town constables to uphold the law (or didn't bother: there was very little crime and certainly I hadn't seen any sort of police presence in Thuhn so far). The chief of each noble family and the head men and mayors formed a parliament of sorts, which met irregularly and could advise the monarch, but after that it was down to appointees of the monarch, and appointees of appointees. Anyone in the kingdom could appeal to the throne if he thought he'd been hard done by in the courts or elsewhere. Suvinder took this part of the job seriously, though Jungeatai Rhumde thought people were inclined to take advantage of the Prince's good nature. He'd suggested a sort of supreme court set-up instead, but Suvinder preferred the old system.

'Aw, shit, no, they're great people. You wouldn't want to confuse them with anybody who gives a fuck, mind you.' Rich was an Ozzie civil engineer. He laughed. 'Some of the fellas disagree, but I think they've got a great attitude to life, but then they think they're going to be reincarnated or something like that, you know?'

I smiled, nodded.

'Who needs crash barriers if God's looking after you and you might come back as something better next time anyway, you know? Fucking hard little workers, though. Don't know when to stop.'

And more circulating. Michel was a French doctor, moodily good-looking but one of those people who makes no effort to be attractive or even interesting beyond keeping their good looks kempt. He was a bit dour, as we say, but provided an overview of medicine in Thulahn, which was pretty basic. High infant mortality, poor ante- and post-natal care in the outlying villages, whole population prone to influenza epidemics which killed a few thousand each winter, some malnutrition, a lot of preventable and/or easily treatable blindness. Goitres and other deficiency conditions a problem in some of the valleys where they didn't get a full spectrum of minerals and vitamins in their diet. No sign of gender-biased infanticide. AIDS known but not common.

On which negative but happy note, the good doctor propositioned me in a bored sort of way that left it open whether he was so used to women falling into his arms that he'd got out of the way of putting much effort into it, or was so frightened of rejection he thought it wise not to invest the suggestion with too much significance.

I did my impression of the Roman Empire, and declined.

*Blue pine and chir pine, prickly leaved oak, Himalayan hemlocks and silver firs, juniper and scrub juniper filled the crannied spaces where any soil had gathered, the last – stunted, blasted by the wind, burned by frost but still just growing – only finally petering out at five kilometres above sea level.*

'This is a pluralist society. We respect the beliefs of our Hindu brothers and sisters. Buddhists tend not to see themselves as being in competition with others. The Hindu faith is like Judaism, providing an ancient set of rules by which one may live one's life and order one's thoughts. Ours is a younger religion, a different generation of thought, if you like, grafted upon a set of much older traditions, but having drawn lessons from them, and respectful of them. Westerners often see it as more like a philosophy. Or so they tell us.'

'Yes, I know a few Buddhists in California.'

'You do? So do I! Do you know— ?'

I smiled. We swapped a few names but, predictably, came up with no matches.

Sahair Beies was Rinpoche, or head lama of Bhaiwair monastery, the biggest in the country. I had already seen it, albeit from a distance, strung across the rock faces above the old palace a few kilometres out of Thuhn. He was slight, indeterminately old, shaved bald and wore very deeply saffron robes and little wire frame glasses behind which intelligent-looking eyes twinkled.

'You are a Christian, Ms Telman?'

'Nope.'

'Jewish, then? I have noticed that many people whose names end in "-man" are Jewish.'

I shook my head. 'Evangelical atheist.'

He nodded thoughtfully. 'A demanding path, I suspect. I asked one of your compatriots what he was, once, and he replied, "Devout Capitalist."' The Rinpoche laughed.

'We have a lot of those. Most are less open about it. Life

as acquisition. Whoever dies with the most toys wins. It's a boy thing.'

'He gave me a lecture on the dynamic nature of the West and the United States of America in particular. It was most illuminating.'

'But it didn't persuade you to move to New York City and become a venture capitalist or a stockbroker?'

'No!' He laughed.

'What about other faiths?' I asked. 'Do you, for instance, get Mormons and Jehovah's Witnesses turning up here?' I had a sudden comical image of two guys in sober suits and shiny shoes (covered in snow) shivering outside the giant doors of a remote monastery.

'Very rarely.' The Rinpoche looked thoughtful. 'Usually by the time we see them they are . . . changed,' he said. His eyes bulged. 'Oh, I find physicists much more interesting. There have been some famous American professors and Indian Nobel Prize winners I have talked to, and it struck me that we were – as one says – on the same wavelength in many ways.'

'Physics. That's our Brahmin faith.'

'You think so?'

'I think a lot of people live as though that's true, even if they don't think about it. To us, science is the religion that works. Other faiths claim miracles, but science delivers them, through technology: replacing diseased hearts, talking to people on the other side of the world, travelling to other planets, determining when the universe began. We display our faith every time we turn on a light switch or step aboard a jet.'

'You see? All very interesting, but I prefer the idea of Nirvana.'

'As you said, sir, it's a hard path, but only if you think of it.'

'One of your American professors said that to study religion was merely to know the mind of man, but if one truly wanted to know the mind of God, you must study physics.'

'That sounds familiar. I think I've read his book.'

The Rinpoche pinched his lower lip. 'I think I see what he meant now, but I could not explain to him that the thoughts of people and the phenomena we seek to explain through physics might all be revealed as . . . subsidiary to the attainment of true enlightenment, which would be like the result of one of those experiments which use high energies to show that apparently quite different forces are in fact the same. Do you see what I mean? That having achieved Nirvana, one might recognise all human behaviour and the most profound physical laws as being ultimately indistinguishable in their essence.'

I had to pause while I let this sink in. Then I stood back a pace from the Rinpoche and said, 'Wow, you guys don't just wander into this job, do you?'

The Rinpoche's eyes sparkled and he held one hand over his mouth while he giggled modestly.

*Amongst and above them snow pigeons, sunbirds, jungle crows, barbets, choughs, warblers, babblers, grandalas, accentors, Himalayan griffon vultures and Thulahnese tragopans hopped, flitted, scurried, dived, wheeled or stooped.*

I was on my way back from the toilet; I nodded and smiled at the little lady-in-waiting as she headed where I'd just been, then spotted Josh Levitsen letting himself out of a door and on to a terrace overlooking the dark town. I followed him. He stood by the stone parapet, swaying, hands cupped in front of his mouth as he fumbled with the Zippo, his face suddenly yellow in the flame as the lighter flared. He looked up as I approached.

'Hey, Ms Telman, you're going to catch your death of cold out here, you know that? Nice dress. Did I say that earlier? You're a babe, you know that? If you don't mind me saying so, that is. Here, you wanna toke? Sun's over the yard-arm and shit, right?'

'Thanks.'

We leant on the stonework. It really was quite cold, though at least there was no wind. I felt the hairs on my arms prickle, goose-bumps rising. The grass was strong. I held it in for a while, but ended up coughing on the exhale.

I handed the skinny joint back to Levitsen. 'Good shit. Local?'

'Thulahn's finest. Every pack comes with a sanity warning from the Lord High Surgeon General.'

'Do they export much? I've never heard of Thulahnese.'

'Na, me neither. For consumption on the premises only.' He studied the joint before handing it back to me. 'Maybe just as well. Prices might go up.'

We smoked in silence for a while.

'It true they have opium poppies in some of the lower valleys?' I asked.

'Yeah, some. That leaves the country, but it's minimal.' He sucked smoke and handed the J back. 'Compared to other places. Tried that stuff once,' he said, pronouncing the words as he sucked more air in. Then he grinned and shook his head until he blew out a cloud of fragrant smoke. 'Just the once, though. Toooo nice. Faaar too nice.'

I shivered. 'Absolutely. Moderation in all things. Here.'

'Couldn't agree more. Thanks.' Silence. 'What you looking at?'

'Can you see the old palace from here?'

'Na. Further round the valley there, higher, too.'

'Right.' Silence. 'Breeze.'

'Yup.'

'Wind getting up.'

'She'll be fine until the east wind blows.'

'What?'

'Nuthin'.'

Silence. 'Jeez, the stars.'

'Cool, huh? Hey, you look cold.'

'I am absolutely fucking freezing.'

'Better get back in. People will talk.'

'Indeed. Good grief, my teeth are chattering. I didn't think that really happened.'

A stiff vodka martini gave the impression that it was counter-acting the effects of the joint. Probably doing nothing of the sort, but I felt like I needed it anyway. I didn't entirely trust myself not to slur my words, or babble, so I circulated in Minimum Speech Mode for a while, standing on the outskirts of groups and listening, or just nodding knowledgeably/sympathetically as somebody else sounded off. I narrowly escaped being collared a second time by the boring Austrian with the factory, but in the course of this manoeuvre bumped into the Prince.

'Kathryn, you are enjoying yourself?'

'Having a total hoot of a time, Suvinder. What a swell party this is. How about you, Princey baby?' Ah, well, Kathryn. Still in Potential Babble Mode, then. Just shut up, you idiot.

'Ha ha! You are a scream, Kathryn. Oh, yes, it is good to be back. And I am enjoying this party very much. Now, listen, as I was saying, I would love to show you more of the country. Langtuhn Hemblu is keen to take a four-wheel-drive and take us all over the place. We might need a week. It is such a beautiful country, Kathryn. Can you spare us that long?' He put his hands together in a beseeching sort of way. 'Oh, Kathryn, please say you can!'

'Ah, what the hell, why not?' I heard myself say. My, that grass was strong.

'Ah, you wonderful girl! You have made me so happy!' Suvinder went as though to take my face in his hands, but then changed his mind and just grasped my hands – they'd more or less warmed up by now, with no visible signs of frostbite – and shook them together until I thought my teeth would start chattering again.

That night I slept very, very well indeed. I had half thought that I might not be spending it alone. There had been a few attractive possibles in the crowd at the reception, which had had a pretty good social, conducive buzz about it, plus I was feeling pleasantly, mellowly receptive and sort of generally well disposed to men, which always helped . . . but in the end, well, I was just too tired, I guess. It had been a good party, I'd met lots of people, encountered an only slightly smaller number of interesting people, gathered a lot of information and over-all just had a fine old time.

I didn't even feel I'd made a mistake accepting Suvinder's offer to show me round the country. I was aware I might, come the chill light of morning, but not then, not right at that moment, not yet.

*Here, too, was a mostly unseen rainbow of animals: grey langurs, red pandas, blue sheep, black bears and yellow-throated martens, their presence – like the leopards, tahrs, gorals, musk deer, muntjacs, pikas and serows that shared the mountains with them – usually witnessed only by their droppings, prints or bones.*

\*      \*      \*

The Prince and I visited the towns of Joitem, Khruhset, Sangamanu and Kamalu and Gerrosakain. Langtuhn Hemblu trundled the old Land Cruiser slowly through dozens of huddled villages where people stopped and grinned and nodded formally, children ran away laughing, goats limped hobbled, sheep wandered indifferently and chickens pecked at dirt. In the ruins of the great monastery of Trisuhl we took tea.

The rhododendron bushes flourished everywhere in the lower valleys, their leaves glossy, thick and so deeply green they were nearly black. The valleys had once been much more heavily forested, and here and there mixed woods still lay across the folded hills and lined the steeper slopes. Where the forests had been, now farms were strewn across the undulating countryside, their terraces looping along the pitched gradients of the land like contour lines made solid.

Relatives, noble families, lamas and government officials greeted the Prince with a variety of reactions that ranged through polite affection, restrained respect, simple friendliness and what certainly looked like unalloyed joy. There were no great crowds of people brandishing the national flag and shouting hip-hurrah, but no cloaked anarchists lobbing bombs either. People waved a lot and smiled.

We visited one hospital. It was clean but sparse, just a building with many beds in many rooms, with little of the equipment the average Westerner associates with institutional medicine. Suvinder took little presents for the patients. I felt rudely healthy, as though my own constitution – which felt pretty sturdy and glowing – was an insult to these sick people.

We went round a couple of schools, too, which were much more fun. We visited the yak market in Kamalu, saw a Hindu marriage near Gerrosakain and a Buddhist funeral in Khruhset.

We took short hikes into the hills to visit half-frozen water-falls, abandoned forts, picturesquely ancient monasteries and picturesquely ancient monks. In the lower valleys, we crossed the milky rush of rivers by open wicker-work tube bridges. The Prince puffed and panted up the trails, using a couple of tall walking sticks, perspiring freely and apologising profusely for it, but he always made it and we never had to stop and wait for him. Langtuhn carried whatever picnic or other stuff he thought we might need and wouldn't let me carry anything other than the pair of binoculars and the Canon Sureshot I'd bought in Joitem.

I was pleased to be able to keep up with Langtuhn, even though he was loaded down with all the gear, had ten years on me at least and – I suspected – was throttling his pace way back to make life easier for us.

It was on one of these walks I lost the little artificial flower Dulsung had given me.

Kkatjats were snacks. We nibbled on a lot of Kkatjats. Pancakes featured strongly. Jherdu was roast millet flour, pi'kho roasted wheat flour. I'd been studying my guidebook and knew words like pha for village, thakle for innkeeper, kug for crow, muhr for death, that sort of thing. Some words were easy to remember because they bore a similarity to their English, Indian or Nepalese equivalents, like thay for tea, rupe which was the local currency, and namst, which was the everyday form of hello.

We stayed in two Thulahnese stately homes (one warm and unfriendly, the other the opposite), a government rest-house (minimalist; big rooms but *a padded hammock*, for goodness' sake. Still, very good night's sleep), the Gerrosakain Grand Hotel, Guest, Tea and Bunk House (long on sign, short on grandness) and a monastery, where I had to sleep in a special annex hung out over the walls because I was female.

Somewhat to my surprise, and much to my relief, Suvinder was a perfect gentleman: no flirting, no hands on knees, no tappings on my door at midnight. All in all it was a very restful and relaxing holiday in a pleasantly tiring sort of way. I'd deliberately left my lap-top and both phones back in Thuhn (the ordinary mobile was totally useless here anyway). It was like a sabbatical within a holiday within a sabbatical. Or something. Anyway, I felt very good. I thought of Stephen a few times, and took out the two discs I had, the CD-Rom with the Business's plans for Thulahn and the DVD with the evidence of my beloved's spouse cheating on him, and held them up to whatever light was available and watched their rainbow surfaces shimmer for a while, before putting them both back in my pocket.

Maybe, I thought, everything will have changed when I get back to Thuhn and make a few calls and send a few e-mails. Stephen will have found out about Emma's infidelity, she'll have taken the children and he'll be winging his way to Thulahn, To Forget. The Business would have suddenly discovered somewhere even better to buy, but donate billions to Thulahn, just to say thanks.

Somehow being away from all electronic contact, even if only for a few days, made this seem much more likely, as though there was a capacitance for change and difference in my life which was constantly being shorted away to ground by all the calls I made and e-mails I exchanged, but which, left alone for a while and allowed to charge up fully, would, when finally released, blast through all problems and light up all and any darkness.

Well, hoping is always easier than thinking.

I stayed up talking to the Prince a couple of nights over a whisky or two. He talked about the long-mooted change to becoming a constitutional monarch, about better roads, schools and hospitals, about his love for Paris and London, about his affection for Uncle Freddy, and about all the changes that would inevitably ensue if – and when, because he talked about it as though it was unavoidable – the Business came in and took over his country.

'It is a Mephistophelean thing, what?' he said sadly, staring into the flames of the rest-house's sitting-room fire. Everybody else had turned in for the night; there were just the two of us and a decanter of something peaty from Islay.

'Well,' I said, 'if you were thinking about this constitutional monarchy thing anyway, you aren't losing so much. Maybe, in some ways, you gain. The Business will probably prefer to deal with a single ruler than a chamber full of politicians, so remaining ...' (I tried to think of a polite alternative to the word that had first occurred to me, but it had been a long day and I was tired, so I couldn't) '... undemocratic for as long as possible will suit them fine. And any pressure for reform, well, they'll just buy that off with improvements if not outright bribes. You should look on it as securing your position, Suvinder.'

'I did not mean for me, Kathryn,' he said, swirling his whisky round in his glass. 'I meant for the country, the people.'

'Oh. I see.' Boy, did I feel shallow. 'You mean they don't get a say in whether all this happens.'

'Yes. And I can't really tell them what it is that might happen.'

'Who does know?'

'The cabinet. Rinpoche Beies has a sort of idea, and my mother managed to get wind of it too, somehow.'

'What do they all think?'

'My ministers are enthusiastic. The Rinpoche is ... hmm, indifferent is not the correct word. Happy either way. Yes. My mother has only the vaguest notion, but despises the whole idea utterly.' He sighed heavily. 'I thought she would.'

'Well, she's a mother. She just wants what's best for her boy.'

'Huh!' The Prince drained his glass. He inspected it as though surprised to find it empty. 'I am going to have some more whisky,' he announced. 'Would you like to have some more whisky, Kathryn?'

'Just a little. Very little . . . That's too much. Never mind.'

'I think she blames me,' he said morosely.

'Your mother? What for?'

'Everything.'

'Everything?'

'Everything.'

'What, like the Second World War, toxic shock syndrome, TV evangelists, the single "Achey Breakey Heart"?'

'Ha, but no. Just for not having remarried.'

'Ah.' We hadn't – ever – touched on the subject of the Prince's short-lived marriage to the Nepali princess who'd died in the helicopter crash in the mountains, twenty years earlier. 'Well, one has to mourn,' I said. 'And then these things take time.' Platitudes, I thought. But this was the sort of thing you felt you had to say. I read once that Ludwig Wittgenstein had no small-talk, no casual conversation at all. How hellish.

Suvinder gazed at the flames. 'I was waiting to meet the right person,' the Prince told them.

'Well, hell, Prince. Your mother can't blame you for that.'

'I think mothers have their own idea of original sin, to use the Christian term, Kathryn,' Suvinder said with a sigh. 'One is always guilty.' He glanced round towards the door. 'Always I wait for her to come through the door. Any door, whenever

I am in Thulahn, and sometimes when I am further afield, scolding me.'

'Well, she does seem kind of committed to her bed, Suvinder.'

'I know.' He shivered. 'That is what's so scary.'

He did touch me that evening, but only in a friendly, companionable way, taking my arm as we walked to our respective rooms. No attempt at a kiss or anything. Just as well: I was set for a struggle with that damn hammock, though once I was in it was very comfortable.

The next day was the last. We headed back towards Thuhn on a fine, clear, cold day and had a picnic lunch in the ruins of the old monastery at Trisuhl.

Langtuhn Hemblu unpacked the little table and two chairs, set the places, arranged the food and brewed a pot of Earl Grey tea, then went off to visit a relation who lived nearby.

The trees growing within the walls rustled where their tops stuck out into the light breeze, and little rose finches and redstarts hopped and jumped around us, almost but not quite accepting morsels of food from my hand. Choughs called out, their cries echoing in the empty shell of walls.

Suvinder chattered a little, and spilled some tea on the table, which was not like him. I felt content and harmonious with everything. I had mixed feelings about heading back to Thuhn and I was surprised to find that, while I was certainly looking forward to getting back to my e-mails and phones, if anything – given the chance – I'd have chosen to continue the tour round Thulahn. But, then, it was a small country. There was not much more to see, perhaps. And I'd been lucky to have had the undivided attention of somebody with as many responsibilities and calls upon his time as the Prince.

It was the sort of time when it paid to remember what

Mrs Telman had said, back in the hotel room at Vevey that night. Appreciate at the time, enjoy the moment, count your blessings.

'Kathryn,' Suvinder said, placing his teacup down. Somehow, I just knew we were suddenly in formal territory.

I turned from feeding the little birds to sit square and upright. Plumped up in our thermal jackets, we faced each other across the little table.

'Your Highness,' I said. I clasped my hands on the table.

He addressed them rather than my face. 'Have you enjoyed the last few days?'

'Immensely, Suvinder. One of the best holidays I've ever had.'

He looked up, smiling. 'Really?'

'Of course really. How about you?'

'What?'

'Have you enjoyed yourself?'

'Well, of course.'

'There you are, then. Hurrah for us.'

'Yes. Yes.' He was looking at my hands again. 'You have enjoyed my company, I hope?'

'Very much indeed, Prince. You've been the perfect host. I'm very grateful for your time. I feel very . . . favoured. I just hope your subjects don't resent me monopolising you for so long.'

He waved one hand dismissively. 'Good. Good, I . . . I'm glad to hear that. Very glad to hear that. Kathryn, I . . .' He exhaled suddenly, an exasperated expression on his face, and sat back, slapping the table. 'Oh, this is no good. I will come right out with it.' He looked me in the eye.

And, dolt that I am, I swear that I still had absolutely no idea what was coming next.

'Kathryn,' he said, 'will you marry me?'

I stared at him. For a while. 'Wi – Will I . . . ?' I said,

eloquently. Then I felt my eyes narrow. 'Are you serious?'

'Of course I am serious!' the Prince squeaked, then looked surprised. 'Of course,' he said, in a normal voice.

'I . . . I . . . Suvinder . . . Prince . . . I . . .'

He searched my eyes. 'Oh, dear, this has been a complete surprise to you, hasn't it?'

I nodded. 'Well, ah, yes.' I gulped. 'I mean, it is.'

'Have I made a complete fool of myself, Kathryn?' he asked, his gaze dropping.

'Prince, I . . .' I took a deep breath. How do you really, clearly, kindly say to someone you've come to like – even like quite a lot – that you just don't love them and so, no, of course you don't want to marry them? 'No, of course you haven't made a fool of yourself, Suvinder. I'm very, very flattered that you—'

He turned sideways in his seat, crossing his legs and arms and casting his gaze to the sky. 'Oh, Prince,' I said, recalling the drunken call in Blysecrag a few weeks earlier. 'I know people have said this sort of thing to you before, used these words. But I mean it. I'm not just trying to be kind. I like you a lot, and I know how much you must have . . . but hold on. I mean, you can't marry a commoner anyway, can you?'

'I can marry whom I like,' he said resentfully, scratching at the tablecloth with one fingernail as though trying to remove an invisible stain. 'My mother and anybody else can go hang. Tradition implies I must marry a princess or someone similar, but there is nothing but this . . . succession of precedents. From an age when there were many more princesses around. This is the twentieth century. My God, it is almost the twenty-first century. I am not unpopular. I have taken the precaution, even though I have resented it, of gauging the reaction of people to you. Ordinary people seem to like you. My ministers do. The

Rinpoche Beies was most taken with you and thought we would be most happy. So it would be a popular match.' He sighed. 'But I should have known.'

'Hold on, they don't *know*, do they?'

He glanced at me. 'Of course. Well, not the ordinary people. But I told the cabinet members in the plane on the way to Thuhn, and the Rinpoche before the reception the other night.'

'Oh, my god.' I sat back, stunned. I remembered them all nodding at me, smiling and nodding at me. They weren't just being friendly. They were sizing me up!

'What about your mother?'

'Her I was leaving till later,' Suvinder admitted.

An appalling suspicion began to form in my mind. 'Who else knows?' I asked, keeping my voice cold and flat.

He turned to me. 'A few people. Not many. All most discreet.' He sounded bitter as he said, 'Why? Are you so ashamed that I have asked you to marry me?'

'I said I was flattered. I think I still am, but I mean did anybody in the Business know?'

He looked defensive. 'I don't know. No, I mean, one or two, perhaps, knew that I, that I might . . .' His voice trailed off.

I stood up. 'This was all *meant*, wasn't it?'

He rose too, reaching out to take my hands in his while his napkin fell to the grass. 'Oh, Kathryn!' he cried. 'Do you really think so?'

I jerked my hands away. 'No, by the *Business*, you idiot!'

He looked mystified and hurt. 'What do you mean?'

I stood there and looked very carefully into his eyes. There was a *lot* of stuff going through my mind in those moments, none of it nice and some of it positively paranoid. So this was what they meant by thinking on your feet. 'Prince,' I said eventually, 'is this the way the Business makes sure that Thulahn is really theirs? By having me marry you? Did they suggest this? Did any of them – Dessous, Cholongai, Hazleton – did they even hint that this might be a good idea?'

Suvinder looked as if he was about to weep. 'Well, not . . .'

'Not in so many words?' I suggested.

'Well, I think they know I . . . that I have very strong feelings for you. I did not . . . And they did not . . .'

I don't think I have ever seen a man look so abject.

Sometimes you just have to trust your feelings. I reached out and took his hand. 'Suvinder, I'm sorry that the answer is no. I like you, and I hope you will stay my friend, and I accept that it was a sincere offer, from the heart. And I'm sorry I called you an idiot.'

His eyes glistened as they looked at me. He gave a small and sorry smile, then lowered his head until I couldn't see his eyes. 'I'm sorry I didn't protest when you did,' Suvinder mumbled at the table. I looked down at the white tablecloth, in the man's shadow, directly under his face. A clear droplet hit the linen surface, darkening it and spreading. He turned away with a sniff and walked off a little way, pulling a handkerchief from his pocket.

'Suvinder?'

'Yes?' he said, still not turning to look at me. He blew his nose.

'I am so sorry.'

He waved one hand and shrugged. He carefully folded the handkerchief again.

'Look,' I said, 'why not tell people that I'm thinking about it?'

He looked back with a smile. 'What would be the point of that?'

'It might . . . No, you're right, it's a stupid idea.'

He returned to the table, pocketing the hanky and taking a deep breath, his head high. 'Oh, look at us, eh? I am ashamed at myself for spoiling a perfectly good picnic, ruining a most pleasant holiday.'

'You haven't ruined anything, Suvinder,' I said, as he held my seat for me.

'Good. I must say, I'm still hungry. Let us eat, shall we?'

'Let's.'

He hesitated as he was about to take his seat. 'May I say one more thing? Then I promise never to raise the subject again.'

'All right.'

'I think I love you, Kathryn.' He paused. 'But that is not why I asked you to marry me.'

'Oh,' I said.

'I asked you to marry me because I think you will make a wonderful wife and because you are somebody I can imagine being with for the rest of my life, when perhaps love, of a sort, of a very important and special sort, might grow between us. I think it is wonderfully romantic to marry for love alone, but I have seen so many people do so and live to regret it. There are some lucky people, no doubt, for whom everything works out just perfectly, but I have never met any. For most people, I think, to marry for love is to marry . . . at the summit, as it were. It must be downhill from there on. To marry for other reasons, with one's head and not just one's heart, is to embark on a different sort of journey, uphill, I suppose,' he said, looking embarrassed. 'My goodness, I do not choose my metaphors so well, do I? But it is a journey which offers the hope that things will become gradually better and better between the people concerned.' He spread his hands and gave a sharp sort of laugh. 'There. My thoughts on the Western romantic marriage ideal. I did not put it, or rather them, very well, but there you are. No more.'

'You put it just fine, Suvinder,' I told him.

'I did?' he said, pouring some more tea from the padded pot. 'Oh, good. Please, another sandwich? We cannot feed them all to the birds.'

*Even moving higher than Thuhn, scaling tracks that seemed to zigzag up for ever to still higher valleys, you could find yourself beneath the lowest limit of an animal's domain; snow leopards that lived perpetually above the tree line and bharals that even in winter never descended below four thousand metres.*

'You what? You go to this remote Himalayan kingdom, the Prince proposes to you and you turn him *down*? Are you fucking *insane*?'

'Of course I turned him down. I don't love him.'

'Ah, so what? Say yes anyway. What girl gets a chance to marry a prince these days? Think of your grandchildren!'

'I don't *want* grandchildren. I don't want children!'

'Yes, you do.'

'No, I don't!'

'You do too. No one's mileage varies that much.'

'I'm telling you I don't, dammit!'

'Yeah, right.'

'Luce, I wouldn't lie to you. I've never lied to you.'

'Oh, come on, you must have. I'm your girlfriend, not your analyst.'

'What a terrible attitude! And I don't even *have* an analyst.'

'Exactly.'

'What do you mean "exactly"?'

'That just shows how much you need one.'

'What? Not having an analyst shows how much I need an analyst?'

'Yes.'

'You're mad.'

'Yeah, but at least *I*'ve got an analyst.'

*Slow-gliding in the air above them all slid the wing-spread shapes of the bone-eating lammergeiers, forever cruising the blade-thin winds that sliced across the frozen peaks.*

'Mr Hazleton?'

'Kathryn?'

'I just had a funny thought.'

'Funny? How do you mean? I thought you'd be ringing about Freddy—'

'Mr Hazleton, I've just received a proposal of marriage from the Prince. Am I supposed to . . . What about Freddy?'

'You haven't heard? Oh dear. He was in a car crash. He's in – what do they call it nowadays? – Intensive Therapy. Kathryn, I'm very sorry to be the one to tell you, but they don't seem to think he's going to make it. He was asking to see you. Though, I don't know, by the time you'd be able to get there . . .'

Suddenly I remembered – or half-remembered – a joke Uncle Freddy had told me once, something about a man, a fanatical hunter who was a great marksman with a double-barrel shotgun and was forever bagging vast quantities of grouse and pheasant but who in the end went mad and sincerely thought he was the piece of cotton on the end of a length of string that shotgun owners use to clean out the barrels of their guns. The punchline was his wife saying, 'But, Doctor, do you think he'll pull through?' This had sent Uncle Freddy into a tearful, knee-slapping frenzy; I could still see him hooting and guffawing and bending and struggling to catch his breath through his laughter.

I said, 'Tell them I'm on my way.'

# CHAPTER
## TEN

I fussed and fretted throughout the rest of that evening and into the night, making calls, sending e-mails, trying to sleep, not sleeping. Suvinder looked shaken when he heard about Uncle Freddy. He arranged for the Twin Otter to bring forward its flight the next day: it would leave at dawn from Dacca and turn around as quickly as possible. Luckily the weather forecast was fairly benign. Tommy Cholongai's Lear wasn't available but there would be a company Gulfstream waiting for me at Siliguri by noon.

The Prince had to pay a belated visit to his mother that evening. I spent most of the time in my room on the phone; my little quilted chattering lady, who was called Mrs Pelumbu, brought me a meal, though I didn't eat much.

I called Leeds General, the hospital in the UK where Uncle Freddy had been taken and eventually persuaded them that I was both a relation and that I was the "Kate" that Freddy kept asking to see. He was in Intensive Therapy, as Hazleton had said. A road traffic accident on the A64, two days earlier, during heavy rain. Four other casualties, two discharged, others not in danger. They wouldn't actually tell me how bad he was straight out, but they did say if I wanted to see him I should get there as soon as I could.

I tried Blysecrag. Miss Heggies answered.

'How bad is he, Miss H?'

'I . . . They . . . He . . . You . . .'

Miss H was reduced to little more than personal pronouns. The small amount of sense I did manage to get out of her only confirmed that Uncle Freddy was very poorly indeed, and in a sense I didn't even need that; just hearing how emotional and distraught this former paragon of stainless rectitude had become was enough to tell me things must be fairly desperate (it also made me wonder if she and Uncle Freddy . . . well, never mind).

Hi, Stephen. Lost Event Horizon here.

Kathryn, I heard about Freddy Ferrindonald. Can you get back there to see him? Is there anything I can do?

I'm starting back tomorrow, weather permitting. You can tell me what the word is in-company. Any details?

Yep, thought you might ask, so I found all this
out. He was driving to someplace on the coast
nearby — Scarboro? — during the evening; it was
raining, he skidded on a corner and hit a car
coming in the opposite direction. Wouldn't have
been too bad but the whatever he was driving was
so old it didn't have a seat-belt; apparently
he went through the windscreen and ended up
wrapped round a tree or a bush or something. Lot
of head and internal injuries. We'd have got
him to one of our hospitals — we had a Swiss air
ambulance waiting at the local airport for him
the next morning — but he's in too bad a way to
move. Kathryn, I'm sorry, but from what I hear he
isn't even fifty-fifty. He keeps asking for you.
I think Miss H's nose is out of joint, and not
just because he's not asking for her. Apparently
there's another woman there keeping vigil;
this is the party he was on his way to visit in
Scarboro.

Uncle F had a fancy woman. Well, that figures.
Look, thanks for collating all that stuff. Do we
have anybody on the ground I can contact?

Lady called Marion Craston, an L5 from
GCM. She's at the bedside too. Well, there or
thereabouts. In case he changes his will or
something, I guess, but also just to have a co.
presence too, most likely.

(Gallentine Cident-Muhel — London, Genève, New
York, Tokyo – are our lawyers. Wholly owned.)

Thanks. We have a number for her?

289

I called Marion Craston at the hospital in Leeds. She wasn't much help; the epitome of lawyerly obfuscation. Basically she confirmed what I already knew. The line was very clear and I could hear that she was still clicking and tapping away on a keyboard as she talked, sort of absentmindedly, to me. This I did not appreciate.

After I hung up I sat for a few seconds thinking about calling GCM and getting her replaced with somebody else, then decided I was upset and possibly just taking it out on her. I had done the same sort of thing myself on occasion (though not when the person I was talking to was a couple of levels above me in the corporate hierarchy; I'd always given them my full attention). But what the hell; one could be too severe.

'Hi again. So, want my analyst's number?'

'No, I do not. Listen, more tribulations.'

I told Luce about Uncle F.

'They have autos without *seat-belts*? Jesus. I suppose it was a right pea-souper, oi, guv'nor?'

'Will you stop that? The poor old bastard's at death's door and all you can do is come on like Dick van Dyke.'

'Okay, I'm sorry.'

'The car's a classic. Or was. That's why it didn't have a seat-belt.'

'I've said I'm sorry. Don't go all prickly-Brit defensive on me. But why does the old guy want to see you? Were you that close?'

'Well, fairly. I was like a daughter to him. I guess.'

'Yeah, like a daughter in the close-knit, down-home, swigging-moonshine-on-the-porch and whistling-Dixie sense. This is still the old geezer who used to grope you up, right?'

'Is this some new Valley phrase or are you in some continuing and pathetic attempt to sound British confusing grope and touch up?'

'Answer the question.'

'Look, we've been through all this. He's my Uncle Freddy who sometimes gives me an affectionate pat on the butt. End of story. He's a nice old guy and now it sounds like he's dying six thousand miles away from me and I've got to wait ten hours before I can even start heading to his bedside and I idiotically thought I'd call *you* for a little understanding maybe but instead—'

'All right! All right! So long as you're sure he never abused you.'

'Oh, not that again. I'm hanging up.'

'No! You've *got* hang-ups! Hello?'


In my dream, in the depths of that cold night, the east wind blew. Mihu, the Chinese servant who looked just like Colin Walker, Hazleton's security chief, cracked open a window in the eastern wall of windows, and the Queen Mother complained of a draught, so the canopy on that side of the bed was dropped. In the night, while the Queen slept, he went out on to the terrace for a while, then slipped back into the chamber and opened the western windows, which led out on to the terrace – the Queen stirred and muttered in her sleep, but did not wake – then, while Josh Levitsen and the little lady-in-waiting looked on, Mihu/Walker opened the eastern windows to let the wind in.

The lowered side of the bed's canopy acted as a giant sail, bulging like a dark purple spinnaker and making the whole framework of the bed creak and flex. The Queen Mother woke up groggily just as the bed started to move. The giant statues with the frayed shining armour stared down, their tattered gold leaf whispering wildly in the gale blowing through the long room; a gibbous moon flared in the cloudless night sky, pouring through the space and scintillating on the tiny strips of tinkling leaf as they tore and lengthened and ripped away and went flying through the moon-dark room like shrapnel confetti.

The bed began to move along its rails. Mihu/Walker decided it wasn't moving fast enough, and put his huge hands on the east side of its frame, and pushed. Contained within a blue-glittering cloud of golden flakes, the bed rumbled along its tracks and out into the night. The Queen Mother screamed, the bed's wheels hit the end of the tracks, but there was nothing there to stop them. The wheels clattered down on to the stones, striking sparks; the bed's canopy, loops and folds and curtains all flapped and snapped and fluttered in the golden-seeded breeze. Still picking up speed, wheels and the Queen Mother still screaming, the bed hit the terrace wall and crashed on through, tipping momentously into the black gulf beyond.

Somehow Mihu/Walker's hand stuck on to the bed and he could not let go, and so he went with it, and Uncle Freddy – trapped in the bed by straps and tubes and wires – screamed as he fell into the night.

I woke from that one with the sweats. I checked my watch. Twenty minutes since the last time I'd looked at it. After that it was a relief to lie and worry about everything.

Uncle Freddy. Suvinder. Stephen. Stephen's wife.

In a bizarre, horrendously guilt-making way it was a relief to have something to *have* to do. I remembered the feeling I'd had when I'd flown back alone from my Italian school trip, knowing that my mother was dead. The tears did not come and I just felt numb, surrounded by layers of insulation that even seemed to muffle the words of people. I recalled the noise the jet made as we flew over the Alps, all feathers of white spread over the land far below.

I was having problems with my ears and gone slightly deaf. The stewardesses were kind and solicitous, but I assumed they must have thought they were dealing with a half-wit from the way I had to keep asking them to repeat things. I really couldn't quite make out what they were saying. There was a roaring in my ears, a compound of the jet's engines and the air tearing past the fuselage and the effects of the pressure on my inner ears. That more than anything else was my insulation, the thing that kept everything at bay.

Then, more than now, you were isolated in a plane. Nowadays you can make calls from your seat phone; then, once you were up in the air, that was it. Aside from the very unlikely possibility of a caller persuading Air Traffic Control or somebody to patch them through to the flight deck, once you took your seat you weren't going to be disturbed. You had that time, that interval between the responsibilities that the ground beneath your feet implied, to detach yourself from things, to take an overview of your life or just whatever problems ailed you at the time.

It struck me only then that maybe that was why I always felt good on planes, why I liked them, why I slept well on them. Shit, did it really go back to that flight from Rome to Glasgow and that roaring in my ears, that strange, numb knowing that I was cut adrift from my mother for ever, and wondering what would become of me? I knew I hadn't really worried – or at least I hadn't worried that my biological father would come and reclaim me for himself and the life I thought we'd left behind – but I did get that detached, Now what? feeling, that impression that everything was going to change and I would too.

And so I kept myself awake all the way through the night thinking this sort of thing, wondering if Uncle Freddy was going to live, and if he didn't whether I'd get there in time before he died, and what it might be – if there was any specific thing – that was so important he was calling for me and not anybody else, and should I let Hazleton let Stephen know about his wife and her lover, and would the Prince, despite all he'd said, hate me for turning him down, and had it all been set up by the Business as the ideal way of tying Thulahn tightly to us, and how else were we going to do it, and should we do it, did the people in the place deserve or need or want to have all that might happen to them happen?

And was this whole thing about planes born in that other flight back after catastrophe, and did it go deeper than that, to layers of insulation I'd been wrapping around myself all my life, to all the hierarchies of contacts and business associates and good reports and executive levels and salary increments and pay-off guesses and colours of credit cards and classes of aircraft cabin and higher-level interest rates and even friends and lovers I'd collected around myself over all the years, not to keep the world away from me, because people were the world, but to keep me away from me?

My last thoughts, as dawn was coming up and I fell briefly asleep again, were that all this stuff about flying beds and aircraft and sleeping on them was making certain that I'd be so tired and sleep-deprived that I was bound to sleep on the plane; the Gulfstream if not the Twin Otter. Then, before it seemed I had really got back to sleep at all, the alarm went off and it was time to get up, feeling groggy and terrible and dizzy with the effects of interrupted sleep, and stumble sticky-eyed to the bathroom.

I stood beneath a tepid shower, listening to the wind moan in the vent to the outside air and making my own moaning noise as I heard it pick up and start to gust.

I dressed ethnic, in the long red jacket and matching trousers. It was only after I'd put everything on that I remembered I'd meant to dress Western. Oh, well.

My bags were already on their way down to the airfield when I did my usual last look round the room for anything I might have forgotten. Just a formality, really: I'm a conscientious packer and I hardly ever forget anything.

The little netsuke monkey. It was still sitting there on the bedside table.

How could I have missed *you*? I thought. I stuffed it in a pocket of my long red padded jacket.

The Twin Otter landed, I thought, spectacularly. Not an adverb I enjoyed settling on as the *mot juste*, in the circumstances. The Prince, bundled up against the cold, stiff wind, took my gloved hand in his. The wind was making my eyes water, so I guessed it was doing the same to his and he wasn't being a big sissy or anything. He asked, 'Will you come back, Kathryn?'

'Yes,' I said. Dark clouds were moving fast across the sky, torn to great rolling ribbons by the high peaks. Swathes of snow dragged down the slopes. The pilots were hurrying the few pallid passengers off the craft and helping with the unloading, loading and refuelling. The crowd was small. Gravelly dust was picked off the football/landing field and thrown into the air.

Everything was late; the plane had been delayed at Siliguri with a burst tyre for an hour. I'd used the time to do a bit of present shopping while the weather worsened. When we heard the plane had taken off and was on its way I wasn't sure whether to feel relieved or terrified. My insides settled on both, which just seemed to leave my lower brain confused.

'You promise?'

'I promise, Suvinder.'

'Kathryn. May I kiss your cheek?'

'Oh, for goodness sake.'

He kissed my cheek. I hugged him, briefly. He nodded and looked bashful. Langtuhn Hemblu and B. K. Bousande looked in different directions, smiling. I saw a way out of our mutual embarrassment and went over to where my little pointy-hatted friends had appeared. I squatted down to say hi. Dulsung wasn't there, but Graumo, Pokuhm and their pals shook both my hands and patted my cheeks with sticky fingers. I tried to ask why Dulsung wasn't there, and they tried to tell me, miming something that seemed to involve lots of twirling and fiddly work.

I distributed the gifts I'd bought earlier. I gave Graumo two presents and tried to make it clear that one of them was for Dulsung, but he looked suspiciously surprised and delighted and promptly disappeared. I hailed Langtuhn, who came over with a big bag of boring but useful stuff like pencils, erasers, notebooks, dynamo flashlights and so on. We presented this to the children, getting them to promise to share it all out.

We'd just finished doing this, and I'd given away the last of the presents, when Dulsung appeared, breathless and smiling broadly. She offered me a little home-made wire-and-silk flower. I squatted down so our faces were level, accepted it from her and attached the new flower securely to my jacket.

I looked round for Graumo but there was no sign of him. I had nothing to present to Dulsung: I'd given everything away. I checked my pockets for a gift I might have missed. Only one lump remained in any of the jacket's pockets. The little monkey. That was all I had left: my tiny dour-faced netsuke piece.

I pulled it out of my pocket, held it in my fingers for a moment, then offered it to her. Dulsung nodded, then accepted it with both hands. Her face split into a huge smile and she reached up with both arms. Still squatting, I hugged her. The little monkey was in her right fist; I could feel its chunky hardness against the back of my head.

Then it was time to go, and so I went.

I left as I'd arrived, just me and the guys up front in the plane. Once the ground had dropped away – along with my stomach – I looked back to see the people I'd left, but by the time we turned after take-off all there was to see was the inside of a big black cloud full of jack-hammer turbulence and glimpses of swirling snow.

The flight was horrific. We got there; we got to Siliguri, but it was pretty damn frightful. One of those flights where you contemplate death and terror so closely that no matter what happens, even if – when – you arrive safely, the you that got on the plane really hasn't survived after all; the you that gets off is different.

I'd given away my little netsuke monkey. What had I been thinking of? Ah, well, never mind. It had seemed like the right thing to do. It still did. Anyway, it was my own fault for almost leaving it in the bedroom; otherwise it would never have been in my pocket in the first place. A superstitious person would have thought that somehow the little carving had wanted to stay in Thulahn. A Freudian . . . well, never mind what a Freudian would have thought. Luce had asked me once Was I a Freudian? I'd told her no, I was a Schadenfreudian.

During one of the wilder bits of the flight, I found myself touching and stroking the little flower in my lapel. My hand was on the brink of jerking away again as my brain thought, Hello, is this some sort of rosary scene going on here? I looked down at my hand as though it belonged to somebody else. Then I thought, No, this is just a childish thing. Comfort, not superstition.

Same difference, I thought.

Of course, a really superstitious person would have thought that the monkey supernaturally knew that the plane was going to crash in the mountains and had made sure it was safely on *terra firma* at the time in the hands of a new owner.

The plane dropped sickeningly and hit another seemingly solid wall of air. I grabbed the flimsy seat arms with both hands. Yeah, very fucking comforting, I thought.

Gulfstream all the way. Siliguri to Leeds-Bradford just like that, in a tad over eight hours; would have been less but for head winds. I'd assumed we'd have to touch down somewhere to refuel, but no. The plane's seats were big and broad and leather in a cabin gleaming with mahogany; there was a rest room with gold and marble fittings, up front there was a no-nonsense flight crew and back with me a welcoming but unfussy stewardess who served hot and cold food and drinks that would have earned a Michelin star back on the ground, plus there were today's papers, this month's magazines – some of them *women*'s magazines, hot diggety – and every TV channel under the sun and over the horizon. I got myself a serious news fix. Oh, and the flight was blissfully smooth.

I changed from Thuhn *haute couture* to a smartly corporate

blouse, pinstripe skirt and jacket, and shoes more suitable for hospital visits in Europe in winter. Dulsung's little artificial flower went in an inside pocket. Contemplating myself in the generously sized and perfectly lit mirror above the deep marble basin, my avaricious side – stunned into shocked silence, like most of the rest of me, by the traumatic transition from Thuhn to Siliguri – woke up briefly to look round the plane and say, I *want* one! While a side I didn't even know I had reared its curious head and with a shake of it said, How sickeningly ostentatious and wasteful. But then both these disputing demispheres fell promptly asleep as soon as I settled my occasionally fondled but assuredly never abused butt into my seat.

I awoke over the North Sea looking down at the flares of oil and gas rigs, the seat fully reclined and a cashmere stole wrapped over my legs. The aircraft and the air roared and shushed around me.

I yawned and made my way past the smiling stewardess – I nodded and said, 'Thanks' – to the rest room to tidy my hair and apply some make-up.

A frustrating delay waiting for a customs official to turn up at Leeds-Bradford, then a smooth journey in a chauffeused Merc – rear seat unforgivingly hard – to the hospital. The air smelled strange and felt thick. Somehow I hadn't noticed this back at Siliguri but I noticed it now.

It was pretty late by then. I'd let Marion Craston know I was on my way as soon as we'd hit cruising altitude out of Siliguri and she'd told the medics, but whether I got to see Uncle Freddy or not depended on how he was. When I got to the IT unit they asked me to turn my mobile phone off. I was allowed to set eyes on Uncle F – tiny, skin yellow-white, head bandaged, almost invisible from some angles because of all the machinery and wires and tubes and stuff – then had to tiptoe away, because he was asleep at last, for the first time, for any length of time, since he'd arrived here. He'd been told I was on my way; maybe he felt able to sleep now. I felt touched and flattered and worried all at once.

Marion Craston and the mysterious geriatric floozy from Scarborough were nowhere to be seen, having retreated back to their respective hotels. I asked if there was any point my staying through the night. I felt well enough rested from my extended snooze on the Gulfstream to handle one of these all-night bedside vigil things, but the medical staff said no; better to come back in the morning. They seemed marginally more sanguine about Freddy's chances than they'd sounded before. I stayed half an hour, just to make sure he really was safely asleep, then left. I still worried, and let myself out of the hospital with a feeling of hopelessness and dread, half certain that, after all, he'd die in his sleep during the night and I never would get to talk to him.

Mercedes to Blysecrag. A red-eyed Miss Heggies, very obviously keeping control of herself. The house felt terribly empty. It should have felt cold, too, and probably would have if I'd come from anywhere other than Thulahn. Instead it felt warm, but still empty and desolate.

I woke up in the middle of the night with a dream of drowning in warm water. Where was I? Warm. Warm air. Not in Thuhn. I felt for my torch, watch and the little monkey, then recalled where I was and flopped back. York room, Blysecrag. Uncle Freddy. I lay looking up at the darkness, wondering if my drowning dream counted as a premonition and whether I should ring up the IT unit to see if there was some sort of crisis. But they had the number here: they'd phone me or Miss H if there was anything serious to report. Better not bother them. He'd be okay. Sleeping soundly. Bound to pull through. I reached out for the netsuke monkey.

Nothing there between the watch and the torch. Of course: Dulsung had it, half a world away. I hoped she looked after it. Actually there was something there, between the torch and my watch: a little home-made artificial flower. I patted it, turned over and went back to sleep.

'Kate, my girl.'

'Uncle Freddy. How are you feeling?'

'Bloody awful. Wrecked the car, you know.'

'I know.'

Breakfast had been interrupted by a call from the hospital to say that Uncle Freddy was awake and asking to see me. There was still half an hour before the car was due to arrive, so I suggested that Miss Heggies and I go together in her ancient Volvo estate. She just shook her head: she'd go when she was asked for.

We opened up the stables-cum-garage and I drove the Lancia Aurelia into town. Miss H would phone the car company to tell them they wouldn't be needed.

Marion Craston was there in the IT unit's small lounge, and the mystery woman. Marion Craston was tall, athletic, a little plain, a little vague and mousy brown. Mrs Watkins, the object of affection in Scarborough, was there too: younger than I'd expected, petite, plump, nicely turned out, lots of brassy dyed blonde hair; soft Yorkshire accent. I thought we might all troop in together, but Uncle Freddy asked to see me alone.

301

Seeing the set-up closer to, I realised we couldn't all have trooped in anyway: there was just about room for one person to squeeze in between all the machines and sit by Freddy's side. The nurse, who made sure I got settled in without tearing out any vital tubes or wires, bustled off immediately afterwards, called to some other emergency.

He looked shrivelled, reduced, lying there. His eyes looked bright in the subdued light, but seemed shrunken back inside their bony orbs, the skin waxy and stretched thin around them. His face and hair were the same yellow-white colour. I patted a few stray wisps of hair back into place.

'Lovely old Delage it was,' he said. His voice was soft and wheezy. 'No bugger'll tell me if it's a write-off or not. Could you find out for me?'

'Of course. Oh, I came in the Aurelia; hope you don't mind.'

'Not at all. They need to be used. Umm. Have you met Mrs Watkins?'

'Just now. She's out there with Ms Craston, the lawyer.'

Uncle Freddy wrinkled his nose. 'Don't like her.'

'Marion Craston?'

'Hmm. Legal eagle. More like legal vulture.' He coughed and wheezed for a couple of seconds before I realised he was really laughing, or trying to. I held his thin, cool hand.

'Steady, now. You'll shake your tubes out.'

He seemed to find this funny, too. His other arm was in a cast; he lifted the hand I was holding away for a moment to wipe at his eyes with a weak, painful-looking delicacy.

'Let me do that.' I pulled out a handkerchief and dabbed at his eyes.

'Thank you, Kate.'

'You're welcome.'

'I hear you've been in Thulahn.'

'Just returned.'

'Did I drag you back, my dear?'

'Well, I was ready to come back.'

'Mmm-hmm. And how is Suvinder?'

'He's well.'

'Did he ask you anything?'

'Yes, he did. He asked me to marry him.'

'Ah. Care to tell an old man what your reply was?'

'I said I was flattered, but the answer was no.'

Uncle Freddy's eyes fluttered closed for a while. I wondered if he'd gone back to sleep, and even if he was conking out on me, but there was still a weak pulse in the wrist above the hand I was holding. His eyes came slowly open again. 'I told them it was a mad idea.'

'You told who, Uncle Freddy?' Oh, shit, I thought. You were in on it too. Uncle F, how could you?

'Dessous, Hazleton.' Uncle Freddy sighed. He did his best to squeeze my hand. There was more pressure from the weight of his thin hand than there was from his fingers. 'That's one of the things I had to say to you, Kate.'

'What, Uncle Freddy? That you knew?'

'That I'm sorry, dear girl.'

I squeezed his hand gently. 'No need.'

'Yes, there is. They asked me which way you'd jump, Kate, how you'd react. They asked me not to say anything to you. I agreed not to. Should have.'

'Was this just Dessous and Hazleton, or did the Prince take part in these discussions?'

'Just those two, and Tommy Cholongai when they brought

him in later. They were only hoping Suvinder would pop the question; dropped a few hints, maybe. But I should have said something to you, Kate.'

'Uncle Freddy, it's all right.'

'They're worried, Kate. They thought they had this all tied up, but then they realised that they were relying on Suvinder's word or, more to the point, on his greed. And it gradually dawned on them he wasn't actually as selfish as they'd assumed. Not like them, I suppose.'

'A cultural thing, maybe.'

'Hmm. Perhaps. But either way, they thought if they could get you in there they'd be going some way to guaranteeing the deal.'

'I bet they did.'

'I expect they'll still go ahead. With the whole thing. Do you think so?'

'I have no idea.'

'I think they wanted to know how ... Damn, I don't know what the word is. Mind's going. I don't know.'

'Take your time.'

'Oh, I don't think so. I don't think I've ... Well, anyway. They wanted to know how you might react to the place, to the country, to the people, I suppose. Would that maybe persuade you, if Suvinder himself didn't? You see?'

'I think so.'

'Take it their fiendish plan didn't work, then?'

'Oh, I don't know. I suppose I did kind of fall in love with the place. But I can't marry the country.'

He blinked a few times and looked oddly surprised. 'Have you met Maeve?'

'What? Mrs Watkins? Yes.'

'Not bad, don't you think?' He winked with a sort of feeble lasciviousness.

'Pretty good, for an old codger like you,' I agreed, smiling. 'I haven't really had a chance to talk to her, but she seems very nice.'

'Very dear to me, Kate. Very dear.'

'Good. That's nice. Have you known her long?'

'Oh, absolute yonks, but we've only been, you know, involved, for about a year.' He sighed. 'Lovely place, Scarborough. You ever been?'

'No.'

'Worth a visit. Road's not really that tricky, either. Just impatient, I suppose. Don't think Maeve thinks it . . .' He seemed to lose the thread somewhat, then shook himself out of it. 'The Prince. Was he upset? I mean, at you turning him down.'

'A little, but still okay about it. More sad than anything else. The ironic thing is I like him a lot more now. I mean, I don't love him, but . . . Oh, it's all so complicated, isn't it, Freddy? It's like you just never get the one you want.'

'Or you do, at long last, but then you go and crash your car on the way to see her and end up in somewhere like this.'

'Well, you'll just have to get better, won't you? Though I think we'll have to get you a chauffeur after this.'

'You reckon?'

'I reckon.'

'I think a chauffeuse, don't you?'

'No, Uncle Freddy. I think a chauffeur.'

'I don't know, Kate,' he said, looking away. 'I don't think I'll be leaving here alive.'

'Oh, come on, now, just stop that. You'll—'

'I'm being honest with you, Kate,' he said softly. 'Can't you be honest with me?'

'I am, Uncle Freddy. They thought you were going to go belly up until last night. Now they think you might just make it. But, then, they don't know you the way I do. In fact, I'm going to warn them that they better surround you with male nurses from now on, or at least make sure no female ones bend over within striking distance.'

He coughed and wheezed again. I dabbed at his eyes. 'I'm sure you are.'

'Well, look, if you—' I said, making getting-ready-to-go movements.

'Don't go. Stay a bit. I have more to say, Kate.'

'Okay, but they don't want me to stay too long.'

'Listen, dear girl, there's something going on.'

'You mean, apart from trying to marry me off to Suvinder?'

'Yes. That bugger Hazleton's up to something.'

'Busy man, isn't he?' I said, thinking of the DVD disc.

'Kate, I didn't get you into any trouble, did I? I mean, by agreeing to invite you to Blysecrag for the weekend. It was Miss H who told me. They had people watching you and that American chap, Buzetski, while you were there.'

'Did they now?'

'Well, I wasn't sure whether to say anything or not. They didn't, I mean they didn't, umm, discover anything, or, or . . .'

'There was nothing to discover.'

'You're pretty attached to the fellow, aren't you? Even I could see that. Didn't need to be told.'

'Pretty. But sadly it isn't mutual.'

'I'm sorry.'

'Me too. But, then, he is married.'

'Yes, I gathered that. That's why I was worried.'

'How?'

'That they might, oh, I don't know, find something that they could use against you, or him, or both of you. Only it was a bit late by the time I found out. Again, though, I could still have said something. I feel bad, Kate. I should have been more open with you.'

'Well, nothing happened, Freddy. I threw myself at the man but he pushed me away, politely. The most sensual we got was me watching him swim and him giving me a peck on the cheek. No blackmail material, if that's what you mean.'

(This was ignoring the fact I'd asked Stephen to take me in no uncertain terms, words any decent parabolic mike or something planted in his suit could have picked up with ease, but apart from causing me a little embarrassment at sounding so desperate, so what?)

'Ah, well, no harm done, then.'

'Well . . .'

'What?'

'See this?' I pulled the DVD out of my pocket.

'CD, isn't it?'

'Digital Video Disc. It does have blackmail material on it. Not of me, not of Stephen Buzetski, but of somebody connected. Hazleton made sure I got this. Thinking that I might use it to get myself something I want, in which case Hazleton hopes I'll feel beholden to him.'

'Crafty beggar, isn't he?'

'Yes, he is.'

'God, I worry for Suvinder, Kate.'

'What do you mean? Why?'

'Because they've got the boy, his nephew. In school in

307

Switzerland. Oh, I don't know, Kate, they might be exaggerating, but they seem to think he's theirs. Willing to do whatever they suggest. Greedy, the way they'd like him to be. If that's true, Suvinder had better watch himself.'

This took a moment to sink in. 'You think they might have Suvinder *killed*?'

'Wouldn't put it past the blighters, Kate. They're very serious about this, you know. Lot of money involved.'

'I know. Lot of people involved, too, in Thulahn.'

'I don't think they care about the people there, Kate, except as obstacles.'

'I think you're right.'

'Oh.' Uncle Freddy sighed, with surprising force. He blinked up at the ceiling a few times.

'You're looking tired, Freddy. I'd better go.'

'No! No. Just in case. You have to listen.' He clutched at my hand, suddenly strong. 'It's this Silex thing.'

'Silex?' I had to think. The chip factory near Glasgow. It seemed like a long while ago. 'What about it?'

'They nobbled our chap. The fellow we had transferred from Brussels.'

'What do you mean, "nobbled"?'

'He's been bought off, turned, whatever you want to call it. Doesn't matter how I know, but I do. He's saying it's all above board up there. Bugger's lying. And I think it's Hazleton again.'

'Are you sure?' Uncle Freddy was starting to sound paranoid, developing a Hazleton fixation. Next, he'd be the one who'd forced him to have the crash.

'No, no, not sure. But his people were there, at the Silex plant. At least one of them.' He winked at me. I had never seen the movement of an eyelid look so laboured and so difficult. 'I had somebody else there. Somebody I knew I could trust. Said that Poudenhaut fellow had been there. Our Brussels chap met him at the factory but didn't mention it. That's how I know.'

I closed my eyes briefly. 'This is getting too complicated, Uncle Freddy. I'll have to think about it later. Come on, you look pretty washed out. I really think I'd better go.'

'Kate.' He kept hold of my hand.

'What, Freddy?'

'Blysecrag.'

'What about it?'

'Oh, Kate, I don't know what to do.' He started to cry; not sobbing, but just crying quietly, tears rolling down his cheeks.

'Freddy, what is it? Come on, don't upset yourself.' I dabbed at his eyes again.

'I'd left it to you, Kate.'

'You did *what*?'

'I'd left it to you, then I changed my will to leave it to the National Trust, because I didn't want to give you an added reason to stay in this country if you might be moving to Thulahn. But . . .' His voice sounded thin and desperate. 'But now I don't know what to do. I can change the will back again if you want the dreadful old pile. I mean, I don't know. You could call in Miss thing, Miss Craston, the lawyer. I could do it now—'

'Hey, hey, hey. Uncle Freddy. Look, I'm *honoured* you even thought of willing it to me. But what would I do with a huge place like Blysecrag anyway?'

'Look after it, Kate, that's all I've ever done.'

'Well, then, I'm sure the National Trust will do a much better job than I could. But you've got to stop talking like this, Freddy. You're not dead yet. Come on, now.'

I had no idea if this pull-yourself-together-old-bean stuff would work with Uncle F. I felt awkward with it, but then how else are you going to feel when you're with somebody who might be dying and who seems convinced they are, or are about to? Especially when he's already crying and you feel you might be about to.

'I'll be all right,' he said, falteringly and unconvincingly. 'Are you sure you don't want it?'

'Positive. I'd just get lost. Look, you're not going to die yet, but I take it you have provided for Miss Heggies, for when the time does come?'

'Oh, yes. Her flat is hers. And there's money.'

'Then there's nothing to worry about. Stop distressing yourself. Good grief, give it a few weeks and you'll be back there yourself, trying to get the damn catapult to work again.'

'Yes.'

'Look at you. You can't even keep your eyes open. Get some sleep.'

'Yes.' He stopped fighting it and let his eyes close. 'Sleep,' he said groggily.

'I'll see you tomorrow,' I said, rising. I let go of his hand and let it rest on the pale green disposable sheet.

'Tomorrow,' he whispered.


'I don't believe this! You're making this up! A fucking for-real prince offers to marry you and you turn him down and take the next jet out of town, then barely a day later an uncle on his deathbed wants to give you some vast estate in England with a house the size of the fucking Pentagon and you turn your nose up at that as *well*! Are you crazy?'

'Oh, right. This from the woman who claims to believe sisters should do things for themselves. And Freddy is not on his deathbed.'

'Look, there's nothing unsisterly in letting somebody will you enormous amounts of realty. Especially when it's an old man on his deathbed. I mean, that's perfect. If he ever did expect you to put out in return, he sounds far too weak to do anything about it now! Even if you were prepared to drop your precious self-righteousness, and your pantyhose, which I doubt.'

'Luce, I swear, talking to you cleanses my soul.'

'You're a fucking atheist, you haven't got a soul. What are you talking about?'

'If ever I start to worry that I might be in any way deceitful, shallow, vindictive, overly acquisitive, exploitative or cynical, I only have to talk to you for a few minutes to realise that I am something close to a saint in comparison.'

'Bullshit.'

'Don't you see, Luce? You're the reason I don't need a shrink. All I need every now and again is to be reminded that I'm not a bad person. And you do that! I should thank you. Actually, I should pay you, but I'm not that saintly.'

'Kathryn, get some help. Your brain has left the building. Book yourself into a clinic. I'm serious.'

'You're not serious, and I'm not ill.'

'You are too! Talk about denial! Apart from anything else, you're denying yourself the chance to own half of North York state or wherever this Blisscraig place is, *and* you're denying yourself to be *Queen* of an entire fucking *country*!'

'Look. Can we come back to this some other time?'

'To talk about what? The archangel Gabriel appeared before you asking you to be the Mother of God for the Second Coming and you turned that down too?'

'Ha ha. No, it's an opportunity I have. I don't know whether to take it or not. Can I run it past you?'

'Why bother? The mood you're in at the moment, you'd turn down the offer of a cure for cancer and an end to world hunger.'

'Well . . . Look, I've been given some blackmail material.'

'Blackmail? Seriously?'

'Seriously. Film of somebody fucking somebody they shouldn't be fucking, somebody they're not married to.'

'So this person is married?'

'Yep, she is.'

'Ah-hah. Anyone I know?'

'No. Thing is, I only have to say the word and the husband gets to see the film.'

'And you get to see the husband?'

'Well, maybe.'

'Ho ho. So is this to do with your beloved?'

'Yes. I can probably destroy his marriage if I want. Of course, whether he falls into my arms is another matter, but . . .'

'Okay. You want to know what I would do?'

'Yes.'

'Let me just check. Are either of the people in the film richer than you?'

'Eh? No.'

'Right, so there's no point in, like, actually blackmailing them.'

'Luce! Even for you—'

'I'm just checking!'

'Okay. Sorry. Go on.'

'Right. Well, I'm very tempted to say, whatever you do, *don't* use the film, just sit on it. I feel I should say that because it seems like you always do the exact opposite of what I suggest anyway, so if I apply a bit of reverse psychology and advise you to do whatever is most against your best interests, you'd end up doing the right thing through sheer cussedness.'

'Whereas really you think I should give the word and let him know his wife's cheating on him?'

'Yeah, do it. If you really want this guy, and you really don't want to ascend to the Yeti Throne or whatever the fuck it is, do it. Give that film the green light.'

'But then I could be blackmailed by the person who got the film to me in the first place.'

'Hmm. Hold on, I've got it.'

'What?'

'The solution.'

'What? What is it?'

'It's this. Be positive. Be affirmative. Say yes to everything.'

'Say yes to everything?'

'Yes. Take the mansion and half of York state; sell it and buy hospitals and schools for the needy of what's-it-called.'

'Thulahn.'

'Yeah, Thulahn. Which I think you should become Queen of. Tell the Prince you'll be his wife, but it'll be one of these formal marriages the Europeans used to have, because you release the film too and do everything you can to be in the right place at the right time to get your guy and carry him off to Thulahn as well, to be your secret lover.'

'So I should suggest to the Prince that we get married but it's never consummated?'

'Yeah. A morganatic marriage, or whatever it's called.'

'I don't think that's what a morganatic marriage means.'

'Isn't it? Shit, and I used to think it meant a good marriage, like rich, from J. P. Morgan? Yes?'

'No, not that either. But that's your suggestion?'

'It is. And if it all works out, I expect a damehood or something, or a fucking tiara loaded with diamonds at the very least. A castle would be nice. Hell, leave Blisscraig to me if you like; it could be your embassy in England.'

'Hmm. I don't know that Suvinder would be very happy with an unconsummated marriage.'

'Oh. Suvinder, is it? Okay then, consummate it.'

'Consummate it?'

'Yes. Is he that gruesome?'

'He's a little plump.'

'How little?'

'Maybe an extra twenty, thirty pounds.'

'How tall is he?'

'About my height. No, a bit taller.'

'That is not grotesquely obese. Does his breath smell?'

'I don't think so.'

'Does his body smell?'

'No. Well, only of scent. Well, I mean . . . Never mind.'

'Teeth straight?'

'The teeth are good. The teeth are an asset. And he's a good dancer. Light on his feet. Even graceful. You could say graceful.'

'Well, that's good.'

'Yeah, but they're old-fashioned dances; waltzes and shit.'

'The waltz may be making a come-back. That's a neutral, for now. Could become a plus.'

'Okay. What else?'

'Full head of hair?'

'Yup. Maybe too full; slightly bouffant.'

'Irrelevant. Hair on a man's head is like the opposite of salt in a dish; you can take it away but you can't add it in.'

'That is so nearly profound it's painful. Keep going.'

'Is he slimy, repellent, actually, like, ugly?'

'None of the above.'

'Can you *imagine* fucking him? . . . Hello? Kathryn? Hello?'

'I just imagined it.'

'And?'

'It wasn't that good for me.'

'Did you imagine having to fake orgasm?'

'Yes. Probably. Maybe.'

'But you don't actually feel sick?'

'Not sick. Possibly a little soiled.'

'Why soiled?'

'I never imagined fucking a guy I didn't actively want to fuck before.'

'You haven't?'

'Never.'

'You're unreal. But anyway, it wasn't that awful, right?'

'Right. But imagining fucking him isn't the same as actually fucking him, is it?'

'That's what your imagination is *for*, you idiot, it's like on-board VR. If it's not that terrible in your imagination it'll probably be even better in reality.'

'So I marry him, fuck him, but keep my beloved as lover?'

'Yes.'

'That may be a little sophisticated. I'm not sure how that'll play someplace where a good wife is worth three yaks.'

'Be discreet. Anyway, he's a man. He'll want to play away, too. Think reciprocity.'

'What about children?'

'What *about* children?'

'What if I'm expected to produce? There's a royal line to be continued here.'

'Well . . . maybe you're not fertile.'

'I am.'

'You checked?'

'I checked.'

'So go on the pill. Tell him they're headache tablets. He'll never know.'

'That is almost plausible.'

'Anyway, once you're in a stable relationship, in fact once you're in *two* stable relationships, with the King-prince *and* your beloved, you may change your mind. You may realise you've wanted children all along.'

'So you would have me believe.'

'Hmm. The Prince; his colouring. Is he, ah, dark-complexioned? Compared to the beloved, I mean. Could you . . . would it be possible . . . ?'

'. . . No, I don't think I want to look down that . . .'

'. . . No, you're right, maybe not.'

'Definitely not. I could get beheaded or something.'

'They behead people for that sort of thing there?'

'Actually they don't have the death penalty at all. More civilised than the US in that respect.'

'Yeah? Well, fuck them. How many aircraft carriers they got?'

'Not a lot of call for aircraft carriers in landlocked Himalayan states.'

'Stealth bombers? Cruise missiles? Nukes?'

'You're right, they're pathetically ill-equipped to enter an escalating correctional-system conflict with Old Glory.'

'You do realise you could end up with three passports at the end of this?'

'Dear holy shit! I hadn't thought of *that*!'

'Well, you—'

'Hold on, I got a call waiting. Oh, shit. I got a bad feeling about this, Luce.'

Miss Heggies was sitting on the parapet at the end of the mile-long reflecting pool, her feet dangling almost in the water, her usually neatly bunned hair hanging down in grey lengths around her undone collar. She didn't look round when I parked the old Lancia on the gravel behind her.

I went up and sat with her on the stone, my legs drawn up under my chin. A very light rain, what we'd call a smir in Scotland, was falling from the bright grey overcast.

'I'm very sorry, Miss Heggies.'

'Yes,' she said dully, still staring at the flat water. 'Sorry.'

I put my arm out tentatively. She inclined millimetrically towards me. She didn't exactly relax and start sobbing, but she leant against me and put her arm round my waist, patting me. We sat like that for a while. In Scotland, sometimes crying is called greeting, and it only struck me then that it was odd that something you usually did when you were saying goodbye to somebody, one way or another, should also mean welcoming.

On the way back to the house I stopped and looked up at the place. So did she, gazing wonderingly at it, as though taking in its baroque confections of stonework for the first time. She sniffed, buttoning the collar of her dress and tucking up her hair.

317

'Do you know what's happening to Blysecrag, Ms Telman?'

'Apparently it's going to the National Trust, but I think only on condition you get to stay.'

She nodded. I pulled a piece of paper out of my pocket. 'And this is my inheritance.'

She squinted at the note. 'David Rennell? He used to be a gardener here. Nice lad. Mr Ferrindonald found him a job with the company.'

'Yes, most recently just outside Glasgow. I'm sorry if this isn't a good time, Miss H, but Uncle Freddy obviously thought this was important and I'd like to talk to Mr Rennell as soon as possible. Would you make the introduction?'

'Of course, Ms Telman.'


I didn't really need the introduction from Miss H, apart from having my identity confirmed quickly; Uncle F had told David Rennell to answer all my questions if I ever got in touch.

'You've been *in* there?'

'Yes, Ms Telman. There doesn't seem to be any big deal about it any more. People are wandering in and out, clearing up and that sort of thing.' He had a nice Yorkshire accent.

'Call me Kathryn. I'll call you David, all right?'

'All right.'

'So, David, what was there? What did you see?'

'Just a big empty room. There were containers for etching materials in there, but I talked to one of the guys; they were empty and just put in there the other day, after everything was moved out.'

'What was moved out?'

'I don't know. Whatever it was it all disappeared in the middle of the night, on the twentieth. Somebody saw a load of desks being shifted next morning. I think some of them might still be around in the warehouse.'

'Could you describe the room in more detail?'

'About ten metres by twenty, ceiling the same height as the rest of the factory, with the usual ducting and so on, carpet tiles on the floor, lots of cables lying around and coming out of opened conduits in the floor.'

'What sort of cables?'

'Power cables. Lots of others, like printer cables and that sort of thing. Ah, I picked up a couple of connectors and plugs and so on.'

'Ah-hah. Well done. Could you possibly do me a favour, David?'

'Certainly.'

'. . . and maybe take some time off?'

I was to meet David Rennell in the car park at Carter Bar, right on the border between England and Scotland. It was a coolish, blustery day. The view from the shallow pass, looking north into the undulating hills, forests and fields of the Scottish lowlands, was moodily dramatic and changing all the time under the clouds that sped and tumbled above. I got a veggie burger from a van at one end of the car park and sat eating it in the car. Very stake-out. Meeting on the border; very cold war.

It had been a good drive. I'd left the phone off for most of it, just driving the Aurelia across the moors on secondary roads, thinking.

Thinking a lot about Uncle Freddy, about what a laugh he'd been and how much I was going to miss him and the occasional invitation to Blysecrag. Probably next time I wanted to go I'd have to pay, and there would be a National Trust shop, and lots

319

of those carmine-coloured ropes with brass hook-ends attached to brass stands that corral visitors into the accepted circular route in your average English stately home. Ah, well. It would mean more people would get a chance to see the weird old place. For the good, in the end. No grouching about that.

Uncle Freddy was another matter. Another one dead. My real mother, Mrs Telman last year (her husband – technically my adopted father, according to the legal paperwork – ten years earlier, not that I'd seen him more than once); now Freddy.

I wondered if my biological father was still alive. Probably not. The truth was I didn't want to know, and if I was honest with myself I'd have to admit that I'd be relieved to discover he was no longer in the land of the living. Guilt about that. Was this the same as actually wishing him dead? I didn't think so. If I'd had the choice, if somehow I could make him alive by thinking him so, I would. But I didn't want to meet him, didn't want some bogus emotional reunion, and anyway it didn't seem fair that he might have survived when the people I'd cared about most, my mother, Mrs Telman and Uncle Freddy, were dead.

What had been his contribution to my life? One drunken ejaculation. Then he'd slapped my mother around, gone into prison for theft, come out to pursue his career as an alcoholic and turned up at my mum's funeral to shout names at me and Mrs Telman. At least he'd had the decency not to contest the adoption. Or he'd been bought off, which was more likely. And – if he knew I'd become, by his standards, disgustingly rich – he'd never bothered me for cash.

I supposed I ought to make enquiries, find out if he was still alive or not. One of these days.

The drive went on; the weather came and went, sending rain and sun and sleet and slush. The high roads across the moors were wild and grey one moment, then sun-bright and fresh with purple heather the next. I stopped at Hexham to put some four-star into the Aurelia's tank and was reminded of the calibratory nature of travelling in a covetable car: if guys in garages start to admire the car more than you, you're getting old. Honours even, then. I drove on into the north.

David Rennell arrived in a dark blue Mondeo. I bought him a burger and a soda and we sat in the steamed-up Aurelia, for all the world like a married-to-others couple having a clandestine meeting towards the end of the affair. Rain beat on the roof.

David Rennell was a tall, wiry-looking guy with short auburn hair. Bless him, he'd brought a couple of Polaroids of the desks they'd moved out of the mysterious, no-longer-top-secret room in the middle of the Silex plant. Not ordinary desks. Too many shelves. Lots of holes in the flat surfaces for cables. He'd brought a handful of the connectors and plugs that had been lying around the place.

'That one looks like a phone jack, except not,' he said.

'Hmm. Did you come up with anything else?' I'd asked him to have a think while he drove down here. The usual no-matter-how-trivial stuff you see in cop shows.

'I talked to somebody who saw one of the trucks that took the stuff away.'

'Any haulier's name?'

'No, they were just plain. They didn't have any markings, but the person I was talking to thought they looked like Pikefrith trucks, though he wasn't sure why. Means nothing to me, I'm afraid.'

Pikefrith were a wholly owned subsidiary of ours, one of

the few European companies that specialised in shifting delicate scientific instruments and sensitive computer gear. Come to think of it, their trucks did appear slightly different from your average lorry, if you looked carefully enough or were into the subtleties of truck design. Air suspension. I just nodded.

'Oh, yes, and the Essex kids have all disappeared. They all seemed glad to see the back of them up there.' (He pronounced it 'oop there', which was really rather cute.)

'Who the hell are the Essex kids?'

'It's what the Silex people called this lot that have just left. They mostly worked in the room and they kept themselves to themselves. Bit brash, though, so they say. Had a big party on the Friday and then never showed up on the Monday. All transferred.'

I felt confused. 'Were they really from Essex?'

'I think they were from south. Don't know about Essex.'

'And Freddy said you saw Adrian Poudenhaut there, at the factory?'

'Yes, just last week.'

I felt my eyes narrow as I looked at him. 'You're absolutely certain it was him?'

David Rennell nodded. 'Positive. I've met him a few times; helped him get some of Mr Ferrindonald's cars started, reloaded for him when he was shooting.'

'Did he see you?'

'No. But it was him, definitely.'

Things that make you go, Hmm.

We went our separate ways. I drove back a different route to Blysecrag, still favouring the picturesque B-roads, even when the sun went and night descended. I had many more miles to think stuff over.

The Lancia really was a hoot to drive.

Uncle Freddy's funeral was in three days. I had plenty of time to visit London.

# CHAPTER
# ELEVEN

S uzrin House stands in Whitehall in London, the only
non-governmental building left on that stretch of the
Embankment. It looks out over the river towards the
sixties concrete brutalism of the National Theatre complex like
an ancient, grizzled gunslinger regarding an upstart cowboy just
arrived in town. It is spectacularly ugly in a brooding, noxious
sort of way.

Its main, dark brown rectangular tower-block slopes inward
slightly and is set back from the Thames, separated from it by

a huge glassed-in section several storeys tall whose roof rises from the Embankment side towards the main block. Enormous ornamental windows stare from the very top of the main tower. I used to wonder why the whole thing looked so familiar from a distance until I realised it was shaped like a giant old-fashioned cash register.

The place is part office, part apartment block. It was where Adrian George worked. I took the train from York to London the morning after Freddy died, calling AG *en route* and arranging lunch.

'I was sorry to hear about old Freddy Ferrindonald.'

'Yeah, it was a shame.'

'Do you have anything in particular in mind for lunchtime?'

'I thought Italian.'

'I meant agenda-wise.'

'Not particularly,' I lied.

We met in a fairly swish French place Adrian George favoured in Covent Garden. He wasn't big on Italian food. He wasn't big on drinking either, citing a heavy workload that afternoon. AG was shortish but trim and dark and handsome. I could remember him when his eyebrows met in the middle, but maybe he'd lost out on too many girls whose mothers had warned them about men with hirsute foreheads, because it looked as if now he shaved that centre line. We conversed pleasantly enough; company gossip, mostly. He was one of those people I got on best with through e-mail, just as Luce was somebody I found it better to talk to on the phone.

I only mentioned his reported sighting of Colin Walker, Hazleton's security chief, in London a month earlier, right at the end of our meal. He tried not to react, laughing it off as mistaken identity. He insisted on picking up the bill.

I said I'd go back to Suzrin House with him. The weather was cool, windy and dry and I thought we might walk along the Strand or the Embankment, but he wanted to take a taxi. He chattered. I already knew all I needed to.

Once we'd gone through Security in the lobby, we went our separate ways, he up to the exec floors, me to the basement to see an old friend.

'That one's a Bell-K connector.'

Allan Fleming was, as usual, a mess. He'd been in a wheelchair for twenty years since a climbing accident in his teens, and despite having a very nice wife called Monica, who was totally devoted to him and turned him out neatly every day, it usually only took him minutes after he arrived at work to look as if he'd spent the last month sleeping rough. Sometimes he accomplished this between the garage – where he parked his converted Mini – and his workshop.

Allan was Suzrin House's resident computer nerd. His work-shop – somewhere deep under the main building and way below the surface of the Thames even at low water – was like a museum of computing, filled to its high ceilings with bewildering amounts of electronic hardware ancient and modern, but mostly ancient (which in computer terms, for the truly, seriously, antediluvian stuff, of course meant about the same age as him or me). We'd known each other since post-grad days, when we'd both been in that year's Security intake, before I'd come to my senses and left to be a proper exec, specialising in hi-tech.

Allan was in charge of computer and IT security, specifically here in Suzrin and the other outlying London offices, but in effect – along with a few other similarly gifted geek-wizards in the States – also anywhere the Business had modems and computers. He was our insurance against hackers: if he couldn't worm his way into your system, probably nobody else could either. I'd shown him the plugs and other bits and pieces that David Rennell had brought me from Silex.

'What's a Bell-K connector?' I asked, staring at his cardigan and wondering how he'd managed to get so many buttons done up through the wrong holes. I bet he hadn't left the house like that.

'It's a specialist phone-line connector,' he said, pulling absently at some of his curly brown hair and twisting it so that it stood out from his head like a tiny horizontal pigtail. 'A dedicated land line, probably; very high capacity, especially for the time. Better than ISDN. Made by Bell Laboratories, as you might expect, in the States. Still copper technology, however; your next step up would be your optical.'

'What was its "time"?'

'Oh, just a few years ago.'

'Sort of thing you might find in a chip-manufacturing plant?'

'Hmm.' Allan turned the little connector over in his hands, then took off his unfashionably large-framed glasses and blew on each lens in turn, holding them up to the light and blinking. 'Not particularly. You wouldn't want it for telephony purposes, I'd have thought, and your standard Parallel, Serial and SCSI ports would handle most non-specialist applications.'

'I though this *was* specialist.'

'Yes, as I said. But this is for specialist telephonic applications.'

'Such as?'

Allan replaced his glasses, asquint, on his nose. He rocked back in the chair and looked thoughtful. 'Actually, the place you'd most likely see something like this would be in the stock exchange, or a futures market, somewhere like that. They use high capacity dedicated land lines. So I understand.'

I sat back in the ancient peeling plywood and black tubing seat, an idea forming in my mind. I pulled the Polaroid of a desk out of my pocket. 'See this?'

Allan sat forward and peered. 'It's a desk,' he said helpfully.

I flipped the photograph round and looked at it myself. 'Well, my copy of *Jane's Book of Fighting Desks* is not to hand. But now you mention it . . .'

He took the photo from my hand and studied it. 'Yes. Lots of holes for cabling. And that extra level, that raised shelf. It does look a little like the sort of desk that might belong to a commodities trader, or someone of a similar nature, doesn't it?'

'Yes. Yes, it does, doesn't it?'


'Kate, I'm in a fucking meeting. What the hell is so important you have to get me called out of it?'

'I'm at your dentist's, Mike. Mr Adatai is quite rightly concerned. I need you to tell him to let me see your file.'

'You *what*? You pull rank on me for that?'

'Look, don't blame me; I thought you were supposed to be here in London. I didn't know you were going to go jetting off to Frankfurt.'

'Yes, to meet some very important – oh, for Christ's sake. What is all this about? Quickly, Kate, please, I need to get back in there.'

'It's very important I see your dental-records file, Michael. I'm going to hand you over to Mr Adatai now. Please authorise him to let me see it, then you can get back to your meeting.'

'Okay, okay; put him on.'

\*    \*    \*

The standard human mouth contains thirty-two teeth. Mike Daniels must have had good, conscientious parents who got him to brush his teeth thoroughly after each meal and snack and in the evening before retiring, because he had had a full set – with just a couple of fillings in lower bicuspid molars – when he'd been drugged in a London club a month earlier, had about half of his teeth removed and then been left in his own bed in his flat in Chelsea.

I sat in Mr Adatai's warm and luxurious waiting room with a bunch of recent *Vogues*, (well, this was Chelsea) *National Geographics* (of course) and *Country Lifes* (I thought of the dowager Queen in her giant bed in the old palace, and – sitting in that warmth – shivered).

I looked at the diagram of Mike Daniels' teeth. I took a note of those that had been taken and those that had been left. I closed the file, stared at a potted palm across the room and did some mental arithmetic.

In base ten, a ten-figure number. Two point one billion and some change. No need to use your fingers at all.

My mouth went dry.

From the start that morning I'd considered staying in London overnight, and had brought a few bits and pieces in a travelling bag, but in the end, after leaving Mr Adatai's – in fact, on the kerb while the taxi was pulling up – I decided to head back to Yorkshire. I rang Miss H to tell her I'd be staying at Blysecrag that night.

We had dinner on the train, my lap-top and I, looking through a load of files I'd downloaded about the Pejantan Island deal and the Shimani Aerospace Corporation. This was the deal that Mike Daniels had been flying out to Tokyo to sign when he'd been dentally assaulted – hence the anguished call to me that night in Glasgow.

Pejantan Island is a piece of guano-covered rock in the middle of the southern part of the South China Sea, between Borneo and Sumatra. It is, to put it politely, undistinguished, except for one thing: it is almost bang on the equator. Shift the place three kilometres south and the zero degrees line would go straight over it. It's less than an hour's flight from Singapore, just big enough for our purposes – or, rather, the purposes of the Shimani Aerospace Corporation, for we were merely investors – and it was uninhabited. The idea was to build a spaceport there.

Now, this is high-horse territory for me – though I do know what I'm talking about, and it is my job – but space, and anything associated with getting into it, is going to be so fucking big, and soon, it's frightening. Space is already very big business indeed and it's going to get a lot bigger in the near future. The US through NASA, Europe through ESA, the Russians, the Chinese, the Japanese and various other minor players are all desperate to grab as much of the launch market as possible, and private enterprise is determined to catch up.

I've seen detailed plans of about a dozen different *ways* of getting into space – even leaving out the exotic far-future stuff like giant elevators, rail guns and giant lasers – using craft with helicopter-like rotors with rockets in the tips or – well, never mind; the point is not that, if we're lucky, one of them might just work, it's that *all* of them might work.

Whatever method you use, the best place to launch stuff into orbit is from the equator, or as close to it as you can get (which is why NASA chose southern Florida for its spaceport and the SU had to settle for the delights of Kazakhstan). The Earth, just through rotating, gives you a free energy boost to help lob your payload above the atmosphere, and that means you can lob more, or use less fuel, than you could if you launched from further up or down the curve towards the poles.

One space-launch concern – in which I am delighted to say we have some investment – is taking advantage of this by using two huge ships, a command-and-control vessel and the rocket-carrying ship itself to send payloads up from the oceans on the equator. The time before last that I was in Scotland I got to clamber over the launch ship while it was in dry dock in Greenock, on the Clyde. It was just techy heaven. These are real ships, built for an entirely pragmatic, unromantic, unsentimental, return-hungry consortium, but they are just such a fabulous, *Thunderbirds*-style idea I'd have been seriously tempted to recommend investing in them just for the sheer mad beauty of the project. Happily, it looks like a good business deal, too.

But you never know. The ships will only be able to handle stuff up to a certain size. To be on the safe side, we're also the major investor in the Shimani Aerospace Corporation's Pejantan Island project, which – if all goes according to plan – by 2004 will be sending state-of-the-art rockets roaring into space with their valuable satellite cargoes.

This was heavy engineering, cutting-edge technology and serious science. The budget was jaw-dropping. So were the returns if we'd all got our sums right, but the point was that the bigger the project and the bigger the budget the easier it is to hide things in both of them.

Like this little item here: a tracking station in Fenua Ua.

Now, why Fenua Ua? I looked up a map of the Pacific. Why not Nauru, or Kiribati, or even the fucking Galapagos?

Sipping my coffee somewhere around Grantham, I used the

mobile and the lap-top's modem to do some more long-range Web searching. Eventually, as the train sped through the night, picking up speed after Doncaster, deep in some otherwise entirely ignorable PR nonsense (which just goes to show you never know where something useful will turn up), I found a little video clip of Kirita Shinizagi, chief executive officer of the Shimani Aerospace Corporation, visiting Fenua Ua earlier this year and inspecting the site for the new tracking station.

Next stop York, the guard's voice said over the speakers, while my head was somewhere between London, Tokyo, Fenua Ua and Pejantan Island.

I disconnected the mobile from the computer. The phone rang. Hazleton's number came up on the display. I hesitated two, three rings before answering.

'Hello?'

'Kathryn?'

'Mr Hazleton.'

'Kathryn, I was so sorry to hear about Freddy.'

'Thank you. Will you be able to make the funeral, Mr Hazleton?'

'Sadly, no. Kathryn, are you able to think straight? Or are you too distraught? If this is a bad time to talk about things, I can always wait.'

'I think I can still string two thoughts together, Mr Hazleton. What was it you wanted to talk about?'

'I wondered how you felt you'd got on in Thulahn. I was going to ask before, but of course we were rather overtaken by events when you realised that Freddy was in hospital. We never did finish that conversation.'

'No, we didn't. I recall that at the time I was about to ask you if you'd had any hand in suggesting to the Prince that he ask me to marry him.'

'You were? I don't understand, Kathryn. Why would I want to interfere in your private life?'

'That's all right, Mr Hazleton. I've had more time to think since then. The question no longer applies.'

'I see. I confess I wasn't entirely sure I'd heard you right when you told me that at the time. However, I've spoken to Suvinder since, and yes, he was, and is, very serious about it. I understand you turned him down. That's very sad. Of course it's entirely your decision and you must do as you see fit, but the Prince did sound very dejected.'

'He's a better man than I thought he was at first, Mr Hazleton. I've come to like him. But I don't love him.'

'Ah, well. There we are, then. This has, as you can imagine, all become rather more complicated because of that development. Are you still thinking of the proposition Jebbet and Tommy put to you?'

'Yes.'

'Good. The amount of power invested in whoever takes up the post there would be very considerable. You might have decided not to become Queen of Thulahn, Kathryn, but you could still be something like the President. What do you think? Have you had any thoughts? Or would it now be too awkward with Suvinder there?'

'Oh, I've had thoughts, Mr Hazleton.'

'You're being very cryptic, Kathryn. Is there somebody there with you? Can't you talk?'

'There's nobody here. I can talk. I'm still thinking very seriously about taking up the post in Thulahn.'

'But you haven't come to a decision yet.'

'Not yet.'

'You couldn't give us a balance-of-probabilities assessment, even? Which way you're leaning, as it were?'

'There are very strong reasons for going, and very strong ones for staying where I am. It's too delicately balanced, so, no, I'm afraid I can't. But once I've made my decision, I'll stick with it.'

'And when do you think that will be, Kathryn?'

'I think another few days should do the trick.'

'Well, we shall just have to be patient, shan't we, Kathryn?'

'Yes. Sorry about that.'

'Of course, there is the other matter, isn't there? I don't want to have to push you on that, too, but it has been a couple of weeks now . . .'

'You mean that B-movie you provided me with?'

'Yes. I was wondering if you'd come to any decision on that, too.'

'Yes. I have.'

Stephen. We need to talk. Call when you can. Voice or this.

Uncle Freddy had a Viking's funeral. His coffin was placed in an old motorboat, one of those polished wooden things with two tandem separate seating compartments and a stern deck that slopes in a curve all the way down to the water. It had been filled with various flammable stuff and moored out in the centre of the lake where we'd fished a few weeks earlier. A crowd of us – a big crowd, too, given that Freddy hadn't had many relatives – looked on.

One of his drinking cronies from the pub in Blysecrag village was an archer; he had one of those elaborate modern bows that looks much more complicated than any gun, with balancing weights sticking out apparently at random and all sorts of other bits and pieces. He loaded up an arrow with a big, bulging head made of bound rags soaked in petrol, another drinking chum lit it, and then he shot it out towards the motorboat. The arrow made a noise I will never forget as it curved up through the clear, cool air. Uncle Freddy's pal was obviously very good or he'd done this before, because that one shot was all he needed. The arrow slammed dramatically into the woodwork, the flames caught and spread and the boat was soon ablaze from end to end.

I stood watching it burn, thinking that there were probably all sorts of terribly British and very sensible rules and regulations about the proper disposal of bodies that were being flouted here. Well, fuck them if they can't take a joke. Freddy: the man who put the fun in funeral.

Uncle F left me a small landscape painting I'd once admired. Not by anybody famous, and not valuable, just nice, and something to remember him by. What do you give the girl who has everything? Your undivided attention, of course. So, having not bequeathed me the entire house and estate of Blysecrag, Freddy did the next best thing and left me something I would be able to pack in a bag and take away with me.

The Charm Monsters – the Business' Conjurations and Inter-ludans division – had been kept at bay by the terms of Uncle Freddy's will. I think Miss Heggies was grateful for that, though there wasn't much she could do about the presence of Maeve Watkins. Still, they seemed to get along politely enough, Miss H serving Mrs W tea in the drawing room with a civility that was one notch up from frosty, and Mrs W seeming slightly embarrassed and modestly grateful.

The company was represented by Madame Tchassot, the other
Level One apart from Hazleton who'd been at the weekend party
at Blysecrag three weeks earlier. I asked to have a word with her
alone. We sat in Blysecrag's toweringly impressive library; she
settled her small elegant frame into a seat, carefully smoothing
her black skirt under her bony legs.

'What is it that concerns you, Kathryn?' She looked around,
then pulled a small container like a powder compact from her
handbag. 'Oh. Do you think it is permitted to smoke in here?'

'I don't know.'

'You don't mind if I do?' Her accent was confusing, half-way
between French and German.

'No, I don't.'

She offered me a cigarette, which I refused. She lit up. The
little container was a closable ashtray; she placed it on the table
at her side. 'I understand you might be moving to Thulahn,' she
said, tapping the end of the Dunhill gently against the edge of
the little ashtray, though the ash wasn't ready to come off yet.

I watched this, trying to judge how much to say, trying to
think back to what I knew of Madame Tchassot. How close was
she to Hazleton? The fact that she was supposed to have a thing
going with Adrian Poudenhaut didn't mean much by itself. If
it did mean anything beyond the purely personal, it might even
mean that Hazleton was using Poudenhaut to keep an eye on
her. Though it might mean something else, too.

'Possibly.'

She blinked behind her small glasses. 'The rumour I have heard
is that Prince Suvinder has proposed to you.' She smiled. 'That is
very interesting.'

'Yes, it is, isn't it? I wondered at one stage if that had somehow
been set up.'

'Set up? How do you mean?'

'I mean that somebody, or some people, at the highest level of the Business, decided that having an agreement with the Prince, legal or otherwise, wasn't good enough to guarantee that Thulahn was really ours, and that having one of our own high-level execs married to the ruler would be a far more satisfactory way of cementing the relationship between us and Thulahn.'

'Ah, yes, I see. But it would be something of a long shot, yes?'

'Not that long, perhaps. The people concerned already knew that the Prince was . . . keen on me. And I was sounded out, first by Mr Dessous and then by Mr Cholongai. I misinterpreted, at the time: I thought they were really trying to find out how suited I would be to becoming a sort of ambassador to Thulahn, which is the pretext that was used to get me to go there. I thought they were worried that I was insufficiently committed, not so much to the company as to the idea of personal monetary success and, I suppose, *laissez-faire* capitalism itself. What they were really worried about, I think, is that I was too committed to those things.'

She blinked. 'Can one be?'

'I think so, if you are hoping that the person concerned might find something in a poor, underdeveloped Third World country that she can't find in her very comfortable existence in one of the richest parts of the richest state in the richest country in the world.'

'I have heard that Thulahn is enchanting,' Madame Tchassot said, persuading some ash to drop from her cigarette. 'I have never been there.' She looked over her glasses at me. 'Would you recommend a visit?'

'In a personal or a business capacity?'

She looked surprised. 'I think one may only savour enchant-ment in a personal capacity, no?'

'Of course. Madame Tchassot, may I ask if what I'm talking about here is all new to you, or did you already know of anything like this before?'

'But, Kathryn, if all that you are speculating about had been spoken about at my level, you would be asking me now to reveal what the Board has discussed. You must know that I cannot do that.' She smiled, and put one hand to her tightly gathered hair. 'However, there are less formal occasions when such subjects arise between Board members, and in that context I can tell you that there was some talk of you being just the right person to represent us in Thulahn, and the point was made that the Prince's high regard for you would be to the good in this respect. I do not think that any of us thought for one moment he would make you a proposal of marriage. For my part, and I mean no disrespect, I would have imagined that he would want to marry, or would be obliged to marry, someone of a certain social class.'

'That's what I thought. Apparently not.'

'Hmm. That is also interesting.' She looked thoughtful. 'Have you made a decision yet, Kathryn?'

'I told the Prince no.'

'Oh. The rumour I heard was that you were undecided. Well, that might be unfortunate, or fortunate. Would you still consider the post in Thulahn?'

'I am still considering it.'

'Good. I hope you did not turn the Prince down only because you thought that we had manoeuvred you into the position of being asked.'

'No. I turned him down because I don't love him.'

She seemed to think about this. 'We are so lucky, aren't we,' she said, 'to be able to marry for love?'

This was probably as distracted as I was ever going to get her. 'Do you know anything about the Silex thing, Madame Tchassot?'

She frowned. 'No. What is the Silex thing?'

'I'm not sure. I thought perhaps you could tell me.'

'I'm afraid I cannot.'

'Then I may have to ask Mr Hazleton.'

'Ah. Mr Hazleton. Do you think he knows about it?'

'He may. Silex is a chip-manufacturing plant in Scotland. There seemed to be something odd about it. I was looking into it.' I paused. 'I think Adrian Poudenhaut was, too. I wondered if he'd said anything to you.'

'Why would he do that, Kathryn?' Now there was a reaction. She coloured faintly. My bet was that Madame Tchassot was either an extraordinarily gifted actress, or she'd been telling the truth so far.

'I hear rumours too, Madame Tchassot,' I said. I gave a small, nervous-looking smile and lowered my eyes. 'I'm sorry if I've embarrassed you.'

'Adrian and I are close, Kathryn. But we do not discuss business . . . how should I say? . . . gratuitously.'

'Of course.' I smiled in what I hoped was a friendly way. 'I was hoping to have a word with Adrian about the matter. But please don't say anything to him. I'll go through Mr Hazleton.'

We talked a little more after that. Madame Tchassot smoked a few more cigarettes.

'Telman?'

'Mr Dessous. Hello.'

'How the hell are you, Telman? What can I do for you? And why did this call have to be scrambled? Yeah, and why aren't you calling me Jeb like I told you?'

'I'm fine, Jeb. You?'

'Mad as hell.'

'I'm sorry to hear that. What's happened?'

'Damn Feds took away my Scuds, that's what.'

'Oh dear. Do you mean Scud missiles?'

'Of course. What the hell else would I mean? Thought I'd hidden them too good. Those fornicating interfering scumbags must have been tipped off. Informer in the ranks, Telman. Least you're not on the list of suspects. I never did tell you where they were hid, did I?'

'Not that I can recall. Where were they?'

'Inside a couple of grain silos. My idea. Grain silos, missile silos. Clever, huh? Thought that would be the last place any-body'd look if they ever did come snooping around.'

'Didn't they do that in a *Man From U.N.C.L.E.* episode?'

'What?'

'I'm sure there was a *Man From U.N.C.L.E.* episode where the bad guys hid missiles in grain silos. Long time ago, of course.'

'Damn! You mean it wasn't an original idea? Hell's teeth, Telman. No wonder they guessed. Never watched the pro-gramme myself. Serves me right for not being more into popular culture, I guess. One of those FBI bozos must have seen the same episode as you, Telman. Maybe we haven't got a turncoat here, after all.'

'Maybe not.'

'So, Telman, what's up?'

'Freddy Ferrindonald, Jeb.'

'Oh, yeah. Sorry to hear about that. You there for the funeral?'

'Yes, it's just finished.'

'So, Telman. Thulahn. Hazleton says you told the Prince to go to hell. That true?'

'No, Jeb. I just refused his offer of marriage.'

'Same thing to a guy, Telman. You going to tell me old Suvinder don't feel like he's been kicked in the teeth?'

'I hope he doesn't feel that. We parted on what I thought were very good terms.'

'Telman, any guy with a nickel's worth of brain cells thinks long and hard before asking a girl to marry him, and if he isn't only asking because he's got her pregnant and he feels he ought to ask then he gets nervous as hell worrying about what she's going to say. This guy's a prince: not only has he got his own future to think of, he's got the future of his whole damn country to think about too. Plus, the way the people round him see it, and probably him too, is he's doing you a big favour and making a huge sacrifice even thinking about asking you, because you're not some princess or lady or something. You're a Level Three exec. You're probably a lot better off than the Prince but that doesn't seem to be what matters to these people. It's breeding. Pile of horse manure if you ask me, but that's the way it is and the fact remains that even if we bumped you up to Level Two you'd still be just some kid out of a project in Scotland.'

'Schemes. We call them schemes in Scotland, Jeb. But I take the point. However, I think I let Suvinder down as gently as possible and I hope we'll still be friends.'

'Hooey, frankly, Telman.'

'You don't think that's possible?'

'I doubt it. You've wounded the man's pride. And if and when the Prince does get hitched and you're around, no self-respecting wife's going to *let* him stay buddies with you.'

'Well, I may not be there, anyway. I'm still thinking about whether to take the post in Thulahn or not.'

'So I hear. Well, don't take for ever, okay? We ain't got that long. So. What you going to do now?'

'I'm going to ask you if you know what happens to Fenua Ua once we complete the deal with Thulahn.'

'Jesus wept, Telman. You be careful what you're saying, will you? This call might be encrypted or whatever you call it but—'

'What happens, Jeb?'

'What do you mean what happens? Nothing happens. That bunch of food-coupon-grabbing good-for-nothing welfare dumb-asses get whatever they can from the US, the French and the Brits before the dung hits the fan, we get the hell out and they go back to incest and alcoholism. Why the hell are you so concerned about them all of a sudden? Jesus, Telman, you haven't gone soft on us just because you saw a few sherpas and their cute little kids, have you? You might get to be our representative to Thulahn, Telman, you ain't our ambassador to the fucking UN. Goddamnit, Telman! Now you've got me swearing! What the hell's wrong with you!'

'Jeb? Mr Dessous?'

'*What?*'

'I suspect we're getting Couffabled.'

There was a near silence at the other end of the line. Listening carefully through the odd lilt of white noise the scrambling circuit added to the connection, I could just hear Dessous breathing. I hadn't even been sure that he would recognise the name of the French exec who'd cheated the Business out of what it saw as rightly its own, over a century ago. Obviously he did. He cleared his throat. 'You serious, Telman?'

'I'm afraid so.'

'Okay. So, how significant is the operation?'

'It's at your level, Jeb.'

Another pause. 'The hell it is, huh?'

'I thought maybe you were in on it, but now I don't think you are.'

'Uh-huh.'

'But I don't know enough yet. And I can't start accusing anybody. I just wanted someone to know.'

'I see. Well. You be careful what you're getting into there, Telman.'

'I'm trying to be.'

In the evening, after the funeral and after all the rest of the mourners had left, Miss Heggies and I sat up round the fire in the little living room just off the main kitchen, drinking whisky and reminiscing.

Madame Tchassot had been chauffeured back to Leeds-Bradford and her Lear jet, the locals had retreated to the pub where Uncle F had put a couple of grand behind the bar for them to have a proper wake to mourn his passing, and Mrs Watkins had returned to her Leeds hotel. Freddy's few relations, all distant, had made themselves so, despite having been invited to stay. I got the impression Miss H was relieved they hadn't accepted. I hoped I wasn't spoiling things by being the only one to stay, and – after a couple of drams – I said as much.

'Oh, you're no trouble, Ms Telman.' (I'd suggested we might

try first names, but Miss H had seemed almost girlishly embarrassed, and shaken her head.) 'It's always been a pleasure to have you here.'

'Even the time I got stuck in the dumb-waiter?'

'Ah, well, you weren't the first, or the last.'

This had happened the second time I'd been brought to Blysecrag by Mrs Telman, when I'd been ten. The first time I'd been so stunned and awestruck by the place I'd barely dared to sit down. When I'd visited a second time I'd been a lot more blasé, and had decided to explore. The dumb-waiter I'd elected to do some of my exploring in had got stuck and it took several strong men a couple of hours to rescue me. Uncle Freddy had thought it was all quite a hoot and had sent down supplies of cakes and lemonade (to my intense embarrassment, he'd also hollered down that I was just to shout out if I needed a chamber-pot lowered to me, too).

'Has anyone ever explored every single nook and cranny of this place?'

'Mr Ferrindonald did, when he first bought it,' Miss Heggies said. 'And I think I have. Though I'm not sure you can ever be certain.'

'You never get lost?'

'Not for years. Sometimes I have to think where I am, mind.' Miss Heggies sipped at her whisky. 'Mr Ferrindonald used to tell me he knew of secret passages that he wasn't telling me about, but I think he was just teasing me. He always said he'd leave the map in his will, but, well . . .'

'I'm going to miss Freddy,' I said.

Miss Heggies nodded. 'He could be a rascal sometimes, but he was a good employer. And a friend to me.' She looked sad.

'Were you glad he never married?'

She looked sharply at me. 'Glad, Ms Telman?'

'I'm sorry. I hope you don't mind me asking. I just always felt that this was almost as much your house as his, and if he'd brought a wife here, well, you'd have had to share the place with her too.'

'I hope I'd have got on as well with her as I did with him,' Miss Heggies said, only a little defensively. 'I suppose it would have depended on the wife, but I would have done my best.'

'What if Uncle Freddy had married Mrs Watkins? Could you have got on with her?'

She looked away. 'I think so.'

'She seemed pleasant enough, I thought.'

'Yes. Pleasant enough.'

'Do you think she loved him?'

Miss Heggies drew herself up in her chair and smoothed her hair with one hand. 'I really wouldn't be able to say, Ms Telman.'

'I hope she did, don't you? It would be good to know that someone loved him. Everyone should have that.'

She was silent for a while. 'I think many of us did, in our various ways.'

'Did you, Miss Heggies?'

She sniffed, and looked into her whisky glass. 'I had a lot of affection for the old rogue. Whether you'd call it love, I don't know.' She looked me in the eye. 'We were never . . . linked, Ms Telman.' She looked at the ceiling and around the walls. 'Except by this place.'

'I see.'

'Any road, in the end it isn't my house, Ms Telman. Never was. I am a servant; he could have dismissed me at any time. I don't mean that he ever threatened me with that, or ever reminded me of it, just that it's always at the back of your mind.'

'Well, that can't happen now.'

She nodded. 'It was very good of Mr Ferrindonald to leave me the flat and to provide for me.'

'Will you stay here once it's handed over to the National Trust?'

She looked mildly shocked. 'Of course.'

'I imagine they might want to employ you. Actually, I think they'd be foolish not to. Would you work for them?'

'I might.' She nodded. 'It would depend. If I was wanted, I'd be happy to.'

'I suspect Uncle Freddy would have liked that.'

'Do you?'

'Definitely.'

She looked round again, took a deep breath and said, 'This has been my love, Ms Telman, this place. I've been in service here one way or another for nearly fifty years, since I left school, for your uncle, his business, the army and the Cowle family. I've never thought to marry, never wanted to. Blysecrag's been all I've ever needed.' She lifted her head up. 'There are those here and in the village who think I've missed out on life, but I don't think I have, not at all. There's plenty of others to fall in love and have lots of children. I've given my life to this house, and I haven't regretted it . . . well, not for more than an hour or two at a time, and then not often.' She gave a small, flickering, vulnerable smile. 'We all have our blues, don't we? But I wouldn't have changed anything, if I could have.' She laughed lightly and swirled her whisky as she looked at it. 'Goodness me, listen to me. I'll be dancing on the tables next.'

I raised my glass. 'To Blysecrag,' I said.

And so we drank a toast to the place, and maybe to places in general.

'Suvinder? Hi. How are you?'

'Oh, Kathryn. I'm sorry. I did not mean to call you. I must have pressed the wrong button. Umm. Are you well? You sound sleepy.'

'That's okay. I'm fine. You all right?'

'I am well, but I had better go or you will be upset with me. Say you forgive me for calling you so late.'

'I forgive you.'

'I bid you good night, Kathryn.'

'Good night, sweet prince.'

'Oh, Kathryn!'

'That's a quotation, Suvinder.'

'I know! But you said it to me! I shall sleep well. Good night, dearest Kathryn.'

I rang Adrian Poudenhaut the following morning. He was in Italy, picking up his new Ferrari from the factory in Modena; he'd be driving it back to the UK over the next couple of days. I told him I wanted to meet up with him and he sounded surprised, so I reckoned Madame Tchassot hadn't said anything to him. We arranged to rendezvous in Switzerland the following day.

# CHAPTER
# TWELVE

Miss Heggies drove me to York in her old Volvo estate. I think we both had slight hangovers. I took a GNER train to London (tea reasonable; opened the lap-top but beyond playing a few variations with the calculator on a certain ten-figure number, didn't do anything, just sat staring out of the window and decided the best bit of the east-coast mainline was definitely from York northwards, not south; played k. d. lang's *Ingenue* on the Walkman and sang along in my head. Where is your head, indeed, Kathryn?).

Taxi to Heathrow (annoying driver; did not take I'm Reading A Newspaper hint and only finally shut up when I put the earphones in). Played Kate and Anna McGarrigle's *Matapedia* all the way along the M4. Folk; not the sort of thing I'm usually into, but just sublime. Degree of tearfulness at some of the tracks; running repairs to face required in lounge rest room; gave self talking to. Swissair flight to Geneva; service coolly correct and flawless as usual. LWB silver-coloured 7-series company car to Château d'Oex; elderly but efficient driver – called Hans – thankfully silent.

Switzerland. Where the money comes. I have mixed feelings about the place. On the one hand it is sumptuously beautiful in a rugged, blatant and snowy way, and everything works. On the other hand they shout at you for crossing the street when there's no traffic visible for miles, just because the crossing signal is showing a red man not a green man, and if you pass them in a car doing a kilometre more than the legal limit, they honk their horns and flash their lights.

Plus, it's where all the Third World dictators and other assorted robbing bastards stash the loot they've sucked out of their own countries and their own people. This is a whole country where money goes to money; this is one of the richest nations on Earth, and some of the dosh comes from some of the poorest countries (who, once they've been bled dry by the latest thieving scumbag, then get the IMF stepping in with orders to Tighten Their Belts).

Somehow, being whisked along the N1 towards Lausanne, in the midst of all the other Beemers, Mercs, Audis, Jags, Bentleys, Rollers, Lexi and the rest, it all looked even more self-satisfied and opulent than it usually did. The snow-topped mountains around the lake alone appeared aloof from it all. Even those, though, didn't look quite the same any more. One of the things I've always liked about Switzerland is that they've civilised a lot of their hills: you can get cable cars up there, you can drive up them, between them, through them and underneath them, or climb into a train and be clunked and trundled to cafés and restaurants at the top where the only things more breathtaking than the views are the prices. Then you can ski back down. I always appreciated that; that accessibility, that refusal to treat each and every peak as something which absolutely had to be left pristine, so that only the mountaineers and the local fauna ever got to appreciate it. And I still liked the idea in theory, yet now, looking at the peaks across the lake, I couldn't help comparing them unfavourably with those of Thulahn, and almost scorning them for being so compromised, so tamed.

Fuck me, I thought, I'm going native. I gave a single snort of laughter through my nose. Hans the white-haired driver glanced at me, saw I wasn't trying to attract his attention, and promptly looked away again. I slipped Joni M's latest into the Walkman, but only half listened.

I'd left my phone off for the journey as far as Geneva. I'd switched it back on when I got into the BMW but deliberately hadn't checked on any messages or previous callers. It rang as we were passing Vevey and turning up into the mountains for the long loop round to Château d'Oex. I looked at the incoming number. I found myself smiling.

'Hello?'

'Kathryn.'

'Suvinder. How are you?'

'I am well. I thought I might call at a more civilised hour and enquire how everything went at Freddy's funeral. It was bad enough that I could not come myself, but, well, there was so

351

much to be done here, and I had just come back. Did it all go . . . I don't know the right word. Fittingly?'

'It did. A Viking's funeral.' (I had to explain to Suvinder about what a Viking's funeral was.) 'And Miss Heggies sends her regards.'

'That is kind of her. She always made me feel most welcome.'

'I used to find her scary at first, but I had a good long talk to her, just last night.' I looked up at the mountains around us.

'Yes? Kathryn? Hello.'

'Sorry. Yes. A good talk. Suvinder?'

'Yes?'

'Nah. Nothing.' I'd been going to say I might be back in Thulahn before too long, but I didn't know how to say something like that to him without investing it with too much in the way of implication. So I settled for, 'How is everybody?'

'All here are well, though my mother learned of my proposal to you and was highly upset. She is still not speaking to me, for which alone I owe you a favour, I think.'

'Suvinder, shame on you for saying such a thing. You should go to her and try to make amends.'

'I will not apologise for what I asked. Nor will I retract my offer to you, not even to please her. She must learn to move with the times. And also that I am the ruler, not her.'

'Well, good for you, but you should still try to make up.'

'I suppose I should. Yes, you are right. I will see her tomorrow. If she will see me.'

'Well, I'd send her my regards, but I don't think it would be a good idea for you to mention that.'

'I think it would be politic not to.' I heard him sigh. 'Kathryn, I must go.'

'Okay, Suvinder. You look after yourself. All right?'

'I will. You too.'

I clicked the phone off. I sat there, tapping its little warm black body against my other hand, looking out at the mountains and thinking.

Château d'Oex is, as I've said, the closest thing we have to a world HQ. The compound starts just above the town itself, on the far side of the railroad tracks. It doesn't look like much, considering: a big old château that looks like it can't decide whether it really is a château or a Schloss, lots of grounds – the sort of grounds that get bigger the longer you look at them, following walls and fences that are as discreetly concealed as possible – and a mountainside scattered with smaller buildings and houses. Blysecrag is a far more impressive sight.

The bit above ground, however, is not even half the story. Some people have tried to nickname the place the Iceberg, because so much of it is hidden under the surface.

In the dusk, Château d'Oex the town looked rich and neat and tidy as ever. It had snowed recently and the place looked quite picturesque, in a neat and tidy way. I swear they clean the slush. The road to the compound swept over the railway and up to a tall set of gates and a designer guardhouse. One of the three guards recognised me and nodded, but they checked my passport anyway.

The gates hummed open with an inertia-rich deliberation that would make you wary of taking anything flimsier than a main battle tank through them uninvited. The 7-series purred upwards past the trees and the crisply white lawns and pastures, its way lit by ornamental light clusters with three softly glowing white globes apiece, and – on about every fifth or sixth lamp – a little CCTV camera.

The château swung into view, tastefully floodlit and looking chocolate-box pretty against the black and white of the wooded mountainside beyond. Above it, necklaces of white road lights wiggled on up the slope to higher buildings.

The mostly male staff at the château went gliding around, white-jacketed, efficient, seeming to do the old Miss Heggies trick of materialising and dematerialising at will. I was welcomed with nods and clicked heels, my bags disappeared apparently of their own volition, my coat slipped silently and almost unnoticed from my shoulders and I was escorted through the baroque and glowing foyer towards the gleaming elevators in the dreamlike state that usually afflicted me here. I nodded to people I knew, exchanged travel pleasantries with the white-jacketed guy carrying my briefcase, but it all seemed dissociated from reality. If you'd asked me when I got to my room and was settling in which language I'd been talking to the guy in the white jacket, I couldn't have told you for sure.

My room looked down the slope of the mountainside towards the town. The mountains across the valley were the colour of the moon. The room was large: the sort of space hotels tend to call a mini suite. It had antique furniture, two balconies, a bigger bed than usual, and a bathroom with a separate shower stall. Flowers, chocolates and newspapers had been delivered, and a half-bottle of champagne. You become very sensitised to the minutiae of Business perks and privileges over the years, and the precise level of luxury that greets you at Château d'Oex is entirely the most accurate guide to how you're doing within your current status in the hierarchy.

This was up to Level Two standards. The champagne was only a half-bottle but, then, I was by myself and it doesn't do to encourage one's guests to get too sozzled before dinner. And it was vintage; big plus. The phone rang and the general manager of the château welcomed me and apologised for not being able to greet me in person. I assured him everything was fine and to my taste.

I took Dulsung's little artificial flower and stuck it in a glass on the bedside table. It looked tiny and forlorn there, even cheap. What if the staff threw it out? I picked it up and put it back on my jacket, in the button-hole, but it didn't look right there either, so I stuck it inside, bending the stalk through the button-hole in the single internal pocket so that it was secure.

Dinner was promptly at eight in the main dining room; there were maybe a hundred or so staffers. I gossiped with the best of them, before, during and after. The château is, usually, the place to find out what's going on in the Business. Mostly people wanted to find out what was going on in Thulahn from me. The quality of the questions they asked indicated the accuracy of the rumours they'd heard, and corresponded pretty accurately to their level in the company.

Had I just come back from Fenua Ua? (No.) Was there some back-up deal being arranged in Thulahn in case Fenua Ua went belly-up at the last moment? (I couldn't say.) Was I going to be president of Fenua Ua? (Unlikely.) Was the deal done yet or not? (I really couldn't say.) Had the Prince really proposed to me? (Yes.) Had I accepted? (No.) So I answered a lot of questions, but I was able to ask a lot in return, and people were happier than they might have been otherwise to share all they knew or felt about a whole host of subjects. At the end of that evening, even if only for a short time, I probably knew as much about the Business as a whole as anybody did, regardless of level.

Madame Tchassot, who kept a house in the grounds, was present at the meal and after it; the only Level One. We talked for a few minutes over brandy in the drawing room and she seemed quite friendly. She would be spending the next few days at her own place, near Lucerne.

'Adrian tells me you're meeting him tomorrow, Kathryn.'

'That's right. I wanted to talk to him.' I smiled. 'He seems very proud of his new car. 355, I think he said. Sounds nice.'

She smiled thinly. 'Red is not his colour, but he insisted.'

'Well, it is a Ferrari. I think it's almost compulsory.'

'You are meeting for lunch?'

'Yes, in a place near the Grimsel Pass. He recommended it.'

She looked uncertain. 'You will take good care of him, yes?'

'Of course,' I said. What was she talking about? She was staring intently at her glass. She didn't think I had any designs on his tumid butt, did she?

'Thank you. He is . . . important to me. Very dear.'

'Of course, I understand. I'll try to make sure he leaves me in one piece.' I laughed lightly. 'Why? He's not a bad driver, is he? I was thinking of asking for a drive in the Ferrari.'

'No, no, he is a perfectly fine driver, I think.'

'Well, that's a relief.' I raised my glass. 'To careful drivers.'

'Indeed.'


In my dream, I was in a great house in the mountains. There was bright moonlight and starlight, but the stars were wrong and I remember thinking I must be in New Zealand. The great house was built on a vast rumpled landscape of spired and crevassed ice tipped between two mountain ranges. It didn't seem in the least strange to me that the building had been constructed on a glacier, though the whole place creaked and trembled as it moved with the rest of our immediate landscape down the vast slow river of ice. With each rumble and creak beneath us, a host of diamond chandeliers tinkled, mirrors flexed and distorted, and cracks appeared in the ceilings and walls, sprinkling white dust. White-overalled servants rushed to repair the fissures, clattering up ladders and shinning up skinny poles to slap fresh plaster across the faults, raining white damp dots. This happened a lot. We held umbrellas above us as we walked through the huge, echoing rooms. Marble statues were real people who had stood too long in one place under the drizzle of plaster.

Teams of yaks moved through constantly branching tunnels in the ice beneath us, only surfacing at the great house, where their smiling, round-faced minders thanked us for soup and their beds in the many tents scattered across the icy scenery.

A masked man I knew not to trust was doing a complicated trick with cups and hats and my little netsuke monkey, shifting them around the table while people placed bets and laughed. The masked man's mouth was visible and he was missing lots of teeth, but they weren't really missing at all: some had been blacked out as though he was an actor.

I woke up, wondering where I was again. Thulahn? Not cold enough. But, then, I'd been moved to a more hotel-like room. But still not Thulahn. I remembered the smell of the Heavenly Luck Tea House. Yorkshire? No. London? No, Château d'Oex. Ah yes. Nice room. Valley view. Alone. Nobody here. I felt groggily across the bed. No, no one here. Monkey gone. This monkey's gone to heaven – wasn't that a Pixies' song? Dulsung. Why hadn't she been in my dream? And who's this 'we' anyway, white man? Na, nothing. Sleep again.

*　　*　　*

357

There was time to kill at the Grimsel Pass. I sat in the 7-series waiting for Poudenhaut, reading the *Herald Tribune*. The phone rang and it was, at last, Stephen.

'Kathryn? Hi. Sorry for the delay. Daniella was running a serious temperature and Emma was away at one of her friend's so I had to do the hospital thing. She's okay now but, well, hence the delay.'

'That's all right. It's good to hear you.'

'What was it you wanted to talk about? Nothing too urgent, I hope.'

'Hold on.' I got out of the car, only just beating Happy Hans, my white-haired chauffeur, to the draw: he had his cap on, he was out of his door and reaching for the outside handle of my door while I was still pushing. He drew the door fully open as I got out into the chill air of the early afternoon. The car park was gravel, uneven. I nodded to Hans and let him put my coat over my shoulders before I walked off, heading away from the quaintly painted old wooden inn and the other cars and coaches.

'Kathryn?'

I stopped at the low wall, looking down the valley at the road winding into Italy.

'Still here, Stephen,' I said. 'Listen, what I have to tell you is pretty bad news.'

'Oh, yeah?' He sounded only a little wary at first. 'What? How bad?'

I took a deep breath. The air was cold; I could feel its raw, numbing touch in my nostrils and at the back of my throat and could sense it filling my lungs. 'It's about Emma.'

I told him. He was silent, mostly. I told him all of it: about the DVD, Hazleton's involvement, the dates and places and the obligation that Hazleton expected of me. He was so quiet

I wondered if perhaps none of this was coming as a great shock at all. Maybe, I thought, they had an open relationship that he'd never wanted to tell me about in case it encouraged me. Maybe Hazleton had been upset that I'd told him I'd made my mind up but that I wasn't going to tell him what my decision was yet, and he had told Stephen.

But no. Stephen was just stunned. He hadn't really started to guess, or if he had entertained any suspicions whatsoever they had been the sort that occur to you unbidden, as purely theoretical constructs, the sort of thing that an imaginative mind throws up as a matter of course, but which the moral self dismisses as preposterous, and even feels shameful to be associated with.

He said, 'Yes,' once or twice, and, 'I see,' and, 'Right.'

'Stephen, I'm sorry.' Silence. 'That's hopelessly inadequate, I know.' More silence. 'I just hope you . . . Stephen, I've thought about this for a long time. Two weeks. I didn't know what to do. I still don't know that I'm doing the right thing. I think it's all pretty horrible, including Hazleton's part in it, and making me have anything to do with it, too. I want you to know I'm not enjoying this. I'm trying to be straight with you, trying to be honest. I could have got Hazleton to let you know without me being—'

'All right!' he said loudly, almost shouting. Then, 'Sorry. All right, Kathryn. I take the point. I guess you did the right thing.'

I looked up at the blue, blue sky. 'You're going to hate me for this, aren't you?'

'I don't know what I'm going to feel, Kathryn. I feel . . . I don't know. Winded. Yeah, sort of winded, like when you fall on your back and can't breathe, but . . . hey, a lot worse, you know?'

'Yeah, I know. Stephen, I'm so sorry.'

'Oh. Well. I guess it had to be done. Jeez.' He sounded like he might be about to laugh or cry. Breath whistled out of him. 'Some start to the day.'

'Is Emma there?'

'No, still away ... Well, just coming back today. God, the bitch.'

'You take it easy, okay?'

'Huh? Yeah, sure. Sure. Ah, and thanks. I guess.'

'Look, call me whenever, all right? Get your breath back. But keep in touch. Call me later. Will you?'

'Ah, yeah. Yeah, right. I'll . . . Goodbye, Kathryn. Goodbye.'

'Good – ' The phone clicked off. ' – bye,' I said.

I closed my eyes. Somewhere down the road, in Italy, I could hear the muted rasp of a high-performance engine, coming closer.


Lunch was a disappointment. Poudenhaut couldn't stop talking about his car, a shiny red 355 soft-top with a black hood. He'd driven me here in it, keeping the revs below five thousand because even though the engine was meant to have been run-in on the bench he just wanted to be sure. Hans and the BMW would appear here later to take me back to the château. We were in a modern glass and steel restaurant in the trees above an archetypically twee village that looked like it was composed of scaled-up cuckoo clocks: on the hour you expected a door under the eaves to flap open and Heidi to bounce out at the end of a giant spring.

We both drank spring water. The food was Swiss-German, not my favourite cuisine, so it was easy to save plenty of space for a pudding, which was satisfyingly rich and chocolaty.

Poudenhaut tore his gaze away from the Ferrari again (he'd insisted on a table with a view of the car park). 'Yes, why did you want to see me?'

Nettle-grasping time again. 'I wanted to ask you what you were doing at the Silex plant the other day.'

His big, puffy face stared at me over our gently steaming coffee. He blinked a few times. I wondered which way he'd jump. 'Silex?' he said. He frowned and concentrated on stirring some sugar into his espresso.

'You know, the chip plant in Scotland. What took you up there, Adrian?'

I watched him decide. He wasn't going for total denial. Something closer to the truth. 'I was looking into something.'

'What was that?'

'Well, I can't say.'

'Was this for Mr Hazleton?'

He stirred his coffee slowly, then brought the little cup to his lips. 'Mm-hmm,' he said, and sipped.

'I see,' I said. 'I take it he had his suspicions too, then.'

'Suspicions?'

'About what was going on in there.'

He put on a serious face. 'Hmm.' His gaze flickered all over me.

'Come to any conclusions?'

He shrugged. 'How about you?'

I sat closer, leaning into the fragrant vapours rising from my coffee. 'There was something hidden in there.'

'In the plant?'

'Yes. Ideal place, when you think about it. Chip factories have brilliant security anyway. You know how much chips are worth:

more than their weight in gold. So the places are really well guarded. Then there's the whole prophylactic rigmarole you have to go through to get into the production facilities; all that changing and delay. Impossible to just charge in. Giving people inside time to hide stuff, if you know somebody who might ask awkward questions is coming in. Plus there are all those deeply noxious chemicals they use, the etching fluids, the solvents and washes; really nasty chemical-warfare stuff any rational person would keep well away from. So as well as all the usual security paraphernalia, the guards and walls and cameras and so on, and the sheer difficulty of accessing the place quickly, you've got a serious health disincentive to go there in the first place. It's perfect, the ideal place to hide whatever. I took a look round three or four weeks ago, but I couldn't find anything.'

Poudenhaut was nodding thoughtfully. 'Yes, well, that's what occurred to us, too. So, what do you think it was? Or is?'

'Oh, it's gone now, but I think they had another assembly line going in there.'

He blinked. 'Chips?'

'What else would you build in a chip plant?'

'Hmm,' he said, smiling briefly. 'I see.' He pursed his lips and nodded, staring at the table where the bill had just appeared.

'I'll get this,' I said, picking up the check.

He reached out too late. 'No, please. This is mine.'

'That's okay, I got it.' I reached down for my handbag.

He snatched the bill out of my fingers. 'Male prerogative,' he said, grinning. I hid behind my best chilly smile and thought, Suddenly you're *far* too full of beans, my lad. He fished his company card out of his wallet. 'So, who do you think was cheating on us, who was behind it? The management at the plant? Ligence Corps? They're our partners there, right?'

'That's right. Obviously the upper management must have known: you couldn't do it without them. But I think it was somebody in the Business.'

He looked alarmed. 'Really? Oh dear. That's bad. Any ideas? What level?'

'Your level, Adrian.'

He paused, blinking again, his card poised half-way to the plate the check had arrived on. 'My level?'

'Level Two,' I said reasonably, spreading my hands.

'Oh, yes.' The plate was taken away again.

'So, did you find out anything? Does Mr Hazleton have any ideas?'

He made a clicking noise with his mouth. 'We have our suspicions, but it would be wrong to say anything at this point in time, Kathryn.'

I waited until he was signing the card slip before I said, 'Of course, it could be a Level One conspiracy. Somebody at Mr Hazleton's level.'

His Mont Blanc hesitated over the tip line. He added a round number that was a little on the mean side and signed. 'Mr Hazleton has considered that possibility,' he said smoothly. He nodded at the *maître d'* and stood. 'Shall we?'


'Grips like nothing else. Just listen to that engine. Isn't that wonderful? I think you hear it better in a cabriolet, even with the top up.'

'Mm-hmm,' I said. I'd been reading the handbook; I put it back in the glove-box with the spare set of keys and the purchase paperwork.

Poudenhaut was a poor driver; even allowing for the fact that he was trying to be kind to the engine, he changed up too early and still didn't seem entirely to have the hang of the car's open gate. His cornering was awful, too, and the fact the car was right-hand-drive was no excuse either: he seemed to think hitting the apex meant driving into the depths of the bend then jerking the wheel round in roughly the correct direction, seeing where he was heading now, then making any necessary corrections (repeat as required until the road straightens). We zoomed and dived along some wonderfully winding, empty mountain roads in one of the best sports cars in the world, but I was getting heartily sick of the experience. He wouldn't even put the top down because clouds had moved in from the west and there had been a few flakes of snow.

'I'd love a shot,' I said between corners. 'Would you let me drive? Just for a bit.'

'Well, I don't know. There's the insurance . . .' It was the most worried he'd sounded so far. 'I'd love to let you, Kathryn, but—'

'I'm insured.'

'But, Kathryn, this is a Ferrari.'

'I've driven Ferraris. Uncle Freddy used to lend me the Daytona when I was staying at Blysecrag sometimes.'

'Oh? Well, yes, but that's front-engined, you see, quite different handling characteristics. The 355 is mid-engined. Much trickier on the limit.'

'He let me loose in the F40, too. And, of course, I wouldn't be going anywhere near the limit.'

He glanced at me. 'He let you drive the F40?'

'A couple of times.'

'I never drove the F40.' He sounded like a disappointed schoolboy. 'What's it like?'

'Brutal.'

'Brutal?'

'Brutal.'

We stopped at a semi-circular gravel terrace on a wide corner near the summit of a pass, just above the tree-line.

He pulled the car up and tapped his fingers on the steering-wheel, then turned to me with a grin and let his gaze fall to my knees. I was wearing a skirt and jacket, silk blouse; just business-like, nothing provocative. 'If I let you have a shot of the car, what do I get in return?' He reached out and put his hand on my knee. It was warm and slightly damp.

I think I made my mind up then. I lifted his hand off and put it back on his own thigh, smiled and said, 'We'll see.'

He smiled. 'She's all yours.' He got out; he held the driver's door open for me. I slipped in. The engine was still running, idling quietly. The door closed with a thunk. I felt in my bag, pulled out my phone and checked the display. We had signal. I clicked the central locking while Poudenhaut was moving round the front of the car.

He hesitated when he heard the locks click, then tried the passenger's door. He bent down, knocking at the window glass with one crooked finger. 'Hello? May I come in?' He was still smiling.

I fastened my seat-belt. 'I think you've been lying to me, Adrian,' I told him. I tested the accelerator, blipping the engine up towards the four thousand revs mark and letting it fall back again.

'Kathryn?' he said, as though he hadn't heard me properly.

'I said, I think you've been lying to me, Adrian. I'm not convinced you don't know more about this Silex thing than you're letting on.'

'What the hell are you talking about?'

'I think you know exactly what I'm talking about, Adrian. And I'd like to ask you a few more questions about what was really in there.' I reached into my bag and waved a piece of plastic and metal at him. 'And needed lots of heavy-duty phone connectors like this.'

He stared through the glass with a look of utter fury, then stood up, glanced around and ran behind the car. I watched in the rear-view mirror while he found a couple of large rocks from the side of the road; he ran back quickly and wedged them on either side of the car's offside rear wheel, stamping them into place. I reached over and tested the glove-box; still open. I pulled the keys out, letting the engine die, locked the glove-box on the key, then restarted the engine. Poudenhaut clapped his hands free of dust as he came back to the window. 'You were a bit slow there, Kathryn,' he said, bending to look in at me.

He sat on the car's wing, looking out at the road. I could still hear his voice quite clearly through the hood's layers of fabric. 'I suppose what we have here is a Mexican stand-off, isn't that what they call it?' He swivelled at the hips and looked round at me through the windscreen. 'Come on, Kathryn. If you're upset I put my hand on your knee, if that's what this is all about, we'll forget it ever happened. I don't know what you're talking about with this Silex thing and phone lines and so on, but let's at least discuss it like adults. You're just being childish. Come on, let me back into the car.'

'What was really going on, Adrian? Was it a dealing room? Is that what you had in there? Was that what the hidden room was all about?'

'Kathryn, if you don't stop this nonsense I'm just going to

have to . . .' He patted his breast pocket, but his phone was in the car, connected to a hands-free kit. He smiled and spread his hands. 'Well, I suppose I'll just have to flag down the next car. The Swiss police won't be very happy about this, Kathryn, if they have to get involved.'

'Were you in on what happened to Mike Daniels, Adrian, or was that just Colin Walker on his own? Well, alone apart from the bimbo and the dentist?'

He stared at me, his mouth open. He closed it.

'And the wheeze of sending a number to Mr Shinizagi like that. What was it – a bank sort code? Account number? That must have been Mr Hazleton's idea, right? He's into numbers and puzzles and shit, isn't he? You can count to over a thousand using your fingers; he ever mention that to you? And, of course, if you use somebody's teeth as binary code, you can count to over two billion, or transmit up to a ten-figure number.'

He came rushing around the car and started pulling at the passenger door's handle. 'You just let me in now, you fucking bitch. You fucking smart-assed bitch, let me in now! Let me in or I'll tear this hood off with my own hands.'

'Your Swiss army knife's in the glove-box with the spare keys, Ade. Oh, what were you keeping the revs down to, Ade? Five thousand, wasn't it?' I blipped the accelerator for longer this time. The rev counter's needle swung sharply up: to six, then seven thousand. The rev counter was red-lined at eight and a half thousand, though it went up from there to ten thousand. The engine screamed, making a wonderful metallic, spine-tingling yowl; a noise that must have echoed off nearby mountains and very possibly exceeded the drive-by noise regulations of several Swiss cantons.

'What are you doing?' Poudenhaut shouted. 'Stop that!'

I stepped on the gas again; the engine responded instantly, producing another fabulous pulse of sound. 'Woah, we were up to eight thousand that time, Adrian,' I told him. 'Nearly into the red.'

He'd given up pulling at the door handle, possibly afraid that he'd break it. He was standing a couple of metres away, looking utterly distraught and trembling, whether with fear or rage it was hard to tell.

I stamped on the accelerator, pushing it briefly to the floor this time. The noise was crushing, vast, furious, like a whole pride of lions screaming in your ear at once. The needle on the rev counter flicked briefly into the red area on the dial, then fell away again and clunked back towards the idling zone. 'We hit the red zone there, Adrian. Can't be doing the car any good.'

'Fuck off! Just fuck off! Fuck you! Fuck you, you cunt! It's just fucking metal. Fuck you!' He looked like he was crying. He turned on his heel and stamped off towards the road, shoulders hunched. I let him get to the metalled surface, then floored the gas pedal and held it there for a few seconds. The car quaked, the engine screamed, wailing like something in the utmost extremity of agony. It would have been a hard thing to do for anybody with the slightest amount of mechanical sympathy, and I wasn't enjoying it but, then, it was a means to an end, and in the end our Adrian was right: it was just metal. No matter what it sounded like, the only real suffering was being done by him. Poudenhaut shook as he heard this noise, then he spun round and came charging back. He beat on the hood with his fists. 'Stop it! Stop it! Stop it! My car! Stop it!'

'Can you smell that, Adrian? Smells like burning oil or something, don't you think? Oh, look, there's a red light on in here. Can't imagine that bodes too well.' I blipped the throttle again. The engine caterwauled, metallic and harsh. 'That sound different to you? I thought it sounded different that time. More of a metallic edge, seemed to me. What do you think? Here, have another listen . . .'

'Stop it! Stop it!'

'You'd better answer my questions, Adrian, or soon I'm going to get bored and then I'll just keep my foot planted pedal to the metal until the fucker seizes.'

'You fucking *bitch*!'

'Here we go, Adrian.'

'All right! What?'

'Sorry?' I said.

I pressed a finger to the window lift, depressing it slightly so that the window cracked open by about a centimetre. He forced his fingers through the gap and tried to shove the window down further. I hit the button again and the window started to lift, trapping his fingers between the top edge of the glass and the fabric-covered metal frame of the hood. He screamed.

'Shit,' I said, 'I didn't think you could do that with a modern car. I thought they were all supposed to have a sensor or something that stopped that happening.'

Poudenhaut tried to pull his fingers free, but couldn't. 'You fucking bitch! My fingers!'

'What do you reckon, Adrian? Are Ferrari above fitting that sort of namby-pamby safety device, or do you think it's just not working? I don't know. I'm still not convinced that Fiat have all the reliability concerns licked. Never mind. Going into the red again here, Ade.' Another swinging, rasping, screaming bellow of noise.

'All right!'

'What?' I lifted my phone and studied the display.

'All right! Fucking let me go!'

'Pardon, Adrian? What was that?' I punched some numbers, listened, then hit some more.

'I said all right! Can't you fucking hear me? All right!'

'What?' I was still fiddling with the phone, jabbing numbers. I held it up to the window. 'You'll have to repeat that, Adrian.'

'It was a dealing room!'

'In Silex?'

'Yes! So fucking what? We could have fucking *lost* money too, you know!'

'The value of your investments can go down as well as up,' I agreed.

'It doesn't matter! It's all over. We sent the money to Shinizagi! That's what he wanted! Daniels raped his daughter; the fucker deserved worse! Who fucking cares anyway? Let me *go*! Ah! My fucking fingers!'

'What's it all for, Adrian?' I asked, still holding the phone up to the window. 'What was the money for? What is Shinizagi supposed to do with it?'

'I don't know!'

'Oh, bad answer, Adrian. Could cost you a brand new engine.' I hit the throttle. The engine zinged monstrously. It really didn't sound right now. I thought I caught a puff of ominously grey-blue smoke in the rear-view mirror.

'I don't fucking know! Something to do with Fenua Ua, maybe, but he wouldn't tell me! You fucking bitch! My fingers are breaking!'

'Hazleton wouldn't tell you?'

'No! I didn't need to know! It's just a guess! I'm just guessing!'

'Hmm,' I said. I let the window down a fraction.

'You cunt,' he hissed, and tried to shove his hands in towards my throat. I leant back and pressed the window up again, trapping him by the wrists. He gurgled, his fingers waving near my face like pink anemones.

I felt in my bag and brought out an aerosol can. 'Not wise, Adrian. This is Mace. Very bad for your eyes and mucous membranes. Could ruin your whole day. I think you ought to back off. I've already called the police. If you behave yourself they may accept it was all a terrible mistake, otherwise I'm going to get very tearful and upset and claim you've been trying to assault me. Put yourself in their place: who would you believe?'

'You fucking bitch,' he sobbed. 'I'll fucking get you for this.'

'No, Adrian. You won't. Because if you try to, I'll do much worse things to you than this. Now, lean back. Lean back on your heels. Let your arms take your weight. That's it.' I pressed the window lift button again; down, then up. His hands pulled free as he staggered back. He stood on the gravel, rubbing his wrists and tenderly massaging his fingers, his face streaked with tears. I held the phone up so he could see it and hit the off button, then dialled Happy Hans and told him where we were.

'What about the police?' Poudenhaut asked, glancing warily up the switch back road.

'Don't worry,' I said. I hadn't called the police, just some-body's answerphone. The Mace wasn't Mace, either; it was a can of Armani. I nodded at the low wall at the edge of the gravel semi-circle. 'Why don't you go and sit down, Adrian?' I turned the car's engine off. It sputtered down to silence, then started to tick and click behind me.

371

Poudenhaut kneaded his fingers and looked at me with an expression full of rage and hate, but he went and sat down on the wall.

Hans brought the 7-series crunching on to the gravel about ten minutes later. He parked opposite, between me and Poudenhaut, then got out and held the door open for me. I waved Adrian goodbye, and got in. I looked back as we drove off. When we were about a hundred metres up the road, while Poudenhaut was staring through the open door at the Ferrari's steering column and turning to look towards us, I lowered my window and threw the 355's keys out.

'Kathryn?'

'Mr Hazleton.'

'I've spoken with Adrian Poudenhaut. He's very upset.'

'Yes, I think I'd be upset in his situation too, Mr Hazleton.'

'Apparently you made some rather wild allegations about me. Which he might have seemed to confirm, though of course it was done under considerable duress. Not the sort of thing that would stand up in court. In fact, the sort of behaviour that could very easily land *you* in court, Kathryn. I'm not sure what you did to poor Adrian isn't against the Geneva Convention.'

'Where are you, Mr Hazleton?'

'Where am I, Kathryn?'

'Yes, Mr Hazleton. We have these conversations on the phone and you quite often know where I am, whether it's in the middle of the Himalayas or on an obsolete cruise liner, but you're always just this placeless, disembodied voice floating in from the airwaves for me. I keep wondering where you are. Boston? That's where you live in the States, isn't it? Or Egham, on the Thames. That's your UK home, isn't it? Maybe you're here in Switzerland: I've no idea. I'd just like to know for once.'

'Well, Kathryn, I'm on a fishing boat off the island of St Kitts, in the Caribbean.'

'Weather nice?'

'A little hot. Whereabouts in Switzerland are you?'

'I'm walking in the grounds of the château,' I lied. I was nearby, but not in the compound itself. I was in a neat but damp little park in the town of Château d'Oex; I could see the château through the trees on the other side of the valley. If things were going according to plan, Hans the chauffeur would be there now, picking up my things from the rather swish two-balcony room.

I walked across springy black rubber tiles and sat on a child's swing. I looked warily around, not so much for Hazleton-controlled Business heavies like Colin Walker as for ordinary Swiss citizens, who'd probably shout at me for sitting on a swing meant for persons of less than a certain height and/or age. Nobody about. I was probably safe. I lifted my feet up and swung gently back and forth.

'There,' Hazleton said. 'Now we each know where the other is perhaps we can discuss more serious matters.'

'Ah, yes. Like your Couffabling antics.'

'Kathryn, you are probably already in deep trouble. I wouldn't make it any worse for yourself.'

'No, Mr Hazleton, I think you're the one in trouble. You're way up ordure inlet with no means of non-manual hydro-kinetic propulsion, and the sooner you drop this patronising now-look-here-young-lady bullshit the better.'

'What a colourful turn of phrase you employ, Kathryn.'

'Thank you. Yes, I'm firing on all cylinders, Mr H, which is probably more than can be said for Adrian's Ferrari.'

'Indeed. As I said, he is very upset.'

'Tough. So, let me run this past you, Mr H: a senior executive in a venerable but still vital business organisation specialising in long-term investment sets up an unofficial and cleverly sited dealing room in a factory which the very people he's cheating on are keeping secure. He makes, oh, I don't know how much money, stashes it in several accounts, probably here in the land of the oversize Toblerone bar, and then sends one of the account numbers to the chief executive officer of a Japanese corporation via an unorthodox route involving somebody's mouth. Oh, and this CEO – according to my latest research – has just resigned and bought himself his own golf course outside Kyoto. Now *that* must have cost a pretty penny, don't you think? However, most of the money will be used to buy a small and very low-lying piece of oceanic land, a personal pocket state for our enterprising exec. It's all a double-bluff, maybe even three-cup trick. The Business is fooled once, by its own decoy in the Pacific, while the Seats are fooled twice, once in the—'

'Kathryn, if I can just stop you there.'

'Yes, Mr Hazleton?'

'I'd just like to point out that the CIA and other US agencies regularly monitor cellphone transmissions in the Caribbean area. They're usually looking for drug-dealers, but I'm sure anything else of interest they happened to hear would be passed on to the relevant governmental department.'

'Such as the State Department?'

'Exactly. Let's just say I understand what you're getting at without you having to go into any more detail. It's all very interesting indeed, in a hypothetical sort of way, but where exactly does this leave us?'

'It leaves you with a choice, Mr Hazleton.'

'And what would you suggest that is? I suspect you're dying to tell me.'

'Beyond a confession extracted – and recorded, I might add – under some duress, a few specialised land-line connectors and some circumstantial stuff, I don't really have that much evidence.'

'Yes. And? But?'

'But the evidence must be there. I'm sure the Essex kids could be traced easily enough, for example, with the right resources.'

'The Essex kids?'

'That's what the regular people at Silex called the eager beavers wheeling and dealing for you in the secret room.'

'Ah-hah.'

'It wouldn't take much to get a serious investigation going, Mr Hazleton. Frankly I'm not entirely sure if there were other Level Ones involved, but I guess just telling all of them would get things moving.'

'That's the sort of thing that might split the Business, Kathryn. If there were other Board members involved.'

'That's a risk one might just have to take. Anyway, I suspect our fellow was acting alone. The point is that even if one or two others are implicated, the entire Board can't be involved or there would be no need to hide everything like this in the first place. No matter how you cut it, the person behind this scam would be in very serious trouble indeed.'

'Of course, they might be rich enough not to care.'

'They were rich enough not to have to undertake all this in the first place. The sort of person who'd organise this sort of wheeze does it because they love the organising, the gamesmanship of it all, the buzz of getting away with adding a zero to their personal worth just for the sheer hell of it, not because they actually need the money to spend on anything.'

'You shouldn't underestimate the developing ambitions of rich people, Kathryn. One might decide it would be interesting to take on Rupert Murdoch in the international media business, for example. That would take a lot of cash.'

'So would buying up a plot as expensive as the low-lying property we're talking about and then what? Selling it on to somebody else who might want their own state? Keeping it banked? Whatever. The person behind all this isn't going to be able to do any of that any more; they've been found out. The game is up and the ball is most comprehensively on the slates.'

'It is?'

'Scottish saying. Are you still with me, Mr H?'

'I think so. So, let's proceed on the basis of this hypothesis then. For amusement value only, of course.'

'Of course. Thing is, there might be a way out of a total loss situation for our hypothetical miscreant.'

'Might there?'

'If the person involved were to present the deal he had struck selfishly for himself to the organisation he is part of, if he were simply to give what he had worked for to his peers, asking for nothing from them except perhaps their thanks, then I think they might be surprised – even shocked – and suspicious, but they would be grateful, too. It would be nod-and-a-wink stuff, but they might decide not to investigate exactly how this *coup* was arrived at. They might simply accept the gift in the spirit in which it was apparently offered.'

'Hmm. Of course, the person doing the presenting might be watched rather carefully in future by the others, in case he got up to any more mischievous schemes.'

'A small price to pay for basically getting away with the crime, even if not actually benefiting from it. The alternative is much worse. Frankly, if I were a fellow Board member I might think about making a very terminal example of somebody who had betrayed my trust so comprehensively.'

'My, you are unforgiving, Kathryn. Perhaps we had better all hope you never make it to the very top.'

'Oh, I'm not totally ruthless, Mr Hazleton. I told Stephen Buzetski his wife was cheating on him without expecting anything else in return.'

'More wasted effort, Kathryn. You could have used that information so much more constructively.'

'Call me a sentimentalist.'

'How did he take it?'

'He sounded as if he was in shock.'

'You realise he will probably hate you for ever for telling him?'

'Yes. But at least I feel better about myself than if I'd got him told on the quiet by your people.'

'So you are quite selfish, in the end, aren't you, Kathryn? Just like me.'

'That's right. It just takes a different form.'

'Indeed. Well, there we are. I imagine if I was in the situation you describe I would start taking steps to do something very like what you've suggested as soon as possible. Deliver that present well before Christmas.'

'That would seem appropriate.'

'Of course, there is a link in all this to that other, diametrically not low-lying, location.'

'I was coming to that.'

\* \* \*

377

I had never felt so frightened. I thought I knew the way we worked, I thought I had an idea what we would stop at, or at least what we would stop at in what circumstances, but I wasn't sure. I felt vulnerable, sitting there in the park, waiting for Hans to return with my bags. What if the conspiracy went beyond Hazleton? What if in some bizarre way they were all behind it? Or just Madame Tchassot, and maybe Dessous, and Cholongai? That only left a dozen other Board members, some of them very inactive. What if I was up against too many of them, what if this was their power base, their stronghold? What if I'd somehow missed some crucial undercurrent of meaning and threat the previous evening, what if I'd totally misconstrued everything?

I swung back and forth, looking through the bare branches at the distant château. Maybe there was a sniper lining me up in his sights right now. Would I get a glimpse of a laser flickering redly around the twigs of the trees between me and the château? Maybe a snatch squad was already on its way from the compound. Maybe I'd disappear into the vaults and catacombs that riddled the mountain behind the château, maybe I'd end up old and out of mind in the Antarctic base in Kronprinsesse Euphemia Land. Maybe Hans had instructions only to drive me towards the airport, and then stop suddenly at a lonely prearranged rendezvous where Colin Walker would suddenly appear, looking regretful and carrying a silenced automatic.

Was I paranoid, or just being sensible? I got a prickly feeling on my forehead and jumped off the swing, walking towards the trees that would hide me from the château on the far slope. I rang Hans on the car phone.

'Yes, Ms Telman?'

'How are things going, Hans?'

'I have your luggage, Ms Telman. Where should I meet you?'

'At the Avis office in town. In twenty minutes.'

'Very well. I shall be there.'

I walked to the Hertz office, hired an Audi A3 and drove it round to a corner opposite the Avis lot, then crouched down and phoned Dessous. Not available. Madame Tchassot then; put my side of the story, assuming Poudenhaut had gone straight to her. Answer-machine. Tommy Cholongai. In a meeting. I looked up the number for X. Parfitt-Solomenides, the guy who'd also signed the Pejantan Island deal but whom I suspected wasn't involved in Hazleton's scam. Not taking calls. I was starting to get really worried now. I actually started to call Uncle Freddy.

Thulahn; the Prince. All land lines out. Luce, then. Luce, please be there . . .

'Yup?'

'Thank fuck.'

'What?'

'You're there.'

'Why, what is it, hon?'

'Oh, just getting paranoid. I think I've just committed commercial suicide.'

'What the hell are you talking about?'

I told her as much as I could. This probably only made the whole story even more complicated than it was anyway, and it was pretty complicated in the first place, but she seemed to get the gist. (Maybe too quickly, a part of me thought. Maybe she's in on it somehow, maybe she's like some sort of deep-entry spy put there by . . . but that was just too mad. Wasn't it?)

'Where are you now?'

'Luce, you don't need to know that.'

'But are you still in Switzerland? Or was this *auto da fé* shit with the Ferrari conducted in Italy, where it is probably a capital offence?'

'Hold on, my luggage has just arrived.' I watched Hans pull up to the kerb across the street in the silver 7-series. No other cars seemed to be following him, or drew up nearby at the same time. Nobody else in the BMW, either. Hans got out and peered through the window of the Avis office as he put on his cap.

I got out of the A3. 'Keep talking to me, Luce. If I get cut off suddenly, call the police.'

'What, the Swiss police?'

'Yeah, or Interpol or somebody. I don't know.'

'Okay. But now I need to know where the hell you are.'

'Yes, you do, don't you?' I said as I crossed the street, dodging honking traffic and gesticulating drivers. 'Ah, fuck you too, asshole!'

'I beg your pardon?'

'Not you, Luce. Hans! Hans!'

'You all right?'

'Shouting at the chauffeur. I'm in a town called Château d'Oex in the Vaud Canton, Switzerland.'

'Right . . . This isn't *that* chauffeur, is it?'

'No. Hans, *danke, danke. Nein, nein. Mein Auto ist hier.*'

'Ms Telman. You are crossing the road in the wrong place.'

'Yes, sorry. Could I just take my luggage?'

'It is in the trunk.'

'Fine. If you could just open it, I'll take it.'

'Where is your car? I will drive to it.'

'That's okay.'

'No, please.'

'Right, okay. It's over there.'

'Please, get in.'

'It's just across the road, Hans. I'll jay-walk again.'

'But this is not a place for crossing. See. Please, you will get in.'

'Hans. There's no need. I'll walk. Okay?'

'But here it is forbidden.'

'You okay, Kate?'

'Fine. Fine so far. Hans, please either open the trunk or get in the car and chuck a U-ie.'

'Yeah! Do as she says, Hans!'

'I don't think he can hear you, Luce.'

'What is a U-ie, please?'

'U-turn. It's a U-turn, Hans. Perform a U-turn.'

'That is forbidden here too. See.'

'Jeez. Anal or what? That guy needs therapy. Let me talk to him, Kate.'

'Quiet, Luce. Please. Hans, look—'

'Oh, you want me to stay on the line but you want me to shut up, right?'

'Right. Hans. Could I have my luggage?'

'Please, you will get in, I will to the other side of the street drive, and all is good.'

'Did I hear that right? Did he really the verb at the end of the sentence put? Well, haw-haw-haw!'

'Luce—'

'Please.'

'No, Hans.'

'But why not, Ms Telman?'

'I don't want to get into the car.'

'You don't want to get into the car?'

'That's right.'

'You tell him, kid.'

'Why do you not want to get into the car?'

'Yeah, come to think of it, why *don't* you want to get into the car?'

'Oh, for fuck's sake. Torture and death can't be any worse than this. Okay, Hans, you win. I'll get in. We're going over there. The green Audi hatchback. Okay?'

'Yes, I see. Thank you.'

'You got into the car?'

'I'm in the car.'

'What's happening now?'

'Hans is getting into the driver's seat. He's taking off his cap. He's putting it on the front passenger's seat. He's putting the car into Drive. He's checking his mirrors. We're driving off. We're in the traffic now. We're heading down the street.'

'Cool. Any nice shops?'

'Will you shut up? . . . We're going quite a long way down the street. We haven't done a U-turn yet. I'm starting to get worried. Hold on. Hans?'

'Yes, Ms Telman?'

'Why haven't we turned round yet? The car's back there.'

'It is forbidden. The signs. See. It is forbidden. Up here we may turn. I will turn there.'

'Okay, okay.'

'Now what's happening?'

'We're slowing down. We're turning up a side-street . . . we're turning down another street . . . and another . . . and back on to the main street. Yeah, heading back towards the Audi. Looks cool. Looks cool.'

'What fucking Audi?'

'My hire car. Right. We're here. I'm getting out. Thank you. No, I can . . . Ah, thank you, thank you. *Vielen dank.*'

'Ms Telman.'

'Thank you, Hans. *Wiedersehen.*'

'Goodbye, Ms Telman.'

'Yes, thank you. Drive carefully. 'Bye . . . Luce?'

'Yeah?'

'Thanks.'

Call me *really* fucking paranoid, but I left the hire car at Montreux, took a taxi to Lausanne and used cash to buy a ticket on a TEE to Milano via the Simplon tunnel (good dinner, pleasant talk to a terribly camp and charming textile designer and his gruffly butch partner; relaxed). Cash again to buy a Tourist ticket on a delayed Alitalia 747 to Delhi via Cairo; upgraded once we were in the air using my non-company Amex (stewardesses less glamorous and more efficient than last Alitalia flight a few years ago; coffee smelled tempting, but avoided). First so empty I could have got up to any amount of shenanigans, if there had been a willing partner. Slept – instead – very well indeed.

In Delhi, going through the formalities, I tried calling Stephen. The phone just rang and rang and rang, the way phones do when the person at the other end is there, hasn't got their answer-machine or voicemail switched on, but can see your number and name on their phone's display and just doesn't want to talk to you. 'Stephen, don't do this to me,' I whispered. 'Pick up the phone. Pick up the phone . . .' But he didn't.

I tried elsewhere.

'Mr Dessous?'

'Telman? What in the hell is going on?'

'You tell me, Jeb.'

'Was it that bastard Hazleton? Is he the Couffabling son-of-bitch you were talking about?'

'I really couldn't say, Jeb.'

'He's called an EBM for Wednesday in Switzerland. Know anything about that?'

'Sorry, Jeb, what's an EBM?'

'Extraordinary Board Meeting. Shows how often we have them if somebody like you doesn't know what they are.'

'Good.'

'"Good"? What do you mean, "Good"?'

'It's good you're having an EBM.'

'Why, dammit?'

'Mr Hazleton may have a pleasant surprise for you all.'

'Oh? It isn't to get you kicked out, then? There's an ugly rumour you assaulted Adrian Puddinghead or whatever the hell he's called.'

'Poudenhaut. Actually it was more his car I assaulted.'

'What? What did you do?'

'I used a search engine.'

'Telman, will you just tell me what the hell is going on?'

'I'm taking up the post in Thulahn.'

'Good.'

'Not necessarily.'

'What does *that* mean?'

'I think the plan we have for Thulahn may be too radical. Too destructive.'

'Oh, you do, do you? Well, I'm sure we'll thank you for sharing those thoughts with us, Telman, but it isn't up to you what we do in Thulahn. You'll be there in a purely advisory capacity, understand? You *might* get bumped up to L-Two, but that still doesn't mean you're on the Board. Am I making myself clear?'

'Abundantly, Mr Dessous.'

'Right. So, we'll see you at Château d'Oex on Wednesday.'

'Ah, probably not.'

'What do you mean, "probably not"? I'm telling you to be there.'

'I'm sorry, Mr Dessous. I can't. I'll be in Thulahn.'

'Cancel it.'

'I can't, sir. I've already assured the Prince I'll be there,' I lied. 'He's expecting me. Could you possibly, like, un-order me to be in Switzerland? That way I won't be disobeying a direct command. There's some delicate negotiating to be done in Thulahn.'

'Jesus! Okay. Get your ass to Thulahn, Telman.'

'Thank you, Jeb.'

'Right, I gotta go, see how that idiot nephew of mine's doing.'

'Why, is there something wrong?'

'You haven't heard? He got shot.'

'What? Oh, my God. When? Where?'

'Yesterday, New York City, in the chest.'

'Is he all right?'

'No, he isn't all right! But at least he's not dead. Probably isn't going to die, either, just cost me a fortune in hospital bills.'

'What happened?'

'The posters.'

'The posters?'

'Yeah. I saw one. Can't believe I didn't spot it myself.'

'What? I don't understand.'

'You know that dumb-ass always wanted his name above the title?'

'Yes?'

'So the posters for his play say, "Dwight Litton's *Best Shot*".'

'Oh, good grief,' I said.

'Yeah. Some crazy asshole took it literally.'

# EPILOGUE

I don't know. What is it that really matters to all of us? We're all the same species, the same assemblage of cells, with the same unarguable needs for food, water and shelter. The trouble is that after that it gets more complicated. Sex is the other big drive, of course, the one after the absolute necessities. You'd think we all need love, in some form, too, but maybe some people can get along without it. We are individuals, but we need to co-operate. We have family and friends, allies or at least accomplices. We always think we are right, and – search as I have

– there is no evil under the sun that somebody somewhere won't argue is actually a good, no idiocy that hasn't got its perfectly serious defenders, and no tyrant, past or present – no matter how bloody – without some bunch of zealot schmucks to defend him or his reputation till the last breath in their bodies – or preferably somebody else's.

So. Why am I doing this? Because it seems like the right thing to do. How do I know it is? I don't. But at least I don't have to tell lies to myself to justify what it is I am doing; I don't have to think, Well, they're not really humans, or, They'll thank me later, or, It's us or them, or, My country right or wrong, or, History will vindicate me. None of that sanctimonious bullshit.

I'm doing what I'm doing because I think good will come of it in the long run, and that almost nothing bad will come of it in the short run anyway, so even if I'm wrong maybe I can change my mind. Though I doubt I will. Either way, nobody's going to die. Nobody is going to suffer. Maybe I'll live to regret it, and it's possible some others will too, but even then I'll try to take as much of the hardship on myself, what little of it – I hope – there may be.

This makes it all sound far too selfless. Actually there's a lot of self in this. All the same, part of me is recoiling in horror at all this. Part of me is thinking, You're going to do *WHAT*? What *is* this shit? Because in one way of looking at it, this is just another example of the same old sad self-sacrificial martyrdom crap I've lamented in my gender throughout my life. We have spent so many generations thinking of others, thinking of our families and thinking of our men, when all they do in return is think of themselves. Just in the last few generations, finally able to control our own fertility, have we been able to act more like men and contribute more with our brains than our bodies. I

388

loved being part of that. I loved feeling that I was helping to make a case for my half of the species being worth more recognition than that due to a womb alone. And yet here I am going back on all that, or seeming to.

But what do we really want? Freedom, I guess. And I demand the freedom to do what seems right to me from first principles, and not the freedom always to behave selfishly, or always to do what a man would do in the circumstances, or always to do the opposite.

'Suvinder?'

'Kathryn. Where are you?'

'I'm in Delhi airport.'

'Delhi? Did you say Delhi? In India?'

'Yes. I'm trying to get a flight to . . . Well, where would you suggest? To connect with Air Thulahn.'

'You are returning so soon? I am . . . I am amazed. My God. This is wonderful! You're really coming back?'

'Yes. Ah, about that flight.'

'Oh, yes. Fly to either Patna or Kathmandu. Let me know which flight you can get. I'll send the plane. Oh, Kathryn, this is wonderful news! How long will you be staying?'

'I don't know yet. That depends.'

'Will you be staying here? In Thuhn? You would be very welcome to stay here in the palace.'

'That's very kind. I'd love to. I'll have my old room, if it's still free. See you later.'

'How wonderful! Yes!'

'You're kidding me!'

'No.'

'You're going to say *yes*?'

'That's the idea, Luce.'

'Fucking *yeah*! You're going to be a fucking *queen*?'

'I suppose I'll have to be, if I'm to take your advice about consummating the relationship.'

'What a total fucking twenty-four-carat weapon-grade *hoot*! Can I be a bridesmaid?'

'Look, it still might not happen. He might have already changed his mind. Or he might change it when he realises it could all really happen. Some guys are like that. It's the anticipation, not the realisation.'

'What the hell are you talking about?'

'You're right; I'm talking nonsense. I guess I just don't want to take anything for granted. I'm nervous.'

'You sure about this, now? You aren't verbalising the chance of it not happening because deep down you really don't want it to happen, are you?'

'I'm sure. I've decided.'

'But you still don't want to fuck the guy.'

'Not particularly. But that isn't everything.'

'Maybe not, but you don't even *love* him.'

'That's not everything either.'

'It's a hell of a *lot*!'

'I know. I might be doing exactly the wrong thing. But I'm going to do it anyway.'

'So why are you doing it?'

'Because he's a nice guy. Because he's a good man, and he needs somebody like me on his side.'

'You've met hundreds of guys like that! You never married them!'

'They weren't in the position he's in.'

'Hold on. So, ultimately, you're only marrying him because he's a prince and he's going to be the King.'

'Umm. Yes.'

'Jesus H. Christ. That's not only, like, not romantic, that's just, like, *breathtakingly* business-like and self-centred. Fucking hell, *I*'d be having severe qualms about doing something like this, and I'm a self-centred, monomaniacal bitch.'

'No, that's not why I'm doing it. I'm doing it because he's in a position of real power in a place I hardly know but I'm already half in love with. And he is a good man. But there's going to be so much change there. Not as much as some people were expecting, but a hell of a lot, and I don't know that Suvinder can handle it all by himself. I don't think he thinks he can, either. And I'd worry about who'd be advising him. Don't you see, Luce? For the first time in my life I can really do some good. Or fail in the attempt.'

'What you're saying is their country needs you.'

'I suppose I am. Sounds a bit presumptuous, put like that, but yes.'

'You're the fucking Peace Corps.'

'I'm the fucking Marines, Luce.'

'Yeah, but seriously, *can* I be a bridesmaid?'


Pip and James – I'd learned the flight crew's names this time – whisked me over the hills and far away, from Kathmandu to Thulahn. Bumpy but clear. Shared the plane with some monks and a lot of freight. Monks very friendly; learned a lot more Thulahnese words. They giggled and looked away when I changed into my Thulahnese clothes. I made sure my little artificial flower was secure and looking spruce.

Thuhn was sparkling under a fresh coat of snow. Langtuhn

Hemblu met me at the airfield with the ancient Roller after the usual dive-bomber landing. There were a few very tiny pointy-hatted children with parents there, but the rest were at school. No Suvinder: he had to be at some important dedication ceremony down-valley.

'I take you there?' Langtuhn asked, smiling.

'Why not?'

We set off down the valley in the crystalline depths of a perfectly clear, blue day suspended beneath the sky-high peaks.

Langtuhn and I had to walk the last bit up to the colourful crowd gathered round a giant newly refurbished prayer windmill the size of a house. There were lots of flags, lots of people, lots of banners and bunting and braziers and fuming censers, all fluttering or guttering in the cool, thin breeze. The crowd of smiling, quilted people parted for Langtuhn and me as we made our way up to the ceremonial platform where three walls of saffron-robed monks looked on and Suvinder, dressed in his own flower-garlanded robes, stepped down from a throne on a dais and held out his hands.

'Kathryn. Welcome back.'

'Thank you,' I said, bowing. I went up to him, took his offered hands, and kissed him on both cheeks. His hands were dry and warm. He smelled of incense. I whispered, 'If the offer still stands, Suvinder, I accept. The answer is yes.'

I pulled away. He looked confused for a moment. Then his mouth fell slackly open, before forming itself into a huge smile. His eyes glistened. Flags and banners snapped around us. A hundred faces looked on. Beyond, the prayer windmill, still bound by ropes and cables, creaked and strained in the wind, waiting to be free. Suvinder nodded, seemingly unable to speak, and with my hand in his, led me to the dais at the rear of the platform.

They found another chair for me, so that I could sit at the Prince's side for the rest of the ceremony.

It was traditional for each guest to offer something to the fire in one of the braziers. When my turn came, I pulled a couple of shiny discs from my pocket and threw both of them into the flames.